# RUNNING FROM THE BLAZE

OFELIA MARTINEZ

READING CACTUS
PRESS

READING CACTUS
PRESS

This is a work of fiction. Names, characters, places, and incidents either are the product of the author's imagination or are used fictitiously. Any resemblance to actual persons, living or dead, events, or locales is entirely coincidental.

First Edition

ISBN 978-1-954906-10-5 (paperback)

ISBN 978-1-954906-09-9 (eBook)

Library of Congress Control Number: 2021921751

*For Anny.*
*We're worse off without you.*
*Know that I miss you every day.*

# RUNNING
## FROM THE
## BLAZE

# 1

## LOLA

Saying goodbye to places shouldn't be as difficult as saying goodbye to people.

But it is.

My teeth chatter as I push open the door to my favorite restaurant. The holes in my ripped jeans do nothing to stave off the cold, and I wrap my olive utility jacket tight around my middle. When I step inside, I find Greg behind the register and smile at him.

"*Bonjour*," I say in greeting.

Greg looks up, his grin spreading wide, then shakes his head. It's so late and near closing time, it seems I'm their last customer. "Lola! Hi. While this is a *crêperie*, no one here is actually French."

"I know," I say with a teasing smile.

"The usual?"

I nod. Greg doesn't yet know I'm leaving. I told myself today would be the day, but I still have a few weeks. I'll let him know in a couple of days when I come back. He hands me a box that warms my hands even through my gray, fingerless gloves. He always throws in a free coffee, and I thank him after he gives me the cup.

"You're welcome." His smile is devious when he leans over the counter. "You ever gonna dump that jerk and let me take you on a date?"

I shake my head. This is the time to tell him I'm moving, but the words still strangle in my throat, and I don't want to cry in front of him. We're not close friends, but I've known Greg for years—he's asked me out for years. He takes rejection rather well but remains hopeful. I'm going to miss his flirting and the way his smile cheers me up every time I see him.

After adding cream and sugar to my coffee, I head out and walk three blocks up Summit Street to my favorite spot. I get to my bridge and take a seat, my legs dangling from the ledge.

Despite the cold, the warmth from the coffee cup and the *crêpe* in my hands comforts me. I look over the Kansas City skyline, pausing on the shiny Kauffman Center, wishing I had gotten to see at least one show there before my time in this city is over.

My eyes prickle with tears, and I take a deep breath. I can't start the waterworks now. I can't be a crybaby over the next few weeks as I say goodbye to everyone I know—to every place I love. Will I even have time to visit all my favorite places before I go? The graffiti alley in the Crossroads arts district where Ethan and I snuck our initials inside a heart next to my favorite piece, an enormous whale swimming in the alley. Or Shawnee Mission Park, where my dad insisted on hosting my birthday parties every year, even after I told him I was too old for birthday parties.

Or the home I grew up in. I take a deep breath. The home I couldn't keep renting on my own. Even if I do find the time to say goodbye one last time, I can't go inside anymore.

A brand-new family lives there now.

I've loved this city my whole life. And now I have to leave it.

I'm not wanted here.

Trying to focus on the positives as much as I can, I'm determined to enjoy all my favorites before I go. And I'm starting with this delicious *crêpe*. Setting the coffee next to me, I open the lid to the box and my mouth waters at the sight of the *crêpe* with butter and powder sugar. I wrap it in a roll like a burrito and it's halfway to my mouth when rain starts falling around me, getting the *crêpe* wet. Now I really want to cry like a pouty child who just dropped her lolly.

I'm considering eating it anyway when my phone goes off in my coat pocket, playing "How to be a Heartbreaker" by *Marina*. I rub my hand over my thigh to warm it up a little and pull out the phone. The name Sofia displays on the screen, and I get excited for a moment. Maybe she has a job for me.

Since I'll be leaving soon, I'm determined to work and save up as much as possible before my move, and she always throws a little extra work my way.

"So?"

"Hi, Lo. How are you?"

"You know me," I say in a teasing voice. "Never good." I look down at my ruined, soggy *crêpe* that I didn't even get to taste. At least my beanie hat is keeping the top of my head warm—even if my long, blond curls are getting wet toward the ends.

Sofia laughs. She thinks my theory that I'm cursed because my parents named me Dolores, which means 'pain' in Spanish, is ridiculous. If only she knew how wrong she is. I'm doomed to misery.

I'm convinced I'm cursed. Apart from the daily glitches in my life, I swear every day something goes wrong—a leaky engine in my car, a bird pooping on my head on my way out of a job, or something as simple as a soggy *crêpe*. It's always *something* with me.

Why did they have to name me Dolores? They so fucked me over with that name.

But not more fucked over than when they revealed on my eighteenth birthday a family secret that derailed my entire future. A secret that froze me in place, and that I'm still trying to escape from. My friends all moved away. So did Ethan, the love of my life.

And I'm stuck.

All my friends are away at college living their best lives, my boyfriend is in California, trying to make long-distance work, and I'm adrift and stagnant. But even if I won't admit it to myself, a little voice inside me whispers that our relationship too, is doomed. Little mocking voice—the curse's voice.

You still don't think I'm cursed?

Let me drive the point home, then. The night my parents revealed their most-guarded family secret, they both went and died on me. At least I learned the truth before they were gone. I turned eighteen that week.

And even with all that information, Sofia does not believe me when I say I'm cursed, as if I weren't an expert in the matter.

"You're not cursed, Lo," she says gently into the phone as she reads my thoughts.

I roll my eyes. "I know. It's all in my head," I say to appease her, then I try to change the subject. "What's up?"

"Do you have a job tomorrow?" she asks.

"I do, but not one I like. I'd be willing to move things around for the right offer."

There's a sigh on the other end. "I actually want you to turn it down, but I promised I'd ask."

"Okay," I say, confused by her shady behavior.

"It's a mansion," she says, and I perk up with interest. "Big money. Cash. No questions."

"I'm in," I say immediately.

"No, Lo. Wait. I'm not done. They've had parties . . . it's . . . I don't know how to say it any better than it's a war zone, Lo. I almost cried when I saw the disgusting mess, and *I* don't have to clean it."

"I'll do it if it pays to match the mess."

"You won't hate me when you see it?" she asks, but I know she's just being silly to cheer me up like she always does.

Ever since she held my hand at the funeral, Sofia adopted me into her family. That's what she does. Her heart is so open and big, when she loves someone, her loyalty knows no bounds. She's taken a big sister role, as has my roommate, Ileana. And they *are* big sisters to me now—just as bossy, annoying, and, most of all, supportive.

Sofia has offered to give me money to help me build a new life, but my pride won't let me take it. I have to work for it. So, she's found a work-around by finding me odd jobs, and then fighting me on the ridiculous rates she sets for the random jobs. It's usually cleaning her bar, or her penthouse apartment. Sometimes it's babysitting my niece, Addy. Then we fight when I return half the bills, and she sneaks them into my coat pocket. And on and on it goes.

I laugh. "I won't hate you. How much does it pay?" I ask.

"I don't know."

"How long do you think it would take me?"

"I don't know," Sofia says.

I blow out a breath. "You are not helpful, So." It's she who laughs then. "Let's do it this way then, by the hour. I'll work for eight hours, whatever I can get done in that time."

"That sounds fair."

"Tell the client I'll charge twenty bucks an hour."

"Absolutely not," she says with determination.

"Too high?"

"Too low! Lola, come on. It's a health hazard."

Geesh, how bad can this place be? Surely she's exaggerating. "Okay, what do you suggest?" I ask.

"I'll tell him a grand, cash. Due to you when you're done. And he's good for it. I'll vouch."

My eyes widen with surprise. "A grand?"

"At least," she says.

"That seems high."

"For a reason. You'll have to sign an NDA."

"A non-disclosure agreement?" I scratch my head, then realization hits me. "Oh my god. It's for Bren, isn't it?" I say excitedly, my pulse racing.

Sofia's partner is the lead singer of my absolute favorite metal band of all time, *Industrial November*. I was heartbroken when I learned he was off the market, but I forgave them both because I love Sofia. I still can't act cool around him. I blame the curse.

And if that weren't proof enough of my curse, the day I met Brenner Reindhart for the first time, the first love of my life even before Ethan, I was elbow deep in Sofia's toilet—cleaning it. There he was, the millionaire rock god from Germany, and I couldn't shake his hand; I was wearing rubber cleaning gloves—bright yellow ones. I went home and sobbed that day at my bad luck.

"It's not for Bren," Sofia says.

"Oh," I mumble with disappointment.

"It's for Karl."

No words. I'm capable of exactly zero words, and my hand drifts slowly to cover my gaping mouth. Karl Sommer is the new guitarist in *Industrial November*—one of the best guitarists alive today, if not *the* best.

Not to mention drop-dead-gorgeous. Blond, perfect pearly-white teeth, blue eyes, and a square jaw sharp enough to cut diamonds. Let's just say I've masturbated to thoughts of him on more than one occasion—and climaxing to his guitar solos, watching those fast fingers expertly strumming the strings, have been some of my best orgasmic experiences.

"Lo? Are you there?"

"Um," I stammer, "yes. I'm here."

"Can I take the silence as a 'yes, Sofia, thank you. I'd love the job'?"

"Yes! Oh my god, yes!"

I'm so canceling Mr. Sanders's scheduled home cleaning tomorrow. I'm going to meet Karl Sommer!

I get off the bridge's ledge so I can hop-dance in excitement.

Oh, my fuck! What am I going to wear?

"Don't get too excited," Sofia says. "He won't be there."

## 2

## KARL

A furious Brenner Reinhart would be more intimidating if this weren't about the hundredth speech of his. It's always the same spiel; *you need to get your head out of your ass. When are you going to get it together? Do we need to replace our guitarist again?*

And on and on it goes, like a merry-go-round of Bren's wrath. I'm immune to it most days, but today is the wrong fucking day. I sit on the couch, elbows to thighs, hands rubbing temples. I have a massive headache—and yes, it's hangover-induced. But that's beside the point.

Today, I'm not in the mood for Bren's tangent.

I lift my gaze to look at any of my fellow bandmates for support. Fritz, our bass player, leans on the back of a couch, legs crossed at the ankles, looking at his shoes. Adrian, our drummer, rests his head on the sofa's backrest next to me, looking at the ceiling. Useless.

Even Roger, our manager, refuses to meet my eyes. What the fuck? This is all his doing. I don't even want this party lifestyle he's imposed on me since I joined the band, replacing their old guitarist.

Finally, Roger speaks up. "Calm down, Bren. This isn't helping any."

"Don't tell me to fucking calm down," Bren roars. "You didn't see what a pigsty his house was when we picked him up. He's not showing up to work when we need him; he's not writing new music, he's not contributing. Apart from looking pretty and playing music Milo *wrote*, what is he good for?"

That stung. I will forever be in Milo's shadow. He was their guitarist before me until he got kicked out of the band three years ago when he refused rehab for drug abuse. Bren loves threatening me with Milo's fate.

But I'm not an addict. Or an alcoholic.

The press assumes that, and Roger lets them believe it— any publicity is good publicity.

But I can't believe my bandmates can't tell the truth from the press lies. As if the press never lied about *them*. My jaw clenches at all the swimming thoughts of betrayal, deepening my headache.

"Please stop shouting," I say as calmly as I'm capable at the moment.

"*Scheisse!*" Bren shouts. "It's too late to get to the studio anyway. Get the fuck out of my sight, Karl!"

"Gladly," I mumble under my breath. This meeting has been a waste of my fucking time. Why did they even drag me out if it was just to yell at me?

One day, I'm going to explode, and Bren won't know what came his way.

All empty threats.

At the end of the day, I want to impress him. He was my hero. The whole band was, before I joined them. Getting through auditions and being picked was the closest experience to winning the lottery I will ever have.

But I've done nothing but disappoint them since I joined.

Story of my life.

Big fucking disappointment. Never good enough. And just like everyone else in my entire fucking life, I'm waiting for them to toss me aside. To discard me and make way for someone better.

Adrian gets in the elevator with me. "Hey, man, you need to cool it a bit for a while."

I turn to Adrian. He's usually the only one who doesn't gang up on me. He gives the band enough trouble himself. "You too, Adrian?"

"Nah, man. Just . . . I'm not supposed to know, so don't say anything. But I overheard Bren talking to Milo on the phone."

Fuck. "They're talking again?"

Adrian nods and says nothing more. He just did me a solid with that warning. Bren swore he'd never speak to Milo again. But if they *are* talking again, something has changed, and Adrian likely suspects the same thing I do—they could trade him back in for me, if they wanted.

After getting off the elevator from Bren and Fritz's apartment building, I pull my phone out and call my stress-relief.

"Miss me already?" Sandy purrs into the phone. I just saw her last night. Already, the headache lifts.

"I need to let off some steam," I say.

Sandy laughs. "I have your relaxation right here, baby."

"No. Come to my place tonight."

---

MY ROOM IS NOT like the rest of the mansion. It's neat and orderly. Even after the maids quit from having to clean up after all the parties, I kept up this room. I actually hate messes.

I'll have to talk to Roger about his plans for me in the

band. I'm tired of this lifestyle he's imposing on me. A lifestyle I have no desire to partake in. And I don't want to lose my spot in the band to fucking Milo for a half-baked publicity stunt Roger concocted.

What a nightmare.

It's eleven at night when the doorbell rings. Having no staff anymore, I go downstairs to let Sandy in. She's wearing an ankle-length winter coat and strappy sandal heels that make me shiver. She must be freezing. But I smile when I meet her face because we both know she's naked under that coat.

She steps inside, and her first order of business is to shove her tongue down my throat. I need to blow off some steam, so I rush her upstairs to my bedroom and rip the coat off her body.

My mouth curves into a half-smile, finding what I knew I'd find.

"Like what you see, baby?" she asks.

I nod, unbuckling my belt. "Drop to your knees," I order.

---

I DON'T REMEMBER when we fell asleep, but I hate it when Sandy sleeps over. When I startle awake with Pixel's barking, I'm pinned under Sandy's leg and arm, and I have to roll my eyes.

Pixel barks again, and I spring up to put on some sweatpants. She never barks. The only person with access to the house is the dog walker, Chase, and Pixel loves him. She'd never bark at him.

Everyone else who has the code to get in knows Pixel: Roger, Fritz, and even Bren are friendly with my baby girl.

Sandy stirs, groggy, as I rush out of the room to get to Pix and find out what's wrong. My heart is racing, and suddenly, I have flashbacks to Berlin. The over-zealous fan I thought was harmless until the stalking became too uncomfortable and who, finally, broke into my apartment. I found her in my bathtub, playing an *Industrial November* song.

I follow the barking downstairs, then it stops. I walk from room to room, looking for her, and finally find her in the kitchen with someone.

There's a woman crouched on top of the kitchen island. She's wearing a massive set of red headphones over blond curls that reach her waist. In her crouched position, I can't tell how tall she is.

And Pixel, my vicious, trained-to-defend this home, German short-haired pointer, is licking this woman's hand. "Pixel, you traitor!" I yell, but Pixel keeps licking the woman's hand. Her music must be blaring because she doesn't hear me shouting behind her.

"That's a good boy," she says to Pixel.

"She's a girl!" I yell, hoping to get through her music, but I don't. I come up behind her and remove her headphones. She startles and spins around, arms swinging, and elbows me in the jaw. Hard. I rear back in pain, and her headphones fly in the air.

"Fuck!"

The woman brings her hand to her heart. "Oh my god, I'm so sorry! You scared me."

I rub my jaw. That elbow packed a wallop. I eye her up and down; she looks so tiny, I'll never live it down if I end up with a bruise from her.

She crouches over the countertop, crawling toward me, and I won't lie and say it isn't the fucking sexiest thing I've ever seen. I'm equal parts terrified she's another unhinged fan, and excited at her cat-like movements as she crawls toward me. She kneels at the edge of the counter and reaches out with her hand to touch my jaw and inspect my face. "Are you okay?"

I nod, looking down at her. She is stunning. I don't know how or why she broke into my house, but I'm rather happy about it even if I should be calling the police. Her eyes are a cool shade of green sea glass, not bright—more like deep, hollow pools with no glimmer—like a doll.

"Here, I'll help you down." I grab her by the waist, pulling her to the ground.

When she's standing, my hands linger at her waist, and I realize she is short. Only about five-five to my six-two frame. Her waist in my hands is slim, fanning out into tantalizingly full hips, and I have an inexplicable desire to turn her around so I can admire her backside.

Her hands wrap around my forearms, and her gaze is frozen to my jaw, a wrinkle between her blond brows. "I'm fine," I whisper, and her eyes meet mine, locking there.

Her lips open slightly and the air becomes thick and electric around us. I get a whiff of something sweet and artificial, like she's chewing gum, maybe watermelon flavor, and it's all I can do not to lick her lips to have a taste for myself.

We're both oblivious to our surroundings, ignoring Pixel, who is sniffing around her feet—frozen in this perfect moment. My eyes dip to her chest, finding small breasts covered in a *Television* "Marquee Moon" t-shirt. My face lights up with the biggest smile. She has good taste in music.

"What?" she asks, still gripping my forearms.

Instead of answering, I ask my own questions. "Who are you? And why did you break into my house?"

She gasps, clearly at a loss for words.

Then I feel a cold stickiness at my jaw and a matching sensation on my forearms. "Ugh! And what the fuck is on your hands?" I finally push her away, breaking our connection and finding streaks of something gooey and brown smeared on my arms. I wipe my jaw with my hand, removing the same substance from my face.

"Oh, um—sorry. It's peanut butter."

"Peanut butter?"

"Yeah, when your dog *attacked me*, I hopped on the counter, and the only thing I could think to do was reach for the fridge and grab something to appease him with. I was looking for cheese or something—and why do you keep your peanut butter in the fridge?"

She is talking a mile a minute now, nervous, and I smile. "Her," I say.

"What?"

"She's not a boy." I look between the island and the fridge. That must have taken some maneuvering to achieve at that long distance.

Guessing my thoughts, she speaks up with a nervous giggle. "It wasn't easy," she admits.

"Impressive."

She smiles with self-satisfaction clear on her face.

"Still, you haven't explained why you broke into my house."

She rears back, clutching the peanut butter jar. "I'm not breaking in."

"You're not?"

She laughs, and the sound seeps warmly into my chest. I want to hear her laugh all the time—but the smile doesn't reach her sad eyes. *Why are your eyes so sad?* "You think that given a chance to break into Karl Sommer's house, I'd steal peanut butter?" she asks.

"Maybe you're homeless and hungry?" I say, defending my theory, though it's far more likely she's another stalker fan. But if she is, the last thing I should do is bring that up.

She shakes her head, places the lid on the jar, then returns it to the fridge. She walks over to the sink to wash her peanut butter-covered hands, pulls paper towels, and comes back to where I'm standing.

I should be afraid she is a potentially dangerous stalker who might have moved into the mansion without me noticing, like what happened to Stephen King that one time. But I'm highly entertained by her.

She grips my forearm again, heating my skin where we connect, and wipes away the peanut butter. "I'm sorry about this," she says, concentrating on cleaning me up. "And for hitting you," she adds.

"Are you a crazy stalker fan, then?" I ask, but can't hide my smirk when I look at her.

She shakes her head again. "No. Sofia asked me to come. I'm your housekeeper for the day."

A housekeeper? "Oh yeah. She mentioned something about getting the place cleaned."

"Please don't tell her I hit you."

I laugh. "And how do I explain the bruise?"

She runs her hand through her hair to scratch her head, making her curtain of curls rustle. My god, she's beautiful. I stick my hands in the pockets of my sweats to occupy them so I don't cup her face between my hands like my fingers itch to. "I'm sure you can come up with some badass story about a fight. It's way better than *a tiny blonde elbowed me in the face after turning my dog against me.*"

"Ouch. Kick a guy while he's down."

She laughs again. "I'm sorry. I'm only joking—"

"No, no. You're right. She's trained to protect me, and she was putty in your hands." I glance over at Pixel, who is now lying down next to the housekeeper's feet. "I'm very disappointed in you, Pix."

"Pix?" she asks.

"Pixel. That's her name. She also answers to Pix, Pixy, Pixy-doodle, and caboodle-doodle," I say and grin wide.

The housekeeper's head tilts to the side, and then she bursts out laughing. "Well, it's nice to meet you both. I'm Dolores Beltran. My friends call me Lola, but I also answer to Lo."

"Lola," I say and smile at her. I'm not sure why, but I want to be the one to lift the sadness from her gaze.

"How'd she get the name Pixel?" she asks.

I crouch down next to Pixel and run my hand through her brindle coat. "See here?" I point to the back of her neck. "There's this white heart shape? Like a pixilated heart?"

Lola's eyes squint as she tries to make out the shape. "Yeah. I see it. It's a great name for a dog."

"I'm glad she didn't bite you."

"Me too. Gave me a good scare, though."

"She's never made friends with anyone so fast," I say as I eye Lola up and down. What is it about her that made her instantly likable to my grumpy dog? "It took Fritz, our bass player, three weeks of coming over nearly every day to get her used to him. I had to resort to taking a sweater from him and putting it in her bed so she got used to his smell."

She grins again and leans down to pet Pixel, who turns over, presenting her front side covered in white fur for belly rubs. Lola laughs but obliges, completely melting me. She likes dogs. More specifically, Lola likes *my* dog—and the admiration, it seems, runs both ways.

Pixel has a mood-lifting effect on most people once she's accepted them, and I watch Lola carefully, waiting for her eyes to stop looking so fucking sad, but even as she smiles, her lids remain at half-mast. When she's done petting, we both stand.

I scratch the back of my head. "So, um, you need help finding stuff?" I ask.

"Nope. I'm sure I can figure it all out if you don't mind me poking about."

"Not at all. I'll let you get to it, then, Iggy," I tease.

Her nose scrunches up. "Iggy?"

I nod.

"As in . . . ?"

"Iggy—"

"Pop!"

I smile with approval that she got it.

Lola laughs. "Oh, I get it." She playfully smacks her forehead. Then she snorts when she laughs in the geekiest, most adorable way. "Because of the peanut butter."

Could this woman be any more perfect?

# 3

## LOLA

**M**y heart hammers in my chest, and not just because of the scare from Pixel's initial attack. Karl tried joking around—to make me feel at ease, I can tell —but now it's a bit awkward. He says his goodbye but then just stands there, not making a move to go away and leave me alone to clean.

It's also awkward because I didn't imagine that moment between us. His hands at my waist, my hands clinging to his forearms, creamy peanut butter smooth between our skin where we touched. It's not like we kissed or did anything inappropriate, but somehow, that moment has me feeling like I cheated on Ethan, and I'm already deep in my guilt about it.

I glance around the kitchen, trying to decide where to clean first. Sofia was right; I almost cried when I saw the mess. But I didn't get the chance to wallow in that thought too long before Pixel launched at me, fangs bared, fleshy gums stretching between her sharp teeth and curled lip.

I'd never been so frightened in my life. But all it took was a little peanut butter.

There's no way I can work in this awkwardness, and I'm

about to dismiss Karl as politely as I'm capable of when the click of heels on the marble floors draws our attention to a stunning woman who joins us in the kitchen.

"Darling." She nearly moans the word out. "Why'd you get out of bed so early?"

She clearly hasn't seen me yet, and she goes to Karl, wraps her hand around the back of his neck, and dives into his mouth. His hand flies to her waist, and he groans into the kiss in the most sensual way.

They're beautiful together, and it takes my breath away. Their tongues massage each other slowly, even as Karl's eyes fly open with surprise and track me in the kitchen as if suddenly remembering I'm here too. He brings his palms up to push her away gently, and she responds by grabbing onto his waistband and pulling his lower body to press against hers. Their kiss and embrace are so erotic; heat pools where my thighs meet.

Ethan doesn't kiss like that.

Finally, Karl frees himself from her grip and wipes his mouth, almost as if he's wiping away the kiss. He clears his throat. "Sandy, this is Lola. Lola, Sandy."

Sandy turns to face me, startled, and smiles brightly. "Oh, sorry! I didn't know we had company. How rude of me. I'm Sandy. Nice to meet you."

I smile back at her. She seems nice. "Lola. Don't mind me. Pretend I'm not here. I'm just going to get started."

"Started?" Sandy asks.

"Oh, sorry. I'm housekeeping for you today," I explain.

"Oh," Sandy says. "Well, thank you. This place could use it." Then she turns to Karl. "I have to go, but call me later?"

Karl nods and finally leaves me to it as he walks her out, Sandy waving at me with a smile.

I explore the house—or rather, the mansion—to take inventory and prioritize what needs the most work. The impressive, gated estate was hard to find hidden behind a grove of trees; I almost missed my turn getting here.

When I first saw the home, I was so excited. Until I opened the door and saw the inside. Now that Pixel is not attacking me, I can take my time assessing the damage, and Sofia was right.

It *is* a health hazard. I almost want to cry. And I'm so grateful she asked for an exorbitant fee because this job is worth a grand at a minimum.

On the main floor, it's the living room and kitchen that need the most work. Beer bottles, shattered glass, and liquor stains mar every surface. It's really too bad because otherwise, the home is luxurious perfection. Sure, there's an enormous floor-to-ceiling slab of quartz as a focal point in the entrance, encasing a double-sided fireplace. Too bad the glass around the fireplace is smeared in something so disgusting, I can only pray it's not human in origin.

Then I look up and wish I had asked Karl if he has a ladder because a bra dangles from the delicate glass chandelier. I have no idea how I'll remove it. And really, what kind of parties is he throwing, and what kind of moves does a woman have to have to land a bra that high? I can only imagine the debauchery that took place here last night. If it was last night, because some of these sticky stains look mighty settled.

I'm not going to cry. I'm not going to cry.

Instead, I take a deep breath, then make my way upstairs. Several guest rooms are slightly worse for wear, but they are not a priority. Then I open the door to what I realize must be the master bedroom.

My eyes grow wide. It's pristine. Not a speck of dust to be seen. The sound of water turning on shifts my gaze to a door on the other side of the room. I smile. Karl must have hopped in the shower. And, huh. He even made his bed.

This makes no sense. How can the rest of the house be the perfect movie set for the pits of hell and his room be the gatesof-heaven level clean? Something isn't making sense here. I gently close the door so he doesn't hear me snooping in his room and walk down the hallway to the other end of the mansion. There's a baby gate propped up on the doorframe, and Pixel's cold, wet nose pops through the bars, trying to sniff me. I jump over the partition and find an entire wing of the house just as clean as Karl's room.

It's full of oversized beanie chairs, and a large television is hooked up with countless video game consoles. The only mess to be seen is the confetti of dog toys scattered over the plush carpeted floor.

*This is where he hangs out with his dog,* I think to myself. Where he spends his time, and he keeps it clean for Pixel.

I'm relieved the house isn't a total health hazard to her, but an unsettling feeling knots my stomach when I walk downstairs again. Something isn't adding up between the floors of Karl Sommer's house.

But it's none of my business.

Getting the kitchen clean first will make me feel better, so I start there. I'm nearly done loading the dishwasher, listening to Patti Smith spelling out Gloria's name and singing along, when I feel a gentle tap on my shoulder. I spin around to find a freshly washed Karl jumping back and away from me.

Removing my headset from my ears, I lower it to rest around my neck.

"You're not punching me in the face again," Karl says with a teasing smile.

"I didn't punch you."

"Elbow-punch." He shrugs. "Potato-potáto."

My mouth dries up as I eye him up and down. I scan his body from shoes up. He's wearing white designer sneakers, jeans that hang low on his hips, and a crisp, white, v-neck t-shirt. I'm disappointed in myself for not having paid attention to his tattoos earlier when he was shirtless, but I was so distracted by everything else. The full sleeve of colorful design disappears into the sleeve of his shirt, and I want to have a closer look at *all* of his tattoos. Does he have any in secret places? I wonder.

A woodsy smell with a hint of sweet clove from either his aftershave or soap overtakes all my senses. His blond hair, which nearly reaches his shoulders, is dripping wet from his shower, and when I get to his face, his mouth is upturned into a smirk.

Oh my god. How much more obvious could I be, checking him out? Earth, swallow me whole. It's the curse at work here— I'm sure of it—tempting me with this rock-god-walking-sex-on-a-stick.

*Ethan,* I remind myself. *You are in love with Ethan, Lola!*

"Like what you see?" Karl asks.

"Uh—" I'm not capable of coherent thought. I'm so pathetic. *Think, Lola.* What do you say to that?

Karl steps closer, shortening the distance between us, and a breath catches in the back of my throat. His arms go past me and settle on the counter behind me, trapping me there, and his head dips, his eyes glued to my lips.

Oh god, is he about to kiss me? My mind flashes to his earlier kiss with Sandy. I bet it was one of those urban-myth kisses that makes you orgasm just from the kiss alone.

I yearn to be kissed like that. Kissed with want and unspoken promises of pleasure to come.

But not by him. He has Sandy, and he only just kissed her.

And I have Ethan.

Ready to find an excuse to pull away—any excuse—my phone rings with "How to Be a Heartbreaker," my ring-tone for Sofia, saving me from having to shoot Karl down. I'm not sure I would have had the strength.

I push past his arm on the counter, and he pulls back. "So?" I say when I pick up. I peer up at Karl, who is tracking me, a grin full of mischief stretching his perfectly molded lips. God. I bet he can kiss the panties right off a girl.

"Put Karl on the phone!" Sofia nearly yells in my ear.

I startle and jump where I stand. "Why?"

"He's not picking up, and I need to talk to him."

Karl's brows furrow when I stretch my hand out to give him the phone. I mouth *Sofia*, and he takes the phone to his ear.

She says something that causes him to wince. "No, I—" he gets cut off by her again. "Sofia—" then his perfectly chiseled face falls for a moment before his eyes snap up to meet mine. He takes a step backward, almost recoiling as if repulsed by me. "No. I didn't know." He lets out a frustrated sigh and turns away from me, running his hand through his hair and pulling it back and away from his face. "Yeah, Sofia. Of course." Silence while he listens. "You know I would never." Another silence. "Yeah. I'll see you later," he says, sounding resigned.

He hangs up the call and spins on his heel to face me again. Accusation in his eyes, his sharp jaw is set with anger. "You're seventeen?" he hisses. "And more importantly, you're Bren's sister-in-law?"

Crap. I close my eyes. Sofia lied to him.

Karl Sommer thinks I'm jailbait and the lead singer's family. I'm neither.

I should correct him. Shouldn't I? I should tell him I'm nineteen, not seventeen, and that Sofia is not really my sister, but more of an *adopted* sister. Then I think about Ethan and how close I came to cheating on him with this man who surely only wants one thing from me. It's better if I have this giant buffer between us.

So, instead of telling him the truth, I find myself nodding.

# 4

## KARL

Seventeen-fucking-years-old.

"And you're Sofia's little sister? When, exactly, were you going to tell me you are Bren's sister-in-law? Fuck!"

I close my eyes and inhale deeply to calm my racing heart down. When I open them again, Lola stands there, looking shocked to the core. What the fuck is she doing cleaning homes at seventeen years old?

She's just a child.

And why would Bren and Sofia let her?

My stomach churns. God, the thoughts I had about her. . . what I just did in the shower, thinking of her. Then I almost kissed her! Brenner Reinhart's sister-in-law. He'd have my balls for this.

I pull my hair back angrily with one hand and toss her the phone to catch.

If I had kissed her, what would have happened? What if it had gone further? My mouth dries up, and I shiver. She's just a kid. My confused body doesn't know how to react at this moment. My brain screams for me to be disgusted—I should be by a minor. But the rest of my body already ignited an undeniable desire—and it sure as hell goes both ways. This has danger written all over it.

Career-ending-danger.

There's too much at stake. Can you go to prison in America? For being with a seventeen-year-old? I make a mental note to ring my lawyer tomorrow. I won't touch her, but what would happen if people assumed . . . if I were accused?

Forget prison. Bren would end me before I had the chance to get locked up.

"Answer me!" I snap when she just stands there.

She nods again. "Yes—yes."

I hang my head. This is a disaster. "About what happened in the kitchen . . ."

"I know. I'm sorry," she apologizes.

"You could end me," I say softly, begging her with my eyes to stay away from me.

"I wouldn't." She shakes her head.

I smile at her. "You could end me without even intending to."

Her face falls, and again my fingers twitch to lift her little face. Those sad eyes looking at the floor tear through my heart with ferocity, and I can't stand it.

"We can't be alone together," I say. Then add, "Ever."

She nods. "Of course. Should I leave? I've barely started the job."

I look around. The kitchen does look a million times better, even if it's not done yet. "No. I don't want to steal your job from you. I'll head out. I'll be back at the end of the day with your payment."

She nods.

"Could you do me a favor and give Pix her lunchtime treat? The treat jar is in the pantry."

"Sure. Would it be okay if I walked her as well?"

"You don't have to. The dog walker comes back at six."

"Oh," she says sadly.

"But you can if you want to," I amend.

She smiles with gratitude. I think she just wants time with my baby girl.

Why does she have to be a minor and so damn perfect?

Then a horrifying thought slices through my mind. Sofia just made her forbidden. Unattainable. I'm disgusted with myself because that thought excites me. What in the hell is happening to me?

I need to get away from Lola—as far away as possible.

I can't be tempted.

"Before I head out, I need to show you something upstairs."

Her eyes narrow, and I want to slap my forehead at how that must have sounded. "About the job. There are special instructions upstairs."

"Oh," Lola says, the tension in her shoulders dropping.

I lead her to the side of the house where I spend most of my time. "If you want to put away Pix's toys in the toy bin, that's fine, but I take care of most everything else in here."

"I was wondering why it's so clean," she says.

"Pixel needs a safe home," I say simply.

"You can dust and vacuum, though I'm not sure it needs it yet. But whatever you do, do not go through that door."

Her gaze darts past me to the closed door at the other end of the room, her head tilting to the side. "What's in there?"

My grin is massive. "I'll show you." I walk to the door, open it, and like in a cheesy movie, I can almost imagine the heavenly light that shines through. The entire wall behind that door is lined with all my babies. Rows upon rows of all my guitars.

"Don't touch my axes under any circumstances."

Lola's jaw is slack in awe.

"You understand?"

She nods.

"I need you to say you understand." I shut the door, and her eyes lift to meet mine.

"I understand. I won't dust in there."

"Good. I have to get going. I'll be back later."

Tying my hair into a low bun, I tuck it under a baseball cap and put on my sunglasses. It's the only way I can go about my business and not be recognized so easily. My instinct is to go to Sofia's bar, *La Oficina*, but *Industrial November* is still connected to that bar ever since she got together with Bren. It's a shame because I like the vibe there. And I really enjoy the Spanish rock she plays. A few of the bands do some exciting things, weaving traditional Mexican music into the metal sounds. But I don't want to risk being photographed, so I find an alternative.

I settle at a table for a few hours, sipping beers, staring at blank pages in my notebook. I've written a few songs, and I always hope I can impress Bren and maybe get him to record one, but I always chicken out before actually showing him any of the lyrics. I'm not the seasoned poet he is.

The blank page stares at me, and I want to write something new, but everything that comes out is cheesy and over-done. After thirty minutes of brainstorming, I look at all the words I listed: Cherry lips, golden hair, forbidden fruit, sad eyes, temptation, biting the apple, Bosch's Garden of Earthly Delights . . .

It's all useless and so damned cliché. And all of it is about my fucking housekeeper. I wonder what she's doing.

The morning passes me by at the bar. I order lunch and eat and keep trying to write something semi-decent. I stare down at the words on the paper in front of me. There's no way I'll show Bren any of it.

It's all crap. I pay my tab, head to the bank to get Lola's money, and go home earlier than I thought.

Earlier than I told her I'd be.

The house is quiet when I go in, and I'm amazed that the living room is spotless now. She works fast, but I don't see her anywhere. Maybe she's moved on upstairs, so I go looking for her there. I head over to Pixel's side of the house, and the door to my ax room is open.

I smile.

She couldn't resist.

I tiptoe over and press my back against the wall next to the doorframe, twisting to peek with one eye into the room. She has a rag over her shoulder, her hair up in a bird's nest bun now, and she's perusing all the guitars. She reaches to touch one but then stops herself, pulling her hand back. I have to clasp my hand to my mouth to stifle my snicker so I don't give myself away.

She looks between the axes as if undecided on which she should pick: *the blue one, Iggy,* I think. *Pick the electric blue ax.* She scans them all one last time, and I have to tell my heart to be still when her hands gravitate to the ax on the middle of the wall. My Blue Dragon. My favorite guitar. It's the least expensive of them all, but my most precious—a gift from the closest thing to family I ever had. The guitar I auditioned with for *Industrial November.*

My lucky guitar.

Lola weighs it in her hands, runs her fingers over the curve of the side body, then turns it over to the other side. She gasps excitedly when she sees the blue dragon painted on the back of the guitar. She is a vision holding that ax, even if I can only see her profile from where I stand by the door.

She brings the guitar close to her body, my dragon kissing her lower belly—lucky-fucking-dragon—and she holds on to the neck of the guitar with her left hand. The ax pressed close to her body, she draws her fingers down the strings, then taps them gently, but she doesn't dare strum them. She doesn't know what she's doing, and her touch is unsure, but she strums the strings once. Her eyes draw closed, either in pleasure or paying attention to the sound. I'm not sure.

But there is one thing I am sure of: I just witnessed Lola's very first spark. When her eyes open again, there is light in them for the first time all day as she looks down at my blue dragon in her hands.

I step in under the doorframe and cross my arms as I watch her. She still doesn't see me even as she puts the guitar back on its display hook. When the guitar is safely out of her hands, I do my best to sound angry.

"I thought I told you to stay out of here."

Lola jumps, startled, her eyes wide and cheeks flushed. "You said you'd be back at the end of the day," she stammers out.

"I finished my errands early. It doesn't matter. If there is one thing I told you not to do, it was to touch my axes."

"You're right. I'm sorry." She drops her head.

"Why are you in here?"

She shrugs. "I don't know. Once you showed me what was in here, I just . . ."

"Couldn't help yourself?" I ask.

She nods, and she looks so embarrassed, it's adorable. "I'm so, so sorry, Mr. Sommer. I'll never come in here again. I swear. I don't know what happened . . ." she trails off.

What the fuck? *Mr. Sommer?* For some reason, her calling me *Mr. Sommer* re-directs all the blood from my brain to my dick, and I have to scold myself inwardly. *She's seventeen, Karl!*

"Don't call me that," I snap, my jaw set.

She throws me a funny look. "Mr. Sommer?" she asks.

I click my tongue. "Yeah. Don't fucking call me Mr.

Sommer. It's *Karl*." I shake my head. I can't have her in my ax room, looking like she does, curious about music, and calling me Mr. Sommer. "You don't need to clean in here."

"Of course. And, um, Karl?"

I nod with approval at her using my first name. "Yeah?"

"It won't happen again."

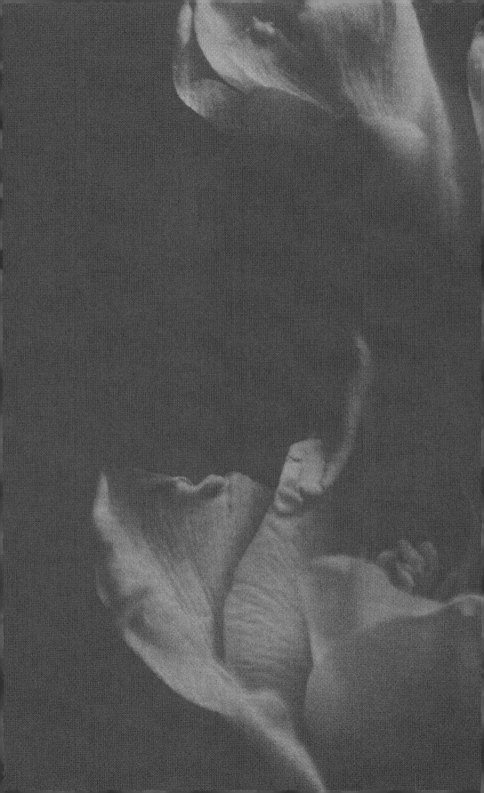

# 5

# KARL

L ola finished cleaning. It was a job for a team, but all full of energy, she hustled and actually finished—to my amazement. I'm glad I doubled the fee Sofia quoted me. She more than earned it. Especially after Pixel attacked her.

There has to be a reason for her to need money bad enough to clean houses when I'm sure she's still in high school. I've only known her one day, so it makes little sense for me to be protective of her, but I feel compelled to help the kid out.

She walks in from the back porch after taking the last of the trash bags out, and I wait, sitting on a stool in the kitchen. After she repositions her headphones to rest on her neck, she smiles at me. Her breathing is hard, and perspiration dots her forehead.

"Oh, hey," she says. "I'm done. I'll get out of your hair."

"You did amazing. Thank you."

She smiles goofily. "You're welcome." She turns to leave, then seems to think better of it. She clears her throat. "Um, Karl?"

"Yeah?"

"Since I'm off the clock, can I be a fan for five minutes? Just a fan talking to Karl Sommer from *Industrial November*, not my client?"

I bite back my smile but nod at her. "Go ahead." I pretend to sound annoyed.

Lola giggles, knowing I'm enjoying the attention. "I've seen you play live twice," she admits.

"We've only been in Kansas City once," I say.

"I missed this last concert here in KC, but I saw you in Chicago, and before that, I was at the first stop in your American tour."

"You were in Boston?" I ask, startled and suddenly uncomfortable.

She smiles knowingly at me. My face heats up, and I start to sweat.

"That fan . . ." she says thoughtfully.

I scratch my jaw. "Yeah, that was, um—an experience."

How could I forget that first concert in Boston? A fan got on stage and stripped for the Arena. Before she was arrested for indecent exposure, I lifted my ax over her head and played an entire song with her between my ax and me—my ax the only thing covering her naked lower body. For a complete song, I played with my erection pressed against her naked ass.

When the song ended, I pulled her off stage and handed her to security to get her dressed and taken away. The crowd ate that shit up. It went viral and made the news globally. To say it pleased Roger would be the understatement of the century.

And innocent, sweet, little underage Lola was in the audience.

"It was amazing," she admits, staring off into space.

"Uh—thanks?"

Lola bounces on her toes where she stands, giddy, like most fans do after concerts. She's so uncool; it's endearing. "I know the big draw to your live shows is Bren's intricate fire show, and it's great and all, don't get me wrong, but hearing you live is something else. It's so much more than just spectacle, you know?"

"Thanks, Iggy," I say, and for some reason, her praise makes me a little bashful.

"Can I ask you a few more questions?"

"Sure."

"How old were you when you started playing guitar?" she asks, leaning over the counter and propping herself up on her elbows.

"Fifteen."

Her mouth falls open. "You're only what, now? Twenty-six?"

I nod.

"You haven't been playing that long."

"Over a decade isn't enough for you?"

"No, uh—that's not what I meant. Most guitarists at your level have been playing since they could hold a guitar up."

I smile. I think Lola just complimented me for a second time. "So, you some kind of music geek?"

She purses her lips, thinking. "Why do you say that?"

"Gee, I don't know," I tease. "Maybe it's the 'Marquee Moon' t-shirt or the fact that you understood the Iggy peanut butter reference."

She smiles, damn pleased with herself. "Oh, that. Yeah. I love music. I swear I was born in the wrong decade. There was a cosmic fluke, and I was really supposed to be Richard Hell's wife."

I laugh at her silliness. "Lola Hell does have a nice ring to it," I say.

"Doesn't it?" she says with a soft giggle. "Anyway, I'll stop fangirling and annoying you."

"Don't forget your pay." I slide the envelope across the kitchen counter. "Here. For today. There's a little extra. I didn't think you'd get everything done, so consider it a bonus."

"Oh, that's unnecessary," she protests even as she opens the envelope. She takes the bills out to count, and her eyes grow to saucers. "Karl, I can't accept this. It's too much."

She tries to shove half the bills back my way, and I cross my arms, not accepting them. I narrow my eyes at her. "How much do you have, Lola? In all the world?"

Her gaze drops to the countertop, and she twists her fingers nervously. "With this, about eighteen grand."

I perk up in my seat. "Why are you saving so much?"

She swallows hard. Whatever it is, it's a source of sadness. Her eyes dim and turn lifeless again. "My aunt owns this restaurant in Mexico. I'm moving there to help her run it."

"And you need so much money for that?" I arch an eyebrow.

"No, I, um, I want to buy a house when I get there. So I'm saving my down payment."

Something isn't adding up here. "Lola, you sound like you're ready to settle down. You should use that money to travel, live a little. There's time for the rest later."

Her smile is sad when she speaks again. "I was going to go to college in California. But it fell through—"

"Why?"

She throws me a funny look. Guess I am being nosy. But I don't care. I want to know what her goals are . . . maybe help her reach them.

"That's a long story. And there are—um, secrets that aren't mine to share. But yeah, the restaurant is my plan B.

Besides, the only family I have left is there. I thought being near them would be nice."

"What about Sofia?" I ask.

She shifts her weight to the other foot. "Sofia and I aren't related like that. I consider her an older sister, but it's more like she adopted me."

Hmmm. Interesting. Sofia didn't say that when she warned me off Lola. "Okay, then answer me this. How long did it take you to get the eighteen grand?"

She taps her chin. "Let's see, I started working right after graduation, so um, I guess just shy of a year."

I narrow my eyes at her. "*After* graduation?"

"Yeah, why?"

"You graduate early?"

"No, why?" And the minute the question leaves her mouth, she clasps her hand over her mouth, her eyes wide above her hand.

Fucking. Busted.

I narrow my eyes at her and stand up. Lola was leaning on the counter but now stands straight, taking a step backward and away from me.

Closing the distance between us, I charge forward, and she presses her back to the refrigerator, leaving herself no safe retreat. "Something you wanna tell me, Iggy?" I ask.

"Um . . ." She looks down at her hands, twisting the hem of her shirt between her fingers.

Resting my forearm on the fridge above her head, I lift her chin with my free hand to force her eyes on me. "Lola? Tell me how old you are."

She hesitates. "Nineteen," she breathes out.

I let go of her chin, incredulous, and step back. Staring at her, I run both hands through my hair, pulling it back. "Why the fuck did Sofia tell me you're a minor?" I roar.

Lola smiles. This is amusing to her. Then she shrugs.

"Sofia? and Ileana . . . they've kinda turned into de facto older sisters to me this past year—since my parents passed. I think Sofia was just being a little overprotective."

My eyes soften as I stare at her. Her parents are dead? Is this why her eyes are so dim? "I'm sorry about your parents," I say lamely.

She smiles the most sad-looking smile I've ever seen. "Yeah. Me too."

I try to change the subject again. I don't want to be the reason for her to remember her grief. "Who is Ileana?"

"Oh, my roommate."

I pace the kitchen. I don't know what to do with all this information.

Then I try to shake off my next thought. Lola is fair game. I can pursue her if I want. She's not jailbait. But she *is* a distraction. One I can't afford if I want Bren to take me seriously—or at the very least, not trade me back for fucking Milo. And I can't forget this makes her *like* Bren's sister-in-law even if there's no real relation.

And why do all these plain and simple facts make the thought of being with her all the more exciting? *Stop it*, I chastise myself.

I grab a beer from the fridge and drain it.

"Can I have one?" Lola asks from her new spot, sitting on one of the island stools.

I shake my head. The audacity! "So you aren't a minor, but I do believe the drinking age in the states is still twenty-one."

She taps her chin thoughtfully, flashing hot pink, chipped fingernails. "I'd like to argue a few points." Her lips upturn into an amused smile. "One, I just did the job of ten people, so a beer sounds about the most refreshing thing in the world. Two, I've had beers before. And three, the crucial point here —I'm not American. I'm Mexican. And drinking age in

Mexico is eighteen, so I *am* of age to drink according to the laws of my country of origin—"

"Wait, you're Mexican?" I ask, completely surprised by that information.

"*Más que un nopal,*" she says with a chuckle.

"What does that mean?"

"Yeah, Karl. I'm Mexican. My name is Dolores Beltran. That didn't tip you off?" she teases.

I shake my head. Lola is a golden blonde goddess with green eyes. Not exactly the first thing that comes to mind when I think of a hot Mexican woman. But what the fuck do I know?

"I know what you're thinking," she says with a teasing smile.

"Oh, yeah?"

She nods. "Did you know that there was a huge German settlement in northern Mexico?"

I shake my head.

"Why do you think Mexican country music sounds so much like polka?" she asks.

I shake my head again but follow it up with an amused laugh. "You really are a music geek."

She shrugs.

"So, you're German?" I ask, excited we might have this in common. "*Sprichst du Deutsch?*" I ask.

She throws me a confused look. "Umm . . . no. Or at least, I have no idea. But I'm sure I have some sort of colonizer ancestry or other."

"Huh." This is all very interesting.

"Anyway, to my last point. Drinking age in Germany is also eighteen—"

"Sixteen," I correct.

Lola smiles, flashing me a hint of the pink bubblegum tucked between her teeth and cheek, and forcing my dick to twitch. I've never been more glad the kitchen island is still between us. "See?" she says. "You wouldn't even be providing alcohol to a minor based on the laws of *your* country of origin."

She is rather insistent. I go to the fridge and grab two more beers, popping them both open and handing Lola one. She smiles triumphantly, and I smile into my beer bottle as I take a sip.

We keep talking music, favorite bands, musical influences I studied as I learned to play guitar, and the afternoon turns into evening.

"Whoa," Lola says when she moves to stand and grabs onto the countertop. She's only had a few beers, so she shouldn't be losing her balance. She smiles, embarrassed. "Empty stomach," she says.

"Lola," I ask, trying not to get angry. "Did you skip lunch today to finish the job?"

She nods, and my fist clenches at my side, my other hand gripping my beer bottle tightly. I'm not sure why her not taking care of herself and skipping meals upsets me, but it does. I take a deep breath and force a smile. "How does pizza sound?" I ask her, and her entire face lights up.

---

HALF CHEESE—AS pizza should be—and half disgusting with pepperoni and pineapple.

Lola smiles goofily as she devours her first bite of pizza. She *was* hungry. She stopped drinking beers after her second one, and her mood is slowly shifting to a tired one. Of course she's tired after that long shift cleaning. If we were more familiar with each other, I'd reach over, take her shoes off, and massage the arches of her feet. *Huh.* I've never had that urge with anyone before.

I scan my living room—as clean as my room and Pixel's part of the house. It matches the rest of my life—my everyday life. The place isn't packed with people like it usually is—I texted them all that I'm not feeling well. Sandy's hands aren't all over my body. I'm sober.

And it's perfect bliss. This is what I want my life to be. Comfortable and in good company. I smile. This is what Bren and Sofia have.

I want it too.

Then, I think, if I found what they have, Bren would have something in common with me, wouldn't he? He keeps me at arm's length because of our age difference, because he thinks I'm a reckless fuckup. But if he saw me settling down, taking someone seriously, taking work seriously, I'm sure he'd respect me then. My spot in the band would be safe, and I might even get to collaborate with him creatively more than I've had a chance to so far.

There's so much I wish could be different. If I could have all that, the eccentric fans would also calm down a bit. I'm not afraid of one energetic fan, but when faced with a mob of them, that's an entirely different story. Even one is a little scary if she's broken into your home.

When Bren finally settled down with Sofia and they had their daughter, I noticed the significant change in the attention he received. Sure, they turned on Sofia those first few months, but then it slowed down. I actually think some of them turned their focus on me, making my fanbase a little more daunting.

A long string of cheese stretches from the third slice in Lola's hand, connecting to her full lips. The stringy cheese snaps and plops down to her chin, stretching down to the collar of her shirt. She looks up at me to check if I'm watching her, and I shake my head. Her goofy smile melts me, and she shrugs. "I eat passionately," she says, not at all embarrassed by the food she's cleaning off her face.

I stare at her in this perfect domestic setting that I want to have so badly, and a lightbulb turns on over my head—and it is massive.

But it's also the most reckless idea I've ever had.

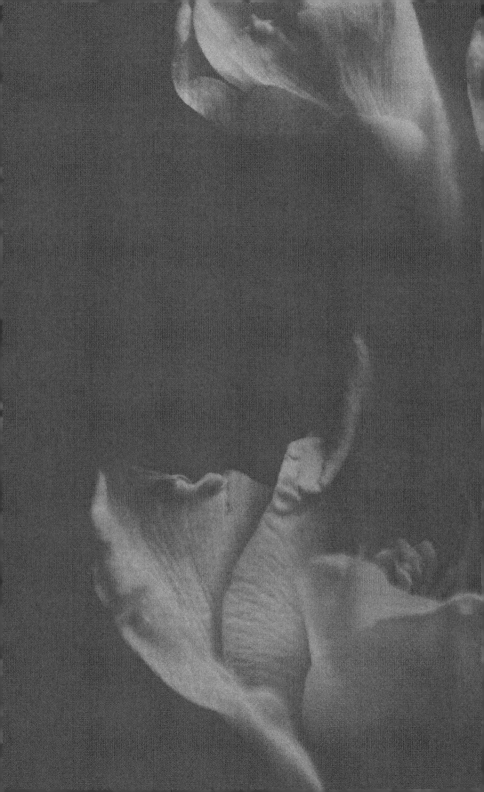

# 6

# LOLA

**K**arl is staring, and it makes me shift in my seat. I really, really—and I do mean *really*—want a fourth slice of pizza, but he's only had two, and what would he think if I dove in? What would my skinny jeans think? I sit on my hands so I don't reach for the fourth—the last slice of pepperoni with pineapple. I should get up and leave. I've over-stayed my welcome by now, but hanging out with Karl is like hanging out with an old friend.

We discussed music all evening, and I can pinpoint most of the influences in his playing now—at least I think I can. I'll go home and listen to the last album, *Breaking this Way*, which was the album he contributed to the most.

But he's still looking at me funny. Brows pinched together, thoughts rolling behind his blue eyes. "What?" I ask finally, rubbing my chin. "Did I miss some cheese?" I wipe my face but find nothing.

"How would you like to double your savings?" he says.

I blink at him. "What?"

"You have close to twenty grand, right? What if I were to double it?"

"Karl, I don't know what you have in mind, but—"

"It would be a better down payment for your house in Mexico, wouldn't it?"

Tilting my head to the side, I study him. Is he proposing something illegal here? Or perhaps something sexual?

Before I can let my thoughts wander any further, he speaks again. "All you'd have to do is pretend to be my girlfriend for a month." His smile is a mile wide, and I burst out laughing.

"What?" I ask, more than a little amused.

"Oh, this is perfect. Pretend to be my girlfriend, help me prove to the band that I'm mellowing, settling down—whatever they fucking call it. Help me dissipate the hordes of women who follow me everywhere. This is brilliant. Just a few months. No partying, serious couple stuff. A few public dinners and early nights in. That kinda thing."

I laugh with a shake of my head. "How much have you had to drink?" I ask.

"I'm sober. And dead serious, Lola. Pretend to be my girl-friend, go to some band practices or events, look dotingly at me, and help me prove I'm actually serious about the band. But more importantly, help me prove to the fans that I'm taken and unavailable." Then his smile turns mischievous. "And you get twenty grand for a month's work."

At a loss for words, I just blink at him again. I take a deep sigh and grab my fourth slice of pizza, skinny jeans be damned. I chew and think. Twenty thousand dollars could do a lot for my fresh start. And I can't believe that for one shameful second, Karl has me contemplating this half-baked idea.

I finally shake my head. "You're insane, and while that kind of money is tempting, I don't really need it. I've saved up my goal already. I don't need the money."

He purses his lips, then his eyes lock on mine. "There must be something else you want, if not money." His words are drenched with meaning.

A little voice inside me whispers, *Yes. I want you.* And I shut it up with thoughts of Ethan.

"Nope. Nothing I need. Besides, it's a terrible idea."

He grins, flashing me those pearly whites. "I think it's a great idea."

"You haven't thought this through. For starters, Sofia would blow a gasket. By extension, Bren would too—"

"Only until they realize how serious we are."

"You have Sandy—"

"No." He shakes his head. "We're not exclusive. I would end it with her, of course—"

"And I have Ethan," I nearly whisper.

Karl's smile vanishes, and his face falls for a moment before he recovers. "Ethan?"

I nod. "He's my boyfriend."

"Lucky guy."

I smile.

"He's in California," I add, though I'm not sure why.

"Long-distance never works," he says.

I look down at the pizza in my hands, a little sad that he's probably right. It's been hard the last few months with Ethan away. Long-distance is tough; it's one thing to make it work with a few states between us, but being a country away? Deep down, I know my move will be the kiss of death for us.

My eyes sting at the thought of losing my first love. My high school sweetheart. I didn't imagine we'd last forever, but we *were* in love once.

*Were?* I think to myself. *Am I already thinking about us in past tense?* I shake my head and reel my tears back in. I should enjoy what time I have with Ethan. He's due to visit over fall break so I'll at least get to spend some time with him before I leave.

"Where'd you go?" Karl asks, looking at me intensely.

"You're probably right about the long distance, but I love him. I want to try to make it work."

Karl nods, and he scratches his jaw. "I'm sorry if I upset you. I shouldn't have shared my opinion on your relationship. Only you two know what goes on there."

I gulp in a big breath and smile, wanting to turn the conversation away from me. I say, "For what it's worth, you could get an actual girlfriend to do this with. Sandy, even . . ." I trail off when he fakes an exaggerated shiver.

"No," he says. "Bren hates Sandy. He hates everyone in the usual crowd—he's a family man now. It needs to be with someone he perceives as a positive influence on me."

I chew on my pizza and think. "My roommate Ileana is the best influence I can think of," I say.

"Is she over eighteen?" he teases.

"Yes." I roll my eyes. "She's in her late twenties. And it would be great, actually. She could move in here, and I could finally have some peace and quiet."

"What do you mean?"

"I babysit for her son in exchange for room and board. I love Isael to death, but he's running me ragged. That's how I saved up so much in such a short amount of time."

"While I like the idea of dating a woman older than me," he says, "you lost me at 'her son.'"

I snicker. "Well, I'm sure you know more than enough candidates. And I'm sure Sandy would jump at the opportunity . . ." Even as I complete that though, a knot forms in my throat, and I don't know why.

Karl shakes his head. "That won't work. Bren hates Sandy," he repeats, annoyed.

Stretching my arms over my head, I stand up from the couch. "Well, good luck finding the perfect girl. I have to get going." I say that and then linger.

I don't want to go. Talking to Karl is like talking to an old friend. Comfortable and sweet. And I've never had anyone in my life I could talk to about music like I did with him today. At least, not outside an online forum. And at the heart of it is this simple truth: I don't want this to be the last time I see or speak to Karl Sommer. But I know once I step outside those doors, he'll be unreachable forever.

Sensing my apprehension, Karl speaks up. "Would you come back and clean again? Keep this place as clean as you left it?"

I fidget with the hem of my shirt. "Sure. Next week okay?"

"Perfect. Maybe make it a weekly job until your move? I don't think we're leaving Kansas City for a while. Bren still hasn't given us an end date for his paternity leave."

I'm much more excited at the thought of seeing him again than I should be. "Same time? Saturday mornings?"

"Yeah. You have the code to get in."

I nod.

Mischief dances in his eyes with a silly grin. "I'll leave the peanut butter out for you."

---

THE HOUSE IS UNUSUALLY quiet when I get home. Ileana tiptoes barefoot out of Isael's room.

"He asleep?" I whisper, and she nods.

Thank the heavens. I plop myself down on the couch, lying down and resting my feet on the armrest. I don't remember ever being so exhausted. The house really was a mess.

"Long day?" Ileana asks.

I peer up at her, smiling at seeing her in her signature maxi dress. Her dark caramel waves fall full around her shoulders. "You have no idea," I say. "Made good money, though."

Ileana grins wide. "Good." She stands to go to the kitchen and comes back with a glass of her famous *agua de jamaica*, setting it on the coffee table in front of me.

Though she's not that much older than me, Ileana is wise

beyond her years, more like family than friend. Since she and Sofia adopted me as a little sister, they've always had my back.

I don't think I could have survived the last year if it weren't for my roommate. She's known profound loss too, and without her advice, I would be in a much darker place now. It took me much too long to learn the most important lesson she taught me this past year: You take one breath, and then another. Day by day, you live one breath at a time. One day, there will be a happy moment that will make all the pain worth it, and that's what you stick it out for.

I'm still waiting for my happy moments. But thanks to Ileana, I stick it out, waiting for it to happen. I'm not sure why, but spending the evening with Karl has me thinking about all this.

My phone rings with "1979" by *The Smashing Pumpkins*, and I smile. So does Ileana when I look up at her. "Sorry," I say. "I have to take this."

I take the drink she poured for me and head into my room. "Hey, baby," I say as I close the door behind me.

"Hi, Lo."

"I've missed you," I say sweetly, but with my heart aching—missing him.

"Uh—yeah. How've you been?" he asks.

My eyes narrow. He sounds . . . off. And he didn't say he missed me back. Maybe he's distracted. "Good. I had a long workday today, but I'm closer to my goal now." Ethan knows all about my savings plan to move to Mexico.

"That's great!" he says, much too happily. He shouldn't be. It means we'll be even farther apart. *Stop it, Lola!* I scold myself. *He can be proud of you for reaching your goals without it meaning anything.*

"I'm excited to see you soon," I say, refocusing the conversation on his upcoming fall break.

"Yeah, about that, Lo . . . that's actually why I called you. I'm so sorry, but something came up. I won't be able to come home after all."

My face falls. "Oh," I say.

"It's an incredible opportunity to be an assistant for one of my professor's projects. A recommendation from him for grad school is just too good to pass up."

I clear my throat. I want to be supportive and try to sound happy when I say, "That's great, Ethan. I'm so proud of you."

"Thanks," he says.

"But . . ."

"But what?" he asks.

"I'm leaving in a few weeks. If you're not coming home for fall break, we won't get to see each other before I leave—"

"I'm so sorry," he says. "We knew this would be hard, right?"

There has to be a way around this. I think of my bonus from work today. It's money I wasn't counting on. I should show Ethan I'm invested in long-distance too, especially if we want to make a go of it once I'm in Mexico.

"How about I visit you, then?" I ask, more hopeful.

He breathes out a long breath. "Lo . . ."

"It's perfect; I'll come up for a week, then come back and pack up to leave. Once I'm settled, you can visit me in Acapulco. Maybe during winter break? Can you just see us? Romantic walks on the beach." I smile at the thought of sand between our toes, Tecate beers in our hands. I keep going, painting the picture for him. "Eating seafood for dinner every evening, dancing all night? I hear Acapulco is so much fun, Ethan. We'll have a blast." I smile again as the montage plays before me. It would be such a perfect time together.

"Lo, you coming here isn't a good idea. I'll be working all day, and you'll be bored out of your mind. We'd only have nights together."

I bite my lip. "All we need are the nights, baby," I say suggestively. I know he catches my meaning because he hesitates.

"As tempting as that is," he says, "I'd feel guilty about neglecting you all day. And some days might turn into late nights working. It's just bad timing. I'm sorry."

"Okay," I say, completely heartbroken. "But you'll visit me in Acapulco, then? Once I'm settled?"

"We'll see. Listen, I gotta go. My roommate is here, and we're heading out to a party. Bye, Lo!"

He hangs up before I can get my "I love you" out.

I'm losing him.

If I haven't already.

# 7

# KARL

F riday morning, we're supposed to meet with Roger and our publicity team, but I get to Bren's apartment early. I smile when I get off the elevator at his penthouse and see the chaotic mess everywhere.

Well, isn't this poetic? Neat-freak Brenner Reindhart's apartment is messier than my place. His daughter's toys are everywhere. Sofa cushions are on every surface except the actual couches. This must be driving him insane. And that starts off my day putting me in the best mood.

Sofia screams from down the hallway, and a tiny wisp of black hair in a ponytail shooting straight up catches my attention as their daughter comes running into the living room. "Addy, get back here! We need to get a shirt on you," Sofia whines.

Addy only giggles, and on wobbly, fat legs, runs to me and crashes into my leg, wrapping her arms around it. I pick her up in my arms.

"Addy-girl, you're getting fast. Once they got you walking, you blazed straight to running, didn't ya?"

She giggles and palms the side of my face. "Io Kal," she

says. I know she means '*tío* Karl.' Sofia has taught her to call Fritz, Adrian, and me '*tío*,' to Bren's annoyance.

"Oh, hey, Karl," Sofia says, surprised. She looks down at her watch. "You're early."

"Don't look so surprised," I tease and hand her Addy for her to put her shirt on. Addy protests, trying to clasp on to my shirt. I think I'm her favorite in the band—well, apart from Bren.

Sofia glances behind her toward the hallway leading to their room. "Bren's in the shower. I thought you were meeting at Fritz's today? I'm sorry it's such a mess."

I shrug. "Yeah, we are, but I was hoping to talk to Bren first. One-on-one."

Sofia smiles approvingly. "Can I give you one piece of advice?"

"I sure could use it," I say.

"He's all bark and no bite. Don't let Bren get in your head. Under that intimidating exterior, he's just a big ol' fluffy teddy bear."

I nod. I'm surprised how well she knows him already. They haven't been together long, even if they share a daughter.

"He in a good mood today? I ask."

"You know him. He's perpetually serious."

We both laugh and both stop midway when Bren's voice startles us.

"Who's serious?" he asks.

Sofia spins to look at Bren. "Addy needs a fresh diaper. I'll leave you two to it."

Bren walks toward me and steps on one of Addy's sharp toys with his bare foot. He winces with pain, closes his eyes, and his nostrils flare, but he says nothing. Oh, this is amusing as all hell. Why haven't I been over more often?

"Why are you here so early?" he asks.

"We need to talk."

Bren nods and leads me to their kitchen table, where he sits across from me.

I want to tell him I know he's been talking to Milo. Remind him of my contract . . . but I don't want to throw Adrian under the bus. A more diplomatic approach will go over better. Reminding myself of his face when he stepped on that toy, I clear my throat to speak. "I wanted to apologize for last week. For not showing up."

"I don't want your apologies, Karl. I want your work ethic to improve—"

"I know," I hurry to say. "And it will. I promise."

"You've said this before."

"I mean it. No more parties. I'm going to buckle down and do better at taking band business seriously."

"What about creatively?" Bren asks.

"What do you mean?"

Bren lets out a long breath. "When you first auditioned, you blew me away. I was in awe of your playing. And all of us, but especially Fritz and me, were excited to see what you could bring to the table. We thought you would add your own flavor to the music."

I shrug. "I don't know. I thought the two riffs in the last album were pretty epic."

"They were, but I want to see you writing more music. Bring ideas. Show us what you can do—what we *know* you can do."

"I'm turning a new leaf, Bren. I promise."

"We always have the same conversation. How is this time any different?"

"You're right. You don't have to believe it because I say it. Let me show you that I'm done with the partying and recklessness. Time will prove I'm serious." I could kill Roger for putting me in this position. I don't revel in being one of my hero's biggest disappointments.

Bren nods with approval. "Why not start proving it now?" he asks.

"What do you mean?"

"Sell me your house."

I nearly jump out of my seat. "What?"

"Sofia liked it when she saw it. I did too. And we need to get out of this apartment. I want Addy to have a yard and more space."

Bren's penthouse is spectacular and has quite a lot of space, but I could see how a one-year-old would make it seem much smaller than it actually is.

"I love my house," I say, hesitant to sell.

"You love it because it's away from any other homes, and you can party and raise hell—but you're telling me you're done with that, right?"

"I am!"

"Good. Then sell me the house. I'll throw in the penthouse if it sweetens the deal. This building has stricter rules, so you can't have the ragers you're used to. Adrian moved into the building too, so you can look out for each other. It's a great plan, Karl." He grins wide. "And it would go a long way to prove you are serious about what you said."

"Pixel needs a yard," I say.

"There's a rooftop garden. Dogs are welcome. And there's a doggy park just a few blocks down."

Damn. He has an answer for everything.

I hang my head. I can't say no to him. Not with everything I've fucked up lately. "Fine," I say. "One week enough to pack and then start moving everything?"

"I'll talk to Sofia, but yeah, I think so. I'll call the lawyer to draw up a contract. We can talk about details later."

After shaking on it, Bren and I leave his penthouse and head a few floors down to Fritz's apartment.

On time.

---

THE NEXT DAY IS SATURDAY, and I get up early again. Lola is due to come clean in an hour, and while the place has stayed mostly clean, Pix and I did a number on her playroom and the kitchen. I jump out of bed and hurry to pick up Pix's toys.

"I need to teach you to put your toys away," I say, pretending to be annoyed, and her little ears pin back—her symbol of shame. Anytime I come home to Pix with her ears pinned back, I know she's in for it. But it also happens when I scold her.

"And yes," I tell her. "Before you ask, I realize I'm a total moron for cleaning up before my housekeeper arrives . . ." Pix's head tilts to the side as she studies me.

Even though today's job wouldn't have taken her that long, I still want it to be done before she gets here. I'd rather spend the morning with her.

Once done, I feed Pix breakfast and let her out into the backyard. When we come back inside, I hear the front door click closed, and I know she just got here. As I smile, Pixel works herself up into a bark and lunges toward the front door. "Pixel, no! It's Lola."

I follow her, and by the time I reach them, Lola is on her knees, Pixel propped up against her, licking her face. Lola squints and makes a disgusted face but leans into Pix's kisses.

And my heart soars. It's the most beautiful thing I've ever seen.

"That's a good girl," Lola says in a playful, deep voice as she pets her. Pix's tail wags with appreciation of the praise.

Then Lola takes something out of her pocket and feeds it to Pixel with a massive grin on her face. Her eyes find me across the foyer. "I came prepared this time," she says.

I laugh. "What is that?" I ask.

"Peanut butter treat. There's this doggy bakery in Leawood near an apartment I cleaned this morning. I stopped by before coming over."

I blink at her. "You already finished a job this morning?"

She nods. "It's a small apartment, and the guy is rather neat, so it doesn't take that long."

My stomach knots at thinking of her alone in a small apartment with a random guy. Is this job of hers safe? I can't ask her, though. I'll sound insane.

She stands up from her petting duties and steps deeper into the house, looking around. "Um, I guess you haven't been home much. It's the same as last week."

"I've been home, but I maintained it."

"Guess you don't need me then?" she says, almost disappointed.

I want to think she's disappointed at the prospect of losing our time together, but it's probably the loss of another big paycheck. "No," I hasten to correct her. "I do need you. If you could dust, so it stays as clean as you left it, that'd be great."

She crosses her arms in front of her. "You want me to just dust?"

I nod. "Maybe clean the countertops in the kitchen? Oh, and you didn't do the inside of the fridge last time," I add, trying to find work that will make her stay. Cleaning up ahead of time was the stupidest idea I'd ever had. "And you'll get paid, of course."

"Fine, but you'll pay me a lot less since the job is so much smaller now."

"Deal."

"And I won't dust your axes," she says with a smirk.

As she works on the few tasks I've given her, I find excuses to go into whatever room she's in and sneak glances at her. I don't understand this need to be in the same room with her, but it brings the biggest, stupidest smile to my face. Pixel, too. Her tail hasn't stopped wagging since Lola showed up, and she's been following her around the house as she works.

She leaves cleaning the kitchen for last, and I sneak in to grab a glass of orange juice before she gets started on the fridge. I sit at the island to watch her work, and there's a hint of a smile in the corner of her lips. She takes her headphones off so we can have a conversation.

"You never told me why you keep your peanut butter in the fridge."

"That's expensive, organic, small-batch peanut butter, I'll have you know. No preservatives. It needs to be refrigerated."

Her hand goes to her hip as she stares at the refrigerator contents. "Ah. Well, you have little else here."

"Don't really know how to cook," I say. "I eat out most of the time."

She closes the door and turns to look at me. Her eyes roam my arms. "How do you stay fit if you only eat out?"

I shrug. "Lucky, I guess? I mean, I work out but don't pay attention to diet."

"Hmm," she says thoughtfully. "The fridge is pretty clean. I guess I'm done unless you want me to make you some breakfast?" she asks hopefully. "I could do your shopping for you, then come back and whip something up."

I smile. She wants to extend our time together too. "You know how to cook?" I ask her.

She nods. "A little. I'm okay. Ileana's been trying to teach me. *She* is amazing. Her food is magic. I swear she needs to open up a Mexican restaurant."

"I love Mexican food. I'd love to try her cooking sometime."

Lola smiles. "Maybe I'll invite you over for dinner one of these days."

I like this. I'm not the only one needing excuses for us to see each other again.

"Let's go to the grocery store, then," I say, getting up from my seat at the counter.

Her head tilts to the side. "You don't have to go with me. You're paying me for my time, remember?"

I scratch my jaw. "Right. But . . . I'm bored. And honestly, I can't remember the last time I was inside a grocery store—"

Lola's laugh cuts me off.

"What?" I ask, amused.

"Your lifestyle, it's . . . straight out of a movie."

"Speaking of, mind if we take your car? Mine is easily identifiable by the paps."

Lola agrees happily, and after tucking all my hair under the baseball cap and putting on my aviator glasses, we head out. We walk down the driveway and get to a shit-brown Suzuki sedan that is older than Lola, by the looks of it. I frown. This car isn't safe for her.

"I don't need to upgrade my car when I'm moving so soon," she says, reading my thoughts. "Besides. This baby and I have been through a lot of shit together. I love her," she says and rubs the car roof lovingly.

I sigh and get inside.

LOLA PICKS out the fruit carefully, weighing each item in her hands and bringing it to her nose to smell before adding it to a bag. I'm mesmerized as I watch her, and I'm glad I'm wearing the sunglasses even inside the store. I pretend to look at items and instead stare at her. Why does she have to have a boyfriend? I'm sure if she didn't, she would have agreed to pretend to be my girlfriend when I asked.

She adds four limes to a bag as she says, "How's Sandy?"

I shrug. "Don't know. The last time I saw her was the last time you did."

Her eyes find mine. "Oh, I thought . . ."

"No. I doubt I'll see her again," I say, surprising even myself. When exactly did I decide Sandy was part of my past and no longer part of my present? *The moment Lola socked you in the jaw, you idiot,* a little voice inside me answers.

"That's too bad," Lola says and pushes the cart away from the produce area. "She seemed nice."

"She is. But for someone else."

We stroll slowly through the aisles, and I know we're both dragging our feet to stretch our time together as much as possible. It's everything I can do to wipe the smile from my face.

"So, what would you like for breakfast?"

"Something easy. Eggs, maybe?" I don't want her busy cooking for hours.

"Easy enough. How do you like your eggs?"

"With ketchup."

Her nose scrunches up in disgust, but she doesn't comment. "All right, let's head to the ketchup aisle."

We round the corner, and I tell her to go on as I select some mustard for hot dogs later. She's nearly at the end of the aisle when a man calls out her name, and I turn to pretend to look at items but slowly inch closer to them so I can hear their conversation.

"Lo?"

She stops rolling the cart, frozen for a moment. Then she jumps up in the air with excitement. "Ethan!"

My jaw tightens. Her fucking boyfriend is here. Just my luck.

Moving past the cart, Lola jumps into his arms, wrapping her arms around his neck, straining on her toes to achieve the embrace. "You came after all! I knew I couldn't leave without seeing you again."

I study them discreetly. Lola's back is to me, and Ethan's eyes are wide in a look of . . . panic? His hands outstretch at his sides as if he's afraid of returning the hug. What the hell?

Another person rounds the corner and joins them. "Ethan? Oh, there you are. I found the basil," a tall, leggy blonde says, then stops in her tracks, seeing Lola in Ethan's arms. She places the basil in Ethan's cart at the same time Lola takes a step back, and then the woman stands next to him, lacing her arm through his. "Who's this?" she asks, looking between Ethan and Lola.

Bile rises to the back of my throat with anger. Lola's heart is about to get broken. This fucker is cheating on her. I pick up another random item from the shelf and pretend to read the label, but keep watching, ready to jump in if Lola needs me.

"This is Lola," he says. Even from where I'm standing five feet away, I see the woman's eyes soften with something that looks a lot like pity.

"Oh," she says in a soft tone. "You're Lola. I'm Megan. It's nice to meet you."

Lola just stands there, frozen, and my heart breaks for her. She's connecting the dots together now. What should I do? I want to go over there, take her hand in mine, and leave with her. But she needs to see this through. I know she does.

"Who—who's this?" Lola's voice is small as it breaks. "Ethan?"

"Megan goes to school with me. She came home with me to uh—uh, Megan? Mind waiting in the car?" Ethan asks.

"Yeah, Ethan. Actually, I would mind," she says coolly, stepping away from him and arching a brow in his direction.

His pasty complexion flushes, his cheeks bright red, and he runs a nervous hand through his dark brown hair. "Lola, I'm so sorry. I wanted to tell you in person . . ."

"Tell me what?" she asks.

God, I wish I could see her face right now.

"I didn't want to break it off over the phone. You mean too much to me . . . Fuck! This is not how I wanted this to go."

"And Megan is . . .?"

Ethan stays quiet, his eyes drifting closed. When he takes too long to answer, it's Megan who speaks up. "I'm his girl-friend. I'm in town to meet his parents."

Nothing from Lola. I expected a gasp. Tears. Yelling. Something. But she just stands there, quiet and heartbroken. I grip the can in my hands, and I want nothing more than to fling it at Ethan's head.

"I'm sorry, Lo," he finally says. "Long-distance was just never going to work out. I should have told you sooner," he adds lamely.

Lola shakes her head. "I understand," she says, barely above a whisper.

That does it. I can't watch this anymore. And I can't stand this awkward moment, with fucking Ethan and Megan looking at her with *pity*. They should *never* pity her, not when they aren't worth enough to lick the bottom of her shoe.

I walk confidently up to them. "Baby, you find the ketchup?" I say with a bright smile. I wrap my arm around Lola, resting it on her shoulder and pulling her into my side protectively. I duck a bit to kiss her temple, getting a whiff of her watermelon bubblegum, and she blinks up at me, star-tled. "Who's this?" I ask, looking up at Ethan, my fake smile plastered on my face.

"Uh . . ." She's confused now.

Ethan speaks up. "I'm Ethan. Who are *you?*" he asks, his eyes narrowed to slits.

I flash him a broad smile and take off my glasses.

"Karl Sommer!" Megan screams and jumps where she stands. "Oh my god, it's Karl Sommer from *Industrial November!*" She rushes to my side and takes my hand in hers to shake it. "I am such a huge fan," she gushes, gripping our handshake too long.

I pry my hand away from her and wink. "Shh, do you mind keeping it down? No one knows I'm here. And no one knows about Lola and me yet."

Ethan's mouth falls open, and Megan pretends to wince, then whispers, "Oh, yeah. Sorry." But she keeps grinning where she stands, utterly unaware of Lola or Ethan's presence any longer.

"What the fuck, Lola?" Ethan asks after a moment of being dumbstruck.

"Like you said," Lola says. "Long-distance is hard, and I didn't want to tell you over the phone—" *Good girl, Iggy,* I think proudly. She's with the program now. "That's why I was so insistent about seeing you over fall break. I wanted to break things off, amicably—if possible."

"So you're with *him,* now?" he asks, throwing me a nasty glare, and I grin wider at him.

"Sorry, mate. You leave a girl this beautiful alone that long? You can't expect she'll be waiting forever." I turn to look down at Lola, and I lift her chin toward me with my index finger. I smile at her, and her eyes grow wide. I give her a moment to pull her attention again to her asshole ex-boyfriend, but she doesn't. Instead, her eyes fix on my lips and even though every cell in my body pushes me to kiss her, I can't. I don't want our first kiss to be here, in a grocery store, in front of her fucking ex-boyfriend. And I definitely don't want it to be to prove a point.

Our first kiss will be real, I decide. When she's moved on from this jerk, and when she's ready for it.

Instead, I kiss her temple again, my eyes closed, savoring the tender moment. When I open my eyes, she's smiling up at me with doting eyes. Is she pretending for Ethan? Or is this moment real? I don't know.

But what I do know for sure is that one day I will taste Dolores Beltran's lips, or my name isn't Karl Sommer.

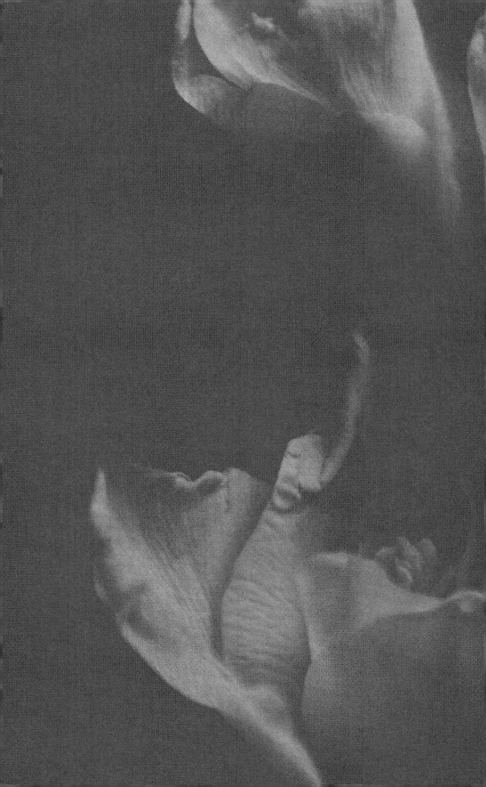

# 8

# LOLA

Karl insisted he drive us back to his house when we left the grocery store, thinking I'd be too upset to drive safely. And he's done nothing but complain about my car since he got in.

When he tried pulling the backrest down, it horrified him that it couldn't move. The seat broke last year, and it's been propped up with the plank of lumber I tied to the back with rope ever since. Karl's horror-stricken face is so comical; I burst into laughter.

"This car is a death trap," he says, but he drives anyway. "I have to say, I thought you'd be more upset than you are."

I run my hands through my hair. "Yeah . . . to be honest, me too. I think I'm more resigned than heartbroken. If I'm honest with myself, I've known for a while this was coming."

"I'm glad you're okay," Karl says.

"Though . . . I think I'm still in shock. When it wears down, I don't know how I'll feel. It was a lot of years, Ethan and me."

Karl nods and says nothing more.

We get to the house, and he helps me take the groceries in. I instruct him to take a seat and wait for his breakfast while I put them away.

But my mind wanders back to Ethan and Megan as I work.

Of course, Megan is perfect. Leggy, blonde, with shiny, straight hair, and she's tall—almost as tall as Ethan. She was so polished and put together in her baby blue miniskirt and white blouse. But the damned curse has struck again. This little run-in happened after I'd already been hard at work cleaning for three hours this morning, wearing my worst jeans and my old, ratty, and ripped *Guns N' Roses* t-shirt. I felt smaller than a grain of sand standing in front of the beautiful couple. No wonder he picked her over me. Because what man in his right mind would choose a gloomy, down-on-her-luck, homely girl when he could have a California dream babe instead?

I don't notice when Karl stands to guide me to a seat. He says something, but I'm not listening. "What?" I ask.

"Sit down. I'll put these away."

I shake my head. "No, Karl. It's my job. Really, I'm okay to work."

He glares at me, but he's smiling, so I know it isn't a serious glare. "You just stowed the milk in the pantry, Lola."

"Oh, I'm sorry. I think my mind is still back there."

He smiles. "I know."

It ends up being Karl who cooks the eggs.

When he sets the plate of scrambled eggs in front of me, the fog in my brain lifts and the tears flow freely. That's how Ethan likes his eggs. Scrambled.

"Shit, doll," he whispers in the seat next to me. "I'm sorry." Karl grabs the chair's legs to drag it closer to him, and he takes me in his arms, his hands rubbing circles on my back. "He's a fucking *drecksau*," he says in a voice so harsh, the German insult must be really nasty.

His embrace is so comforting, I only sob harder into his neck. It finally sinks in.

Ethan is horrible. He lied to me. He's been lying to me for a long time. How long has he been dating Megan? I need to drown my cell in a glass of water before I'm tempted to text him a million questions.

And his lies didn't end there. He lied again today. He said he waited because he wanted to break it off in person, but he lied to me about not coming home for break. Ethan never intended to break it off with me. He was going to string me along for . . . how long? Was he planning on having me as his side-piece in Mexico when he vacationed and keep Megan as his girlfriend at home? When did he turn into such an ass? He's not the Ethan I know. Not the Ethan I fell in love with freshman year. Not the Ethan who held me up so I wouldn't fall apart at the funeral. He's someone different now, I guess.

I break away from Karl and smile through my tears, embarrassed. "Do me a favor?" I ask him.

"Anything."

"Confiscate my cell until I leave? I don't want to be tempted to call and ask Ethan my million questions. He's not worth my time."

"You got it."

I pull my phone from my jeans pocket and hand it to Karl. "Thank you."

"Can I ask you a favor in return?" he asks.

"Sure."

"Hang out with me today. Not as an employee. I enjoy your company. You're not . . . *fake* like everyone else I hang out with. And it'll make me feel better to know you're okay."

I smile at him and nudge him under the table with my knee. "You're sweet, Karl Sommer. You know that?"

He smiles wide. "I do know that, Dolores Beltran."

The afternoon passes by as we talk about everything and anything under the sun but mostly music. In the evening, when my tummy rumbles, I offer to cook something, but Karl shakes his head and proposes pizza again. I smile. This is my second Saturday night pizza . . . date? No. This is not a date.

After eating, we relocate to Pixel's part of the house, and I sink into a giant, comforting bean bag chair. Pixel can sense my sad mood because she curls up next to me, and the chair is big enough for both of us. Karl takes the chair across from us.

I hug Pixel tightly. "I really did love him," I say and wipe a lone tear from my cheek.

"I know."

"When my parents died, he was my rock. And so incredibly understanding. If it weren't for him, and Ileana, and Sofia . . . I don't know what would have happened to me."

Karl's eyes darken as he nods.

"Until he had to go away to college, Ethan was the sweetest."

"People change, Lola. And college, that's an entirely different environment."

I nod. "You know, when he first went away without me, I think I knew. He'd continue to learn and grow, and I'd be stuck in the same place. I knew we'd never last."

"Don't say that, Lola. Life teaches us more than college does."

"Did you go to college?" I ask him.

Karl rolls his eyes. "Like you aren't a super fan who already knows everything there is to know about all of us in the band?" He raises an eyebrow at me.

I try to remember if I ever read about his educational background. "Well, I know Bren, Adrian, Milo, and Fritz all met at university in Berlin. But I don't think I ever read about you going to college."

"I went for one year before dropping out."

"Why'd you drop out?"

He scratches his jaw while he thinks. "For one, I knew what I wanted to do. I wanted to play guitar in an awesome metal band. College would not get me there. But I didn't enjoy it. It was more about kissing professors' asses than it was about learning." He pauses for a moment, thoughtful. "I guess I wanted to start living, and I didn't feel I was in those cramped dorm rooms."

I smile at him and look at the surrounding luxury. "Guess it worked out okay for you."

He smirks. "It did. And it will work for you too. You'll see."

I shake my head, a little sad. "Don't think so."

"Why not?"

"You had a passion—something you were pursuing. I've never felt that way about anything. The best I can hope for is a quiet life in Acapulco, running my business, owning my home."

"Bull," Karl says.

"What?"

"Bullshit. You have a passion."

"Oh, yeah?" I ask, amused.

His eyes widen in an *isn't it obvious?* look. "Music. You're passionate about music."

I laugh. "I love music, but I don't want to make it."

His eyes narrow. "Don't you? When you were in the ax room, I saw the look."

"*The look?*" I ask with a laugh.

"Yeah. There was a spark there. I think you should think about playing guitar."

I mull that over for a minute. I've always loved listening to music and reading about it. But I've never contemplated making it. "Maybe," I say. "It could be fun just as a hobby."

Karl shakes his head. "Trust me, that look was not a hobby look."

"What was it then?" I ask.

Karl doesn't hesitate even a second before answering. "That, Iggy, was a look of passion and desire." He smirks. "You covet my ax."

My mouth falls open. Is there a double meaning in his

words? I shake the thought away. No. He's trying to distract me, that's all, to take my thoughts away from Ethan.

He's being incredibly sweet, and letting me curl up with Pixel is one of the nicest things he's done for me. Another tear falls, and he must sense his failure at distracting me because he proposes watching a movie instead.

When he asks what I'd like to watch, I smile wide. "American Psycho." I'm in the mood for violence.

"You like horror?"

I shake my head. "Not really, but Christian Bale's naked ass sure goes a long way to cheer me up."

"You're a pervert, Lola." He shakes his head but finds the movie and presses play.

But I don't watch the movie. My eyes drift to the door next to the television—the one leading to the room I know houses all of his world-famous guitars. Is Karl right? Am I passionate about guitar? The one note I played when he caught me holding his guitar is the only time I've held a musical instrument in my hands. I need to get hold of another guitar to test this theory out.

Suddenly, I find myself concerned more about the future—about what I want to do—and less and less about my shattered heart and the jerk who broke it.

I don't even notice as I fall sleep, but wrapped around a warm puppy, I drift off into an untroubled sleep as Patrick Bateman continues on his rampage in the distance.

I'm barely aware of someone shifting me, but I feel the comfort of being laid down on fresh linens and getting tucked in. I smile at the memory of Mom when I was little. She always tucked me in. Then I drift again into a deep, content sleep.

SOMETHING cold and wet presses against my arm hanging off the mattress. I open one eye to find Pixel staring at me from next to the bed. I startle out of bed. "Pixel, you creepy dog. You can't just stare at people sleeping."

She wags her tail.

I blink. It's light out. Where am I? Looking around, I realize I'm in one of Karl's guest rooms—the one next to the master bedroom, to be more specific. It was dark out when we went upstairs to talk and watch a movie. He must have put me to bed. I look over to the door, and my shoes are next to it. I smile. He carried me to bed, took my shoes off, and tucked me in.

I run to the restroom and wash my face and brush my teeth. "Come on, Pix. Let's go find your sweet, sweet dad."

We head downstairs together to find Karl making coffee. "Good morning," he says brightly, seeing us walk in.

"Morning. I'm sorry I fell asleep—"

"I'm glad you did. You feeling any better?"

I sigh. "Yeah. It's sunk in. I can move on now."

"Go sit at the table. I'll bring breakfast over."

"You cooked again?"

"God, no. I went out for donuts."

I roll my eyes. "Of course."

He sets a glazed donut in front of me, and we sip our coffees and eat the pastries. "Thank you for breakfast. I'll get going."

His face falls a little, making me smile. He likes me here.

I stare at my coffee, thinking. As much as we talked about everything else, we never broached the subject of his surprise attack boyfriend role and him kissing my forehead. With everything else going on and all the emotions, I haven't had time to dwell on it. But it had to be just a friend helping me save face, right? It wasn't a genuine kiss. I decide not to ask him about it. He hasn't brought it up, so surely he was just helping me out.

I'll always be grateful to him for that.

"Before you head out, can I ask you something?" Karl asks.

"Sure."

"Will you reconsider my offer from last week?"

I set my coffee mug down. "What? You mean, about pretending to be your girlfriend?"

Karl nods, his face stern. "You no longer have a boyfriend, so . . ."

"I can't, Karl. I'm moving in less than two weeks."

"Push your trip. It's not urgent, right? Come on, Lola. Where else are you going to make twenty grand in just a couple of months?"

I smirk. "You said one month. Now it's a couple?"

"I'll take whatever you're willing to give." His statement is full of meaning, and my breath catches in the back of my throat.

I shake my head. "I don't need your money, Karl. And more importantly, I don't want it."

"Why not?"

"I have everything I need. I'm set for my fresh start. I'm ready to move on and start somewhere else. With new people—"

"I'm new people," he says.

I laugh. "Yeah. You are. But like I said, there are a million girls who'd jump at the opportunity—"

"I don't want a million girls. I want you."

My heart somersaults at those words from his lips, but I have to be practical. "I'm sorry. There's absolutely nothing you have that I would want."

"Everyone wants something, Lola. Even you. Come on. What is it?"

An idea pops into my head, but I'd never voice it out loud. Would I?

Karl leans over, propping his elbows on the table. His hand rubs his chin. "What about guitar lessons with the best guitarist in the world?"

My jaw slackens for a moment before I recover, then I

decide to tease him a little to lighten the mood. "You can get me guitar lessons with Slash?"

His mouth gapes with fake shock, and he nudges my knee with his under the table. "Hilarious."

We both laugh.

"But how about it?" he continues. "Two months. Twenty thousand dollars and two months' worth of guitar lessons while you're here."

"My plane ticket is non refundable," I say before realizing how stupid that sounds. It wouldn't matter with twenty thousand extra dollars in my pocket.

Karl rolls his eyes. "Fine. Guitar lessons, twenty thousand dollars, and one plane ticket. Or you can take the private jet. Fritz is always going off to Mexico. I'm sure he'd love an excuse to go, and he can take you when the two months are up."

"You have a private jet?" I ask.

"Not me personally, but the label does, yeah. But, Lola, *focus*. What do you say?"

I twist the hem of my shirt between my fingers. He's tempting me. And as tempting as his offer is, there's something I want more than his money. But I'm too ashamed to ask for it.

"You're thinking about it," he says approvingly.

I chew the inside of my lip. "Is the offer open to negotiations?" I ask in one breath, but I can't meet his eyes.

When I look up again at him again, he's smiling, and amusement flickers in his eyes. "I knew there had to be something you want."

"There is." My face feels a million degrees as I break out into a sweat.

"Lola, you're flushed," he says, amused. "What is it?"

"I, um—" I clear my throat. God. How do I say this?

"Spit it out, Lola. It can't be that bad."

"I don't want the money."

"Okay, what *do* you want?"

"The guitar lessons, for one. . ."

"*And?*"

"And." Oh god, I'm going to pass out from embarrassment.

"And what, Lola? What else do you want?" Karl takes my hand in his and squeezes it reassuringly, urging me to go on. I stare down while he rubs the back of my hand with one calloused finger.

I smile down at our linked hands, and without looking up, I close my eyes and blurt it out in one breath before I chicken out. "Guitar lessons, and you take my virginity."

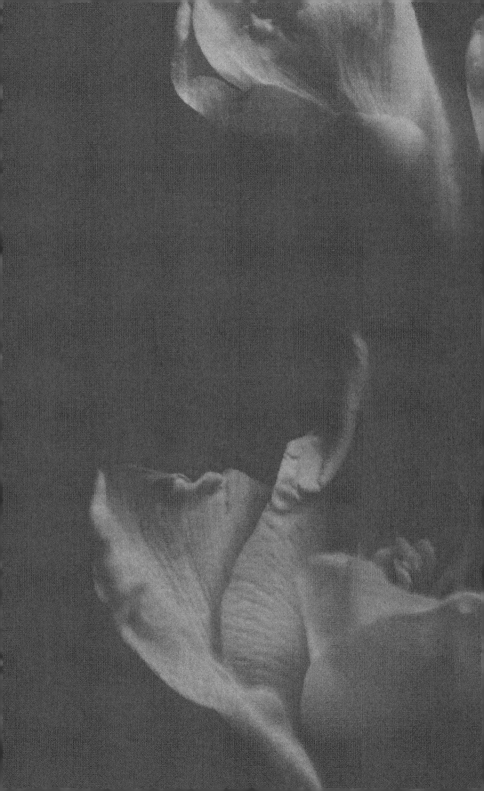

# 9

# KARL

All the air leaves my lungs, and I drop her hand like it's a hot burner. Did I hear her right? I shake my head. The chair creaks as I stand and pace the dining room.

"You're a virgin?" I ask, stunned and staring at her in awe. Lola nods and looks down at her hands again.

"Lola, no—"

"Just, please, listen first."

I shake my head, but I say nothing.

"I want it to be with someone who is a friend. Someone who I know will be kind."

"You were with him throughout high school, right? It never occurred to you to have sex with Ethan?" I ask, even as the mere thought of it rises bile from my stomach.

Lola nods. "Of course I thought about it. But . . . Ethan—" She bites her lower lip, the fabric from the hem of her shirt twisting in her fingers. "He's really religious and—and I tried to be respectful of his beliefs. He's been my only boyfriend, so I've never . . ."

My blood pulses loud in my ears. She's asking me for

something that I want—something that my body *needs*—but something I can't give her. I won't do it.

"Lola, I'm not having sex with you for your first time."

"Okay," she says.

"Okay? What does that mean?"

"It means okay, Karl. I'm not going to force myself on you or anything—"

Crap, she looks so dejected. That's not what I intended. "It's not that I don't want to, Lola. Don't look like that."

Her head tilts to the side, big green eyes blinking at me. "Then why not?"

"Because. You're special. I want your first time to be with someone you love."

Lola scoffs.

"What?" I ask.

"I'm done waiting for the perfect person—for the perfect moment. I want to have sex, Karl. I respect you don't want to —with me. And that is totally fine. But even without you, I *will* have sex. It's what I want."

How do I tell her the truth?

How can I convey with words what an empty feeling it is to wake up to a stranger? How hollow and gutted it feels when you realize you're being used, for your body, for your money, for your fame?

While her situation isn't exactly the same, picking up a stranger will surely mean having sex for the first time with a man who wants something from her, only her body, but not *her*.

If I could get her to understand the depth of that emptiness the morning after, I know she'd agree with me.

That emptiness has been the only kind of experience I've ever had. I don't want to drag her down here with me, to this wretched place where you feel more used and discarded than a roll of toilet paper. She deserves so much more—especially her first time.

For the first time in my life, I think *I* might deserve so much more too.

My fists clench at my sides, and I pace faster. She's going to have sex with some random jerk who might not even treat her right. "Lola, you can't just have sex with someone random for your first time. You should love the person you—"

"You said it wasn't that you didn't want to. So you would want to if it weren't my first time?"

"Lola—"

"How about a wager then?" she asks, her face hopeful.

"A wager?"

"Yes. Let's bet on it. A game. Any game you want. Poker, whatever."

"I hate poker."

"How about *Lotería*? It's like Mexican bingo."

I can't believe I'm considering this. "What's the bet?"

"If you win, I pretend to be your girlfriend for two months in exchange for the twenty grand and guitar lessons. But if I win . . ." Her smile is mischievous. "If I win, I get the guitar lessons, and you fuck me."

My jaw drops, and I have to sit back at the table to hide my hardening erection. She's killing me here.

"Lola, your first time shouldn't be a fuck. You should make love your first time. Preferably with someone you care deeply about."

She shakes her head. "That's not what I want."

"You say that now—"

"Please don't insult me by assuming I don't know my own mind."

I sigh and run my hands through my hair, pulling on it. This woman is testing all my self-control.

"Karl Sommer? Are you a romantic?"

I roll my eyes. Then I smile, because maybe I am. Instead of answering her, though, I ask my own question. "And the money?"

Her brows knit together in confusion. "What?"

"You said if you win, lessons and—and—having sex. But you didn't include the money."

She scrunches her nose up in distaste. "I'd feel funny about getting money from you if we have sex."

God. She couldn't be more perfect if she tried. I like that she has a moral code, even if it's dodgy at the moment with regard to her virginity.

"Why me?" I ask, wanting to understand her.

"I like you. We share a lot of interests, which makes me feel like there's a connection, so it wouldn't be like doing this with a total stranger. And you *are* very handsome." She smiles approvingly as she eyes me up and down. "You've also been very kind to me. I want someone who knows I'm a virgin, someone who I know will be gentle."

My eyes snap up to meet hers. "What? Do you even like me?" I ask, more hopeful than I enjoy feeling.

"Of course I do." She stops for a moment like she is thinking of how to word something right. "Being around you alone . . . it makes me feel things . . . how you held me by your side in front of Ethan . . ."

I sit up tall in my seat. "Oh?"

She nods. "I know it was for show—that you only did it to help me save face with Ethan and Megan. I'm not delusional; I know what it was. Even so, being so close to your body made my entire body feel hot."

My eyelids fall to half-mast with arousal. I want her. I want her body. And I want to—more than anything—be her first. "What else did you feel, Lola?" I ask hoarsely.

"My pulse . . ."

"Yeah?"

"I could feel it in . . . new places." Her gaze goes past me as she studies the wall behind me.

I lean in close enough to smell the sticky sweet scent of the donut on her breath. "Where did you feel your pulse, Lola?"

Her lips part, and her chest rises higher with each heaving breath. "Between my legs," she whispers.

I bunch my fists over the table and press them down hard to force them to stay. I can't touch Lola. But god, I want her. I want her more than I've ever wanted anyone.

And for the first time, I'm considering letting go of my self-control.

Nobody would ever accuse me of being anything other than impulsive. But nobody knows I have self-control of steel—secret self-control—self-control that only Lola has ever managed to tempt.

Then I look at her across the table. Lola's hair is a bedhead mess. Her black *Guns N' Roses* t-shirt is ripped at the collar on the left side, revealing the dip above her collarbone, and there's a hole right under her left breast. She looks like she stepped straight out of a sixty's punk, underbelly-of-New-York dream. Then there's the small amount of donut glaze nestled in the corner of her lips that I want nothing more than to lick off her. She looks edible. My jaw clenches. I do not know how I'm *not* touching her right now.

Fuck it. Let the fates decide.

"Deal. I'll take the bet. We can play the game you mentioned. What was it? Lorry?"

"*Lotería*," she says, her face lighting up. "You mean it?"

I nod. Whether or not I lose the bet, I get what I want— more time with her.

LOLA GOES HOME to freshen up, run some errands, and get the game that will decide if we have sex or not.

I take that time to jerk off. I don't want to lose all self-control when she's offering herself up on a platter. Fuck. Why does she have to be so hot? I jump in the shower and stroke myself as I play back our conversation in my mind. She felt her pulse between her legs when I touched her. My blow erupts from me in less than three minutes. I lather up with soap, and before I'm done showering, I'm hard again.

I have to force myself to come two more times before I can get out of the shower. And even then, I'm semi-hard as I get dressed. I have no idea how I'm supposed to stop myself from touching her tonight. Why did I have to agree to the stupid bet?

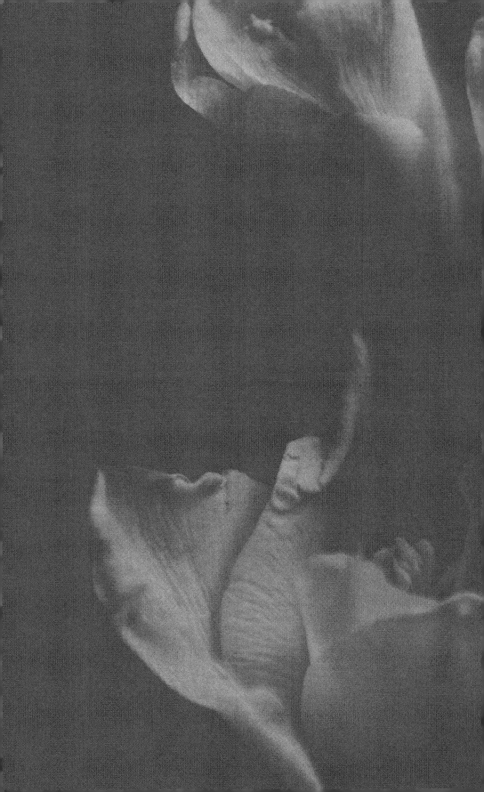

# 10

# LOLA

W hen I get home, Ileana is gone, and I remember she was taking Isael on a playdate with Addy at Sofia's house.

I rush to the shower and shave . . . everything. I've never gone completely bare, and the task takes me longer than I'd like, but if I'm having sex tonight, I don't want Karl—the hottest man alive—to find me lacking more than he already will with my inexperience.

After I pick out an outfit that hopefully doesn't scream 'trying too hard,' I go on a hunt for our game, trying to remember where we put it away the last time we played it.

In the middle of this search, I get a video call notification and pull out my phone. Only one person ever calls, and I smile immediately.

"Tía!" I squeal. It's been a few days since I've seen her. We keep our conversation in Spanish—mine is getting so much better since I started talking to her regularly. "How are you?"

"Good, *mija*. Just wanted to check in—"

"That's not true!" I hear a voice in the background that I recognize as Fernanda's, my aunt's favorite waitress.

"Hi, Fer," I yell into the phone and Fernanda comes into view.

"She wants to know when you're coming down. The holidays are a high season around here, and if you won't be here by then, we need to hire another person."

I watch as *tía* Elena swats at Fernanda's arm to get her out of the frame. I laugh.

Then the laugh dies inside me. I've already pushed my move date twice, trying to avoid the inevitable. And my aunt has been more than understanding of my cold feet, but I sense her getting impatient to have me home. Since she couldn't be at the funeral, I think she sees me as her last connection to my mom and wants me with her. I've told her Sofia and Ileana are like family, but she still wants me home in Mexico—with my blood family.

I clear my throat and straighten my spine. Then I lie. I lie like the little shit that I am. "I um, had an unexpected expense, so I'll need to work a few more months to make up the dip in my savings.

Elena sighs. "My love, you need to come home. I know it's hard. That you love it there. But your new life is waiting for you here."

"I know. I promise I'll be there before the spring-break high season. Deal?"

"Okay, *mi vida*. We're all here waiting for you."

We say our goodbyes and end the call. With the game now in my hands and more determination than ever, I head back to Karl's.

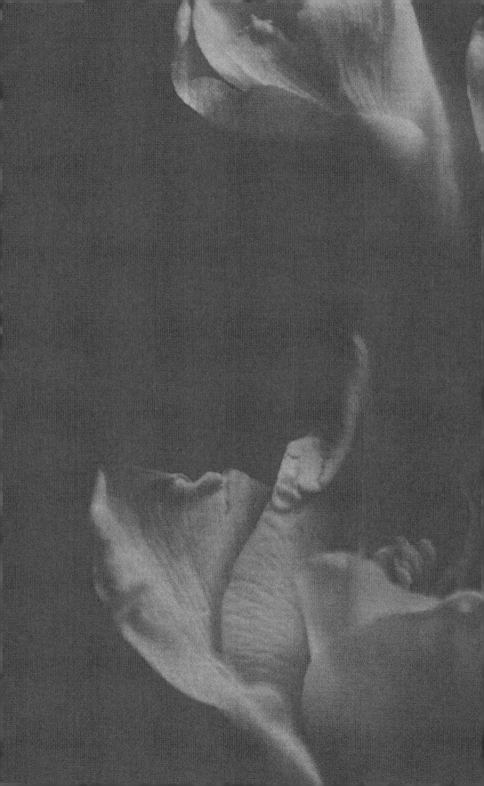

# 11

# KARL

When Lola comes back, I'm in the living room, anxious like I've never been before. Then I see her, and my heart skips a beat. She's beautiful. She has showered, and her hair is still damp in the most sensual way. Her makeup looks natural, and the shade of soft pink on her lips gives them an edible look.

She kicks off her shoes like she feels perfectly at home, and I watch her come sit next to me. She's wearing tight jeans and a simple, slate gray, long-sleeve sweatshirt. It's tight on her body, like a second skin, highlighting every curve, every dip in shadow, every peak prominent, and I have to peel my gaze away from her.

She plops her oversized purse on her lap when she's sitting next to me. "I got the game." She grins, patting the bag.

"Before we play, we should discuss terms," I say, trying to sound casual. Like this is an ordinary business meeting.

No matter what, I have to win this game.

"Okay," she says. "What do you have in mind?"

"If I win, I'll pay you the first half now and the second half in two months when our arrangement is over—"

"No." Lola shakes her head. "You don't need to pay upfront. I know you're good for it."

She trusts me, and that thought spreads a smile on my face. If I do happen to lose, trust will be necessary. "Okay. Thank you," I say with approval.

"What else?" she asks.

"You stay more and more nights here . . ." I stop when I see her grin. "In the spare bedroom," I add, and her face falls a little, but she keeps faking her smile. "Eventually, you'll move in. We'll announce our relationship publicly and go out a lot. Let the photographers catch us looking serious. If I have band practice or other band-related events, you'll come with me—"

"And help convince Bren your party days are over, and deter the women that flock to you," she adds.

"Exactly. Also, neither of us will be seen with other people while we want the world to think we're together."

"And if I win?" she asks.

"If you win, the timing has to be right before—before . . ."

"Before you have sex with me?" she finishes for me.

"Right. And if you change your mind, tell me. We don't have to go through with it, Lola." I pull my hair back. "And it will not be soon. You just got dumped. You're heartbroken, and I need to make sure you're not just lashing out in anger. I need you to have time to wallow in your breakup. Then, if you're still sure this is what you want . . ."

She smiles tenderly at me, and it melts my heart a little. I'm hoping if I give her time, then she could grow feelings for me.

"I have some terms as well," she says.

"Okay. Shoot."

"You must follow all the rules of the game. All of them—"

"Of course."

"And no cheating," she adds with her eyebrow arched.

After swallowing the lump in my throat, I stretch out my hand. Lola takes it in hers, and her shake is firm. I let my thumb rub the top of her slim hand. I don't want to hurt her. This bet . . . I'm not sure she'll come out the other end with her heart intact because I'll never be good enough for her. But I have to try.

If I lose, maybe I can convince her she should wait for love. With renewed purpose, I smile at her.

"Let's play."

---

LOLA KNEELS on the floor next to me and in front of the coffee table. She sets several large cards with colorful images on the table and a smaller deck of cards next to those. Next, she produces a small Ziploc bag full of dried beans. "Uh," I say. "Why do you need beans?"

"It's what we use to check off the boxes."

This game is weird. What have I gotten myself into?

"Okay, so you select one of the large cards. They're all different, and you should get the one that draws you in."

"Okay." I peruse the cards. I don't understand most of the labels on each image, but I settle for one that includes the image of a fish, a spider web, a skull, a man holding a guitar, a hand, and I understand La Rosa means rose, written under the image of the red rose. "This one," I say.

She nods, then takes the stack in front of her to study them carefully. She fans them out on the coffee table and runs her fingers over them with eyes closed.

I chuckle. "What on earth are you doing, Lola?"

Her eyes fly open, and she smirks at me. "It has to speak to me, Karl," she says, sounding annoyed, as if it were the most obvious thing ever.

"Right." Dolores Beltran can be so amusing.

She finally settles on one, then sets a hand full of beans next to my card and another next to hers.

"Okay, here's how this works. We'll take turns drawing from the deck of the smaller cards and flipping the card over so we both can see it. If your game card contains an image that matches the card we just pulled from the deck, you place a bean over that image on your game card. Just like bingo, but with images."

"Easy enough," I say.

There's a grin on her face when she speaks again. "When you place the bean on the image, the other person removes an article of clothing."

My eyes snap up to her face. "What the fuck?"

"It's strip bingo," Lola says calmly.

I stand up and pace the living room. "I'm not playing fucking strip bingo with you, Lola."

"Karl—"

"I told you we are not having sex soon. You need time—"

"Who said anything about sex?" she asks me, much too calm from her spot on the floor. "It's just a game, Karl. Don't be so uptight."

"No. I'm not stripping."

"You shook on it."

I stop in my tracks and I gape at her. "What?"

"You promised you'd follow the rules of the game—"

"I didn't know it was fucking strip bingo!" I roar.

Lola giggles. Oh, I'm glad she finds this amusing.

"No fucking way," I say again.

Her eyes narrow. "I didn't think you wouldn't be a man of your word."

"What? I am a man of my word!"

"Then play. You said you'd follow all the rules, and we shook on the terms."

I run both hands through my hair and pull back

painfully. Lola is going to drive me insane for the next two months.

At least she'll be here, spending time with me.

I huff as I retake my seat on the sofa. "Fine. How do I win this fucking game?"

Lola smiles. "You have to get a row of four, vertical, horizontal, or diagonal. But to win, when you get to four, you must yell out *Lotería.*"

"Why?"

"Because if we both get to four with the same image, whoever yells out the name of the game first, wins."

I can't believe I'm doing this. "What's the word again?"

"*Lotería,*" Lola mouths slowly. The way her tongue rolls over the roof of her mouth as she shows me how my mouth should move to pronounce it sends goosebumps up my arm. There's no way I'm surviving this night.

"*Lotería,*" I try the word.

Lola only scrunches her nose. "Nope." "Lo. Te. Rí. A." she says, breaking down the word for me.

"*Lotería,*" I try again. She looks proud when I can pronounce the 'r' like she did.

Lola laughs. "Close enough."

"You won't disqualify me if I mispronounce it when I win?" I ask, joking to get the playful mood back.

"No, I wouldn't. But you won't get the chance, Karl Sommer. I'm going to kick your ass at *Lotería.*"

"I need a drink for this," I say, standing to go to the kitchen. "You want a beer?"

"Please!"

When I get back, I hand Lola hers and drain half of mine in one gulp. Lola giggles, probably at how nervous I'm acting.

"You ready?" she asks.

I nod and pull the first card from the deck. Lola peers at it and calls out, "*El Gallo.*"

Neither one of us has the rooster on our game card, and she pulls the next card as she sips her beer. "Fuck yes!" she squeals. "*El Gorrito*! I have *El Gorrito*!" She lands a bean on top of the hat image on her card, and I roll my eyes. I don't have the hat, which means . . . "Strip!" she orders, finishing my thought.

With trepidation, I peel the shirt over my head. Thank god I wore socks. This gives me two more beans before I have to take my sweats—or worse—my underwear off.

We pull several cards from the deck, taking turns, and I swallow hard. I have to win this game but winning also means that Lola will be either naked or nearly naked by the end of it. What a fucking mess.

And what a fucking temptress. She knows exactly what she's doing to me.

The following several cards aren't on either of our play cards until she pulls the image of a frog, and with shaky hands, I place a bean over my game card.

Lola smiles darkly at me, and her eyes lock with mine as she slowly takes her top off. My mouth falls open. Underneath, she's wearing a bright, flaming hot-pink bra. It has lace at the edges of the cup and darker pink dots on the mesh of the cup. And it's fucking see through. I can clearly make out the large areolas and pebbled nipples straining against the mesh material. Fucking hell.

When I have to grab a cushion to cover my lap, Lola doesn't miss it, and she chuckles. As if nothing has happened, she pulls another card, and we keep playing. My jaw sets tight for the rest of the game because all I want to do is to lunge up and over her body and take her—claim her.

*Mine.*

She gets two more on her game card but is nowhere near connecting a line of four. Still, it means I'm down to my sweats and underwear. She calls the boot, and that's another point for me, and one of Lola's socks comes off. A few more cards, and again, the point goes to me—another sock, revealing hot-pink toenails that match her bra.

My heart races. This was the worst fucking idea ever.

When I get the next point and she unbuttons her jeans to shimmy out of them, I groan. Out loud. I finally have to say something. I lean sideways and bite the sofa cushion. "Lola," I groan again. "You're killing me here."

She grins wide and shakes her glorious, full hips playfully as she steps out of her jeans. She twirls in an exaggerated, if playful, modeling move. The matching thong in hot pink lace has a double waistband separated by a thin strip of fabric in the middle and a little pink bow. As she turns, I get a glimpse of the triangle strip of cloth that disappears into her perfect, plump ass. Did I mention the thong is also see-through? And I get a clear glimpse of her bare flesh before she sits down again, crossing her legs under the coffee table. She's completely shaved. I shut my eyes tight and sneak my hand under the cushion on my lap. I grip my shaft tightly, begging it to go down.

"Don't be so dramatic, Karl Sommer," she says with a smirk, and we keep playing.

The next point goes to her, and I spin around to take off my sweats, grabbing the cushion to cover my front when I turn around again to sit. No way I'm letting her innocent eyes see my dick print through my underwear.

"You're cheating, Mr. Sommer," Lola says, and my eyes narrow at her.

I feel the pre-ejaculate seep out of me when she calls me Mr. Sommer. "I told you not to fucking call me Mr. Sommer," I bark.

She rolls her eyes and sips her beer. When I pay attention to the game again, realization hits me like a bolt of lightning. We're both one point away from winning. The same point.

*The hand.* My line of four horizontal will be complete if *the hand* comes up, but so will her line of four vertical.

My pulse quickens as we take turns drawing cards. I have to scream *Lotería* first. I just have to. As we pull cards, we're both on edge, and I'm repeating the word over and over in my head, *Lotería, Lotería, Lotería.*

Then I peek at the corner of the hand as I flip a card over, and before she has a chance to, I scream, "*Lotería*" at the top of my lungs. I spring to my feet with excitement. I beat her to it; I did it. When I look at her, her mouth hangs open.

When I stood up, the cushion fell off my lap, and my hard cock is straining to get free of my boxer briefs. "Lola!" I snap. "Look away. For fuck's sake."

She giggles and turns her attention to stacking the cards neatly and sticking items into the game box.

I put my sweats back on and sit next to her again as she puts everything away.

"Guess this means no sex for me," Lola says with mock disappointment.

"That's right. But you'll be twenty thousand dollars richer and will become a kick-ass guitar player."

"That's too bad. I guess I'll have to wait to have sex in Mexico."

"What the fuck did you say?"

She turns to me with a questioning look in her eyes. "What? You said no seeing other people while we're pretending to be together, so the two-month countdown begins now."

"Lola," I breathe out, closing my eyes with pain. I open them again and grab her chin between my index and forefinger, forcing her eyes on mine. "Lola, don't have sex just to have sex. You deserve to do it with someone who loves you—"

"Did you?" she asks.

"Did I what?"

"Did you love your first sexual partner?"

I intake a deep breath. "This isn't about me, doll. You're special—I just know it. And you deserve everything good in this world."

Her eyes drop to my lips, and I want to kiss her. I do—but I don't dare do it. I also can't move, so it's Lola who goes in for it. I feel like the biggest asshole on earth, because I turn my face away, giving her my cheek instead. Her lips are soft against my cheek. She's been chewing the watermelon gum; I can tell because even after drinking beer, the overpowering fruity smell lingers on her breath, so close to me. I want to give in, to kiss her, but I know I shouldn't.

Lola doesn't seem fazed by my rejection.

With our eyes locked, Lola repositions herself to come up and over me. She straddles my lap and grinds her hips over my erection through my sweats. I groan into her neck, and it feels so damn good.

Somehow, I manage to stop myself. I twist my hand around her hair a few times and pull her away from me. Both our chests are heaving with labored breaths, and we look at each other, a little stunned.

Without letting go of my grip on her hair, I dust her cheekbone with my thumb. "Lola, listen to me."

She nods, and I keep talking. "I want you. I really, *really* fucking want you. I need you to know that."

"Then have me," she says in a small voice that attacks my defenses.

"No, doll. I need you to know I want you because I don't want you to feel rejected. I'm not rejecting you. But I can't have sex with you. Do you understand?"

She chews her bottom lip, and though her face can't fall with my grip on her hair, her eyes drop to my bare chest. Then she nods.

I caress her soft neck with my thumb, then drop it to dust her collarbone. "It's not that I don't want you, Lola. I do. But it's too soon. You just broke up with Ethan yesterday. And I'm not some asshole who will take advantage of your heartbreak and vulnerability."

She smiles sadly now, but I think I got through to her. She has to know I'm right about this.

She gets off my lap and gets dressed.

# 12

## LOLA

It's early morning when I tiptoe into the dark house. I'm relieved that Ileana and Isael are still asleep—until the light flicks on in the living room as I make my way across it toward my room.

Busted.

Ileana smirks at me. "Morning," she says.

Crap. I'm holding my shoes in my hand, looking guilty as all hell, and I wince. "Morning, Ileana . . . I uh—"

She chuckles at seeing me squirm. "You're a grown woman, Lola. You can have fun. And you don't owe me any explanations." She hesitates, then adds, "But I'd love to hear what's going on in your life—if you'd like to talk about it. That's two nights now you've been out all night."

I plop on the love seat in front of her.

"I'm sorry. I don't enjoy being so secretive with you, but I had to."

Ileana's hands wrap around a warm mug of tea, and she keeps it close to her body. "You've never kept secrets before. Have I said something—"

"No, god, Ileana, no. It's just new, and I'm not sure how you're going to take it."

She smiles warmly as she takes a sip of her tea. "Try me."

After I drop my shoes and bag on the floor, I take a deep breath. If I'm moving in with Karl soon, I need to give her notice so she can find alternate babysitters for Isael. It's time to tell her. "You know how Sofia had me clean Karl Sommer's house?"

Ileana nods. "Oh, we didn't talk much about that. You were so exhausted after." She grins wide and perks up in her seat. "What's his house like? Did you find any dirty secrets?"

I shake my head. "No. But he was there."

"But I thought Sofia said they'd be working—"

"Bren canceled their meeting with some music executives last minute, and he overlooked telling Sofia."

"Wait," Ileana says. "So you *met* Karl?"

I nod, and Ileana squeals with excitement.

"Shhhh, keep it down! You'll wake Isael up."

She winces, and we both freeze for a moment, listening for sounds, but none come, and I keep talking.

"He's really nice. The house was a mess, but he made up for it with great pay. Then we started talking music, and he ordered pizza. Honestly, Ileana, it felt a little like a first date once I clocked out."

Her jaw goes slack. "What?"

"I know. Then he asked me to come in a week—that was Saturday—and the house was spotless. Like, I think he cleaned before I got there."

We both smile. "That was sweet," Ileana says.

"It was, but then he had to scramble to find things for me to do. It was kind of funny, actually. In the end, he went grocery shopping with me."

Her head tilts. "Really?"

"Believe me. I was as surprised as you. But then, get this. Guess who we bump into at the grocery store?"

"Who?"

"Ethan!"

"Ethan? I knew he'd change his mind and come see you before you leave—"

"But guess who he was with?"

"Who?" Ileana asks.

"Megan," I say casually.

"Who is Megan?"

"His girlfriend."

"Shut up! That little weasel is cheating on you?" Ileana hisses the question.

God, I can't believe this story myself, so I'm not surprised at Ileana's shock as it unfolds, but her reactions are rather comical.

"Yep. He wasn't even going to tell me he was in town," I say, my blood boiling all over again.

Ileana's brows furrow with concern, her face twisting in anger as I keep telling the story. "What did you do?" she asks.

"I was so shocked, I froze. But then Karl came to the rescue. He pretended to be my boyfriend, like I'd been cheating on Ethan too."

"What?" Ileana nearly spits her tea out.

"Yeah, he wrapped his arm around me, and Megan went berserk when she realized who he was. The worst part, though, was that for a moment, Ethan actually looked like he was angry I was with someone else. I don't know what bothered him more, if it was the fact that he thought I cheated too—which, what a hypocrite—or if it was that he thinks I cheated with a celebrity."

"Who cares!" Ileana says. "And way to go, Karl. I would have paid to see the look on Ethan's face."

"It was pretty epic. It gets better." I pause. "He kissed me—" I whisper, "Well, my forehead, but still."

"What?!" Ileana really shouts that time.

"Yeah. In front of Ethan."

"Shut up! What did he do?"

"What could he do? Megan would have slaughtered him if he'd acted jealous, so he just . . . stewed."

Isael walks into the living room, his blankie trailing behind him, his thumb in his mouth. His harsh brows draw together in anger. I have to bite back my smile. He's always so grumpy when he wakes up. He needs to be eased awake, or the day goes to hell.

"Morning, *mi terremoto*," I say softly and outstretch my arms. Wordlessly, Isael crawls onto my lap and wraps around my torso, resting his cheek on my chest. With his thumb in his mouth, his eyes drift closed again, and I rub his back, making me think of Karl and how he comforted me after the Ethan debacle.

Ileana and I whisper the rest of our conversation. "He was wonderful, Ileana. I had a breakdown at his place after we got back from the store. He comforted me and spent the entire day trying to either cheer me up or distract me from thinking about it."

"This is unreal," Ileana says dreamily. "From what Sofia has said, he's super famous, isn't he?"

I snort. Ileana doesn't follow pop culture, and she enjoys rock and metal even less. She listens to pop, country, or Spanish pop mostly. I envied her so much for how normal she was when Sofia first introduced her to Bren. I wish I'd been that cool. "Yeah, he is super famous," I say, though even that is an understatement.

"Anyway, I came home to change and grabbed some board games. I went back to his place, and we played a long while—"

"You didn't . . ."

I shake my head. "No. We didn't have sex." *To my annoyance*, I think.

"So how come you stayed over again then?"

"Oh, while we played board games, we were drinking beers. I had a few too many and didn't want to drive home last night."

"I'm glad you aren't totally heartbroken over Ethan. You look happier than you have in a long time, actually."

I grin at her. "Karl makes me smile. He is so interesting. Oh, and I didn't tell you, he offered to teach me to play guitar."

I don't tell her what it felt like to hold a guitar for the first time. How those confusing butterflies fluttered in my chest, or how my fingers twitched over the strings like they were finally home after a long odyssey.

"Really? I was wondering when you'd pick up an instrument or start singing."

"What?" I ask in surprise.

"It was just a matter of time, Lo. I mean, I have to hum 'Sweet Child o' Mine' or Isael never goes to sleep. Same goes for Sofia and Addy. If she doesn't play her 'Marquee Moon,' Addy stays awake. She's still mad at you for ruining a classic. Or so she says." Ileana pauses her rambling, and I snicker. I can't believe my roommate doesn't like rock music. She keeps talking. "What I mean is, you've always been passionate about music. I'm glad you're taking guitar lessons. I think it can be a great source of purpose and happiness for you." Her smile is wide when she finishes.

This is the woman who has seen my darkest days—the days I considered ending the pain. She's cried with me, and she's picked me up. I know seeing me happy brings her some sense of hope that I'll be okay—that she can stop worrying about me.

"Anyway, I have a feeling I'll be over at Karl's quite a bit more."

"If you're worried about Isael and me, don't. Between Sofia and me, we can work out a schedule to trade sitting Addy and Isael."

Ileana works at Sofia's bar, and it would be easy for them to get on opposite shifts and trade sitting duties. I'm glad I'm not leaving her in the lurch. "I should start paying you rent if I'm not going to earn my keep with babysitting as often—"

She shakes her head. "I won't hear it. You're leaving soon, and you need your savings for your fresh start. Besides, you know we're taken care of."

"Thank you," I say sincerely. "I do still want to sit some, though. I love Isael, and I'm going to miss him. I'd like to spend time with him before I go." I tighten my hug around the little bundle of love in my arms. Isael is a living earthquake, full of energy, and some days he makes me cry with the messes he makes—not unlike someone else I recently met—but he is also the sweetest, most loving kid I've ever known. I'm reminded I have to leave him too, and tears spring to my eyes.

Her eyebrow arches. "Just him?" she asks.

I laugh through the hurt. "No. Not just him. I'll miss you too."

# 13

# KARL

After our game of *Loteria*, Lola and I have but brief moments to hang out this week. Most of them are over me packing for my move to Bren's penthouse and letting movers in to bring all of his and Sofia's crap in boxes.

I didn't want to hire anyone to help pack because I don't trust strangers with much, and especially not my axes, so I let Lola help me with this task instead.

By the end of the week, we're both exhausted, and Lola stays over for the first time on Saturday night. It's becoming our little tradition, Saturday night pizza dates, and that's precisely what we do tonight.

When I told Lola I was trading homes with Bren, saying she was ecstatic would do her reaction a disservice. She adores Bren's penthouse and is over the moon about living there for the remaining month and three weeks of our arrangement. We're at the mansion for one more week, and she hasn't moved in full time yet, but I'm hoping she'll at least stay through the rest of the weekend, and maybe Monday.

Tuesday too, if she wants.

To my delight, she does.

We argued once—which is better than I thought we'd do. She's still working most mornings, and I told her she doesn't have to, but she won't take my money. As much as I'm bothered that she's wasting her time cleaning homes and potentially putting herself in danger with strangers, I won't lie and say I'm not a little proud of her work ethic.

It's a work ethic I share—even if no one fucking knows about it.

And we haven't started guitar lessons. Not only are all the axes packed, but we're usually exhausted by the end of the day, and we agreed to start once we settle into the penthouse.

"I didn't bring enough clothes," Lola says from her place at the breakfast table.

I look up from reading the news on my phone. "Huh?"

"I'll have to go home today. I didn't bring enough clothes to get me through Wednesday."

I throw her a look like I think she's an idiot. "Just use the laundry room, Lo."

Her head tilts to the side as she studies me. "You want me to stay?"

"Yeah. I know we said you should move in gradually, but I like having you here. If you're comfortable and want to stay, you're welcome to be full time whenever you want."

"Oh," she says. "I wasn't sure when you wanted to transition."

"I don't have a timeline. Things should progress naturally," I say pointedly, and she chuckles.

---

THAT NIGHT, I hear Lola as she starts the laundry. It's late and I'm tired, so I head into the shower before bed. When I get out, I head to my dresser and start pulling out clothes and tossing them on the bed so I can change. I'm naked and in the middle of this task when a gasp turns my attention toward the door. Shit. I didn't close it all the way.

Lola is staring at me through the crack in the door, and even as I catch her, she stays frozen, her eyes wide and fixed on . . . my penis. Under her gaze, it hardens, and her jaw falls slack as her eyes widen even farther, if that were possible. She grips the laundry basket tightly, and her eyes never lift from my lower body, watching as I harden completely. Her headphones are on, and she clearly hasn't realized I'm watching her watch me.

My pulse quickens loud in my ears with my rising arousal. I grip one hand around my shaft and pump once. Her sharp intake of breath is just loud enough for me to hear. *Is this the first time she's seen a penis in person?* I wonder. Has she ever seen a man naked before in the flesh? I have to push the arousing thought aside.

She's wearing a black sweater with the collar cut off, and it falls off one shoulder. I don't know how I'll make it two months with her here and not touch her. I pump my dick a second time, studying her features intently, and this time her eyes lift to meet mine.

I smirk, and she returns it. Look at the guts on her. She doesn't flinch when she's caught. Doesn't move. Doesn't retreat. She keeps watching, my sweet, brave doll, my little pervert. I stroke myself a third time with our eyes locked.

As I walk to the door, I keep stroking myself. She swallows hard as I approach her, and her tongue darts out to lick her lips. I grip the door and shake my head at her with a teasing smirk, then close it gently in her face.

AS BRAVE AS she was last night when I caught her staring, Lola can't meet my eyes today. She's flustered and jumpy. I find her in the kitchen making coffee, and I grin wide at her. Oh, I'm going to have fun with this.

"Morning, Lola. Sleep well?" I tease.

She wraps both hands around the coffee mug and sips before saying, "Uh-uh."

"Any sweet dreams?" I ask.

Her cheeks flush a deep red, and it is so freaking arousing. Teasing her is backfiring in the worst way. I'm starting to understand my fate for the next two months is to live all day with a full erection. Fuck. This is going to be painful.

Lola shakes her head. "Nope. No dreams."

As I brush past her to grab a cup from the cabinet, I get my mouth close to her ear, taking in the smell of her shampoo—something sweet and tart. Green apple, maybe? I whisper in her ear, "Oh, I had a glorious dream."

"Oh, yeah?" she asks, and her voice squeaks, making her wince.

"Yeah. It was about this peeping Tom—"

"Karl!" She rushes to take a step away from me, and I can tell she's forcing herself to look me in the eye and pretend to look unaffected. "I'm sorry about last night. It wasn't on purpose. It just happened, and then . . . I—I don't know what happened. I just froze."

"Relax, Iggy," I say, more playful now. "I know it was an accident."

"Good." She grips the hem of her shirt and pulls it down. "Can we pretend it never happened then?"

"You got it." I grin widely and sip my coffee. "So, what do you wanna do today?"

LOLA IS EVIL.

And she has me by the balls. How can a seemingly sweet, nineteen-year-old have so much power over me?

The rest of our day together is normal. She goes to work. We have dinner together. We walk Pixel in the evening. I honestly think we've both forgotten about what happened last night.

But Lola hasn't.

And she's been scheming all day. I just know it.

Lola goes to bed by ten, and she's been playing loud music for the last twenty minutes. She keeps playing the same song. It's *FKA Twigs's* "Two Weeks." The ultimate sex song if I've ever heard one. And it's blaring. What the fuck are her headphones good for if she's going to play music this loud? It's on purpose. It has to be. I try to ignore it. She's just trying to get my attention.

But then it plays a second time. She's playing it on a loop, I realize. What the fuck is she doing? That's it. I can't take it any longer. I stomp over to her door, ready to pound on it and yell at her to turn the music down. But when I get there, the door is cracked open. To my horror—and delight—she's on the bed . . . writhing and naked.

The lights in her room are off, but she has some sort of red-tinted nightlight that outlines her body perfectly. Her legs are outstretched into the perfect diamond shape with her hot-pink toes touching, her hand between her legs. She moves her hand, stroking up and down slowly, and I catch a glimpse of something dark pink in her hands. It looks like a bullet toy of some sort. My jaw is so tight, I might break a tooth.

Lola will be my undoing.

I storm into her room, find her phone on the bedside table, and shut off the song. At first, she startles at the interruption, then smiles when she sees me. Her eyes were shut tight before, and she didn't see me come in.

She smiles up at me but keeps moving the toy between her legs. A sheen of perspiration on her skin glows under the red light. I hover over her, my face an inch away from hers, and I grab her jaw between my fingers angrily. She winces a bit. And it must hurt, but I'm so angry, I don't care. "Masturbate all you want, doll," I say. "I'm not going to fuck you. You lost the bet."

Her eyes hold mine with challenge clear in those twin green pools. "I know," she breathes out and writhes some more under her hand.

I chuckle bitterly and shake my head, then make my way to the door. "Last fucking warning. Keep the fucking music down," I hiss and slam the door with too much force.

———

BUT SHE DOESN'T KEEP the music down the next night. Only the song this time is "Barely Legal" by *The Strokes*, and I have to laugh out loud. My poor, sweet doll is getting desperate, and she's taunting me. And she's fucking doing it with the best musical selections.

I run my hand over my face in frustration and turn to scream into a pillow so she doesn't hear it—not that she would over the music. Then I cover my ears with the pillow and drift off into the most restless sleep of my life.

When she does it again a third night in a row, to none other than *Halestorm's* "I Get Off," something snaps inside me.

That fucking does it.

I storm into her room again, but this time I don't shut off the music. I let the song play on a loop. I nearly tear the shirt off my body and rip my sweats and boxers off. Anger seeps from my every pore. She props herself up on her elbows—a dark smile on her lips. She thinks she's fucking won.

*Oh, doll. You can't play with fire and not get burned.*

I crawl on top of her and bite her neck. Her eyes shut tight in pain, and I bite her lip, but I don't dare kiss her. She jerks back in shock. "Is this what you want?" I yell over the music.

She shakes her head, her eyes a bit frightened now under the glow of the low red light. "You want me to stop?" She thinks for a moment, then shakes her head again, and I smirk at her. My tongue tastes the delicate flesh leading to her shoulder, and I grind my erection on her stomach but don't go any lower. She reaches with her hand to touch herself again, and I pin her hands together above her head, forcing the toy out of her hands. The bullet lands next to us on the bed, where it buzzes against her hip. I shake my head at her. I keep licking her neck, her clavicle, letting her feel my length on her body, but get nowhere near where she wants me.

I work my way down her body, dragging my tongue down her neck, between her breasts, down her abdomen, and when I reach her mound, she lets her knees fall to the sides, opening up to me. And fuck. She's perfect.

I part her flesh with two fingers but don't sink them inside any deeper, and fuck—she is dripping wet. My eyes draw closed in reverence. What would it feel like? To let go and let myself feel her, let myself be inside of her? Bliss. It would be bliss.

But I won't. Not even with fingers. *Has* she had her fingers inside? Toys? I lick her inner thigh and whisper into her skin, "What secrets does your body keep, my sweet doll?" But she doesn't hear me.

With that thought, I find her center and dart my tongue out to find her clit. I circle it slowly, and her moan rises above the music as the song starts over. "Karl!" She moans and writhes under my touch, but keeps her legs wide open for me. I pick up the speed, and her thighs shake in my hands. She yells my name again and says something else, but it gets drowned out in the chorus. I pull away for a moment to locate the toy. I position it at her entrance, swirling it, teasing her. I have no fucking idea if she's had toys inside or not—I've only seen her play with the toy on her clit—and I'm afraid of pushing it in any farther and instead let it stay there, right at the opening, buzzing gently in my hand. I peer up at her, and she seems to enjoy it. Her hips lift, wanting it deeper—I know. But I'm not giving her what she wants.

Not tonight.

Even as her own body begins to ever so gently suction the toy inside, I tug on it to keep it out. Fuck, this is the hottest thing I've ever seen, but I keep my grip on the bullet, tugging against her body's gentle suction to not let it in, and return my tongue to her clit.

Within minutes, her every leg muscle tenses under my grip, and she comes hard on my tongue.

I'm ready to explode, so I have to let go of her thigh and fist the bedsheets tight to stop myself from taking my dick in my hand until she's done climaxing.

When her body is down to soft quivers, I drag my mouth down the length of her thigh to clean off most of the wetness with her skin and come up and over her again. I bite her lip again, still not kissing her, with open eyes to see her reaction at tasting herself on my mouth. Her eyes grow wide, and then she lifts, trying to kiss me, but I pull away.

After managing to avoid her kisses, I lean back, kneeling above her, and stroke myself furiously. Her eyes widen with horror as realization must strike. She shakes her head, and I read her lips saying, *No.* Her hips lift off the mattress, trying to buck me so I'll be closer to her entrance. She wants me inside her, not jerking off above her.

But I'm so ready by the time I start jerking off, it takes no time before I explode over her stomach. I keep stroking, emptying myself over her body. My muscles are tight knots as I jerk out the last of my cum, letting it pool in the dip of her belly.

Her jaw is slack, like she can't believe I didn't fuck her— not the way she wanted me to. *Two can play this game, doll. You're in for it now.* But I won't give in. I won't accept that last piece of her virginity even if she begs me to because I would never do that to someone vulnerable after a recent breakup.

Her heart is at stake here.

I won't let her regret me.

Because she *will* inevitably regret me.

I'm not good enough for her. And I know I could never be the type of man worthy of her. She'll thank me one day when she finds him. Even if the mere thought of it sours my stomach, for some reason.

My heart rate is in the process of calming down as I take deep breaths when she gets that look in her eye, the one she gets when she's thinking.

She smiles up at me, and it's the last fucking thing I think she'll do.

Without breaking eye contact, she lowers an index finger to her stomach, traces a circle, dipping the pad of her finger in the thick liquid, then brings it to her mouth. Her eyes draw closed as she savors it. When she looks back up at me, I can only shake my head. Fucking hell.

I jump off her, pull my sweats on, and kill the music. I should go grab a washcloth and help her clean up. I should . . . so many things. Instead, I fake my anger. "Last fucking warning. Keep the fucking music down," I hiss and leave her in her room, drenched in my cum.

WHEN I WAKE up in the morning and remember it wasn't a dream, my stomach grows hot. The way I treated her . . . remorse slices through my chest. I hope she'll forgive me for my behavior—but even I know I don't deserve it. I didn't succumb to fucking her like she wanted, but does it matter after everything else I *did* with her body? I was so rough with her. The things I said . . . the things I did. She has no experience, and the first taste of it I gave her was degrading and rough. I wince as I recall every single second of last night.

She's reading my copy of *Please Kill Me: The Uncensored Oral History of Punk,* Pixel curled by her feet on the couch when I find her. She must not have work today. "Lola, can we talk?"

She looks up from her book and nods. After setting it down next to her, she asks, "What's up?"

Nothing seems out of the ordinary. She's acting like she does every day. Like nothing happened last night. Did I imagine it, or was it a dream? No. It was too visceral to be a dream.

"Um, are you okay?" I ask.

"Yeah, why?"

Is she kidding me? "Lola, the way I treated you . . ."

"Yeah?" She looks confused.

I rub my temples. "I'm sorry," I breathe out.

Her face twists a little. "For what?"

"Are you kidding?"

She shakes her head. "No. I'm fine, Karl. Last night was fun." She smiles. "We should do it again soon."

What the fuck? "Lo—I didn't want your first sexual experience to be—"

"Why do you think that was my first sexual experience?" she interrupts.

"What?" I ask. Did she lie to me before? Is she not a virgin? Not that it matters, but why lie? "I thought you said—"

She laughs, and I blink at her. She's insane. I can't believe I invited a total psycho to move in with me. "I said I was a virgin," she explains. "Not a nun. I've obviously done *other* things."

My mouth falls open with the shock of her statement.

"What?" Her eyes roll as she crosses her arms in front of her. "Let me guess? You thought because I haven't had inter-course, I'm some sweet, demure, innocent little thing. Inex-perienced and dumb?"

"Uhhh . . . I'm not sure I'd put it quite like that, but—"

"Karl, I've done things. Many things. I had a serious boyfriend for four years. Of course, we had a sex life—of sorts."

"You did?" I should be angry at the thought of her fooling around with Ethan, but a big part of me is relieved. I didn't taint her last night, and more importantly, I can't be a hypocrite and be mad at her.

She nods. "Yeah. I've obviously explored my own body too. Wait—" her eyes narrow. "Did you think your penis was the first one I've seen or touched?"

I nod, at a loss for words and astonished at all of this information.

"I'll admit it's the biggest," she says with a chuckle, "but not the first." She stands to get close to me and peers up at me through her thick lashes. "And I know how to make it feel good, Karl. I'm really good at sucking dick," she whispers and licks her upper lip to drive her point home.

I should be horrified.

But I'm not.

I'm more fucking turned on than ever.

# 14

## LOLA

Holy hell, Karl Sommer's tongue is magic. If he can do that with just his tongue, what can he do with the rest of him? I swallow hard at the memory of his massive shaft. It was huge. So huge, my insides clenched, almost sensing pain from the threat of his size, even as he refused to take what I know he wanted. But I had the best sleep of my life after he finally barged into my room to play with me.

Took him long enough to give in. But he's a gentleman, and even as he defiled my body in the most delicious way, he refused to cross that last line—or to so much as kiss me, even though we were both dying for it.

He thinks I'm still hung up on Ethan, but honestly, Ethan is the last thing on my mind these days. The first is getting my hands on a guitar again, and the second, wondering how long Karl thinks I need before I'm ready for him to really claim my body.

I'm lying on the floor with my legs propped up on the couch, staring at the ceiling, thinking a mile a minute. I'm wondering if I should dip into my savings for a guitar, but surely Karl will let me use one from his stash of what—thirty guitars? Pixel is next to me, getting belly rubs, bringing the biggest smile to my face.

"I'm heading to the gym at Bren's," Karl says, interrupting my thoughts.

I sit up to look at him. For a moment, I'm considering asking if I can tag along. Watching Karl work out would be a sight for the ages, and I'd hopefully get to see the rest of the band if they work out together. But we've been spending a lot of time together lately, and the last thing I want is to be that clingy annoying girl. So instead, I just say, "Okay. Have fun."

Once he's gone, I can't help myself, and I go snooping in his room. I go straight to his closet. It's mostly empty now except for a few changes of clothes. Most everything is in boxes because he moves into Bren's building this weekend, and I'm thinking I will too.

I run my hands across his shirts. I snort. God, I feel like a creepy stalker fan. Guess I am, a little, if I'm honest. And if I'm already a creepy stalker, I have to think about what creepy stalkers do. Glancing at the dirty clothes bin at the back of the closet, an idea tugs my mouth into an evil smirk. I rummage through the bin until I find what I'm looking for. The deep red hoody is perfect. I bring it to my nose and smell him.

*God, Lola! You are being so creepy*, I think. But my eyes draw closed with pleasure as I sniff the fabric. And there it is. That intoxicating manly and woodsy aroma, with just the slightest sweet hint of clove. It's his aftershave, not a cologne, I've decided, mixed with his natural manly smell. Last night when he had his mouth on my neck, I smelled it on his jaw, and I know he had shaved earlier that day.

Before I head out of his room, I glance at the stack of books on his nightstand. A David Bowie biography, a Lou Reed biography I'll need to read after the current book of his I'm reading, and *Just Kids* by Patti Smith, one of my favorite books of all time. I love that about him, how well-read he is, and how he immerses himself in books about his craft. It highlights a level of dedication and passion for music that, for some reason, turns me on so damned much. Maybe I'm a sapiosexual.

I put on the hoody and go to my room to listen to music in bed, but it's so warm and cozy I fall asleep. I'm not sure how long I'm out before I hear Karl calling out my name. I startle awake and peel the hoody off to hide it. I stuff it under my bed just before he knocks at my door.

"Lo? You in there?"

"Yeah, one sec," I call out and straighten my top and run a hand through my hair to tame it. I open the door. "Hey, how was your workout?"

"Good," he says. I eye him up and down and panic. He's freshly showered and changed already. Did he see me sleeping in his hoody when he got home? No. My door was closed, and he just knocked. He wouldn't have opened it. "What's wrong?" he asks.

"Nothing," I say.

"Okay, weirdo. I was wondering if you're hungry."

"What time is it?"

"Noon."

Shit. I slept all morning. "Yeah, guess I am a little hungry."

Karl smiles. "Good. You ready to be seen together in public? Let the news get out?"

"Sure. Let me just change."

"I'll wait for you downstairs." He turns to leave, then turns back around to face me. "Oh and, Lo?"

"What?"

"For the love of all that is holy, don't wear an *Industrial November* shirt."

I smirk at him. "Slash then?"

He shakes his head with amusement. "How about no other rock bands over your chest for our first public date?"

"What should I wear then?"

"Jeans. Be casual. We aren't going anywhere fancy."

I haven't brought over too much clothing since I'll be moving it to the penthouse anyway, so I panic as I pull out all the contents of my duffle bag on the bed.

What does a rock star's girlfriend even wear? *Don't panic, Dolores.* He said to be causal, and casual I have. I think about Sofia and what she wears. She's usually in jeans, comfortable tops, and her leather moto jacket. Sometimes she wears dresses for Bren, but I don't think this is a dress kind of date. But she wears a lot of black. I brought my black ribbed turtleneck. It's chilly out, so this should do fine with my good jeans.

I didn't bring any other shoes, so my black ankle boots will have to do. I quickly do my makeup in a simple, natural way for daytime, and remember I have my black skull ring in my purse. I retrieve it and put it on my middle finger. I look at myself in the mirror. Not bad for having so few options. I wish I had my black crossbody purse, but I don't think my oversized boho one goes well with this, so I will go purseless. Instead, I accessorize with my Audrey Hepburn-style oversized sunglasses.

I'd say this is pretty rock star girlfriend-like. At least it is for this rock star's fake girlfriend, and it will just have to do.

When he sees me, Karl smiles in that boyish way of his. "You look perfect, Iggy," he says.

He takes my hand in his and leads me out to a beautiful gray sports car. I whistle. "Hot damn, that's a nice car." Karl only chuckles. I step around it all the way to check it out, and my mouth hangs open when I see the logos on the back: *Porsche* and *911 Turbo S.* "I don't think I've ever even known what a Porsche looks like. Just hear about them all the time," I say, in awe of the beautiful car.

"Germany's finest for the finest German," he says with a cocky grin.

I just roll my eyes and get in.

When we get close to Sofia's bar, I gape at him. *"La Oficina?* We're having lunch at *La Oficina?"*

"What? Food is great here."

"I know it is, but are you insane? There will for sure be paparazzi here!" Ever since news broke out about Sofia and Bren, there has been at least one photographer or reporter staking out the bar.

"That's kinda the point," he says and pulls up to the front of the bar.

Instantly, two photographers recognize the car and get close to it, doing their best to photograph past the tinted windows. The guy trying to get the image from the passenger door moves to the front of the car and snaps pictures from there.

It's intrusive as all hell, and I twist my fingers in front of me. *I can do this,* I think as I let out a deep breath.

Karl must sense I'm nervous because he takes my hand in his and kisses the back of it. "It'll be okay. I'm right here. If they throw questions at you, don't answer. Stay in until I get the door for you."

He leaves the car to walk over to my side of it, and my heart is pounding loud in my ears. Fuck. What did I get myself into?

He opens the door and offers me his hand.

"Karl! Karl! Who's the babe?" One photographer calls out. Karl only shields me from the camera protectively, but it doesn't matter because the other photographer is on my other side. We rush inside the bar, and they don't follow.

"That was intense," I say.

Karl shrugs. "You'll get used to it."

---

WE GRAB a table in the center of the restaurant, close enough to the windows to be photographed, but not close enough that it looks as intentional as it is. I'm so nervous, the smile on my face so forced, Karl has to coax me into relaxation.

And he knows how.

"I have to confess something," he says.

"What's that?"

"I hate *Guns N' Roses.*"

My mouth hangs open. "Impossible. Nobody hates *Guns N' Roses.*"

"I do."

"If you do, it must be professional jealousy. Slash is your only real competition."

"Nope. Not professional jealousy. And loads of people don't like them."

"In that case, you're probably getting on the bandwagon like a sheep. I didn't take you for a music snob, Karl Sommer," I tease, all thoughts of the photographers outside gone now.

Our food arrives, and Karl dives into his tacos al carbon while I eat my elotes. Sofia really does have the best food in town.

"How long do you think before the pictures are out?" I ask.

Karl looks up from his taco. He shrugs. "Within the hour, probably."

I'm stunned and push my food away. Oh god. This is getting too real, too fast. Twenty thousand dollars, I remind myself. That's what I bargained for.

And guitar lessons.

***

WITHIN THE HOUR, the photo of us in Karl's car as he kissed my hand was on every online tabloid imaginable. My name isn't out there yet, but Karl says it's only a matter of time.

I think I'm going to be sick. I didn't give this enough thought.

Then fear slices through my very core. I should never have agreed to take this public.

What if they find out the truth about my family? I'm not sure I'm ready to let them drag my family name through the mud, not when they're no longer here to defend themselves. But it's too late to go back now. The best I can hope for is that they are satisfied enough with the sensation of Karl Sommer finally having a serious girlfriend to not dig into my family's past.

We're lounging in the living room after a few hours of packing the last of Karl's things. He's playing a video game, and I'm leafing through his copy of *Steel Hard Rock* magazine when the doorbell rings. Karl opens the door, and Brenner Reindhart, looking like a raged bull, storms into the house. His house now, I suppose.

"Do you have a death wish?" he roars.

"Calm down," Karl says.

"Didn't we just talk about you taking things seriously?"

I rush to the foyer to let Bren know I'm here too and listening.

"Oh, hi Lola," he says. "I'm sorry for yelling."

"Hi, Bren. Is Sofia here?"

"No. She's home with Addy, but I can't stop her from murdering Karl."

I snicker. "What's going on?"

Bren looks between Karl and me, waiting for an explanation, but we both just stare back at him.

"I thought Sofia told you to stay away from her, that she's seventeen," Bren says, in lower volume but no less furious-looking.

"No. Sofia *lied* to me that she's seventeen," Karl explains.

"So help me god, Karl. Lola is like family to Sofia. She's like her little sister. She's under my protection—"

"I'm right here, you know," I say. Bren just blinks. I walk up to Karl and lace my fingers through his, leaning on his arm sweetly. "It's okay, Bren. I'll talk to Sofia soon. As far as Karl and me, we've just started spending time together and are getting to know each other. There's no reason to overreact."

"Karl—"

But Karl cuts him off before Bren can say anything else. "You wanted me serious about the band and to stop the partying, right? I've spent all my evenings with Lola. No parties, no going out except with her. We're starting guitar lessons soon, and I'm even dabbling in some lyric writing. I'll be showing you drafts soon. Lola and me, we're . . . like she said, getting to know each other," he pauses and scratches his jaw thoughtfully before continuing, "in a serious way."

Bren blinks, but there's a hint of surprise in his eyes. "You've been warned," he says, then turns to me. "Sorry, Lola. It was nice to see you."

"Yeah, you too."

"Call Sofia, please. She's raising hell at home."

"I will."

# LOLA

After one more glance to make sure I didn't forget anything in my room, I seal the last box with packing tape and carry it to the living room. I thought this moment would come when I was ready to leave Kansas City, but because I still have a month and a half here, it doesn't seem quite as devastating as I thought it would.

Isael is on his play mat on the living room floor, one hand wrapped around Addy as they watch cartoons with the volume on low. I smile, watching the back of their heads, his covered in wispy, light brown curls, hers in straight black strands that shoot straight up in her ponytail, almost like a cartoon character. After setting down the box on the counter, I grab my cell from my back pocket and snap a picture of the sweet moment.

I don't let myself get teary-eyed about not getting to watch them grow up or even visit them again. I can't go down this rabbit hole because I still have a few weeks to enjoy them both.

Sofia looks up from her spot on the sofa where she and Ileana sip tea together.

"You sure you aren't moving too fast?" Sofia asks.

I shake my head. "We're just having fun," I say. "Promise. And

I promise Karl Sommer isn't going to break my fragile little heart."

"That's not what I—"

"Has it ever occurred to you that he's not using me and that maybe I'm using him? Maybe after a four-year-long relationship, I just want some fun with no strings," I say in a huff. "Moving in with him is just convenient. That's all. I'm still going to move to Mexico; this is just a temporary detour."

I don't miss the way Sofia and Ileana eye each other, but both give me the courtesy of biting their tongues. They already said their piece when I first told them my plans to move in with Karl. I'd let Sofia scold me as if I was still a little kid, but after they both calmed down and vented, I regained my composure. They both seemed impressed, and when they realized I wouldn't be moved from my decisions, they agreed to be supportive—even if they didn't entirely mean it at the time.

"Are you ready?" Ileana asks.

I nod. Ileana takes me into one of her signature soul-soothing long hugs. The kind of hug that comforted me when Mom was no longer here to do it. I squeeze her tight in my arms. When we break away, her eyes are glassy despite her face-splitting grin.

"When you get settled, I'll come help you cook and have a little housewarming. Just us and Sofia, and the band."

"And the kids," I add, looking over at the toddler pair in front of us.

"Isa," Ileana calls. "Your *tía* is going. You have to say goodbye."

Isael's little head turns to the side only a millimeter, one eye still on the television. Instead, I go to him and kneel next to where he's sitting. I hug him from behind and kiss the top of his head. "I'll see you soon, *mi terremoto*," I whisper next to him. He is entirely ignorant this is goodbye for now and that soon it will be goodbye for good.

I smile at the back of his head and ruffle his curls with one hand. I wish I still had the bliss of innocent ignorance.

Knowledge isn't always better, and being sheltered provides a sense of security, even when it's a false one. And the harrowing fall to the realities of life . . . well, the landing from that fall is astoundingly painful. *Stay a kid, Isael. If you can.*

---

BREN and his security guard stand outside the Escalade where they wait for us. When they see us, Andreas, Sofia and Addy's security guard, approaches me to grab the box from my hands and places it in the trunk. The moving truck already picked up everything else yesterday.

Andreas has a look about him that would almost have him pass for Karl's brother. He's not quite as tall but nearly as handsome and with a similar length of blond hair. I've barely met him, though, so I don't know if their personalities are shared as well.

As we ride away from my latest home, I sniff back my tears. Is this what my life is like now? Bouncing from home to home, aimless? This neighborhood was my entire life. The solid foundation I could always return to if the real world spat me out. Or so I thought.

Now my security blanket is nonexistent.

I watch as the suburbs, encased in arching trees, pass us by and turn into the hard architectural lines of the city where Karl's new penthouse awaits. From the front seat, I look at the rearview mirror and catch a glimpse of Bren and Sofia in the back, Addy's car seat between them, and Sofia's arm outstretches to rub the back of Bren's neck.

It's all I can do to hold in a sob deep in my chest before it gurgles out. Mom used to do that to Dad. She did it so often, I thought nothing of it at the time. I just remember Dad would be driving, and Mom would rest her arm on his backrest and rub the back of his neck or run her fingers through his hair.

God, I miss them. But I'm still so damned mad at them. Angry for leaving me so soon, when I still need them. Mad for everything they kept from me.

"If you change your mind," Sofia says from behind me, "I'm one phone call away. Ileana would take you back in a heartbeat."

"And so would we," Bren adds. "We have plenty of room at the new place."

I know, I think, and smirk, my mood lifting again. If they only knew I've stayed there already.

Maybe my future is unsteady at the moment, but what I can do is enjoy my present. And my present, luckily, is on the arm of the man voted the sexiest man alive by nearly every magazine worldwide.

Maybe the curse is breaking.

---

AFTER BREN AND SOFIA LEAVE, I look around at my new room in Karl's penthouse. It's mostly unpacked now, and I stare at my temporary future. Watching Sofia and Bren is so much like having a younger version of my parents around. I tried distracting myself by holding Addy and playing with her the entire time. But now they're all gone, and I'm left with nothing but my longing for my family.

A soft knock at the door breaks my wandering thoughts. "Come in."

Karl comes into view, and his wide grin vanishes at the same time his face falls when he sees me. "What's wrong?"

"Nothing," I lie.

"Come here." In three long strides, he reaches me and wraps his arms around me. I press my cheek to his hard chest, and he cups the back of my head in the most tender way while rubbing circles on my back. "Your nose is red, and you're about to cry."

"No, I'm not." I let out a nervous giggle.

"Listen, Lo. If you don't want to move in, you don't have to. Say the words, and I'll get the movers to take your stuff back to Ileana's. We can still date or just be friends if you want out of the bet. Just don't cry, doll."

I laugh and wipe the corner of my eye, and take a step away from him, so he has to let me go from his embrace. "I don't regret moving in. It's just . . ."

"What?" Karl asks when my thought trails off.

"It's silly. Really. It's just being around Bren and Sofia together. I don't know how to explain it, but seeing them together . . . I've just been thinking a lot about my own parents today. That's all."

Karl laughs. "You know, even before Bren met Sofia, all of us in the band would call him 'Dad' as a joke. He hated it."

I laugh. "Really?"

"Yeah. He's always been so serious, and . . . paternal. Like the dad of the band, you know? Of course, the more he told us to stop, the more we called him that. And then when Addy came along, well, he could no longer fight it."

"Thanks, Karl," I say.

"For what?"

"For cheering me up."

Karl leaves me to explore my new home. I've been here before, visiting Sofia or sitting for Addy, but it's different now that I'll be living here for a while.

My favorite features in the apartment are the black marble floors and the entire wall of windows that displays the Kansas City skyline. I've always loved this view, and I can't wait for nighttime when I can sit by the window with a hot beverage and watch the city nightlights turn on all around us.

The main room is an open space. Beyond the foyer, the

living room and dining room are in view from the elevator entrance. Karl gave me a key card to access the top floor from the elevator. Having no front door, only an elevator, seems unreal. What my life has come to seems surreal.

There are four bedrooms, though he has turned one into an office and I'd bet that's the space Karl will use for his ax collection. We settled all of Pixel's things and the playroom in another guest bedroom.

He also insisted on me taking the bigger guest room next to his. I haven't been able to stop smiling since he insisted. He played it off as wanting to give me the bigger of the two guest rooms. But I know the truth.

He wants me close.

---

As I push the vacuum with too much force, "You Drive Me Wild" by *The Runaways* works me up even further into my seething anger. I had an argument this morning with Karl when I left for work. Of course, he'd insisted I quit cleaning houses. For a moment, I thought he would be ashamed if it got out that he's dating a housekeeper, but that's not it. Even if I quit today, that information will inevitably get out.

He simply doesn't see why I have to work.

Of all the entitled, jerk things to say. But what really rubbed salt on the wound was that he chose the day I clean my most difficult customer's house to pick the fight.

Before I even had my morning coffee!

Worst morning ever.

I need to focus on my task, though. Mr. Sanders insists I vacuum in such a precise way that the visible track lines from the vacuum form a lattice of perfect, overlapping 'Vs.' What a douchebag. It's not like he and his family won't ruin the pattern within ten minutes as they walk all over the carpet.

When I'm done, I find Mr. Sanders in his office, and I knock softly on his open door. "Mr. Sanders?"

"Yes?"

"Do you have a minute?" I've always hated that he makes me ask for my payment. All my clients leave my fee by the entrance so I can just grab it on my way out and I can stay out of their hair.

He looks up from his computer and gestures for me to sit in the second chair in his home office.

"I'm all done for today," I say.

Mr. Sanders opens his desk drawer and pulls out a small stack of bills he slides over his desk. "Thank you, Dolores."

"Of course." I move to stand and take the bills in my hands to roll them up. I slide them in my back pocket, and I haven't turned to leave when he speaks up again.

"You know, Dolores, I've never said anything because I don't want you to feel uncomfortable."

*Then don't say it now.*

But he keeps talking. "I think you are very beautiful."

I smile tightly, and fuck, why was my gut reaction to smile? "Uh—thanks."

"I mean, you don't look Mexican at all. If you hadn't told me you were, I'd never have thought that." He smiles at me. He actually fucking smiles.

My brows draw together, and I'm not sure how to handle this. "So when you say I'm pretty because I don't look Mexican, that's supposed to be a compliment?"

"Calm down, sweetheart. No offense intended. Just wanted to pay a pretty lady a compliment. That's all."

"By telling her she's pretty because she doesn't look Mexican?"

"Now wait just one second, that's not what I said—"

"It's not?" I arch a brow and take two big gulps of air and count to ten in under two seconds. I'm pretty sure that's not how that calming technique is supposed to go. I don't need to take this shit. I've saved up my goal. And I have a rock-star boyfriend. Who cares if it's fake? I don't need to clean this *viejo rabo-verde*'s toilets one more day. "You know what, Mr. Sanders? I quit."

I storm out of his office and can sense him hot on my heels. "Dolores, please wait. I meant no offense."

"But you did offend, Mr. Sanders. I'm very proud to be Mexican. And if I'm beautiful, I happen to think a lot of that has to do with my Mexican roots. I take after my Dad. But my mom looked 'Mexican,'" I say and pause to do air quotes for him, "and she was the most beautiful woman you'd ever set eyes on." I'm clenching my jaw so tightly it hurts. "You have a month to find a housekeeper before you need your next cleaning. I'd start looking now, Mr. Sanders," I spit out and shut his own front door on his face.

Asshole.

---

I DON'T SEE Karl anywhere when I storm into the apartment, and I rush into my bedroom, shed my clothes, and jump in the shower. I need to get the grime of this infuriating day off of me, and I dip my head back under the rain showerhead, letting the warm water soothe me.

After I wrap myself in a towel, I startle when I look over at my bed. I stormed into the shower in such fury when I first got here, I didn't even glance in that direction.

My hand floats to my chest.

I left my bed unmade this morning. But someone—Karl— has made it for me. And on top of it, he's neatly placed a beautiful little black dress. It is a flared mini-dress with a single layer of ruffle at the hem. Triangles of black fabric wrap the bodice under the bust and meet at the center in a gold clasp with a design of Medusa. It's very rock and roll but super elegant at the same time. The double spaghetti straps have mini versions of the gold clasp. I approach the dress tentatively and read the label: Versace.

I take a step back. I've never been in the same room with a designer garment before, not unless cleaning for wealthy clients counts. I'm almost afraid to touch it. I'm pretty confident these types of dresses cost in the thousands. And I'd bet my signed headshot of Robert Trujillo this dress is worth more than my car. I laugh at the thought of me in this dress behind the wheel of my car—my car with the plank holding up the backrest.

What has my life come to?

There are two boxes next to the dress, wrapped in shiny gold paper. I take the envelope sitting on top of the boxes and set it aside to open the first box. From it, I produce a black clutch with a golden chain strap and a gold "V" with leaf details in the metal on the face of the bag. Does Karl have some type of deal with Versace or something?

When I open the larger box and find shoes, I half-expect them to match the brand. But they don't. They're Jimmy Choo's. The shoes I've only ever heard mentioned on television. And they are fucking spectacular.

Shoe porn. They are fucking rock and roll shoe porn.

The black suede platform heels are sky high and exactly my size. I hurry to try them on, and my eyes close with pleasure. They fit like a glove. I squeal with excitement I can no longer contain.

I tear open the note next.


"Iggy,

I'm sorry we argued this morning.

You're right. You should work if that's what makes you happy.

Please let me make it up to you.
Be ready at seven. We're going on a date.
~K"


WHEN I'M DONE READING the note, I frown. He called me Iggy in the note. The name he uses when he is being playful or detached, not wanting to show his attraction to me. If this were an actual date, he'd have addressed the note as *doll*, the nickname he uses when he's turned on or being sweet. Maybe this is just for the press. Not an actual date.

*Stop it, Lo. You're reading too much into it. Just let yourself enjoy this.*

It's been so long since I've been on an actual date. My stomach flutters with both excitement and nerves. I finish getting ready, and I'm only ten minutes late when I walk into the foyer and find Karl waiting for me. He stands by the elevator doors, and his face beams when he slowly draws his gaze from my toes to my face.

I straightened my hair for tonight, something I rarely do because I don't want to fry it, and am wearing a heavy, smokey eyeshadow with about a million coats of mascara and thick winged eyeliner. I'm going to freeze in this outfit, but I'm not ruining it with my stupid jacket. Besides, it'll only be for a brief moment when we get out of the car and into the restaurant.

Karl cleans up nice too. He's wearing black slacks and a crisp white shirt with the top two buttons undone. His sleeves are rolled up to his thick, veiny forearms, giving him a bit of a relaxed look. Despite that, he looks dapper. Or as much as a metal head can look dapper.

"You clean up nice," I say with a smile.

He takes my hand in his and spins me around, whistling slow and making me giggle when I find his face again. "You look stunning, doll." He lifts my hand in his and kisses the back of it.

Then grabs a suit jacket that matches his slacks and throws it over his shoulder as we head out.

My heart flutters. *Why, stupid heart?* Because he called me *doll*. That's why.

Game on.

---

IT WAS in June of 1970 in Cincinnati when James Newell Osterberg, Jr—best known by his stage name, Iggy Pop—decided to crowd-surf in the most unconventional way. He walked over the audience's hands with incredible balance, and they didn't let him down.

In one infamous act, a fan handed him a jar of peanut butter, and Iggy—still standing on the hands of his fans—took the jar, sunk his fingers in the condiment, ate some, smeared some over his naked chest, and flung some in thick clumps at his audience.

There was complete abandon when he performed that night. He was living life, right there for that moment and for that moment only. There was no past. No future. No worries about absolutely anything. Only the present.

It was him and his performance, his art, and his connection with the crowd.

I've always admired people who can live like that. I want to live like that.

I want freedom.

That kind of freedom is what I'm chasing, but the very act of running to find freedom in itself makes the goal unattainable because instead of running toward something, I'm running from something else.

If there is a time that I get to let go completely, it's tonight.

I laugh hysterically most of the way to the restaurant, and Karl has been staring at me like I've grown two heads—or like my hair has turned to snakes like the Medusa medallions on my dress.

"You're sure you aren't high?" He asks for the third time during our ride to the restaurant in our limousine.

*Our* limousine.

I've laughed so hard; I'm risking tears ruining my makeup. I carefully dab the corners of my eyes with my fingers.

"I'm sorry," I say between guffaws.

At first, I snorted when the limousine pulled up in front of us, and Karl opened the door. And then he told me we were dining at the Ampersand, the most upscale and exclusive restaurant in Kansas City. And I couldn't help it. I can't stop laughing.

"Are you going to tell me what's so damn funny?" Karl asks with mock frustration, but the amusement dancing in his pupils tells me he is far from frustrated.

"It's just, I drive past the Ampersand to go to work most days. It's in the rich part of town, and I always trudge into this neighborhood in my *carcacha*, barely on fumes. I never thought I'd get to eat there. And look at me now!" I scream and laugh harder. "In a limousine, wearing a dress that costs more than my car, driving past clients whose toilets I've cleaned only this week. And my date is freaking Karl Sommer!"

Karl laughs, amused at my antics.

This is it.

What Iggy must have felt that night. Or something close to it. When nothing matters but the perfect little moment that this messed up life offers you. A little gift that you must seize before it's taken away again. And you do; you want to sink your fingers into something thick and tangible and smear it over your body to graze at the raw nerves that are feeling life to the fullest. It's raw, gritty, and honest. What life is for.

It's rock and roll.

"Are you done yet?" Karl asks.

"Yeah. I'm done. But Karl?"

"Yeah?"

"Don't call me *doll* tonight."

His lips disappear into a thin line before he asks, "Why not?"

"Just for tonight, I want to be Lola. Not Lo. Not Dolores. I don't even want to have a last name. Just Lola."

He smiles, though he's still eying me like he doesn't believe I'm not high.

But I guess I am. I'm high on life. And I just want to be me. Not my parent's daughter, not the housekeeper.

Lola.

"You got it, Lola."

# 16

# KARL

Lola is giddy.

And it's amusing as all hell, but damn, this woman is easy to please. One little dress and a nice dinner, and she's high on life. I like that about her.

She's not materialistic as far as I can tell, but she's taken to being pampered rather well.

And she looks stunning tonight. My heart nearly stopped when I saw her. Little sex kitten that she is, decked out to the nines in Versace. I'll have to thank the personal shopper I hired to make her feel like the heavy metal goddess she is.

I wanted to treat her to a nice night before our guitar lessons start because I'll be taking those seriously, and she'll likely hate me when she realizes how demanding a teacher I'll be.

So yes. Maybe I am sweetening her up a bit.

Lola orders a bottle of champagne, and the waiter pours our glasses and sets the bottle in the ice bin next to our table.

"Are we celebrating something?" I ask her.

"Yes. Life!"

We cheer at that, and we both take a sip. Then she speaks again. "And I quit today."

"You did?"

She nods. "I realized I'm worth more than shitty customers. I have some nice clients, but I think I'm done with that, you know? I was hesitant to move on. Work . . . it's been my safety blanket this past year, and I was hesitant to let it go. But it's time."

We cheer again, and she laughs, and my heart somersaults when her smile reaches her eyes. She's genuinely, incandescently happy tonight. I did that. For some reason, I'm mighty proud of that.

We're on a second glass of champagne when the waiter brings our salads, and Lola is all smiles for him too.

"Can I ask you something?"

She looks up at me from her salad.

"Sure."

"Why do you only want to be called Lola tonight?"

"It's like a stage name—"

"Like Iggy?"

"Sort of. I mean, I'm turning a new leaf. I'm learning who I really am, and I just want to be undeniably me tonight. Feel what it's like to be Lola without all the damned baggage, without all the worries."

My brows furrow together. I want to ask her what her worries are about, but I want tonight to only continue to bring out her smiles and laughter, so instead, I change the subject. "Speaking of who you really are. We start lessons tomorrow."

Lola perks up. "We do?"

"Yes. Intensive. You're going to take this seriously," I say, but it's not a question. It's an order.

Lola's hand bunches into a fist, and she screams as she punches the air, "Fuck yes!"

I laugh because either she is oblivious or doesn't care that diners from several tables over are staring at us now, eyebrows near their hairlines. Lola couldn't be more perfect.

We eat our steaks, and Lola rambles on animatedly about her favorite guitar solos, making lesson requests that have me rolling my eyes. She's getting so ahead of herself. We need to start with the basics, but her enthusiasm is encouraging. She'll likely be an excellent student.

By the time we leave the restaurant, photographers are lined up next to either side of the entrance. They are yelling questions about my date and who she is. We push past them and duck into the limo.

When I look over at Lola, she's breathing hard, her palm pressed to her chest.

Security.

Why didn't I think of security? The first thing Bren did when news broke out about Sofia was to get her personal security. I'm a fucking idiot for not thinking of it.

I'll have to talk to Bren and Andreas tomorrow about assigning Lola her own security guard.

"We're fine," I whisper and rub the back of her hand with my index finger.

Lola smiles up at me as her breathing slowly returns to normal. "I know. It's just hard getting used to it, you know?"

I smile. "I do know."

She turns thoughtful for a moment, and her hand drifts to her stomach.

"What is it?" I ask.

Her mouth twists like she's biting the inside of her cheek. "Umm . . ."

Not this again. The last time she was embarrassed like this, her request wasn't one I wanted. "Just spit it out," I say. I'd rather know what she's thinking.

"Those portions were tiny. Don't you think?"

I let my head fall back with laughter. "Yeah. They were. You still hungry?"

Her cheeks flush a little, but she nods.

"Me too," I say with an encouraging smile.

"I know a great place, but we'll have to ditch the limo," she says.

I ask our driver to lose the cars trailing us, and he drops us off at a gas station. Lola orders a car with her phone app, and ten minutes later, we're on our way to get ourselves a second dinner.

"A food truck?" I ask, aghast at where she's led our driver.

Her smile is wide. "Best tacos in the world. Come on."

I smile inwardly. She noticed I ordered tacos when we ate at Sofia's bar together. Several food trucks surround multiple picnic tables and benches. We get out of the car, and Lola walks toward the taco truck in the center.

As we walk, her hands go to her arms, and she rubs them. I should have asked the personal shopper to get her a coat to go with the outfit. I'm so stupid. Taking off my jacket, I wrap it around her shoulders. "Here," I say and rub the spot over the fabric now covering her arms.

"Thank you."

After the last person in line ahead of us orders, Lola yells out her order. "*Dos ordenes de tacos al pastor por favor,*" she says.

The man taking the order does a double take when he sees her, then his smile grows exponentially.

"Lola? Is that *you*?"

She nods with a goofy grin, and he rushes out of the truck. He takes Lola in his arms and lifts her off the ground, spinning her around. "Oh my god," he says, setting her down again and eyeing her up and down. "You look incredible!"

My jaw clenches. *Hands off.*

Then the man looks up at me, his arm still wrapped over

Lola's shoulder, my eyes glued to where they connect. "Who's this?" he asks.

"This is Karl. My boyfriend. Karl, this is Paco. He keeps me fed."

Paco turns a startled look at Lola. "So you finally dumped that piece of shit, Ethan?"

Her face falls, and my chest constricts. "Yeah," she whispers.

"Good riddance!" Paco says and finally lets go of Lola to offer me a handshake. I take it, and he holds my hand tight in his grip. "I hope you're a trade up," he says, looking me dead in the eye now, "but if you hurt her, I'll free you of your tongue to make *tacos de lengua* with it. You got it?" Despite his threatening words, he is smiling, clearly glad to see Lola with someone other than Ethan. And if he recognizes who I am, he doesn't care.

"I would never purposefully hurt her," I say.

"Good, now what was it you said you wanted?"

"*Al pastor*," I say, rolling the 'r' like Lola had. Paco smiles approvingly at me.

"And two Coronas," Lola adds.

Paco nods and goes back inside the truck to make our order.

When our tacos and beers are in front of us, I watch as Lola devours her food. "So you're friends with the taco truck guy?"

She smiles around her taco, waits to swallow, then laughs. "Pro tip—always make friends with the *taquero* in your town."

I laugh. This woman is amazing.

Not wanting to look like a total creep staring at her as she eats, I finally take a bite of my taco. The medley of spices, pineapple, and pork, seasoned with onion and a spicy salsa verde, bursts over my tastebuds. I've never eaten anything so delicious. I just spent hundreds at a three-Michelin star restaurant, and don't get me wrong, the food was excellent. But it does not compare to the tacos that Lola has insisted on buying.

When she pulled out the rolled-up, crumpled bills from her Versace purse, I was stunned.

I don't remember the last time anyone has treated me to so much as a cup of coffee. The free swag I get in the mail from companies in hopes of free promotion doesn't count because it isn't selfless. Not the way her buying me dinner was.

She spent less than twenty dollars, including beers, but the gesture was worth billions to my jaded heart.

When we finish eating, I stand to get us more beers. I rejoin Lola at our table, and we keep sipping beers into the night.

"Did I tell you how beautiful you look tonight?"

Her little nose is rosy from the alcohol, and heat creeps up to her cheeks in a matching shade. She nods.

"Thank you. Really, Karl. This has been the best date of my life."

There's an enormous speaker outside Paco's truck now, and he is playing a slow song in Spanish I don't recognize. Then, a scattering of lights turn on above us, the string of bulbs connected to the roof of each food truck. I glance over at Paco, and he gives me a thumbs up with a huge smile, and I tip my chin in appreciation. Paco and I could be good friends.

I stand and hold out my hand. "Would you do me the honor?"

Her nose scrunches up. "I have a hard time *walking* in these shoes. I don't think I can *dance*."

"Just the slow songs. I won't let you fall," I say, my hand still waiting for her to take it. "I promise."

She drains her beer and finally takes my hand. I wrap both arms around her, the side of her face nestling between my pecs as we sway gently. "Mmm," she moans against my shirt. "You're warm."

I chuckle. "Thank you for dinner, Lola. You don't know how much that meant to me."

"Next time, pick somewhere with fully-grown-human portions, please."

We both laugh and fall silent for a while. The song changes to another slow song in Spanish, and she looks up at me. "I love this song."

"What's it about?"

"The title in English means traitorous butterfly. He's singing about a girl he loves, but she's too free for him. She's always flying away, and he wants her to feel his pain, so he tells her this time, he won't come back to her."

"That's sad," I say. "They're both doomed to sadness."

"Yeah. But he still loves her. He always will."

Our eyes lock, and the air becomes thick around us as I breathe it in with effort. I brush a strand of hair away from her cheek with my thumb and tuck it behind her ear. Her eyes fall to my lips at the same time she lets go of her arms around me to instead take my collar in her fists, so she can pull me down to her level.

And I let her. I don't want to keep fighting this. And more importantly, I *can't* keep fighting this.

Our lips mold together gently, and I smile into the kiss.

I try not to chuckle. I've imagined kissing her a million times. I always assumed when I finally had the chance to taste her, she'd taste like the watermelon gum she's constantly chewing. Instead, the taste of *al pastor* and beer with lime lingers on our tongues as they massage each other. I file the sensation away with all my most treasured memories.

We break away, and she smiles. "You can *really* kiss, Karl Sommer."

I chuckle for real now. "So can you, Lola—"

And for one panicked second, I almost called her Lola *Sommer* but stopped myself just in time.

*What the actual fuck?*

# 17

## LOLA

When we get back home, our home—I still can't believe it's *our* home—Karl has to help me with my balance.

The perfect Jimmy Choo's that fit like a glove have pinched my skin raw to within an inch of its life over each pinky toe. And let's not forget the two glasses of champagne and two beers that we used to wash down our two dinners. I suck in my belly, hoping it's not too noticeable in the second-skin dress. And all this means I have very poor balance, and Karl has to help me out of the car. Our hands lace together as I lean on his arm for support.

As we ride the elevator up to the penthouse, I let my head drift to his arm. It's the most content moment until the elevator doors slide open and reveal a party taking place inside our apartment.

Karl's hand tightens around mine as he leads me toward the crowd. It's a small party, only about fifteen people, but that's fifteen more than I want here tonight. And I'm sure fifteen more than Karl wants around after his talk with Bren.

But what has me freezing on the spot is the sight of Sandy

sitting on the couch, a handsome man on either side of her, as she sips from a martini glass, holding court. She laughs at something one man says until her gaze cuts to us and her eyes drop to Karl's and my hands still laced together. The man next to her follows her line of sight, and he stands and walks over to where Karl and I stand frozen.

I look up at Karl, his every muscle taut with strain. I can even feel the vibrations in my hand from his shaking.

He is pissed.

"Karl, man!" the man greets, reaching us. "Who's this?" he asks, looking at me.

"Lola," Karl hisses. "My girlfriend."

The man's eyes widen with surprise, and he quickly recovers. "Well, hello, darling," the man says. "I'm Roger—"

"Kemp. Yes, I know," I say. I try getting my hand back from Karl, but he only grips it tighter, as if I am his support beam.

Roger Kemp is the infamous band manager for *Industrial November*. I'd know him anywhere.

"What the fuck is going on?" Karl says in an eerily soft tone.

"I thought we'd have a little housewarming—"

"Lola and I have a housewarming planned. And it includes none of these people, and it certainly doesn't include you." Karl's eyes are narrowed to slits, daring Roger to challenge him.

"I think I'll head to my room," I say, feeling uncomfortable as all hell.

"No," Karl says. "You aren't going anywhere. This is your home now, and you won't be made uncomfortable in it." His eyes never leave Roger, though. "You," he pokes Roger in the chest with his index finger, "get everyone the fuck out of my house."

"Come on, man, they just want to see how you've been—"

Roger's words die in his mouth when Karl finally drops my hand and rushes over to the sound system to cut the music.

Everyone turns to look at him now. Even the bartender they apparently hired looks up from the drink he's mixing.

"Everyone get the fuck out," Karl roars.

Everyone in the room turns to Roger for direction, and Roger hesitates.

*What the fuck?*

I'm starting to understand the dynamics here. These people think Roger is in charge of Karl. Band manager or not, this is a gross invasion of Karl's privacy.

Roger gives a subtle tip of his chin. Everyone sets their drinks down, then slowly trickle into the elevator until only four of us are left. Karl, Roger, myself . . . and Sandy.

Sandy uncrosses her legs and stands to face Karl. "The housekeeper, Karl? Really? You're with *her* now?" She sizes me up slowly, disgust etched in her twisted mouth. I can't blame her for her animosity toward me, given our last interaction. I feel a little sorry for her. Based on the way she looks at Karl, with so much pain, I think she might actually have feelings for him.

Karl sticks his hands in his pockets. "Yes. I'm with Lola now."

"But I thought we—"

"No," he says. "I was clear from the start. You and I—"

"Karl!" I snap, and he stops mid-sentence to look at me. "This is really uncomfortable for me." I throw Sandy a sad smile. "And I'm sure for Sandy too. Why don't you go into the office to talk?"

Sandy squares her shoulders as she follows Karl down the hallway, and I spin on my heel to look at Roger.

"I'm sorry about this," he says.

I narrow my eyes at him, emboldened either by alcohol or the anger I feel on Karl's behalf—I'm not sure which. "Are you?" I ask him.

Roger sets his drink down, and I study him. He is polished despite the casual jeans and t-shirt number he wears. 'Expensive' comes to mind. He is fit and handsome and wouldn't be out of place next to the band members on an album cover. "What's that supposed to mean?" he asks.

We stay quiet for a long moment as we size each other up. "You use him," I say simply.

Roger chuckles. "What?"

"You use him. All the parties, the women . . . none of it is Karl, is it? All the photos on all the tabloids, it's all you? You stage it to make it look like, like . . ."

"He's no innocent little thing, Lola. Karl enjoys being a rock god."

*Lies.*

I think about that first day I cleaned his house. How bad the first floor was. That was Roger's doing. But the top floor where Karl lived was pristine. And it's stayed that way since I cleaned that first time. Anything that is currently a mess in Karl's life is a direct byproduct of Roger's meddling. I'm sure of it.

I shake my head. "No. He likes making music. He likes performing. And sure, he probably likes the money too. But this little charade"—I wave my arms around the room—"this nineties clichéd rock-star image you've conjured up, it's all you. I see it now. Your hand is in every leaked photo, in every spilled secret, in every police report after a rager got out of hand." I tick off on my fingers a long list of grievances, suddenly grateful for all my years of stalking the band online.

Roger cracks his neck. I've hit a nerve with my accusations. *Bingo.* He steps closer to me, doing his best to tower over me, and though I'm much too short to try to intimidate him back, I keep my posture tall and lift my chin up in defiance.

His eyes narrow.

"Does he know?" I ask.

"Does he know what?"

"That he's your puppet? And more importantly, does the band know? That who you've made him out to be isn't who he is?"

"Fuck." Roger runs a hand through his light brown hair. "You've known him all of two seconds, and you think you know him? You don't know anything."

"I know manipulation when I see it."

"It's for the good of the band—"

"Not for *everyone* in the band. It's not good for Karl. It's not good for the band dynamics. Bren is half-ready to trade Milo back in."

"He wouldn't do that. The label wouldn't allow that."

"Wouldn't they?" I bring my hands to my hips as if that will help me drive my point home. I have no idea if that's true, but planting the idea in Roger's head seems like a good battle tactic at the moment.

Roger stays quiet.

"Here's what's going to happen," I say, and bring my hand up to silence him when he tries to open his mouth. "This is going to stop. You are going to let Karl work on his art and pitch music to Bren. You are going to give him the space to concentrate and work. The parties, it's all done. It's not what he wants."

"There's an image he agreed to uphold when he signed on to the band."

"You can tell the press whatever you want, but you will lay off his *time*. Do you hear me?"

"Or what?" Roger asks with defiance. "You think you're going to last?"

That stung, but I don't let him see it, and I definitely don't falter when I answer him. "Or I will turn into your worst nightmare. I'm Karl's girlfriend for as long as he wants me around. I moved in with him. Has he ever moved in with anyone before?" I raise a brow at him. Suddenly, I'm grateful Karl wanted this fake relationship to look as serious as it does. "Whose side do you think he'd take if he had to choose?"

Roger takes a step back to eye me up and down like he's considering me in a new light. "You're pretty smart, aren't you?"

His mouth upturns into a half-smile, and for some reason, I'm no longer as angry as I'd been a second ago. This man is trouble. He could disarm you if you let him.

"I care about Karl. He isn't happy with how things are," I say.

Roger lets out a long breath. "Fine. We'll try things your way for a while, but if the band's popularity dips and sales drop, we will have to reassess his public image."

"Thank you," I say.

"Welcome to *Industrial November*," he says as he turns to leave.

Roger is waiting for the elevator to return when Sandy rushes to join him, and they leave together.

Karl is looking at me funny, and he sticks his fists in his pockets. "I'm not his puppet," he says when we're alone.

My jaw goes slack. "You heard that?"

The clicking of nails on the marble floors announces Pixel as she approaches me eagerly. She sniffs my feet. They must have locked her in a room while the party took place. Another strike against Roger Kemp.

Karl nods. "Some of it. I agreed at the start . . . I just assumed the band knew, but it's become clear lately Roger kept this from them. I actually half-think he is trying to save their feelings."

"What do you mean?"

"When I came on, Roger was worried that as the guys got older, interest in them would drop. That's why he wanted someone younger. He pitched me as new blood. They're all slowing down in terms of their personal lives, and the parties don't hold the same allure to them that they once did."

"What does this have to do with their feelings?"

"I think Roger didn't want to make them feel old."

I laugh. "I'm sorry. They're millionaire, handsome, rock gods. I don't think aging will bother them." I pause. "Still. I'm sorry for insinuating you're his puppet."

Karl takes several steps forward and stops an inch away from me. "Thank you," he says, his eyes locked on mine.

"For what?"

"Standing up for me. Tonight, you've done two things no one has done for me in a long time." His voice cracks when he says that, and I think he might actually cry. "No one's ever . . . defended me so passionately," he admits.

Something moves inside my chest. I suddenly realize I know nothing about Karl, his background, his upbringing. Everything has been all about me. How can I be so selfish? Is he alone in this world like me? I want to ask him, but now doesn't seem like the time, when he was just ready to murder Roger on the spot.

He retrieves his hand from his pocket and caresses my cheek sweetly, but I pull away. "What are you doing?" I ask and step away from his touch.

His brows furrow at my retreat from his physical space. "I was thinking about our kiss."

I laugh nervously. "Right. Sorry about that."

"Don't be sorry—"

"The two guys at the table next to us recognized you. They were trying to take photos with their phones without us noticing."

"What? I didn't see anything."

"They were behind you when we were sitting," I say with a slight shrug.

I watch as the hard line of Karl's jaw tenses, the muscle above it ticking visibly. "That's why you kissed me? For the photo?"

"That's what tonight was about, right? Our official debut as a couple?"

He's silent as he seems to come to some sort of decision. He sticks his hands in his pockets again. "Right. Well, goodnight, Lola," he says, his tone harsh. Then, he goes to his bedroom.

I blink after him. What did I do now?

THE FOLLOWING MORNING, I lay awake in my room with Pixel curled around my feet as we wait for Karl to go on his run. At seven on the dot, the soft knock at my door comes. "Come in," I say and sit up in the bed.

Pixel stirs and stretches before getting off the bed.

"Sorry. Did I wake you?"

I shake my head. "No. I've been up for a bit."

"Come on, Pix," Karl says, looking down at Pixel. "We're going on our run. When we get back, we're starting lessons, so get ready."

"Really?" I beam up at him. I rush to stand on my bed and jump up once excitedly. "Hell yeah!"

Karl chuckles and leaves with Pixel, shaking his head until he is out of view. "And clean up that mess," he yells from down the hall.

There's no way I'm cleaning my room. Spend a year cleaning professionally, then tell me you have any desire to ever clean again. I don't care that half my things are in boxes. I can live out of boxes. Besides, what's the point when I'll have to ship them soon, anyway? Instead of cleaning, I go on a mission.

Since moving in, I've been tempted to snoop in his room again, but so far I've managed to refrain, at least since I stole his hoody at his old place.

After last night, I'm more curious than ever. The smell of him is long gone from the hoody, and it's time I replace it with something else.

Double-checking he's gone, I sneak into his bedroom and toss the hoodie in his laundry bin. I have to roll my eyes at how neat Karl keeps everything. He is completely unpacked, and I swear the man dusts daily. What a neat freak. Rock-star party monster, my ass.

I'm perusing his closet, thinking about what new garment I

can steal, when a thought crosses my mind. I know I have at least an hour before he comes back, so I head toward his bathroom.

I haven't been in this bathroom before, and my eyes bulge when I take it in. It's larger than my room was at Ileana's. The his-and-her shower has two rain showerheads with an assortment of detachable nozzles. I have no idea what they're all for. Man, Sofia really is living the high life now. This was her room not too long ago.

There's a built-in bench carved of stone all along the edge, and I'd kill to shower in here. The bench is perfect for shaving my legs.

A small thrill runs through me, and I jump in place. Between Karl announcing we're starting lessons today and being in Karl's private space, I can't stop myself from what I'm about to do.

I undress and step into his shower. I don't think about the consequences or care that when he gets back from his run and jumps in the shower, he'll notice it's wet.

The water runs hot down my body, and I close my eyes with appreciation. Wondering if he has a sound system in the shower, I call out, "Play *Industrial November*." A soft chime sounds, and a soothing voice answers. "Playing *Industrial November*, Metal Red Day." I squeal as one of my favorite songs comes on, and the volume is blaring through the shower.

Best shower ever.

I grab the bottle of body wash and bring it to my nose. It has an earthy smell I've caught a whiff of on Karl before when he doesn't shave and skips the aftershave. Lathering some in my hands, I wash my body, letting the smell of Karl envelop me in the steamy shower. I look over at the wall with handles and attachments and zero in on a detachable showerhead.

I don't know if it's the smell of Karl, the steaming shower, the luxury of the bathroom, my favorite song playing, or me just being horny, but there's only one thing to do next.

After adjusting the main showerhead to aim at the bench, I take a seat under the rainfall and spread my legs wide, bringing the detachable showerhead to my seam.

The water pressure is out of this world against my clitoris, and I moan with pleasure.

I close my eyes, thinking back to our kiss last night.

The most perfect first kiss in the world.

Karl's arms around me as we swayed to the music. His hand caressing mine reassuringly when I was afraid of the photographers yelling. His touch, so innocent and so scorching to my skin.

Several minutes pass, and my breath turns ragged when that familiar tight coil of pressure builds in my core. When I open my eyes briefly, I startle for a second when I find a second person in the large shower with me.

Karl is watching me from the other side of the shower. How long has he been in here with me? Watching? The water is on above him now too, letting the water ripple down his torso, those perfect pec and ab muscles spraying off water in all directions, giving the impression of a light glow coming off his body. I didn't hear him come in over the music. He could have been here since I started pleasuring myself with thoughts of him, or only one minute. It doesn't matter. Either way, it's the biggest turn-on of my life.

I only falter for an instant when I first see him because this moment is too hot. Too perfect.

Our eyes lock, and his jaw tightens, but he stays where he is, frozen. I resume my work with the water pressure over my clit, and Karl's eyes turn dark. He yells over the music to change the song. I snicker. He probably doesn't want to do this listening to Bren's voice, and I can't blame him. Instead, he plays "Closer" by *Nine Inch Nails*. What a great song for what we're about to do. I smile my approval. That is precisely how I feel about him right now.

His chest rises and falls, and his fists ball at his sides.

He likely can't decide if he's more turned on or furious at me. Because furious, he is. He doesn't like me tempting him like this. I know that for certain. Tempt him like I did that night when he came over my stomach. Like I'm doing now as water slides down my body, my toes curling against the natural stone floor at the sight of his perfect body. What it would be like to reach out and touch him right now. To feel his slick, wet skin under my fingertips.

My gaze drops to his erection hanging heavily between his legs, and my mouth dries up, making me lick my lips. His resolve to only watch must waver because, in two long strides, he is in front of me, his penis inches from my face.

I keep working myself with the water pressure and dart my tongue out to lick off the bead of precum that has risen to the tip of him. The taste of him overtakes my tongue, and I moan with pleasure. This man is divine.

He struggles to grip my dripping wet hair in one hand, forcing me closer, and I have no choice but to take him deeper in my throat. I'm so close to coming, I lay off the pressure a bit. I want to enjoy him longer. Karl's hips pick up speed as he fucks my mouth, and I gag around him. I bring my free hand to his powerful thigh to push away, but his grip is too strong.

Fuck. This is hot. His possession. His need for me.

He can't keep fighting this—us. We are inevitable.

I know it.

And it's time Karl Sommer knew it too.

Unable to stave off satisfaction any longer, I let myself fall. Ecstasy overtakes my body as I tighten with my release. When Karl lets himself fall right down here with me into this depth of pleasure, I drink up the last drop of hot liquid, enjoying every bit of him as he comes.

The song stops after its second loop, and Karl orders the sound system to stop. The loud rush of water around us veils

Karl's increased breathing, and he pulls out of my mouth. Our eyes lock as he brings his thumb to trace the shape of my upper lip. I stand, trying to find him, but he won't concede to my pull around his neck to kiss me.

My face twists with his rejection, and he responds by wrapping a tight arm around my waist, wiping away water from my brow. "I'm not fucking you, Lola. Pull all the stunts you want. I'm not going to be your first."

I raise a brow at him in defiance. "But you'll fuck my mouth?"

His face falls with shame. He's clearly not proud of what pleasures he gives into when it comes to me.

"Hey," I say, nudging him gently. "I liked it. A lot. I don't see how much different it would be to just fuck me. Don't you want to, Karl? To feel what it would be like to be inside me? Feeling me clench around you?"

His hold around my waist tightens, and his other hand drops to my hip bone, pushing me painfully. One arm bringing me closer to him, his other hand pushing me away. Even his body is undecided about giving in.

"It just can't be me, Lola. Will you just drop it?"

Fuck-drunk and sated, I smile sweetly up at him. "For today."

He laughs, and the sound breaks the tension mixed in the steam from the shower.

# 18

# KARL

L ola walks out of her room in a cropped *Pretty Reckless* shirt paired with the shortest shorts ever known to man. They might actually be underwear more than shorts. I track her as she joins me on the sofa, and I bite my tongue hard so I don't yell at her because I know what she's doing.

Her hair is still wet, and she is toweling it as she sits next to me.

I can't believe I let myself go like that. I wasn't supposed to see her, and I know she didn't intend for me to walk in on her like that—though that simple fact doesn't soothe my anger any. But I forgot my headphones in my room, so after Pixel did her business, I came back to grab my headphones before our run.

Then I heard the water running.

Does she do this often? How many times has she showered in my shower when I've been gone? Does she masturbate in my bed when I'm not here? My sweet little pervert.

"Good band," I say, smiling at the band logo splayed over her small chest.

"One of my favorites." Her smile is vast, and she doesn't seem at all riled about what we just did. How I just fucked her mouth.

Right. I stretch over to the side of the couch to pick up the electric guitar. The blue dragon is the Gibson Les Paul I learned on, and now she gets to as well. Her eyes grow wide, and she clasps her hands over her chest in excitement.

"I get to learn on an electric guitar?"

I raise an eyebrow in question. "Why wouldn't you?"

"I always thought you had to learn on acoustic first."

"No. You should learn on the instrument that will inspire you enough to keep you practicing. It's actually a little harder to learn on acoustic. The strings are thicker."

"Oh."

I toss her nail clippers, and her brows furrow together. "What's this?"

"What does it look like?"

"My nails are short," she says.

I scoff. "Not enough. Trust me. Get that shit real short."

After completing her task, and I approve of her work, Lola nods and tentatively brings her hand to the guitar on my lap. She searches my eyes for permission, and I tip my chin.

She's allowed to touch now.

She runs her hand over the guitar, feeling the shape of it with her fingertips, a face-splitting grin on her face. She is so a guitarist.

I map out the guitar from top to bottom, going over each element with her. Headstock, tuners, neck, frets, pickups, tailpiece—everything. We go over and over every part until she has it memorized, and an hour later, her smile is long gone.

Frustrated now, she rolls her eyes. "Can we get started with the lesson?" she whines impatiently.

I try not to chuckle with my amusement. "No. You need to learn the strings, what your practice amp settings are, and then we can start playing."

Another painstaking lesson on the amp and what it can do, and Lola is ready to strangle me. When we've gone through everything a few times, I finally concede. "Fine. If you can remember the string names, I'll teach you your first riff."

Lola beams at me.

"Easy," she says, trying to remember the order. "Eddie Ate Dynamite. Good Bye Eddie. E.A.D.G.B.E!"

I laugh. "Yeah. You got it. All right. Grab the dragon, hook it up to the amp, and let's go."

She takes the ax with tentative hands. "Like this?" she asks.

"No." I shake my head. "You want the smallest string near your thigh."

Lola rolls her eyes. "Show me then." She stands, guitar in hands, and sits in front of me, directly between my legs—her back pressed to my chest, legs sprawled in front of her, those cute toes in hot pink polish sparkling in my view.

The smell of my soap and shampoo coming off her body is thick in her hair, and I have to clench my jaw. "What are you doing, Lo?" I ask, annoyed.

"Show me the riff. Move my fingers for me."

I grumble but try to help her. Wrapping my arms around her, I guide her movements and take over the pick, letting her watch.

Placing my fingers over hers, I guide them behind the first fret. "Here, see?" I ask. "If I say one, you place your finger here behind the fret. If I say another number, you press down behind that fret. Press down, and for now, only strum the E string."

Lola nods, and with my hands, I guide hers.

The note plays, and Lola squeals with excitement, causing her body to squirm, my erection hardening between us.

What the fuck? I just exploded in her mouth not too long ago. Will it never be enough? Will I never have enough of her? I try to ignore it and concentrate. "Good," I say. "Now, move the pickup selector toward the strings."

Familiar now with the terms, Lola does as I say.

"Then reach for the amp, and press that button that says 'O/D.' The overdrive."

She reaches over to do as I say, and I groan when a red lace thong peeks out of her shorts. She's doing this on purpose, and I won't acknowledge it. I won't admit how powerless she makes me.

"Try the same note. Don't fret at first, so zero, then three, then five. Stick with the E string still. Practice zero, three, five, then backward, over and over until you're comfortable with it."

She nods, but as soon as she strums the chord for the first time, her hands fly away from the guitar, letting it rest against her body. The new settings have that heavy metal sound she loves. I smile at her in awe.

As soon as the note resonates, heavy and distorted, her toes curl against a couch cushion, and her chest heaves. "Wow," she gasps. Then she wiggles on the spot with excitement, causing her ass to shake gently, and my cock hardens like concrete against her booty shorts.

I smile, looking at the back of her head, wishing I could see her face right now, as her eyes roam the guitar and she revels in the magic she just made.

"Is it always like this?" she asks.

"Like what?"

"You know, that tingling in your body—resonating from your chest and going all the way down to your toes."

"More so at the start," I admit. "But even now, when I'm in

the middle of an epic riff, or when I get lost in a solo, yeah. It's like that a lot."

"Fuck, Karl. I think I'm addicted."

I laugh. "I knew you would be." I let her collect her thoughts for a few moments until her hands go back to the ax in front of her, and she snuggles back against me, rubbing her ass against my now rock-hard erection. "What are you doing, Lo?"

"Practicing guitar," she says playfully, then grinds her ass just a little bit more.

"You're trying to kill me; that's what you're trying to do."

She laughs.

"Do you need a little motivation?" I whisper against her ear, catching the shell of it between my teeth.

"Mmm-hmmm," she moans.

My hand reaches around her middle between her and the guitar. With one finger, I tuck the fabric of her shorts and thong to the side. My other hand spreads her lips wide, leaving my dominant hand to strum.

"Alright, doll, follow my rhythm," I order.

"Wha—"

But before she can get the complete word out, I strum her clit once. "O," I say, then strum a second time. "Three," another dusting of my fingers over her clit. "Five. Like that."

Her entire body shudders with each soft graze of my fingers against the delicate nub.

"I can't concentrate like that," she breathes out.

My hand remains where it is, spreading her wide for me. Exposing her, making me wish I could see, but even if I were sitting in front of her instead of behind, the guitar would hide the view.

"You said you wanted motivation. Here it is. Now follow," I say more sternly now. "O, three, five," I strum my fingers, and she shudders but places her hands where they should be, one wrapped around the neck to fret, making me wish it was my cock in her hand instead of the instrument. "Good girl," I whisper. "Just stick with E. Now backward. Five. Three. O." She follows my movements, her fingers mimicking mine, and I smile against the shell of her ear. "Good girl, doll. You are such a good student. Now. Again."

I pick up speed, following the same pattern, over and over. She mirrors the movements until her body shudders so hard against mine, she drops the guitar and pushes it away from her, letting it fall on the couch.

My fingers get wetter and wetter as she comes in waves, and I keep strumming long after she's abandoned her lesson.

"Karl!" she cries out when I don't ease up on her clit— when it becomes too much for her. "Karl! Please," she begs. Her hand snakes behind her back to wrap around my shaft through my sweats. "I need you inside me. *Please.*"

I stop playing with her flesh and sober back down to reality.

"Lola!" I snap, pushing her off me and stand up, creating as much space as I can. "Stop this. Just fucking stop it." I shake my head.

Her eyes grow wide, and her nose turns red like she might cry. "I'm sorry," she whimpers. "I wasn't trying to . . ." She shakes her head, startled by my response.

I run my hand through my hair with frustration. Fuck. I know I'm giving her mixed signals, but I can't help it. She looks edible, all flushed from her orgasm, and all I want is to bury myself balls-deep in her body.

I'm just that far gone into my desire for her. I want her more than I've ever wanted anyone, but if she made one thing clear on our date last night, it's that this relationship is still fake to her. I thought it was to me too, but after our date, I'm not so sure that's all I want anymore. But she does.

And thank god she does. She deserves better than me.

And she sure as hell deserves to love the man she ends up with. I pull at the roots of my hair. At the bottom of it all, I understand it's too soon for her to be over Ethan yet. Giving in to her vulnerability after her breakup would be a dick move. I wouldn't take advantage of her like that.

In the meantime, I need to find a way to make her stop prancing around naked, testing my determination like she does.

"We're done for today. Tomorrow we keep going where we stopped," I snap and head to my room. I need to not fucking see her right now.

When I'm alone, I text Roger.

Me: Send me a girl tonight.

Roger: What happened to Lola?

Me: Fuck off. I don't owe you explanations. Send me a call-girl tonight.

Roger: To the penthouse?

Me: Yes. At ten.

Roger: You got it.

# 19

# LOLA

**K**arl hasn't left his room since he stormed off this afternoon. I'm worried he didn't even come out to have dinner. I've been tempted to knock on his door and apologize, but I didn't do anything wrong. I wasn't trying to come on to him during our lesson, but I know that's what he thought. And yeah, maybe once I realized how turned on he was, I may have pushed his buttons a little.

So I took Pixel on a short walk after dinner. We're listening to music on the couch, Pixel curled up next to my thigh, and me leafing through magazines when we hear Karl's door finally open.

"You okay?" I ask him.

"Yeah. Took a nap."

*All evening?* I want to ask but don't. He goes to the elevator and waits in front of it.

"We expecting someone?" I ask him.

"None of your fucking business," he snaps.

Pixel's ears pin back at his tone, and I pet her to soothe her, but if I had ears like that, they'd be pinned back just like hers.

The elevator doors open, and a beautiful woman walks into

our home. She's wearing a trench coat, sky-high clear heels—hooker high heels if I ever saw any—a fiery red wig, and obnoxious makeup with full red lips. What the fuck is this?

I stand, and Pixel follows. "Karl?" I ask. He doesn't turn to look at me.

Pixel begins to growl from behind me, then she rounds me in a protective stance between me and the woman. She barks once at the stranger.

"Pix, stop!" Karl growls. Her ears pin back for a moment, then she lets out one more bark. I bend to pet her, which seems to calm her.

"Karl?" I'm hoping for an explanation.

He still doesn't turn to look at me. Instead, he walks to the woman. "Scarlett," he says like he knows her. The woman smiles at him and takes his outstretched hand.

"Karl?" I ask again. He needs to tell me what's going on. "Who is this?" But he won't look at me.

Instead, he walks to his room, leading Scarlett by the hand. I wait for the door to slam shut or click as he closes it, but it never does.

I'm frozen where I stand. What the fuck just happened? We agreed we wouldn't be seen with anyone else while we pretended to date. But I suppose if he hired a sex worker, no one would see them out together.

My chin trembles, and I can't explain this cold and heavy feeling settling in the pit of my stomach. Karl and I are just friends—not even that. I'm his employee and his student. God, I'm so stupid. This shouldn't feel like this. We're not together, and were not a couple, so I shouldn't care. Right? Do I have feelings for him? I shake my head. I can't. This is temporary. I'm leaving soon. I refuse to fall in love with Karl Sommer.

For long minutes, I stare down the dark hallway until low moans float into the hallway. Scarlett moans. Moans, the direct result of Karl's touch. Is he fucking her? Of course he's fucking her. What a stupid question.

A lone tear rolls down my cheek, and I angrily wipe it away. He won't fuck me, but he'll hire an escort when I'm right here? For only one second, I let myself feel dejected. But that's not it. I know he wants me. He just doesn't want to be my first. If he'd only give me a straight answer as to why. Is he afraid I'll get clingy or fall in love with him if we take that step?

Would I? If I didn't have some sort of feelings for him, it wouldn't hurt to hear him fuck someone else, would it?

I head to my room, and their voices increase in volume as I pass his room and go in mine. I don't close my door. Maybe it's self-punishment, or maybe I want to hear them, but I sit on the edge of my bed, listening closely.

The longer I listen, the more my blood boils as I seethe on my bed. Eventually, the anger gives way to surrender. Each of my muscles unclenches, and resigned, I fall to my bed. I grab a pillow to place over my head, pressing it tightly to my ears as I curl into myself.

Something unrecognizable sours my stomach so much that it's hard to breathe. Why am I feeling like this? I don't even feel the tears until they cool on my face. I bring shaky fingers to my cheeks to confirm the wetness there, and yep, there they are. But why?

Why does it hurt so much to hear him with someone else?

He is doing nothing wrong. Our agreement only stated we couldn't be seen in public with anyone. We never said anything about what happens in private.

The hurt is still there though. I'm not betrayed, but I feel it.

What did he just do to us?

I STARTLE AWAKE when my bedroom door flings open. A murderous Karl grabs the door jamb tightly with one hand, while the other grips the doorknob.

I sit up and realize I slept in my bra and panties. Instinct has me grabbing for the bedsheets to cover myself, but the way he looks at me forces me to freeze. His eyes are dark, roaming, roaming all over my body.

His jaw is set as he stares at me, so I don't cover myself. I let him stare.

"Be ready in an hour. I'm going for my run. And stay the fuck out of my room."

I blink after him as he leaves.

Well, he's not kicking me out or ending our arrangement, at least. That's something.

I sit at the kitchen island, drinking my coffee and trying to make sense of everything that happened last night when Karl comes into the kitchen after his shower.

He grabs a cup of coffee and sips it in front of me, his eyes narrowing as he looks at me. He's been slamming doors, drawers, and snapping at Pixel all morning. The poor girl has been seeking refuge behind my legs since he got back from his run, and that's so unlike her. The strip of bacon I gave her turned her day around, though.

The more I watch him and how riled up he is, the more I'm convinced Karl regrets what happened last night.

Shouldn't someone who had sex all night be more relaxed in the morning? That's what I'd always assumed. Unless they faked it. For some reason, the very thought makes me smile, so I don't cower under his glare.

"Sleep well?" I ask, syrupy-sweet.

"Not even a little."

"Scarlett sleeping it off?" I ask easily like I don't care at all.

"No. She left last night."

I set the coffee down. The last thing I want is for him to

know I was upset last night. "So. Want me to cook you some breakfast before our lesson today? Sounds like you burned off some calories."

His jaw sets, and I wonder if he knows I'm faking my indifference.

"That's all you have to say?"

"What do you mean?"

"You don't care I slept with someone last night?"

"Why would I?" I lie. "We agreed we wouldn't be seen with anyone during our arrangement, but she came here. No one saw you or photographed you together, so I don't see a problem."

"So you wouldn't mind if she came back again tonight?"

I offer him a slight shrug. "Should I care?"

Karl freezes, a stunned expression on his face. I don't miss his death-grip on the coffee mug or the white knuckles encasing it.

He definitely doesn't have the afterglow I'd expect to see after a good night of sex.

---

As MUCH As I teased him about it, I don't continue to offer myself up on a platter. For one, I'm starting to feel pathetic. Even though I know he wants me as much as I want him, a girl can only take so much rejection. I do have some self-respect, damn it.

And I don't want to push him into inviting Scarlett again to deter me. My heart can only take so much.

During our lesson today, I keep my distance. I don't touch him. I don't insinuate or speak with double meaning. We keep our conversation on topic, and I think I make great strides on the guitar. Even Karl can't hide his satisfaction at my progress.

After we finish work, I offer to cook dinner, despite how raw my fingertips are. I set the guitar down and stretch my hands, hoping to ease some of the pain. Karl catches a sight of my movements and says, "Come here." He pats the spot next to him.

"What?"

"Sit next to me," he says.

I blink at his hand on the cushion. I've kept a respectable distance all through our grueling lesson today. He moved on from strings to actually teaching me a few chords. While nothing resembles anything rhythmic yet, my hands are getting used to the movements.

But now it's Karl closing distances between us. When I take too long to concede to his request, he leans forward, tucks an arm under my legs and the other behind my back, and scoots me over next to him. "Now relax," he says, taking my hand in his.

He massages the tender muscle between my index finger and thumb. It's painful at first as the overworked muscle and tendons scream at the kneading of Karl's strong fingers, but then they ease into a calm relaxation, and I let my head fall to the backrest. I melt into the couch as Karl massages my hands and moan with pleasure at each firm, yet tender, massage.

"That feels amazing," I moan—eyes closed.

Karl chuckles. "Maybe one day you'll return the favor."

After a thirty-minute massage, my stomach rumbles. We're supposed to get a snow storm rolling in soon, and the frigid weather has me craving caldo de pollo.

Karl finds me in the kitchen when dinner is almost ready.

"That smells amazing," Karl says as he grabs a glass of water.

"Thank you. It's my mom's recipe."

"Tell me about her."

I shake my head, my tears building even as I stir the broth in the pot. "I'm not ready for that. They've only been gone a year. When I do talk about them, I want to be able to think of them fondly."

"And you don't think of them fondly now?"

"No. I'm still in the anger stage. I'm so freaking mad at them, Karl. I swear."

"Oh," he says uncomfortably like he doesn't know how to follow that up.

I smile sadly. "I'm working on forgiving them still. But yeah, this is how my grandma used to make this soup. And my mom taught me."

Karl nudges my arm. "And one day, you'll teach your daughter?"

Before I can answer, Karl gets a call. He steps away to take it, and I'm serving our soup when he gets back.

I keep stirring in ingredients, cooking the soup at a low and steady flame. That question had never come up, and while I like the idea of passing on mom's recipes, I don't think I want kids.

Wow. I don't want kids. I love kids, but I don't want my own.

I'll teach Addy and Isael my recipes, I decide, when they come to visit me in Mexico as I'm sure they will.

"So a couple of things," he says, setting his cell on the counter. "Pictures of us at the taco truck are everywhere. The word's officially out since we've been photographed together now. Roger wants to talk to us about how to handle the situation."

My stomach knots, but I nod. "And the second thing?"

"We have to babysit Adrian day after tomorrow."

My spoon falls into my soup, splattering it everywhere. "Your drummer?"

"Yeah. Fritz usually stays with him, but he has to go out of town for Christmas, and he's leaving tonight. Mind if Adrian stays with us some nights? He lives in the building."

My jaw drops. "How did I not know Adrian lives in the building?"

Karl shrugs. "I don't know. You seem to know everything else."

"And why does he need to be looked after?"

"He doesn't trust AA to keep his secrets, so he can't get an official sponsor. The band take turns keeping him on the straight."

"Adrian is an alcoholic?" I ask. I mean, I kind of know, everyone does, but I'm never sure what's true and what's fabricated in the media.

"Recovering," Karl corrects, taking his first bite. "This is delicious, by the way."

"Thank you."

Huh. I'll be living with not one but two rock stars. Life can be so surprising sometimes. "Well then, that's great. I'll hide all the liquor."

Karl smiles approvingly. "Thank you."

ROGER PAYS us a visit before I get a chance to meet Adrian—though I'm sure Roger orchestrated the timing perfectly.

Karl and I are seated together at the couch like a couple of school kids, while Roger stands, looming over us in his black suit, on the other side of the coffee table. He places two pieces of paper in front of us, and Karl and I take one each.

"What is this?" Karl asks.

"Your schedules," Roger says simply.

"Our what?"

"Your schedules. Tomorrow you have an interview with Joanna Elliott—"

"Shut up!" I shriek. "From *Steel Hard Rock* magazine?"

Roger's face remains passive, as if bored, while my heart is racing so fast I'm sure he can hear it from where he stands. "Yes."

"Oh my god," I squeal. "Joanna Elliott is interviewing us!" I look over at Karl who seems just as bored as Roger. "How are you not excited?" I demand.

"Should I be?" Karl asks.

"Yeah! She's only the best music writer ever!"

Roger and Karl exchange a look.

"What?" I ask them.

"You're just, kind of a nerd, Lo," Karl explains.

"Whatever."

"Anyway," Roger says, now sounding more annoyed than bored. "She'll be here tomorrow with a camera crew. Make sure the place is clean. Coordinate your outfits or whatever it is couples do."

"Fine," Karl says followed by an exaggerated sigh.

"This weekend you'll be attending a fundraiser Sofia is helping with. It's for a cancer patient. Lola, you'll volunteer too. I'll have photographers on site. Bren and Karl will sign head shots and pose with fans. Sofia has assigned you to the ticket booth for them."

"Sofia told me about it. Happy to help out."

Roger continues going through our itinerary. "At the end of the month, Lola will accompany you to Los Angeles for the Steel Hard Rock Music Awards—"

"What!?"

"Lola, do you mind?" Roger snaps when I interrupt yet again. "We'll never get through the itinerary if you stop to freak out at every item."

"Sorry," I say. I bite my lips together. I'm going to be Karl's date at an event featuring all my living heroes.

"Win or lose, Bren wants to host a New Year's party the following night. He's rented a property just outside L.A. You will be staying there with the band. Lola, Sofia already has wardrobe and stylists on board for the trip. All you have to do is show up. You will be at all of these events and be happy to be photographed together."

I look over at Karl, but his expression gives nothing away. Is he upset about all this? "Karl? I don't have to go to these things if you don't want—"

"You're coming with me," he says firmly. "End of discussion." And I know he means that's our deal.

"What's in it for you?" I ask Roger, more than a little worried about why he's helping us appear so serious when not too long ago, he was so set against dropping the party charade.

Roger looks at Karl. "You didn't tell her?"

"Tell me what?" I ask.

"After the failed housewarming party," Karl says, "I had a talk with Roger. He's agreed to help me clean up my image and give this a try."

"If it fails, we can always reevaluate," Roger says.

I study Roger, considering him in a new light. He's willing to work with Karl and compromise, to give him what he needs to thrive in the band. Maybe Roger isn't as bad as I originally thought.

# 20

# KARL

Lola is a dog whisperer. With her around, it only takes Pixel five minutes to accept the invasive camera crew that has shown up to interview us.

Joanna Elliott, our interviewer from *Steel Hard Rock Magazine*, will conduct the interview that will also be filmed for their social media platforms. For me, it's par for the course, but I can sense Lola's nerves.

They've arranged two chairs together for us, Joanna sitting in front of us, a small table between us with tea and water. Bright lights and mics intrude on our space. I bring Lola's hand to my thigh, so I can rub the back of it with my index finger. I know this calms her down a bit.

"You'll be great, Lo," I reassure her.

She peers up at me and flashes me a nervous smile, then squeezes my thigh, leaving her hand there throughout the interview.

"We're here tonight with *Industrial November*'s newest band member, Karl Sommer, and his girlfriend, Dolores Beltran," Joanna starts. "Thank you for speaking with *Steel*

*Hard Rock* magazine and inviting us into your home," she says with a warm smile.

"Of course," I say, squeezing Lola's hand again. Here we go.

When I signed on to the band, part of my contract included me being the gofer for publicity to ease off the other guys a bit. Roger's plan has mostly worked, and I've done hundreds of these interviews, it seems. But Lola is stiff and nervous next to me, so I keep our hands laced together while we speak.

"So." Joanna turns her attention to Lola. "Dolores—"

"Lola. Please," she says with a sweet smile.

"Of course. Lola. You are public enemy number one since you snagged the most eligible bachelor in the world—named sexiest man alive by nearly every magazine."

Lola laughs nervously. "Well, I haven't snagged anyone. Let's start there. Karl and I, we're new, but it's special. We're getting to know each other—"

"From the outside, it seems much more serious than that. You moved in together, is that right?"

"It's hard," I jump in, "for us to go on normal dates like other new couples can. Not if we want privacy. So while we get to know each other, we thought it would be easiest to live together."

"Lola," Joanna cuts back in, and I'm having a hard time focusing attention away from Lola. I guess she'll just have to hold her own. But I know she can. Joanna continues, "Fans are curious about you. What can you tell us about yourself, your family—"

"I don't talk about my family," she cuts in, her features a little angry, and I squeeze her hand a bit. "But I'll answer anything about myself you'd like to know."

"Why don't you start by telling us, who is Lola?"

"Not much to tell, really. I grew up in this city; it's been my home since I can remember. I'm so glad *Industrial*

*November* ended up temporarily settling down here so that I could meet Karl—"

"And how did you meet?" Joanna takes Lola's bait. *Good girl, Iggy,* I think proudly.

"I cleaned his house. I used to work for Sofia—"

"Bren's partner?" Joanna asks with new interest.

Lola nods. "Yeah. That's how I got the job at Karl's. Sofia is like family—more like an older sister than a friend." She doesn't go into the private details of Pixel and her attack that first day. That special memory is only for the two of us. Lola is really good at this. She baits the reporter expertly so that Joanna asks what Lola wants to be asked about and skillfully dodges subjects she doesn't want to discuss. She'll be a natural at this—when the time comes.

"A true rags-to-riches story," Joanna says.

"I don't see how," Lola shoots back without hesitating even for a second. "I'm not rich. Karl is. And I'm in no rags. I work hard to provide for myself. I'm smart with my money and don't need Karl's—or anyone else's—financial support."

Joanna smiles nervously, knowing she put her foot in it, so she pivots the conversation. "What can you share with Karl's fans about him that they wouldn't already know?"

Lola smiles at me, and it's tender and sweet. I tip my chin, trying to convey that it's okay for her to answer honestly. I'm actually quite interested in what she has to say.

"He's not what he seems, what the media paints him as." She arches a suggestive brow at Joanna, and she smiles nervously, egging her to go on. "I admire him. From what's printed about him, you wouldn't know how deeply dedicated he is to his art. He has the most determined focus I've ever seen from an artist. Music is his true love, and he gives one-hundred percent of his dedication to it."

I blink down at her, stunned at her assessment. I don't know what this feeling is, but I've never had anyone defend me or praise me like she has just done, and something moves in my chest. I clench my jaw because the last thing I need is to cry on camera like a little baby.

"So, you've seen him working on new music?" Joanna asks.

"She has," I jump in. "And I'm teaching her to play guitar."

Joanna's brows raise to her hairline. "You're a musician too?" She asks Lola.

"I didn't know I was. I've always loved rock and heavy metal. I've been a fan of *Industrial November* since the band first formed, before Karl was even a part of it. But since meeting Karl, he's helped me realize that making music is also important to me."

"How is he as a teacher?"

"Grueling." Lola holds up her hands, presenting her fingers to Joanna. "See these calluses? They're entirely Karl's fault. It's a full-time work schedule, and he expects me to practice in my own time."

"Sounds serious. Are you planning on starting your own band?"

"Maybe one day," Lola answers. "For now, I'm just learning the instrument, learning to respect it and letting it guide me. We'll see what the future holds."

"Is she any good?" Joanna directs her question to me.

I smile wide when I answer. "She's a natural. There are two types of players. One is the dedicated player, that through enormous discipline, dedication, and time can learn to be a good guitar player. That's what I am. I'm not naturally talented. But what I lack in natural talent, I make up for in grueling practice hours. Ig—" I clear my throat. "Excuse me. Lola is not like that. She won't need the years I did to master our instrument. She's a natural talent. I actually hate her a little bit for it." I laugh, trying to keep the conversation light.

When I look at Lola again, her eyes are rimmed with red,

and they are glassy like she's about to cry. *Come on, not in front of the camera, Iggy.*

"Lola? What do you have to say to that?" Joanna asks.

She wipes the corner of her eyes. "What *do you* say to that? When the best guitar player alive today dishes out praise like that? It means the world, you know?"

"I see a lot of love between you two," Joanna says, and both Lola and I stiffen.

We eye each other, considering Joanna's words, and it's Lola who speaks first.

"Can you blame me? Who in their right mind wouldn't love this man if given half the chance?"

My jaw slackens as I'm rendered stunned by her words. Does she mean this? Is this for Joanna, for the cameras? Or is this what's in her heart? Everything is so muddled.

But she is also so incredibly wrong. There are plenty of people who couldn't love me. In fact, no one has ever loved me, not unconditionally. And I can't tell if Lola is one of them. I can't tell if she's acting right now. Nor can I force myself into being something I'm not—someone worthy of her.

# 21

# LOLA

The next morning, I wake up to snow. Instead of making coffee, I make my mom's hot chocolate with cayenne pepper and sit on the floor next to the floor-to-ceiling windows to stare at the snowscape. Below us, every building is capped in three inches of white fluff.

I sigh longingly. Growing up in Kansas City, snow used to get so much higher than it does nowadays, but still, I love it, and waking up to the city nestled under a blanket of snow brings me both comfort and sorrow.

Comfort because I love snow and am hoping the weather keeps it up so we can have a white Christmas next week. Sorrow because I've always loved Christmas. It's my favorite holiday, but this will be my second Christmas without my parents. Without my family.

"Hey, are you okay?" Karl asks when he finds me crying on the floor.

I wipe my eyes. "Yeah. I'm fine. I made some hot chocolate. It's on the stove if you want some."

Karl grabs a mug of chocolate and sits in front of me on the floor. "This is good," he says.

I smile at him, and his socked foot nudges mine. "What is it, Iggy?"

"I just used to love Christmas so much. Not so sure I do anymore. Last Christmas was hard, and I thought this one would be easier, but I think it will only get worse every year." I'm not sure why I'm so chatty this morning, but I let Karl see just a little deeper into me than usual. "You know what I missed the most last year?"

Karl sips his chocolate, eyes locked on mine, his gaze soft and tender. "No. What?"

"Waking up to buñuelos and this hot chocolate. Mom used to make buñuelos every Christmas morning and New Year's too. Then she'd send Dad and me to deliver stacks to our neighbors."

"What are bunyellows, or whatever you just said?"

I snort a little when I laugh like a dork. "Buñuelos. It's a pastry. Like a deep-fried flour tortilla sprinkled with cinnamon and sugar. They're delicious and go great with hot chocolate."

"It must have been nice," Karl says, "to grow up with traditions like that and to have those memories of your mom."

I remind myself I know nothing about him. "How about you? You have family Christmas traditions growing up?"

His drink stops midway to his lips. "No," he answers simply. I want to ask him to elaborate, but he distracts me with his guitar. He obviously doesn't want to talk about it, so I let him lead me to our guitar lesson for the day. Clearly, we both have demons we want to avoid.

Early in the morning, we take a break, and I call Ileana to walk me through a recipe for the thousandth time. I tell her we're having guests, and I want to make her slow-cooker barbacoa, so I picked up ingredients yesterday. I want to throw it all together early, so it's ready by dinner time when Adrian joins us.

Karl watches in awe as I sear beef chunks before tossing

them into the slow cooker. "You could help me peel some garlic," I tease him.

He shakes his head. "I can't cook."

"Peeling garlic isn't cooking," I say with a laugh.

Eventually, he decides to help, and he tosses more garlic than I think will be necessary, but Ileana has reassured me garlic is the key.

"Usually, this recipe goes with red wine, but I'm leaving that off for Adrian tonight."

"Is that typical for barbacoa to be cooked in wine?"

I snort. "No. But Ileana is a maverick in the kitchen. Believe me, if I can get it half as good as hers, this will be orgasmic."

Karl chuckles and rests his chin on his hand while he keeps watching now that his task is done. "What are those?"

"Smoked cardamom," I say as I toss the pods in between layers of beef.

After throwing everything in the slow cooker and setting it on medium, we return to our grueling guitar lesson. Karl is kind of a hard-ass, but I can tell he is proud of how fast I'm learning.

I'm proud of myself, to be honest. I never thought I'd love playing an instrument as much as I do.

We work into the evening, and at six sharp, Adrian shows up. I run up to him. "Adrian, hi. I'm Lola," I say with a giggle. *God, who am I? Be cool*, Lo.

Adrian shakes my hand as he blinks down at me, then he finds Karl serving himself dinner.

"Roger told me you had a girlfriend, and I didn't believe him. Guess it's true."

My cheeks feel hot under his gaze. God, he is beautiful. Longish raven-black hair that hits his jaw, with a deep widow's peak in the center over a perfectly symmetrical face. I know men don't appreciate being called beautiful, but Adrian Köhler is just that—breathtakingly beautiful. Tall, lean, with a sharp face that reminds me of modern Hollywood vampires in teen movies, but with an older look to him shaded by barely-there scruff.

"That's right," Karl calls out. "So hands-off."

I blink down at my hand in his, and I realize I never let go. Adrian smirks and steps around me to say hi to Karl.

"Are you hungry, Adrian?" I ask when I find my voice.

"I wasn't, but that smells amazing."

I stack a tower of tortillas in front of the men, a bowl of red salsa, and chopped onion and cilantro. I need to start feeding Karl something other than tacos, but it's so enjoyable to watch him eat them. His head bowed, tilting to the side, moaning with every bite. It's almost erotic, and a girl could get used to that.

Now I stare at both of them, bowed and hovering over their plates, so they don't make a mess.

"So, where did Fritz have to go?" I ask to kick off the conversation.

Karl rolls his eyes, and Adrian chuckles.

"What?" I ask, missing the joke between them.

"We have no fucking idea," Karl says.

Then Adrian jumps in. "He's always sneaking off, not telling us why. We were able to find out from the pilot that he is flying in to Mexico, but we have no idea where in Mexico, or why. We're taking bets."

I perk up. "Oh? What are the theories?"

"Bren thinks he's a closeted accordion player and in a mariachi band," Karl says.

"And you?" I ask Adrian.

"I think he's involved in some dark shit. A cartel, maybe. Maybe he's a drug mule."

I wrinkle my nose. I highly doubt that. "What's your bet, Karl?"

"I think he's going down there to party. He's probably just taking a break from everything and lying on a nude beach somewhere enjoying the view if you know what I mean." He waggles his eyebrows, and I roll my eyes.

"How much is this bet?" I ask, thinking I want in on it because I already know what Fritz is going to Mexico so often for. I have a gut feeling based on what they've said. And I can get it out of him when he takes me to Mexico when I'm ready to go.

"Five k," Karl says, and I can't hide my disappointment. "Why, Iggy? You want in or what?"

"Iggy?" Adrian asks.

"Long story," Karl says. "But do you? Want in on the bet?"

"Not for five thousand dollars. Geesh."

"Care to share your theory anyway?" Adrian asks.

I roll my eyes. "Men can be so dim."

Karl and Adrian look at each other, then just blink.

"Do I have to explain everything? Fritz is . . . elegant. Polished. Stoic. He's not out there partying on the beaches. You're definitely out," I say to Karl. "He's a millionaire—"

"Billionaire," Karl corrects, and my jaw drops.

"What?" I ask.

"Fritz is a businessman first, musician second. He invests his band millions wisely."

"Even worse. There's no way he's involved in any crime or running drugs. Just no way."

I know my gut is right.

"And the Mariachi?" Karl asks.

I laugh. "Seriously? You know how disciplined he is, how seriously he takes his work. Do you think he'd stray his focus for a mariachi band?"

"I'm out," Adrian says.

"Me too," Karl agrees.

I shake my head at the two idiots in front of me. "It's a woman, you dummies. Fritz is in love, and whoever she is, she's in Mexico. It's probably a secret, so the media doesn't cover it. If he is a wise businessman, he understands his allure is greater to a female fanbase if he is single. Not taken."

"Why hide it from us, though?" Karl asks.

"That, I'm not sure about." I shrug. "Maybe she's famous too, and he's signed an NDA."

"Fuck," Adrian says. "I think she's right."

"I'll find out when he takes me home."

"What?" Adrian asks.

I meet Karl's eyes, and his gaze is cold and distant when he explains to Adrian that I'll be moving to Mexico soon and that Fritz will likely be escorting me.

I'm surprised when Karl and Adrian offer to take on the dishes since I cooked. It's a wonder they're so normal when I've had them on a pedestal ever since I got heavy into metal music. But they're both sweet guys at the bottom of it all.

"Would you guys like to play a game?" I ask when they're done cleaning up.

Karl spins around to spear through me with his dark glare. "We're not playing *Lotería*," he roars, and I laugh.

"That's not what I was thinking," I say. And honest, it wasn't. I want to keep Adrian distracted and entertained. Kind of like I do with Isael when I babysit him. "I was actually thinking poker or dominoes or something," I say.

Karl's shoulders relax, and he looks a little embarrassed. "I have dominoes," he says and heads to his room to retrieve them.

We settle into the night, playing games and talking. I'm craving some beers with this conversation but want to be respectful of Adrian.

"Adrian, what can you tell me about Karl? He refuses to dish anything up."

Adrian's dark smile is mischievous. "Oh, this could be fun. Let's see, he's a sad little orphan—"

Karl smacks Adrian in the arm. "I'm not an orphan. My parents aren't dead." He pauses, then adds, "I don't think."

Adrian chuckles. "They dropped him off at a fire station, so, same difference—"

"They did not!" Karl whines with embarrassment.

I watch him carefully. He's being playful, but the hurt is there in his beautiful blue eyes. Is this why he didn't have Christmases growing up, and why he won't talk about himself?

Adrian clears his throat and continues. "He was a little street urchin like Gavroche," Adrian jokes.

I laugh. "Well, he's had a better ending than poor Gavroche."

"Who is Gavroche?" Karl whines.

I roll my eyes. "Pick up a book or something," I joke because I know how well-read he actually is, and he'll take this as a challenge.

"Will you just tell me?" Karl snaps.

"He was a street kid in a classic. Adrian is saying you were a street kid like him."

Karl shifts in his seat. "I wasn't a street kid. I grew up in foster care."

"Oh. I'm sorry, Karl. I shouldn't tease you about that," I say.

Karl smiles a sad little smile, then turns to Adrian. "And you need to be more sensitive. Lola here actually is an orphan."

"Ouch," I say. "That stung." The truth of the matter is, I never thought of myself like that, but I guess I am.

Adrian's eyes lock on mine. "I am too," he says.

"I know. I'm sorry," I say.

"How long have they been gone?" Adrian asks.

"Just over a year."

He nods, and a silent moment of understanding passes between us. We're made of the same stuff now, Adrian and me. Regret, pain, longing, feeling left behind, and worst of all, guilt.

"They named me Dolores," I say, getting ready to explain my curse. "It means pain in Spanish—" but before I can get the full explanation out, Karl interrupts me with a snort.

"More like *pain in the ass*," he says.

Adrian chuckles, then stands. "I'll be right back. Need to wash up."

He heads into the bathroom, and Karl whispers so Adrian can't hear us from down the hallway.

"Don't ask him about his parents," Karl says.

"Why not?"

"It's a hard subject for him. He watched as they were murdered. I think that's why he's as messed up as he is. He was just a kid."

My hand floats to my heart. "Oh." I know from interviews and media coverage that his parents were gone, but the details aren't public knowledge.

I can't begin to imagine what that must be like. I didn't witness my parents dying, and even if I had, they weren't murdered before my eyes. No wonder Adrian looks like he's always in pain. My heart constricts thinking of such a beautiful man masking so much darkness.

"You know," Adrian says as he rejoins us, "I was thinking we could form the Sad Orphan Club."

I laugh.

"Can I be in it?" Karl asks.

"You just said your parents aren't dead," Adrian says. "You can't be an orphan if your parents are alive."

"You know," Karl says, looking at me now, "the Sad Orphan Club would be a great band name."

"How gloomy, though. Maybe for an emo band. Besides, I already have a name for my band," I say triumphantly.

"You play?" Adrian asks with interest.

"Just started. Karl is teaching me."

"She any good?" Adrian asks Karl, but I answer.

"It's only been a couple of days."

Karl flashes his toothy grin when he answers. "Iggy's a natural."

And for some reason my brain can't understand, Karl's

praise lands in the same section of my heart that houses my mom's comfort chicken soup. I don't know if it's his praise because we're friends, or because he's the best living guitar player in the world, or simply because I care about him, but the compliment does wonders for my playing confidence.

"Thank you, Karl," I say, only a little teary-eyed.

He rolls his eyes. "Well, don't cry about it."

A COLD, wet slug swipes over my face. Fast. Too fast to be a slug. I startle awake to find Pixel standing over me, licking my face. "Pix," I hiss. "You creepy dog. You have to stop waking me up!"

In response, Pixel pulls on my bedsheets to get them off my body. "Do you have to go out?" I ask her. She just stares at me, which means she doesn't. When Pix has to go outside to relieve herself, she bolts to the door when we ask her.

She pulls on the bedsheet again. I wipe the sleep from my eyes at the same time that I hear a small whimper. Where is that coming from?

I get out of bed and follow the sound, Pixel trailing behind me. It's coming from the other guest room. Adrian's room. We stayed up so late talking, he ended up crashing here. I press my ear to the door and can hear him grunting and talking in his sleep. The words are jumbled, and I can't understand most of them, but I hear a "no," and "stop" clear as day. I twist the door-knob gently, and he's under the covers. I walk up to the side of the bed. His face sparkles with perspiration under the moon-light, and his neck looks like he's straining.

Fuck. He's having a nightmare. What do I do? Do I wake Karl up? Would he even know what to do? I follow my instincts because if I were him, I'd want to be woken up. I nudge him gently.

"Adrian," I whisper. "Adrian, wake up. You're having a nightmare."

He finally startles awake and gulps air like he was drowning. He looks around the room frantically as he becomes oriented to the time and place. "What—"

"You were having a nightmare."

He blinks a few times and shakes his head. "Sorry. Did I wake you?"

I shake my head and smile sweetly at him. "No. Pixel did, but then I heard you through your door. I wasn't sure what I was supposed to do. I'm sorry if you didn't want to be woken up."

He grabs my hand, clinging to it like Isael does sometimes. "Thank you," he says.

I pat the space on the bed next to him and call out to Pix. "Here, girl." She jumps on the bed with a clink of her name tags and curls up next to Adrian. I sit on the other side of him on the bed, resting my back on the headboard. "You wanna talk about it?" I ask him.

He shakes his head.

"Okay. How about I stay here quietly until you fall asleep?"

"You don't have to do that, Lola," Adrian says. "I'm not a little kid."

"I know. But I want to."

Adrian lays back down and wraps himself around Pixel, effectively spooning her. I smile. I bet he doesn't have another nightmare tonight.

With his back to me, I decide if he doesn't speak, I will.

"I had a fight with my parents the night they died," I whisper into the quiet room.

Adrian stays in his spot, not turning around to look at me. "What about?"

"They had just told me I wouldn't be able to go off to college after all. We fought; I screamed at them and ran out of the house. They thought I'd go to my boyfriend's house, but when they called him later, and I wasn't there, they worried." I swallow the dry knot in my throat before I continue with a story I've never told before. "So, they went looking for me, driving around in the rain. The downpour was so heavy; visibility was terrible that night."

"I'm sorry," Adrian whispers.

"Yeah. Me too. I didn't see it happen, but I often have nightmares where I can see it clear as day. There's this guilt I can't shake off, you know?"

"It wasn't your fault," Adrian says.

"Wasn't it? If we hadn't fought . . . if I hadn't run off . . . if so many things. But I think the bigger guilt I carry is that the last words I said to my parents were that I hated them for ruining my life."

Adrian's chest expands with a deep sigh.

"And I used to love the rain. Now it only brings on the nightmares. It's one of my biggest triggers for that nightmare."

"I don't have triggers," Adrian says. "They happen . . . all the time."

"I'm sorry," I say, and we let silence fill the room for a long moment.

Then Adrian breaks the silence with an attempt to change the subject. "Do you love him?"

I feel like a shit for lying to him. He doesn't know our relationship is fake. "I care about him."

"Hmm," Adrian says. "I guess I'm thankful you're honest. But, do me a favor?"

"What's that?"

"Be careful with Karl."

"What do you mean?"

"He acts like nothing bothers him, but don't let that fool you into thinking he's happy. He's just as messed up as me and more fragile than he lets on."

My brows furrow together. This doesn't sound like Karl at

all. "Are you sure you're not projecting?" I ask Adrian, and he shakes his head.

"No. He has rejection issues. First his family of birth, and then anytime he was relocated in foster care, he felt like those families didn't want him either. Then he gets to our band, and Bren, our parental figure in the band, rejects him. It's hard on Karl because Bren was—is—his idol, so his rejection stings."

"Wow," I say, stunned. "I had no idea."

"Karl hides behind the playfulness, but he's never felt good enough for anyone—for anything."

"How are you so sure about all this?"

"Get a little whiskey in him, and it's like Veritaserum to Karl." Adrian laughs.

"Adrian, I honestly couldn't love you any harder." I smile, thinking of this broody man with a scowl on his face as he read *Les Miserables* and *Harry Potter*. What other secrets does he keep?

But I know Adrian is deflecting from the real conversation at hand. And while I will heed his warning and take gentle care of Karl's heart, it's Adrian I'm concerned about tonight.

"But, back to you, my friend. Do you have anyone you can talk with about your demons?" I ask.

Adrian considers that for a moment. "How many people have you told about your parents?" he asks, deflecting yet again.

I laugh a bitter little laugh. "You're the first," I say. "At least the full story. Only you and I know the last words I ever said to my parents."

"So you know. It's hard to have this conversation with someone who hasn't been through it."

I nod even though he can't see me. "I'm always here if you ever need to talk."

I head to Lola's room to wake her up before my workout as it's become our routine, but she doesn't answer the door when I knock. I open it to find her bed is unmade and empty. It's rare for her to be up before me. I head into the kitchen, thinking I'll find her making coffee, but the apartment is quiet. Where did she go? Pixel is nowhere to be seen, so she must have taken her out.

Next, I head to Adrian's room to ask him if he wants to work out with me, though I already know the answer will be no.

Only, when I gently open his bedroom door, there are three forms on the bed instead of one.

What the fuck is this?

Adrian is sleeping in the middle, one arm wrapped around Pixel. She snores softly into his chest. And Lola— Lola is behind Adrian, in a similar position with one arm over Adrian's naked waist.

I try not to snicker at this ultimate betrayal from my supposed best friend and supposed girlfriend.

Instinctively, I know what happened. Adrian had a nightmare. The entire band and regular entourage all know about his nightmares. Lola heard him and came in here to wake him up. Then in true Lola fashion, she wanted to talk to him —to comfort him.

This was innocent at best, thoughtless at worst, but I know nothing happened. And still, I could have fun with this.

The mess of curls is splayed over her face, and I move them away gently with one index finger.

"Lo," I whisper. "Wake up."

"Mmm," Lola moans.

I nudge her shoulder, stretching over Pixel and Adrian. "Lo. Wake up."

"Wha . . ." Her eyes flutter open, and she pulls her forehead away from Adrian's naked back. Her brows furrow with confusion, then her eyes grow wide. I raise a brow at her when she finally looks up at me, a smirk tugging the corner of my mouth.

She shoots out of bed like it's made of lava. "This is not what it looks like," she whispers, though she still manages to sound alarmed. "Adrian had a bad dream," she continues as if she might run out of words if she doesn't get them out quickly enough. "I just came to wake him up and let him have Pixel. I thought she might help. Then we got to talking, and I must have fallen asleep."

With my chin, I point to the door and wait for her outside. Neither Pixel nor Adrian stirs as we leave their room and gently close the door behind us.

"What the fuck, Iggy?" I ask, but I know I'm not looking quite as annoyed as I want to be.

"It was an accident. I swear. We just . . . slept. I didn't mean to sleep in there; it just happened." Lola looks at the closed door with regret painted on her sweet features.

I caress the back of her hand with one index finger.

"Relax. I know he has bad dreams. I don't think I've ever seen him sleep so peacefully." I pause, unsure I want to say it, but in the end, I do. "Thank you," I say honestly.

Lola lets out a long breath, clearly relieved. "Why are you thanking me?"

I lead her toward the kitchen because I don't want to risk Adrian hearing us through the door. "For soothing him," I answer her. "For being there for him. He's a good buddy. Probably my closest friend when it comes to the band. He's always had my back."

"Thank you for trusting me and not reading into this," she says, her eyes searching mine.

"I trust both of you," I say honestly.

Lola crosses her arms. "Don't you mean all three of us?"

"Three?"

"Did you not see your daughter with him too?"

I chuckle as she starts making our coffee. "Yeah. Talk about a betrayal," I say, thinking of Pixel still with Adrian, protecting him from the monsters under his bed.

---

LOLA'S CELL is on the counter as she makes breakfast for us. I sit at the island and watch her, making a lesson plan for the day.

"I'm going to head out," Adrian says, making his way to the elevator. "Thanks for dinner, Lola."

Lola spins around, spatula in hand. "Oh, you're not staying for breakfast?"

Adrian shakes his head. "After that huge dinner, I'm not really hungry yet."

"Okay. Come back anytime you want to hang out with us."

"Thank you. But Fritz gets back in tonight; I'll let you two lovebirds have privacy."

"See ya, man," I say just before he leaves.

Lola turns her attention back to the tomato sauce she was in the middle of simmering down to pair with eggs and doesn't notice when her phone lights up on the counter. I glance at it, grabbing it to hand to her, but my hand freezes when I see the name displayed on the screen.

Ethan.

Is she still talking to him? Even after everything that happened? My shoulder blades constrict tightly as my nostrils flare. "You have a call," I say coolly. "Would you like me to pick up?"

"Who is it?" she asks, and I relax a little, realizing she's not hiding anything.

"Ethan."

Her entire frame freezes. "No. Send him to voicemail, please."

"Lola." I try to grab her attention, but she only keeps stirring. "Lo. Look at me, please."

She turns around slowly, and the hurt is billboard-sized in her eyes. I lick my lips, my heart racing. Does she still have feelings for him? She wouldn't be so hurt if she didn't. Of course she has feelings for the scumbag. They were together for four years.

"Are you talking to him?"

Lola shakes her head. "No. He's called a few times since my name was released and the photos of our date night went viral."

"What has he said?"

She bites the inside of her cheek, then turns to keep stirring the pot. "I haven't picked up, though . . ."

"Though what," I ask?

"He's left voice messages."

"Oh?"

"Yeah."

"You listened to them?"

She nods. "I couldn't help it. But yeah. He said he broke up with Megan and that he's really sorry—"

"And that he wants you back," I finish for her.

She turns the stove off and shifts to look at me, her eyes holding mine. "Yeah. He said he wants me back. But I swear, Karl, I won't break our agreement. I wouldn't get back together with him, not while we're still pretending to be in a relationship."

I see red. Not while we're in a contract, but what about after? My stomach clenches when I think for a moment that she is considering getting back together with him. "You want to be with him again when we're done with our agreement? Because you don't have to wait, Lola. We can end it now if that's what you want."

"No, Karl." She hesitates, trying to find her words. "That's not what I meant. I don't want him back, not even after."

My eyes narrow as I consider her. "You sure? Don't do me any favors."

"Ethan is my past. We were good together at first. But we grew into different people, and we're no longer compatible. I want him to stay in my past. At least as far as anything romantic is concerned."

Her words are reassuring, and my body relaxes. I may not be good enough for Lola, but Ethan sure as hell isn't either.

# LOLA

Karl and I are on our way to a fundraiser. Sofia's best friend, Carolina, has teamed up with our local church to raise funds to cover cancer treatment for one of the hospital's patients.

Roger, of course, jumped at the idea for positive band press, and both Bren and Karl volunteered to sign autographed headshots and pose for selfies with fans.

Adrian and Fritz are on their way to Mexico for another short trip. I secretly tasked Adrian with spying on Fritz to find out who wins the bet, though I'm sure none of them do because I'm right.

We get to the community college gymnasium hosting the event, and I'm impressed at what Carolina managed on such short notice. I've met her briefly through Sofia, but her reputation as a beloved local physician precedes her. She'll do anything for her patients—even if that anything is begging Sofia to offer up her husband and his band to endure grueling hours of fan interaction—with zero compensation.

The gymnasium is full of carnival-style games and a few food stands, including Paco's Tacos, and I wave at him, but he's so busy, he doesn't see me. It seems the entire neighborhood showed up despite the frigid cold.

"So, why are we doing this again?" Karl asks me as we maneuver to find where we're supposed to be.

I volunteered to sell the selfie tickets and direct fans toward a line to meet the band. "Cancer treatment for a young mom."

"But why isn't her treatment just covered?"

"She's not eligible for health insurance," I say simply.

"Why not?"

"She's undocumented, so she can't pay for treatment. Her options are to pay out of pocket or return to her home country for treatment, but her kids were born here, and she refuses to take them out of school and relocate them. At least, that's as far as Ileana explained the situation to me. I don't really know the full details."

"Oh, is Ileana going to be here? I want to meet her."

"No, she stayed home with Addy and Isael so that Sofia and Bren could be here."

As we get to work, it doesn't escape me how much longer the line is or how different the demographics are in Karl's line compared to Bren's. Karl's fans are a bit younger, primarily female, and wait in line as they check their pocket mirrors and adjust necklines lower on their cleavage.

*Hoes.*

Okay, that wasn't very nice, but could they get a little self-respect?

The line is moving swiftly, and the guys have a couple of security guards to ensure nothing gets out of hand. And I have to admit, it's a little funny watching how happy and glowy every girl looks going toward Karl and then how sad they look on their way out.

Mid-shift, I notice Sofia, who is helping one of the food stands hand out plates, and she pauses to glance over at Bren. As if he can sense it, Bren's eyes raise to meet hers, and he looks at her with a smoldering gaze like he wants to eat her alive.

I sigh dreamily. I want someone to look at me like Bren looks at Sofia—how I look at pizza.

"Two, please," someone says, annoyed, and I glance up.

"Oh, sorry. Two tickets. That'll be ten dollars." I take the cash from the annoyed woman and give her change, moving her along toward Karl's line.

We all work for three more hours, and the crowd starts to dwindle a little, so Roger announces that Bren and Karl are taking a short break.

I, on the other hand, keep selling tickets but smile when Karl darts straight toward Paco's food stand. I really need to find a way to get him off this taco diet.

I lose sight of him for a while after he finishes eating, and for an hour, I have no clue where he's gone.

Only when he comes into view, he isn't alone. He walks in from a door leading to who knows where, Carolina all giggles and long lashes batting as she walks next to him. Have they been gone together this entire time? They pause to face each other and keep talking. He says something, and she laughs, then brings her hand to his forearm, squeezing it a bit.

She is *so* fangirling, and could she be more obvious? Okay, I know that's not Carolina. Maybe I'm imagining things?

My mouth dries up. They look so perfect together. Carolina is almost as tall as Karl and so beautiful. She is so elegant when she moves, so poised. Always put together.

The pillar of her community, Carolina exudes a grace that makes men fall at her feet. And the way Karl is looking at her, and that smile of his so warm and inviting, makes me feel a little bit sick.

Has he asked her out? Because what man in his right mind wouldn't?

I have no doubt Karl will honor our contract, but maybe

they're making plans for after I leave. As they walk away from each other, Karl's hands go into his jeans pockets. He heads back to his table, not once glancing over at me.

When they call an end to the festivities, I sell my last ticket and watch as Carolina grabs a microphone and stands on a small stage set at the end of the gymnasium. She calls attention, and everyone stops to look at her.

She is unaffected by all the eyes on her. "Thank you," she starts, "for being here tonight. I couldn't be prouder of this community and how we always come together when someone is in need. Today is for Lucinda. Many of you know her. She is a hardworking mom of three. She always has a smile on her face, and she's been there for many of us when we've needed her help. Always quick to give a kind word and a hand, she is more than just part of this community. She is part of our family. She can't be here today. She didn't ask for this fundraiser, and she actually was embarrassed when I told her I was doing this." Carolina pauses to laugh. "But I have my ways. Still, she sends her deepest gratitude on her and her sons' behalf." Then she smiles wide. "And I have great news!" she all but squeals. "We raised over ten thousand dollars today to go toward Lucinda's treatment. In addition to that, we have received an anonymous donation of eighty thousand dollars to cover the rest of Lucinda's treatment and her rent for the next year."

The collective gasps flutter through everyone at the event. Roger directs photographers and a reporter covering the fundraiser like a stage manager.

Could it have been . . .? I look for Karl, not finding him anywhere in the crowd until I realize he's right next to me. He looks down at me with a smile. "You ready to go?"

On our drive back home, I wait until we're close to home to ask him. "It was you, wasn't it?"

"What are you talking about?" Karl asks.

"You're the anonymous donor."

His lips purse, but he keeps his eyes on the road. "It was an anonymous donation, Lo. You don't get to know who it was."

"But I saw you. You went away with Carolina, and when you both came back, she made the announcement. It was you."

He throws me a mischievous side glance but admits to nothing.

This man.

Could he be any more perfect?

# 24

## LOLA

On December twenty-fourth, I wake up to the smell of grease. *What is that?*

When I get to the kitchen to investigate, I find Karl and Adrian arguing over a pan on the stove. When I call out to them, they both turn around, and I have to bite back my smile. They're both wearing aprons, looking absolutely adorable. The backdrop to the scene is a heavy snow falling in thick plumes outside our windows.

I rush back to my bedroom to grab my phone and call out to them again—my phone ready—and catch them off-guard.

"What are you two doing?" I ask them.

"You weren't supposed to be up yet."

"The smell woke me up," I say. "Whatcha making?" I step toward the kitchen island and lift a tea towel covering a mountain of something. Underneath is . . . something that looks a lot like flour tortillas.

"Those, uh, didn't turn out so great," Adrian admits, scratching the back of his neck.

I pick up one of the soggy tortillas, and it wilts, limp, over my fingers. It's translucent with oil and looks rather sad.

"I told you the oil wasn't hot enough yet," Karl whines, flipping something over with tongs.

There's something grainy on the surface of the greasy tortilla. I dab my finger in it and bring it to my mouth, tasting sugar and cinnamon.

"Uh, dude," Adrian says after a moment, nudging Karl.

"What?" Karl snaps.

"I think you made her cry."

Karl turns to look at me, and now both men are studying me curiously.

My voice is chopped when I find it. "You—you, you're making buñuelos?"

"Well, we're trying, but I'm not a damned cook, and Adrian was supposed to help, but he's done nothing but get in the way—"

After I set down the pastry abomination, I cut Karl off as I surprise him with a hug, clinging to his neck and sobbing into his chest.

"This is the sweetest thing anyone's ever done for me," I say. "Thank you."

Karl's strong arms wrap around me, and he lets his cheek fall to the top of my head. "Don't cry, Iggy. This was supposed to be a happy thing."

"They're tears of joy," I whimper, then let go of him so I can hug Adrian. "Thank you too, Adrian."

I have to laugh through my tears because it's almost as if Adrian doesn't know what to do with a hug. He's stiff, and his arms hang like dead weight at his sides. I nudge him. "Hug me back," I tease.

One arm, only one, comes up to pat my back awkwardly, and I laugh, pulling away from him.

"Thank you. Really," I say to both of them as I dab my tears with my shirt. "Now, give me those tongs."

I make the rest of the buñuelos and fix a pot of hot chocolate. When I set the stack of flaky pastry in front of them, Adrian picks one up, breaks a corner, and tastes it. He then smacks Karl's arm. "I told you they were supposed to be crispy."

"But you didn't know how to make them crispy," Karl shoots back, and we all laugh, nearly spitting out our hot chocolate.

BE careful what you wish for because sometimes, miracles are a double-edged sword. Waking up to a beautiful snowstorm on December twenty-fourth was the stuff of dreams. But now the Weather Service is advising against driving, and I don't take those warnings lightly anymore.

This means we can't go to Ileana's for dinner as planned. She sounded disappointed when I called her to let her know, but she agreed staying safe is best. Plus, she said she could save us leftovers. She and Isael are going to have a feast.

We invited Adrian to stay this evening, but he declared that Christmas isn't his thing and that he feels good today, which I think means he feels strong enough to not drink tonight. I did, however, ask him to come back in the morning for gifts.

So Karl and I are alone. We don't have much grocery-wise, so I pop a frozen pizza in the oven after a short guitar lesson.

"So what shall we do this evening? Any other traditions I can make happen for you?" Karl asks.

I think for a moment. "My Dad and I would usually have a Quentin Tarantino marathon."

"You're not serious," Karl says, aghast.

I laugh. "We did. We always said we'd watch *Django*, *Inglorious Basterds*, and finish up with *Pulp Fiction*, but Dad always fell asleep halfway through *Basterds*."

"And your mom was cool with that?"

"She said she wasn't and always complained how sacrilegious it was, but she liked the movies too, especially Django, so she'd sit and watch with us." I pause for a moment to think. "I haven't seen any Tarantino movies since they died."

"We don't have to. We can start our own traditions," Karl says.

I smile sadly. "No, it's fine. That's actually a happy memory. Maybe it's time I remember them with a little more kindness in my heart." I start to feel the anger toward my parents crumble just a little.

"So *Django*, then?" Karl asks.

"If you don't mind."

WHEN I FEEL myself being moved, I wake, cradled in Karl's arms. I must have fallen asleep. "I can walk," I moan.

"Shhh," he whispers.

When he lays me down on my bed, I grab onto his hand tightly. "I don't want to be alone tonight. Stay?"

He blinks down at me, his hand at his hip now. "I don't think that's such a good idea."

"No funny business. Just . . . company."

He sighs but then nods. "Okay. Let me just go grab some pajama bottoms."

After a few minutes, Karl walks into my room in sweats, shirtless. I feel the bed dip as he gets under the covers next to me.

I turn to face him, and Karl is staring at the ceiling, one arm behind his head, the heavily tattooed arm in perfect view. I hadn't paid close attention to its underside, but right there, on his inner-bicep, is a completely blank space. I tentatively bring a finger to the spot and trace circles on it.

"What's this space for?" I ask.

His head tilts to look at where I'm touching. "I'm leaving that space open for someone special," he says.

Accepting his short answer, I flip on my side to face away from him. My heart summersaults when his large fingers curl over my hipbone, adjusting me on my side, and his hand wraps over my waist, not unlike how he found me with Adrian this morning.

I was so mortified! I can't believe I slept with Adrian before I slept with Karl.

I cradle my hand over his, and I fall asleep with the biggest smile on my face.

In the morning, when I wake up, there's a light snore coming from behind me. Karl is spooning me, and at some point during the night, his chest has come to be pressed flush to my back.

The room is bright with the curtains open, revealing snow still coming down hard. And there's something extremely hard nestled between my butt cheeks through my leggings. A long, thick, and hard-as-steel pipe nudging my rear in the most tantalizing way.

I smile and scoot back, increasing pressure on his penis, then close my eyes again. "Karl," I whisper. "It's Christmas morning."

He moans and stirs, his arm tightening around me, his hips thrusting forward, poking me harder with his shaft.

I ignore the slickness collecting in my underwear. "Karl," I say and giggle. "It's Christmas morning!"

With every ounce of self-control I can muster, I peel his arm off me and get out of bed. Then I head the two floors down to Adrian's apartment.

I bang on the door much longer than I thought I'd need to. A groggy and grumpy Adrian opens the door, rubbing sleep from his eyes.

"Lola? What the hell? What time is it?"

"It's Christmas morning; it doesn't matter what time it is. Now come on," I grab his hand to lead him back to the elevator, but he holds his ground.

"Hold on, let me grab a shirt and some shoes."

"Okay, I'll meet you upstairs," I call after him and head back up to get ready.

I'm trying to get excited about Christmas, I really am, but a big part of me still carries this darkness, so even though I didn't have it in me to get a Christmas tree and decorate, I did get gifts for Adrian and Karl. I sit both men down on the couch in front of two boxes, one for each of them waiting on the coffee table.

Karl scowls when I hand Adrian the larger box and him the much smaller one.

"Well? Open them!" I say, and the men look at the boxes on their laps like they think I'm giving them snakes or something. I roll my eyes and grab my phone to take a video.

"One at a time," I say. "Adrian, you go first."

"Uh." Adrian looks up at me. "I didn't get you anything."

"You made me buñuelos yesterday. That is a way better gift than what I'm giving you," I say honestly.

"Tried," he corrects.

"What?"

"We *tried* making you buñuelos."

"Will you just open the gift already?"

I bite back my smile when Adrian tears the wrapping paper slowly, unfolding the corners and carefully removing tape. It's almost as if he doesn't know how to open gifts. I'm also trying not to jump where I stand with excitement, trying to avoid getting a shaky video.

He peruses the items inside the box once he's opened it and pulls them out one at a time. A thick, leather-bound sketchbook. A set of charcoal, a set of graphite, a set of conté, and an assortment of pastels. The complete artist's starter guide.

"I'm not an artist," he says gently like he's afraid to hurt my feelings.

"Have you ever tried?" I ask him with a grin.

He shakes his head.

"You, Adrian Köhler, have the heart of an artist. You should give it a try. I think you will surprise yourself. And an artist friend of mine once told me it can be cathartic to release all your pain onto a canvas."

"Thanks, Lola. I will give it a try."

"Okay, you next," I say to Karl, and he grabs the box on his lap. He rips apart the wrapping paper to shreds just as gifts are meant to be opened.

Then he opens the plain box that gives no indication of what's inside. When he pulls out the item, he laughs.

He holds the peanut butter jar in his hand. It has a custom-made label in a green shade close to my eye color. I took the jar to a local screen-print shop so they could make the custom label for me, with a decorative letter "I" for "Iggy" that looks almost vintage.

Karl stands and wraps me in his arms. "It's the best gift I've ever gotten, Iggy." He pulls away from me for a moment.

Adrian scratches the back of his neck, looking at the jar. "Uh, okay," he says, confused. Karl and I both laugh but explain nothing.

"Inside joke, man," Karl says instead. Then, "Okay, hold on right here." Karl disappears down the hallway and comes back with a massive box in a rectangular shape that hints at its contents.

Stunned and frozen where I stand, Karl grabs my hand and leads me to the couch. He takes the phone from me so he can record me now and watches as I stare at the box in awe.

"Karl . . . it isn't . . . ?" I choke off the words, then start tearing through the hot pink wrapping paper. When I finally open the box, there's a large case inside, and I know, just know in my gut, it's a guitar case. Discarding the box and wrapping paper to the side, I gingerly unclasp the case's lid and lift it open. My heart plummets, free-falling with excitement, gratefulness, and some other emotions I can't identify. Something blooms in my center, making my fingers twitch as if they're being resuscitated from a coma.

I blink away the tears as I stare at Karl, my hand pressing down firmly on my chest lest my heart explode. "Thank you," I say, and I don't miss that his own eyes are teary behind the phone he's holding to record this with.

I grab the neck of the guitar to pull it out and run my fingers over the strings on the Fender Stratocaster. It has a hot pink body with black details. So girly. So heavy metal. So me. He got it perfect.

Karl clears his throat. "It's what—"

"What Hendrix and Clapton played," I say much too excitedly.

He nods with approval. I bring the guitar to my chest and hug it tightly to my body, letting my tears fall to my chin. My very first guitar is fucking spectacular.

After setting the guitar back in its protective case, I jump to hug Karl again. This time, our hug is prolonged, and we forget Adrian is here and barely hear him leave when he does.

"Thank you, Karl. Really."

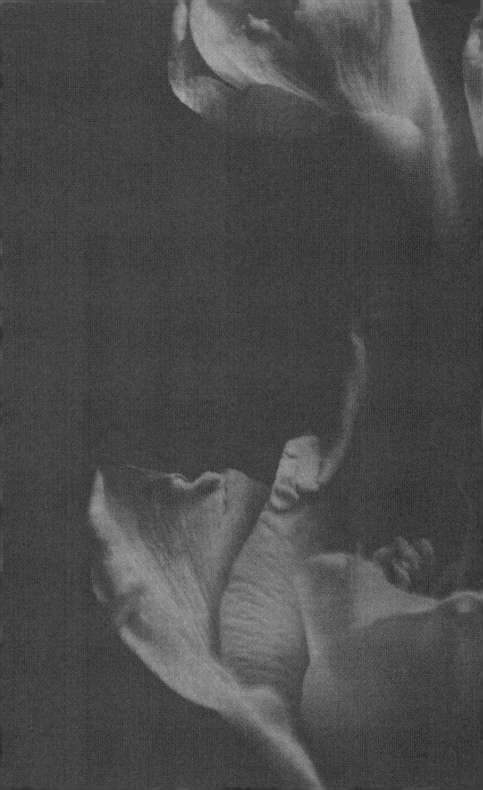

## LOLA

I'm lying down on the floor, and Isael is pretending my curly locks of hair are curvy roads for his car toys as he drives them from root to scalp. He giggles as he makes car noises. When he pulls on my hair much too painfully for about the hundredth time, I sit up.

"That's it," I say. "You're gonna get it!"

"*Tía*, no!" He screams as I roll him onto his back and start tickling him.

"Calm down, you two. Waffles are almost ready. Go wash up," Ileana calls from the kitchen.

"Come on, *mi terremoto*, let's go wash our hands."

Isael pouts, his little chubby cheeks twitching in the most adorable way as he discards his toy car on the carpet. "Kay," he says and takes my hand.

As we walk back out from the bathroom, we hear a knock.

"That must be Karl," Ileana says cheerily. "Can you get the door, Lola?"

"Sure," I say.

I came early to help her with Isael so she could cook breakfast. Once the roads cleared, she insisted on having Karl over so she could meet him.

Karl is smiling when I open the door. He's wearing his aviator glasses, dark denim, and a form-fitting ribbed sweater that conceals his tattoos. He's trying to impress Ileana, I realize. He's also holding a bottle of champagne in one hand and a bottle of orange juice in another. "For mimosas."

"Thanks." I take the bottles, and he follows me to the dining room.

"Um, Lo?"

"What?"

"You have a toy car hanging from your hair."

I spin on my heel to look at him and sigh, resigned. "Karl, there are at least five cars stuck in my hair at the moment."

I know for a fact Isael rolled my hair into those wheels nice and tight. I have no idea how I'm going to free my hair from the toys without resorting to cutting it.

"Isa, *mi amor*. Come here. I want you to meet someone."

Isael crashes onto my leg, and I lift him in my arms. "Isa, this is Karl. My good friend."

For all his hyperness, Isael is really shy with strangers, and he lets his little head fall to nestle on my neck under my chin.

"Hey, buddy," Karl says, taking off his sunglasses. He holds out a fist for Isael to bump, but Isael just stares at it. I squeeze him in my arms.

"It's okay," I reassure him, then bump Karl's fist. "See? Like that."

The gesture must seem interesting because Isael sits upright in my arms and blinks at Karl's fist. "Go ahead," I tell him. Gently, Isael bumps his fist.

"Atta buddy," Karl says.

Then, Isael turns his little head back to me and asks, "*Tío?*"

My head falls back with laughter. "No. He's not your *tío*."

"That's what Addy calls me," Karl says. "I don't mind if he calls me uncle too."

I sigh, resigned. "Fine, Isa. You can call him *Tío*."

I settle Isael in his highchair as Ileana joins us, holding a large serving plate of Belgian waffles I know she made from scratch. My mouth waters.

"Karl, hi!" She smiles brightly, setting the plate down. Then she makes her way around the table to kiss Karl's cheek. "It's so nice to finally meet you. I won't even bring up the fact that you moved Lola in with you before meeting me. I'm like an older sister to her, you know. Her only family."

Karl laughs. "Well, thanks for not bringing it up."

"Come on, are you hungry?"

We all sit, and I cut up Isael's waffle into bite-sized pieces, then drizzle the cream Ileana has made and add small bits of the candied peaches.

"This looks amazing. Thank you for inviting me," Karl says, and we all dig in.

"So, how are lessons going?" Ileana asks as she pours some of the mimosas.

"Great," Karl says, then gives her a similar answer to the one he gave our interviewer Joanna not too long ago. Which makes me wonder when the interview will be released, if it hasn't been already.

"Karl actually got me this awesome guitar for Christmas," I say.

Ileana sets down her fork and raises an eyebrow at me. "Really?"

"Yeah. It's too expensive, but I love it too much to decline."

Karl laughs. "It's not too expensive."

"So, Karl. Tell me about yourself, and I mean before *Industrial November*. I want to get to know the real you."

"Well, let's see, born and raised in Germany—"

"Really? I can't really hear an accent."

Karl laughs. "Oh, it's there, though very faint. Fritz is kind of a hardass about how we all have to be fluent in English for interview purposes, so I had to shed as much of the accent as I could."

"Did you always know you wanted to play guitar?" she asks.

"Not really. But when I was a teenager, I got a job at a petrol station run by a man named Ernest. He was the closest thing I ever had to family up until that point. I lived with foster parents at the time, but there were a lot of us, and it was crowded, so Ernest let me spend a lot of time at the station or at his place."

I eye Karl, wondering why he hasn't shared any of this with me before during the million and one conversations we've had about how he learned guitar. But I suppose he did always leave anything about his past kind of vague.

Karl continues his story for Ileana, who is listening intently. "Ernest was this old-school blues cat, you know? He could make an electric guitar weep like no other." Karl pauses to snort-laugh at a memory. "And he had this guitar over the mantel at his place. He explained that it was a priceless guitar, not meant to be played or touched and that I wasn't allowed to touch it— ever. I could do anything else I wanted at his place. Nothing was off-limits, except for the guitar—"

"Hey!" I whine, the forbidden guitar story hitting a little too close for comfort. "That's what you did to me! You told me I couldn't touch your guitars. Were you just using reverse psychology on me?" I ask, horrified he played me like that. And even more horrified it worked.

Both Ileana and Karl burst out laughing. "Sorry, Lola. It worked so well on me, I thought I'd try it on you."

"It's good you had a mentor who shared his love of music with you," Ileana says, and Karl nods, a little sad now. "Do you still get to see Ernest?"

Karl shakes his head solemnly. "No. He was in his seventies

when I met him as a teenager. He passed after my first year at college. But he left me his guitar."

I gasp. "The blue dragon?"

Karl nods. "Yeah. It's not priceless in the way he made me think it was. If you tried to sell it, you couldn't get much for it. But it's worth the world to me personally. I never had a father figure in my life, and Ernest was the closest thing to that. The fact that he trusted me with his guitar and handed down his legacy of music to me means I'd give up all my fortune before I would give up that guitar."

"People can be amazing sometimes, can't they?" Ileana asks, her eyes a little glassy at hearing Karl's story.

"Oh, my goodness." I startle out of my seat when I see Isael drenched in the cream sauce from forehead to chin, bits of peach stuck to his cheeks like glue. This kid. What a mess. "I'll go clean him up." I pick him up, turning away, so nobody gets a glimpse of my welling eyes.

# 26

# KARL

Lola only slightly protested when Roger showed up at the apartment with an entirely new entourage yesterday morning. Trailed by estheticians and their assistants, stylists with racks of evening gowns and their assistants, and a personal shopper who styled Lola's travel wardrobe, Roger orchestrated our trip to Los Angeles for today.

Our last album, *Breaking this Way*, was nominated by the Steel Hard Rock awards for best album, best metal performance, and the hit song "Girl from Kansas City" is up for best lyrics. This is Brenner Reindhart's year.

I was also relieved that when we introduced Lola to Matt Dalton, her new personal security, she accepted his presence immediately. And I could have kicked myself for not getting protection for her sooner.

Now we're on our way to L.A. in a private jet. Fritz, Adrian, Bren, and Sofia, plus our primary security team, means the plane is at full capacity—a first for the band.

Lola's head is resting on my shoulder, my t-shirt

drenched through with her drool on the spot on my shoulder directly below her mouth as she snores. Adrian peers up from his sketchbook, which I'm surprised he's actually using, and smirks at me.

"She always snore like that?" he asks.

I raise a brow at him. He's already slept with her, and he has no idea. "Yes," I say, and he chuckles, then returns his attention to his sketch.

Before we descend and before I wake Lola, Adrian hands me a piece of paper. I look at a sketch of Lola sleeping on my shoulder.

It's a simple sketch with crude lines and not much dimension, but it's pretty spectacular for someone who only started drawing this week. "Dude, you're actually good at this," I say, awe-struck at his hidden talent.

"I know, right?" He flashes me a smile before I wake Lola.

---

SIX CARS PULL up to the jet to pick us up so we don't have to deal with the mass of L.A. photographers at the airport.

Lola is bouncing with excitement since she has learned where we're going. Just the thought of meeting any of her rock and roll idols has her squealing and nervous, and it's the most adorable thing I've ever seen.

"We're not going to a hotel?" Lola asks as we get past the gate at what will be our home for the next two nights. "Nope." We have rented a mansion just outside of L.A. because even Bren feels like raising hell on this trip. "We rented this place so we can host a New Year's party tomorrow night."

Tonight, the awards show, and win or lose, tomorrow a New Year's party. I've never particularly looked forward to a

New Year's party, but the prospect of Lola being the one I get to kiss at midnight exhilarates me more than I would have imagined.

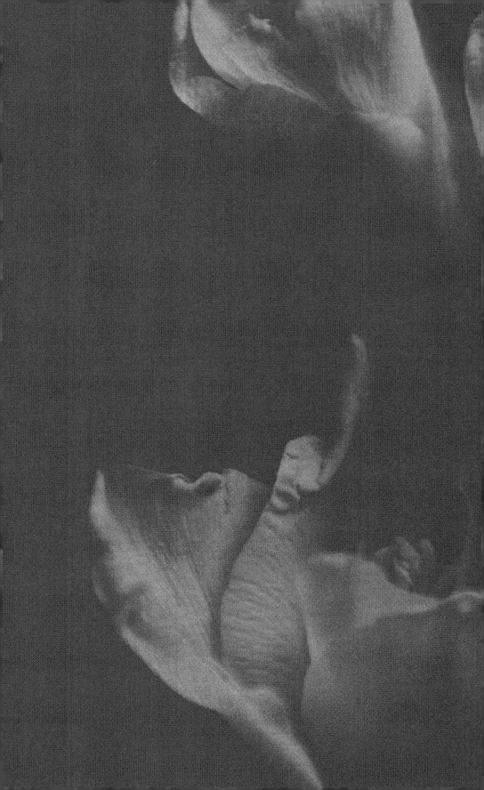

# 27

# LOLA

The shock of the estate where we're staying isn't so great now that I have lived at both Karl's mansion and Bren's old penthouse. I never thought I'd see the day I'd get used to this lifestyle. And I'm only a little ashamed that I'll miss it when I move to Acapulco.

What I won't miss is the security. I actually have a personal security guard now. I wanted to seem unaffected when Karl first introduced me to Matt. I'd thought we could be buddies, but with stony features and unshakeable quietness, he's kept me at arm's length. He's like a shadow, never intrusive, and already I can tell I'll forget he's at my side half the time.

I need to be more careful with what I say and do.

Sofia drags me to the master bedroom, where racks of dresses await us. I'm amped with nerves and excitement but glad to have a friend to go through this with.

"You're not at all nervous?" I ask Sofia.

"A little. It's my first major public event with Bren too."

"I know. After tonight, if we can walk down the street without getting tomatoes tossed at our heads, I'll be surprised."

Sofia laughs. "Which reminds me," she says, leading me by

the arm to sit on the bed. "Are you sure about what you're doing? You're not moving too fast here?"

"I'm just having some fun, Sofia. I swear."

She lets out a sigh. "I'm not blind. I see how much he makes you smile. But I'm worried you'll fall for him. From what Bren tells me, he doesn't really do the girlfriend thing. Bren doesn't think he's ever been in love. And I'm afraid you will fall for him and not have it reciprocated."

I understand where Sofia's concern is coming from. If Ileana picked me up from hell a year ago, Sofia was on my other side, helping her with the weight. Ileana and Sofia are like twin pillars that propped me up at the time of my life when I was crumbling, and they didn't let me fall completely apart. So I can't be too annoyed at Sofia's meddling. She's invested in me now.

"I'm not falling in love with him," I lie. I'm growing feelings for him, sure. But I'm not in love. "What's the harm in letting a little loose, just this once in my life?"

Sofia takes me into her arms for a hug. "You know I just care about you and would hate to see you hurt, right?"

"I know. And I won't be hurt. I promise."

She smiles at me and stands again to look through the dress racks.

"How are things with you and Bren?" I ask, turning the conversation away from me.

"Amazing. He's growing into this amazing father, and it only makes him all the hotter."

She laughs, and I join her.

"It's a little gross, to be honest, that you two can't keep your paws off each other."

"We're making up for lost time," she says with an enormous grin as she pulls a dress off the rack and holds it up for me to see. "I think this is the one for you."

My mouth falls open. "You're insane! I can't wear that in public."

"Oh yes, you can. This is the dress. Karl won't be able to keep his eyes off you . . . or his hands."

Somehow, Sofia, this lovely friend I think of as an older sister, convinces me to select one of the most scandalous pieces on the rack.

The rest of the afternoon, we're pampered with massages and champagne, and then the real work begins.

Sofia's beauty team works on me too, and I won't lie: the professional makeup and hair look spectacular. After three grueling hours of work, Sofia and I stand in front of the mirror.

I take a deep breath. "This 'rock-star girlfriend' enough?" I ask her, more than a little nervous.

She shakes her head, then her smile grows. "No. Not rock. That dress is metal as fuck."

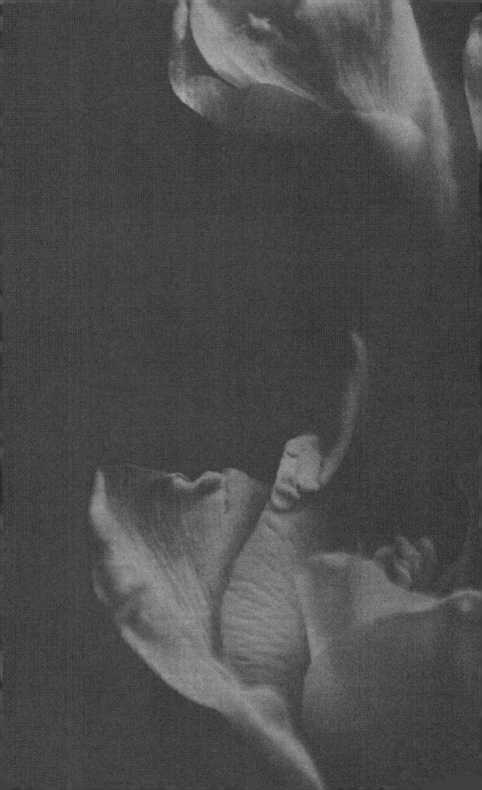

# 28

# KARL

The guys and I are all waiting for the women to grace us with their presence. Estheticians showed up earlier and whisked them away to be pampered, scrubbed, buffed, polished, or whatever it is women do. I don't know. I'm glad Sofia thought to set all this up for Lola too, because I'd have no idea what to do with all this.

Fritz hands me a small tumbler with just one finger of whiskey, and I thank him with a tip of my chin as I take it and toss it back. I'm not up for an individual award, and yet I'm nervous—which is unlike me. I wonder if having Lola in the audience has something to do with that. Her approval means something to me, I decide. What that *something* is, I have yet to figure out.

Bren is leaning back on a brown leather chair, swirling his own drink, a cigar in his hand.

"That was a good interview," Bren says, looking at me. Both Fritz and Adrian turn to look at me too.

"I didn't know it was out already," I say truthfully.

Bren nods. "It came out this morning. All that shit she said true?" Bren asks.

I swallow hard. God, I hope so. But to Bren, I lie. "Yeah. It's all true. I meant it, Bren. There have been no parties since before the move. And there won't be any more unless it's with the band, like tonight and New Year's."

Bren nods approvingly and blows a ring in front of his face. His smile is barely there, but all the same, the unease about the security of my place in the band starts to dissipate like the smoke in front of his face.

"She's a good kid," Adrian chimes in with regard to Lola.

"She's not a kid," I snap.

Adrian only laughs.

"You got lucky with that one," Fritz says.

"Sure did," I admit.

Bren takes another puff of his cigar and shakes his head. "I'm not thrilled about it. Lola is like Sofia's little sister. You hurt her, we're going to have problems."

I shake my head. "I wouldn't. I care about her, Bren. You have nothing to worry about."

Before we can take the conversation any further, Sofia walks into the room in a black satin gown with only one shoulder strap. There's a black leather detail above her cleavage, and she looks stunning. All of us stare at her in awe.

She makes her way over to Bren and sits on his lap, and it seems he's forgotten anyone else is in the room with them. She's the only thing he can see. The man is putty in her hands. She grabs his cigar, and his now-free hand drifts to her waist.

"Hello, boys," she says, still locking eyes with Bren. Then she takes a puff of the cigar and blows the smoke into Bren's mouth.

"Will you two get a room?" Fritz barks, and we all bust out laughing at him.

*Someone needs to get laid*, I think. Fritz is grumpier than usual.

The laughter only dies when Lola walks into view. All the air gets sucked out of the room as I forget to breathe while I watch her. Her smile is wide as she finds me and walks straight to me.

I stand slowly, waiting for her to reach me so I can kiss the back of her hand and spin her around. As I do, Sofia whistles.

Lola is wearing a skin-tight latex gown in a peachy-nude shade with a slit so far up her left thigh, it's almost indecent. The bust and torso area look like some sort of corset in the same latex material. You almost have to look at her twice, or you'd think she's naked. Her blonde hair is in thick, loose waves cascading down her shoulders, and her makeup is minimal but sultry.

Lola looks fucking edible. My dick twitches in appreciation as I spin her a second time, this time focusing on the latex material hugging the perfect curve of her full hips and ass.

I get close to her ear, taking in the intoxicating smell of a new perfume I don't recognize, and whisper, "You're breathtaking, doll."

"Thank you," she says. "You clean up rather nicely yourself. You all do," she says, spinning around to address the other guys.

"I picked out that dress for her," Sofia says with a huge smile.

"You can dress Lola any time," I tease, and Sofia shoots me a wide smile.

For all her complaining at the start, Sofia seems to be on board with the idea of us now. I think she, like Bren, realizes what a good influence Lola is on me and how much she seems to smile around me—a smile I have to remind myself was mostly absent from her features when I first met her.

She's brightened up, like the scorching sun, and her warmth is inviting to anyone around her.

---

OUR SECURITY DETAIL encases us as we exit our limo and walk toward the red carpet. I don't miss Lola clutching at the material of Matt's jacket sleeve. Has she felt unsafe? Being in public? Or is she anticipating the attention now that the interview is out there?

But her shoulders seem to relax as she looks from face to face, her eyes widening then dropping in embarrassment as she finds famous person after famous person walking ahead and behind us on the red carpet.

Photographers yell out Bren and Sofia's names since they're just in front of us, but as soon as they get a glimpse of Lola, they go wild. Flashes go off in quick succession as they try to capture my delectable date, and they yell her name. Only, they don't call her Lola. They keep calling out Dolores.

We stop to pose for a few pictures together, and I correct them, "Lola. Her name is Lola."

Her grip is tight around my waist, and I realize she must be nervous, but I'm so damned proud of her because, in front of the cameras, she hides it well.

The thought is also unsettling because she could have faked everything she said during our interview.

I take her hand and lead her inside.

---

WHEN *INDUSTRIAL NOVEMBER*'S name is read off a card announcing the winner in the best album category, it's Sofia who jumps to her feet first, followed closely by Lola. The guys and I all stand, and we get hugs from the two ladies with us.

When we get on stage, the guys all say short speeches I can't hear because my heart is pounding loud in my chest.

"Breaking this Way" was the first album I wrote music for. I helped create these songs with the band, and to be up here for an album that Milo had no part in creating is a small form of validation that I'm meant to be here. In this band.

With this woman.

Fritz clasps my shoulder and leads me to the mic when he's done speaking.

I clear my throat nervously. "I would like to thank Bren, Adrian, and Fritz for giving me a shot. To Ernest, my dearest buddy, for making one fateful guitar so forbidden, I had to have it." I pause to send a solemn and silent 'Rest in peace' to Ernest. When I open my eyes again, I continue. "When I wrote music for this album, I didn't know Lola." I pause to find her in the crowd and lock eyes with her. "But if there is any soul or any heart in any of the notes I play on the album, it was a love like hers I was dreaming of—that I was waiting for." Lola's hands are fisted over her heart, and even from this distance, I can tell her nose is red and tears trail down her cheeks. The sheer pride in her features plunges my heart into a freefall from my chest. I swallow hard because there's only one thing I must say, and I mean it more than I've ever meant anything before. "I love you, doll."

The crowd cheers as they grace us with a standing ovation. The guys and I line up and hold hands like we do at the end of concerts and take a bow. When we look up again, Sofia has her thumb and forefinger in her mouth, and her whistling is so loud, it reaches us over the applause, making us all laugh.

When I find my seat next to Lola, all cameras, it seems,

are on us. Both her hands go to the sides of my face, and her forehead presses to mine. "I'm so damn proud of you," she says, and I lift her chin to kiss her.

We kiss for the longest time, the applause a sound so far-off into the distance, I hardly notice it.

# LOLA

There was champagne.

So much champagne.

At the dinner. At the multiple after-parties we attended.

I drank it to steel my spine so I wouldn't fangirl over my rock heroes and embarrass Karl or the band.

And then I drank it some more. On the shared limousine drive home, there's more champagne.

I'm not alone. Sofia is red-nosed, half-wrapped around Bren, and we're both giggling with the excessive tipsiness that is nearly bordering on drunkenness.

Karl asks the driver to stop at In-N-Out for burgers. We go through the drive-thru, and the cashier begs the driver to let him see who's in the limo. Sofia and I both giggle inside the car. When he finally hands the driver the bags filled with burgers and he's about to drive away, I yell out the window, "It's *Industrial November!*"

Now this, I'm not proud of. Karl tries to get me to eat so I can sober up, but I'm so petulant, I refuse. Everyone else scarfs down the burgers, and I just roll down my window and rest my head on the window frame, letting the night air cool my face. I watch the night lights of the city whip by, and I smile into the sky. What a perfect night.

Eventually, the lights begin to disappear, and when we pass the gate, I know we're almost home.

How sad. I was having such a great time.

Adrian left early and didn't participate in the partying, so I can only imagine he's already sleeping. As soon as we all get inside, Bren ducks to throw Sofia over his shoulder and takes her upstairs like a sack of potatoes. Fritz shakes his head as he goes to his own bedroom.

"What time is it?" I ask Karl when we're alone.

"Two-thirty."

The night seems like a blur now, but it was one of the most fun nights of my life—second only to the taco truck night. Then I feel Karl's fingers between mine as he leads me toward the kitchen.

"Where are we going?"

"You need to eat."

"I'm not hungry."

"And I need to get some water in you, or you'll feel like hell in the morning."

I stop fighting it. The night is officially over, so I let him lead me to the kitchen. I squeak when he surprises me by holding on to my waist and lifting me onto the kitchen island.

I snort.

"What?" he asks. He rummages through the kitchen until he finds coffee and puts a pot on.

"This is how we met. I was on the kitchen island at your old house."

He hands me a glass of water that I gulp down. A small smile curves those perfectly molded lips. "I remember."

"Only, Pixel was trying to kill me." I pout. "I miss her."

"Me too. But she loves Chase, so you know she's in good hands."

I watch as Karl halfway unwraps a burger and hands it to me. "Eat."

I shake my head. "I'm not hungry."

"Eat anyway."

After sticking my tongue out at him, I get a whiff of the burger and my stomach growls. "Maybe just a bite."

I devour the burger, and when I'm done, he hands me the coffee.

"Drink."

"You know, you're very bossy tonight." I press my thighs together at the mere thought of a bossy Karl.

"If it makes you feel better, I'm drinking the water and coffee too."

I think back through the night. I realize he hasn't had half as much to drink as I have. In fact, that is partially my fault. I was so nervous, whenever I finished my drink, I'd steal his and down it too. No wonder he's the voice of reason now, I realize, as I start sobering up.

"Thanks for taking care of me," I say.

He's in front of me now, and I run my fingers through his long blond locks, like I've wanted to so many times. "Your hair is beautiful."

"You're still drunk," he says, but the crooked smile has grown. "Come on." He grabs me by the waist again and my feet find the ground. "Can you walk okay?"

I nod.

Unsure I can keep my balance in heels, he grabs my hand and leads me up the stairs.

Earlier, when Sofia and I were getting ready, we were in the master suite, so I never found out where my room was.

When Karl leads me to it and I peer inside, I squeal at the

luxury, and the inviting perfect bed reminds me how tired I am and how much my feet hurt. I turn to thank him for helping me find my room, but he's in here with me, and the door is shut behind him.

"Uh—Karl? What are you doing?"

"What do you mean?"

"You're in my room." I take off one of the uncomfortable high heels.

That hint of a smile appears on the corner of his mouth again. "Our room," he corrects me.

When he says that, I trip and nearly fall as I try removing the second heel. He lunges for me and holds on to my elbow to steady me.

"What?"

"They think we're together, remember? We can't have separate rooms."

I look over at the bed and gulp. "Where are you sleeping?"

He sighs, but he's still smiling. "I'd hate to sleep on the floor, but I will if you want me to, Lola. I'd say the bed is big enough. We can barricade with pillows."

He's looking at me differently. And he has been since he was on stage. I'd thought his declaration of love was an act. Fake. Like our first kiss at the taco truck. For press . . . but the way he's been looking at me . . . I'm not so sure anymore. That's another reason I kept gulping down the drinks. I was so nervous, I kept slamming them down like shots.

Did he mean it? How could he? We hardly know each other. We're faking a relationship. It's all going to plan. Bren seemed happy with him tonight. The hate mail was diverted from him to me, and there have been no more incidents of women trying to break into places for alone time since I've been in the picture publicly.

If the plan is going so perfectly, why, then, is this starting to feel anything but fake?

Sharing a bed after his admission of love, whether it was fake or not, sounds like a terrible idea.

Even so, my body gravitates to him. I may not be in love with Karl, but I'm definitely in lust with him. And I like him.

I approach him, intending to embrace him and kiss him, but he stiffens.

"Easy," he says. More soothingly, he draws his thumb up the length of my cheekbone. "You'll stay on this side." He pats the bed. "And I'll stay on that side."

Famous last words.

I drop to the bed in the dress and in the makeup, too tired to change or wash my face. And I feel it when he places the pillows between us before he dozes off.

And yet here we are the next morning, the pillows gone, and Karl is wrapped around me.

Wrapped around me in a familiar way that would suggest we wake up together like this all the time. There's a warmth on my chest and I smile when I realize he's cupping my left breast. His nose is also nuzzling the side of my neck. Has he been doing this all night?

He's slept with me once before, on Christmas when I was so lonely. But that was so different.

I try moving, and he stirs. He lets go of my breast and rolls onto his back, still asleep. I sit up, and peer at him. And holy hell, the tent he's straining on the bedsheet is massive.

Inviting.

I want to reach over to pull him out of his boxers. At least he had the forethought to undress before crashing.

I think about it. Seriously think about it. I imagine peeling the bedsheet off him, sneaking my hand into the opening of the boxers, and freeing him. Asleep, he wouldn't notice at first, not until my mouth would be around him.

But I don't.

He's made it clear he doesn't want to touch me, and I've

already pushed myself on him enough. I need to respect his wishes. I remind myself of the night we had. Of the stupid questions that were swimming in my drunken head last night. Of course he doesn't love me.

This is fake.

# 30

# KARL

The collective chant is deafening around us.

"Five!"

"Four!"

"Three!"

Lola is holding a glass of champagne, and she sets it down. We lock eyes, and I wrap both arms around her waist.

"Two!"

Her gaze drops to my lips, and I smirk.

"One!"

"Happy New Year!"

Her arms fly around my neck as she pulls me down, and my mouth dives to find hers. She opens my mouth with the probing of her tongue, and I smile into the kiss. Her tongue finds mine, letting me taste the faint hint of champagne lingering there. We both limited ourselves to this one drink after the morning we had, full of headaches and nausea. It could have been worse, I remind myself.

She drops one hand to my waistband, fingers curling around my belt, tugging my hips closer to her, and I groan into her mouth. Fuck this.

I lift her over my shoulder like a neanderthal, like Bren did to Sofia last night, and take her back inside the house. I ignore the looks I get from Bren, Fritz, and the entire party as I stalk across the lawn, get inside the house, and take us to our bedroom.

I bring her to her feet once we're in our room, and I start unbuttoning my shirt to the sound of fireworks outside our window.

"Naked," I bark.

Lola jumps a little at the tone in my voice, but then her own little dark smile twists her mouth, and she hurriedly undresses.

I steal another kiss from her hungrily, letting my dick press against her smooth stomach, and she whimpers into my mouth. When I break away after a long moment, Lola is panting. "You are going to sit on my face," I tell her.

"What—"

I smile at her. "I'm going to lie down on this bed, here"—I point next to us—"and you are going to sit on my face. You're going to let me taste that sweet, sweet pussy. You hear me?"

Lola nods, wringing her hands in front of her. I lift her chin. "No. You won't be embarrassed. Do you understand?"

She nods.

I run my hand down her thigh. "You're going to spread these pretty little legs, and open up your perfect cunt for my tongue, aren't you?"

"Yes," she breathes out. Her cheeks are rosy from the champagne, and I'm finding it difficult to keep control here.

I bring her body over me as I lie down and instruct her to support herself with her palms to the wall above the headboard. She does as I say, but she is so nervous.

"Sit," I order her.

Gripping my shaft in one hand, I feel as she slowly lowers those lips to my mouth.

I lick her once, tentatively, and her body shudders.

"Karl," she moans.

"Do you know how perfect you are, doll?" I lick again, stroking myself and looking up at her body, her breasts tantalizing with hard nipples I want to suck but can't reach with my hands occupied spreading her lips and stroking myself.

I let my eyes fall closed as I find her clit and circle it with my tongue. I bite it gently, then tease it some more. Allowing myself to enjoy the taste of her, I feel as her thighs begin to shake around my face.

This is not the New Year's kiss I had in mind, nor the one I was expecting.

But I sure as hell am not complaining.

# 31

# KARL

The following day, as we arrive back at our building, it seems every news reporter in Kansas City is waiting outside the gate to the garage.

"What the hell is going on?" Lola asks.

"They're probably going apeshit because I said I love you publicly."

Lola's eyes drop to her hands as she wrings the hem of her shirt. Since I said "I love you" in front of the rock and roll elite in L.A., she still has not acknowledged my declaration. I haven't brought it up either. It was a whirlwind two days, and it seems we hardly had a moment to ourselves, and when we did, I usually opted to eat her out instead of talking.

Not a bad tactic, really.

But she also never said it back. I know she doesn't love me. It's too soon. Half of me realizes it's too soon for me to be in love with her too, but I can't help how I feel.

I can't pinpoint the moment it happened, I only know that in the best moment of my life, when Bren finally extended an olive branch publicly and I was recognized for my musical contributions, the only person I wanted to share that moment with was Lola.

Bren's acceptance, my peers' acknowledgement of my contribution, none of it mattered as much as I'd imagined it would. The only person I cared about being proud of me that night was her. Iggy. What I said in my speech was nothing but the truth.

I've been waiting a long time—all my life—to find my true love, something real. And I know Lola and I have that potential if she can only let herself be vulnerable enough to try again after her heart has been shredded into thin and delicate ribbons.

And I'm okay knowing she doesn't love me back because I know her feelings are growing, and one day she could. I just need to be patient.

Luckily for us, patience is my forte.

"Right," Lola says.

I open my mouth to reassure her she doesn't have to say 'I love you' back, but my phone goes off in my pocket, interrupting. "Uh, sorry," I say as Matt parks and we get out of the car. I frown when I see Roger's name on the screen. I talked to him before our flight, so I wasn't expecting a call tonight.

"Is it true?" Roger demands as soon as I pick up.

"Is what true?"

"The story on Lola. Is it true?" Roger asks again. "It's not a big deal, Karl, but I need to know this kind of shit ahead of time. Taking the offensive position is the best form of defense. You know that. What were you thinking, hiding this?"

"Slow down. I don't have any idea what you're talking about."

"Where are you?"

"We just got home. About to get in the elevator and will lose the call."

"Turn on the damned news when you get upstairs and then call me back."

Roger ends the call, and I blink at the phone in my hands. What the hell was that? "Lo?"

"What?" she asks.

"Is there something you need to tell me?"

"About what you said at the—"

"No." I shake my head. "Have you been keeping anything from me?"

She looks to the sidewall of the elevator and bites the inside of her lip. That's all the answer I need.

"Roger said to turn on the news when we get inside and call him back."

"The news?" she asks, her eyes wide with panic.

"Yeah. There's apparently some sort of story on you."

She shakes her head as all color drains from her face. "No, no, no, no," she says over and over as she dashes out of the elevator and lunges toward the remote to turn on the television.

We stare at the television as a gallery of images rolls through the screen before our eyes. Pictures of a man and a woman in their mid-forties. The man, blond and green-eyed just like Lola, gives it away, but it's the woman's lips, with that perfectly symmetrical cupid's bow, that are a direct replica of Lola's. It's her parents, I realize. Then their images roll away, and the image of a car, or what's left of it, scrunched up like a soda can, fills the screen.

"Oh, fuck, Iggy, you don't need to see this shit." I move to take the remote from her to turn it off, but she raises a hand to stop me and turns the volume up.

"We're back with more on Karl Sommer's partner's tragic story. We have confirmed reports that Dolores "Lola" Beltran, the nineteen-year-old girlfriend of Industrial November's guitarist, is, and has been for the last eighteen years, in the United States without documentation. Her parents, Patricia and Gabriel Beltran, also undocumented immigrants, died over a year ago in a tragic vehicular accident—"

I shut off the TV. She doesn't need to see this. Lola's tears are dripping from her chin as she keeps staring at the black screen, her sniffles the only sound in the room.

"It's true, then?" I ask her.

She nods and wipes some of the tears. "I—" She clears her throat. "I didn't know. I found out the night they died."

"You didn't know what?"

"That they were—that I was . . . am . . ."

"Undocumented?"

She nods again.

"That's why you couldn't go to college?"

Another nod. "Dad had been saving, hoping to be able to pay out of pocket. I had plans to turn him down and use financial aid and some savings, but I couldn't because of my status. I just didn't know it."

"And you found out that night?" I ask her.

Her tears well in endless streams. "Yeah. That's why we fought. They were out in the rain looking for me. They're dead because of me."

"Oh, come here, Lo. It's not your fault." I pull her into my arms and let her sob into my sweater for several minutes. "It's okay, love. I've got you."

"I'm so sorry," she whimpers.

"Why are you sorry?"

"To drag you into this."

"It's me who's sorry. If it weren't for me, no one would be trying to dig up shit about you. Is this why you're moving to Mexico?"

Lola nods in my arms. "I don't want to be where I'm not wanted," she croaks.

"Shit, Iggy." I sigh, my own tears threatening to spill over. Talk about the ultimate rejection. I know how much she loves this city and the people she's come to think of as family, but this country doesn't want her here. No wonder she used to be so sad all the time. I can't imagine walking through life knowing that the very place that made you, the place you love, wants you out. "They're so stupid for not wanting you. Do you hear me?" I tighten my grip around her.

She laughs, a wet, teary laugh.

"I mean it. You're so talented. One day, you're going to be in your own famous rock band. And if these idiots here don't want you or your talent or your money, Mexico does."

She nods again, her sobs lessening. "And so does Germany," I say, teasing her. "We'd take you in a heartbeat, Iggy."

She laughs and pulls away from me, dabbing her tears on her shirt collar. "Thanks, Karl. And thanks for not being mad."

"Of course I'm not mad."

After leading her to bed, I make her a cup of tea and set it on her nightstand. She takes a few sips, and I sit on the side of her bed and run my fingers through her hair gently until she nods off to sleep. Once she's out, I text Roger the statement he should give the press. I really don't want to talk to him, so I shut off my phone after sending the text.

---

I'M NOT surprised when Sofia shows up unannounced. I smile when I see her step off the elevator. She really is like her over-protective older sister. "Hey, Sofia."

She takes the sunglasses off, and I don't miss her swollen eyes from recent crying. "Where is she?"

"Asleep."

Makeup-free, wearing jeans and a grey t-shirt, Sofia sits next to me and pats my leg. "How bad was it?"

"She's heartbroken," I admit. And somehow, Sofia's strength is enough to let myself go for one moment, to let her carry some of this weight with me, and I let a tear fall. A single tear for my beautiful Lola, so precious, so talented, and so damned unwanted. "And so am I," I say.

"Me too," Sofia says.

We stay like that for a long while, Sofia not commenting on my tears. "Is there anything we could do to help her stay?" I ask, grasping at anything to make this better.

"There was a pathway for her to go to college."

"Great, I'll pay for it if that's what it takes. If what she really wants is to be here, I'll give her an anonymous scholarship."

"It's not that simple," Sofia says.

"But it *is* an option, right?"

She lets out a breath. "It is, for those who want it bad enough. Lola doesn't. What you have to understand is that children brought here under age can go to college on their own dime, with zero financial aid. And they have to be so above perfect, so ahead of the curve, it's not a real option for most."

"I don't understand."

"It's a long legal process. Those kids live holding their breath, while at the same time keeping ridiculous grades for a small shot at the few merit scholarships they *are* eligible for. It's very competitive. They can't get in trouble at all, they can't be kids when they're in college. They have to be models of society to warrant taking up space in a way that the rest of us don't. The bar is set so much higher for them, when they did nothing to deserve such a prejudgment of their character."

"Lola could do it."

Sofia laughs. "Of that, I have no doubt. If she wanted it. If she'd had a specific career goal in mind, she probably would have. But undecided dreamers aren't the best candidates for that pathway. Do you think they'd view an aspiring metal guitarist as the model of society I mentioned?" she asks, a brow arched. "People who go through that process want it bad enough to make all the sacrifices worth it. Not Lola though. She is so hurt by not being wanted here. You've heard her say that by now, I'm sure—"

I nod. "Yeah. I have."

"Would *you* want to be where you're not wanted? If you had a choice?"

I shake my head. Fuck. This is so complicated. No wonder she was so angry with her parents. They hid this from her until . . . until it was too late.

"Lola has a choice. A beautiful one. One with a fresh start, her own business, and her only living family. As much as it breaks my heart for her to leave, I'm so excited for the future she's chosen. She's one of the lucky ones, to have an option like that. She'll do great when she's home. And even from afar, I'll always be there to catch her if she falls."

I swallow hard, but it lodges heavy in my throat. I can't fix this.

I can throw all my money at the problem to help her stay —and I would, every last cent if that's what it took—and she wouldn't want it, because if there's one thing I know in my marrow, it's that you can't force yourself to be wanted by anyone.

"Well, I don't want to wake her. But tell her I was here and have her call me when she wakes up. I'm sure Ileana will be worried too, so she should probably call her first."

We stand, and Sofia embraces me for a long moment before she leaves.

I sneak into Lola's bed and watch her sleep, a million

thoughts racing through my mind. Lola isn't out much longer after that, and when she wakes up, I smile at her from the spot next to her.

"Feeling better?" I ask.

"Yeah. Sorry for crying all over you."

"I'm always here for you. You know that, right?"

She nods. "What do we do now?"

"I sent Roger a statement he can give to the press if he wants. Made it clear you didn't know and that you have plans to move soon."

"Thank you."

I brush her hair away from her face. "You know what I love most about rock?"

"What's that?" she asks.

"It's for the rejects. I found my home with metalheads. Whenever I was feeling lonely or left behind, I'd show up at a concert, any concert, and I felt . . . embraced, I guess."

"I never thought about it like that."

"I grew up feeling that way, Lo. I got really good at being comfortable with rejection. You didn't. One day your life was perfect—you were loved by your parents, had a bright future, aspirations. The rug was just . . . pulled out from under you in so many freaking ways at the same time."

"What's it like? Getting used to rejection so deep?"

"It's only bad until you find the people that *do* embrace you. You know, like Sofia, Ileana, your aunt in Mexico, *me*," I say with a grin.

"You're silly."

"But seriously, I'm a little worried about you. When I met you, I thought maybe you were depressed, and I think I was right. I think you still are."

She sighs. "I don't know."

"Have you seen a therapist yet?"

Lola rolls her eyes. "You sound just like Ileana now."

"Think about it. It helps."

"You've been to therapy?" Lola asks, clearly not expecting me to say yes.

"I have. I have a regular therapist in Germany. Haven't seen her in a while, though. Since I've been here. But it does help, Lola. More than you can understand until you go through it."

"I'll think about it," she says.

"Good. As soon as you get to Mexico, find someone. I'll pay for it if that's what it takes."

"You're too kind, Karl. Too generous."

I let the topic drop, and we're both silent for a moment. We stay like that, just staring at each other, our breaths in perfect sync, until we fall asleep.

We wake up much the same way, just staring at each other.

"Can I ask you something since you were being all serious and open last night?" Lola asks.

"Sure."

"You said you love me."

I nod. "I did."

"But you won't have intercourse with me. Why?"

I sigh. This again. I hold her gaze so she knows I'm serious when I answer. "Because you don't love me—"

"Karl—"

"It's okay, doll. I know you have feelings for me. And I think you could get there—that *we* could get there. You just need to be a little patient."

We both fall silent, and I don't know what else to say, how else to comfort her. Before I realize what's happening, Lola rolls over on top of me, making out with me.

She grinds her hips over mine, forcing an erection out of me.

"Please, Karl," she begs. "I need you."

"I will happily make you come if that's what you need, but we're not ready for that step yet," I say with the best smile I can offer. With what she's been through today, seeking hollow comfort from the flesh wouldn't be quite the same as choosing to make love to someone for the sake of loving them, would it?

She bunches my shirt in her fists, and she begs once more. "I need your closeness. I want to feel you inside of me. *Please.*"

God, how can I resist this? When she's so perfect, begging for me, wanting a physical connection to soothe her aching heart. I want to give in. She may not love me yet, but having sex with her could be a step in that direction.

It's a bad idea, I know it is, but I've held off as long as I can humanly hold off.

At the end of the day, I'm just a man—a mere mortal.

My patience and resolve waver, and for one moment, I consider giving in—giving her what she wants. I know she deserves better than me, and if I were a better man, I'd make her wait for that.

"Why me, Lola? You don't love me, so it's not love. Why does it have to be me?" I ask her.

She stops grinding on me for a moment and thinks. "I've thought a lot about it. As I've said before, you're my friend, and I know you would be gentle my first time."

I nod. "I would."

"And at the end of the day, I want someone experienced. Your reputation as a sex god precedes you." She chuckles. "My first time, I'd love to be with a man who knows what he's doing."

*What the fuck?* I grimace, and I grab her by the arms to pull her off of me and set her aside, then stand up. "Wait, *what?*" I ask her, my hands fisted at my sides.

"What's wrong?" she asks.

"You want me to fuck you because you want my *experience?*"

"Well, yeah," she says like it's not the most insulting thing anyone has ever said to me.

She doesn't want *me*. She maybe doesn't even have feelings at all for me like I'd thought. She wants my body, my experienced dick, but not me.

As much as the rejection hurts, it's also exactly what I expected. I shouldn't be surprised. It also strengthens my resolve.

I grab her face angrily like I did that first time I watched her touch herself, my fingers digging into her jaw, not caring enough when she winces to let go of her face.

"Get this through that pretty little head," I growl. "I'm not going to fuck you. Ever."

# 32

# LOLA

"Oh," I whisper, pulling away from his hold that is hurting my face. I try to hold the shameful tears in. "I'm sorry, Karl. That's the last time I try to touch you. I thought maybe you wanted me to—"

"I don't," he snaps.

"I see that now." My lip trembles as I try to mask the hurt. "I'm sorry I read everything wrong. It won't happen again."

The hard lines of his jaw are taut, and that muscle in his right cheek twitches visibly, but he just stands there, considering me for far too long. "If you don't mind, I think I'd like to be alone now."

Karl nods and closes the door after he leaves my room.

I hug the pillow where his head had been, sniffing it, and let my tears fall.

But I'm not crying for the news story, not anymore.

Why did he say he loves me if he doesn't? Because he can't love me, I've decided, not when he insists on pushing me away.

I'm also mortified at how many times I've come on to him. I thought he liked it. I thought he wanted me too—that he was considering giving in and only pushing me away because he thought I was still hung up on Ethan. But that's not it at all. He honestly doesn't want me.

I don't hear a peep out of him for over an hour, and the only time I see him again is when the dog sitter brings Pixel home, and Karl cracks the door open to let her in my room.

"Hey, old lady," I whisper as she curls by my feet. "I've missed you too, girl."

***

"WHERE ARE YOU GOING?" I ask Karl later that morning as he waits for the elevator.

"I'm flying to New York," he says coolly, not looking at me.

"Oh. How long will you be gone?"

"Just flying in and out. It's for a stupid photoshoot Roger signed me up for. Should be back by nine tonight."

"You weren't going to tell me?"

"Just did."

His frigid temper pierces through me after he was so incredibly supportive last night when the news of my parents broke. It's like he can flip off his warmth so easily, like a switch.

"Goodbye," I say just as the elevator doors shut, but I'm not sure he heard me.

I've overstayed my welcome yet again, I realize too late—that familiar pain crushing my heart.

My time in this city just ended, and so did my time with Karl Sommer.

I spend the next hour making calls and packing, and I somehow manage to transfer my flight to this afternoon.

When I'm nearly ready to head out, I sneak into Karl's room one last time. I pull the guitar case from under his bed, open it, and take out the blue dragon. In its place, I leave the pink guitar he gave me for Christmas, topped off with my goodbye letter. I then transfer the blue dragon into my guitar case. He'll probably be mad at first, but he'll understand when he reads my note.

The dog sitter comes out of the elevator as soon as I leave Karl's room. "Hi," he says.

"Hi, Chase. Thanks for taking her back so last minute."

"Happy to help."

"Let me say goodbye, okay?"

"Sure."

I sit on the floor and call Pixel to me. She sits in front of me and stares at me with wide eyes.

"Hey, Pixy-girl. I have to go now. You've been such a good girl." I scratch her favorite spot behind her left ear. "And I'm going to miss you so much. Take care of your dad for me, okay?" She licks my face once, and I do my best not to cry through our goodbyes.

I hand Chase the leash and watch them leave.

---

WHEN I LAND in Acapulco and turn on my phone, I have fifteen missed calls from Karl, three from Roger, and seven voice messages. I don't listen to them. I also don't read the flurry of texts that came through while I was in the air. I pocket my phone and decide to change my number the first chance I get.

After retrieving my guitar case and single suitcase carrying my life's belongings, I head to the arrivals bay. I instantly recognize my *tía* Elena. I'd known from our video calls how much she looks like Mom. Mom always told me stories about how people used to confuse them when they were growing up, but I wasn't prepared for such a striking resemblance in the flesh.

I freeze when I see her, almost sure I'm looking at Mom. An inch shorter than me, and a slightly stockier frame than my Mom's, *tía* Elena clasps her hands over her heart.

"Lola!" she screams, causing everyone around us to stare,

then she runs up to me. I set the guitar case down next to me just before she reaches me and takes me into warm, welcoming arms.

My tears dot her shirt over her shoulders as we embrace. I've never before met this woman in the flesh, and I never knew why until my legal status became clear to me. I should have guessed why we never traveled outside the country when we had family here.

I've spoken to Elena on the phone so many times, and she's always said how happy she was to have a niece because she never had children of her own. Though our relationship has been entirely over the phone, being in her arms now feels like home.

Elena pulls away from me and hands my bags to a man who I didn't realize was standing just behind her. "This is Ricardo. He works at the restaurant with me." She hands my suitcase to the older man, who has a thick mustache and severe brow, and he leads us out of the airport. I step out into a sticky, high-eighties day that instantly matts my black *Alice in Chains* shirt to my skin. I close my eyes and tilt my head up at the sun, letting the rays filter through my closed lids.

I'm home.

## 3 MONTHS LATER

I SETTLED into my new life quite quickly. Elena has fostered a great family out of her staff at *Mariscos Elena*, her seafood restaurant, and they welcomed me with open arms.

It's different, feeling so wanted and free at the same time. I don't have to worry about what will happen if I get pulled over or need to go to the emergency room. No matter what, I'm going to be okay.

And it's so damned freeing.

It's hard to believe that my life has almost become routine now. I spend most of my time at the restaurant. On my few days off, I try to slowly decorate the small but charming two-bedroom bungalow I bought for myself. Sometimes I sit at the beach and watch the waves roll. I even have a therapist who is helping me through my depression. In so many ways, my life feels like it should . . . in so many ways except *one*.

But I try to avoid thinking of that—something my therapist insists is unhealthy, but he has agreed we can tackle one demon at a time, so he's let it go for now.

I've made new friends too. Fernanda, for one, whom I'd met briefly via video calls when I was still in Kansas City. She's the quietest woman, with the most angry-looking face in its resting state I have ever seen. But her heart is also as big as the chip on her shoulder. With hot pink hair and a nose ring Elena keeps asking her to remove before work. But Fernanda refuses; she marches to the rhythm of her own drum.

Then there's Mariela, second in command in the kitchen after Ricardo. Her love for cooking almost rivals my love for music. She makes the best shrimp *ceviche* and *pescado a la talla* on the entire coast—I'm sure of it. Though I'm not as close to her as I am with Fernanda, I know we will be . . . in time.

Fernanda is hard to crack, so I focus on her first, but when she finally lets me in, I know we'll be friends for life. It's like she picks people, and she's selective of who she will let in her heart, but when she does, that heart will cherish you forever with a fierce loyalty that almost makes me weep.

Not like my high school friends who moved on and all but forgot about me. Somehow, in the deepest part of myself, I know that even if we end up with a distance between us, Fernanda and I will remain friends.

We bonded over our life stories a month after I arrived,

laughing through the pain over a bottle of mescal and *Chavela Vargas* tunes.

I told her all about my life in Kansas City, carefully leaving out any mentions of a certain perfect blond man I try not to think about—and given she's a huge *Industrial November* fan, she probably wouldn't have believed me anyway. She hugged me when I told her about my parents, and we drank to their memories together.

And she told me about her life too. Her parents aren't dead, but according to them, Fernanda is dead to them. They kicked her out of her house at seventeen when they found her in bed with her girlfriend. At the time, she was working part-time with Elena, and my beautiful, nurturing *tía* took this discarded girl and gave her a home.

Ever since, Fernanda has worked full time at the restaurant, and when she saved enough, she got herself into a small apartment. I'm trying to convince her to become my roommate, but she keeps saying she loves living alone—at least for now.

But I hold out hope she'll move in with me because the truth is, I'm pretty damn lonely without Ileana and Isael everywhere like I'd become accustomed to.

We've gotten to know each other well—or I thought we had, which is why when I head into the back of the restaurant to drop off dishes and I catch her singing, I am floored.

Her voice is phenomenal.

"Fernanda!"

She jumps and spins on her heel to smile wide at me. "What?"

"You can sing?"

She shrugs.

"Let me rephrase that. You can *sing*."

She laughs. "Yeah, I like to sing. You know, just while I'm working, or around the house. For fun . . ." She trails off, and she looks at me with her head tilting to the side. "Why are you looking at me like that?" she asks.

"Like what?"

"Like a *paleta de hielo* in a desert."

I grin wide at her. "We're starting a band," I say.

"What?"

No one at the restaurant knows about my secret guitar playing.

When I first got here, I cut my hair to shoulder-length and dyed it a warm shade of brown. That was enough to not be recognized from the press storm that haunted me in Kansas City.

And perhaps it was too painful to play. But sometimes, late at night, when I can't sleep because I'm thinking about Karl and Pixel and how much I miss them, I'll pull out the guitar and practice into the early morning hours, howling at the vanishing moon.

If I'm honest, I've become quite good, and I know I'll do my former teacher proud one day.

"We're starting a band," I repeat.

"I don't like *banda* music," Fernanda says.

I laugh. "Not that kind of band. We're starting a heavy metal band, and *you* are going to be the lead singer."

Fernanda stares at me for a long moment, blinking like she's deciding if I am serious. Then she shrugs and says, "Okay."

"Okay?"

"Yeah. All right. I'll sing in your band."

"Well, first we have to find drums and bass. I got guitar covered."

"*Chido,*" is all she says and heads back to work.

THE SPRING BREAKERS are slowly starting to trickle into the city, and I'm excited about the extra business.

I sank most of my savings into a down payment for the house. Luckily, business is great since Elena's restaurant is in a great location with ocean views. Otherwise, we'd never be able to afford the prices in this neighborhood now.

I didn't realize, when I was growing up, that Mom used to send her money to Elena, to help her set up this business. Elena is thrilled for me to take over when she decides to retire. In her mind, it's all a perfect circle.

I'm behind the bar, mixing a drink for a customer, when I hear a voice I haven't heard in months.

"Hi, Lo," he says, and my shoulder blades instantly tighten.

I spin on my heel to confirm the voice belongs to him, and it's not my imagination.

# 33

# LOLA

"Ethan?"

Ethan grins wide at me. "Hi, Lo. How are you?"

My brows pinch together as I remember our last conversation at the grocery store. "Busy," I say and keep mixing drinks.

"Come on, Lo. Don't be like that. We were friends once. Remember that?"

I turn around to face him again. "Yeah. I remember that, Ethan," I hiss. "That friendship died when you decided to cheat on me and then lie about it."

No doubt seeing murder on my face, Fernanda joins me behind the bar. "Who's this?" she asks.

"Ethan," I say.

Fernanda knows all about Ethan, and she raises a brow at him, her hand going to her hip. "What do you want?" she asks him in a tone so cold, it's clear he's unwelcome, but Ethan keeps looking only at me.

"To talk to Lola. And apologize. I owe you that much, don't you think? Please, Lo?" he pleads and throws me those signature puppy eyes of his. "Just give me five minutes."

I roll my eyes and hand Fernanda the *michelada* I just made. "Take this to table seven? Then take over? I'm taking five."

"You got it, boss," she says.

"For the millionth time, I'm not your boss," I call after her, and she throws me a wave as she walks away.

"Come on," I say to the jerk in front of me. I don't want anyone to hear our conversation. I toe off my shoes and let them dangle from my fingers as we walk down the beach.

I snort.

"What?" Ethan asks.

"I used to daydream about this—us walking down the beach together. But it was so . . . different."

"Lola, I'm so, so, sorry. Breaking up with you was the dumbest thing I ever did."

"You didn't," I say.

"What?"

"You didn't break up with me. I found out you were with Megan, and it just ended."

"Right." He pauses to scratch the back of his head. "Well, she was not you. I didn't feel for her what I do for you. Not even close. I still love you, Lola."

"I don't love you," I say honestly. "Not anymore. But I did once if that makes you feel better."

"It doesn't." He pauses to scratch the back of his neck. "I get the feeling you'll always be the one that got away." He sighs deeply. "Will you at least consider forgiving me?"

The thing is, I'm not as angry with Ethan as I thought I'd be. I'm so beyond caring, it isn't funny. My heart is now broken over a different man, a man I didn't realize I was in love with until it was too late for us. But it doesn't matter because that man never loved me, even if he once said he did.

But Ethan—he was my rock once. He held me while I cried at the funeral, brought me food for weeks, and made sure I showered and ate when I couldn't function. He saw me through the worst of it. I can't hold this grudge if only for the respect I owe the friendship we once had.

"Yeah, Ethan. I forgive you," I say honestly. "Now, let's start heading back."

"Thank you, Lola," he says.

The restaurant is at a lull when we get back, and I ask Fernanda to join us as we sit, drinking *aguas frescas*. Having her at the table feels less intimate, more like friends chatting. I stir my straw in the glass as I catch up with Ethan and everything he's been up to since I last saw him.

"So, what are you ladies doing tomorrow night?" Ethan asks.

---

I LOOK at myself in the mirror and can hardly recognize the woman looking back. I'm not used to being a brunette yet.

"You look hot," Fernanda says from her spot on the bed. She came over with a few options to let me borrow an outfit since I don't have many pieces in my wardrobe appropriate for nightlife.

"Thanks," I say, pulling down the short cream-colored miniskirt. "And thanks for coming out with us tonight. I don't want Ethan to think it's a date."

"I know," Fernanda says, running her fingers through her hot-pink locks.

"Are you sure this isn't too revealing?" I ask for the second time. The miniskirt she's let me borrow is more like minuscule, and my fuller hips and rear are testing the skirt's limits. To go with the skirt, Fernanda has lent me a gold sequined halter top that leaves my back completely bare.

"Just enough for the club we're going to," she says.

"You look killer too, by the way." Her strapless deep-blue dress fits her like a glove.

We meet up with Ethan at the dance club, a mid-scale venue

next to the water that Fernanda insists has a good vibe, and if we get tired of dancing, we can always bail to the boardwalk.

Ethan's mouth hangs open when he takes me in, and his gaze rakes my body from the top of my head down to my toes. "You look great," he nearly screams in my ear over the thumping bass while he hugs me hello.

"Thank you," I yell back, pulling away from his embrace. Despite how dark it is, I can tell his eyes are hooded with arousal, but I pretend not to see it. We're just friends now.

And I'm determined to enjoy myself. To let loose a little, for once. I've worked so hard to learn the ropes of running the business with Elena, to move into my new place, to work on myself with my therapist, picking up yoga at the insistence of my therapist to do something physical. After all that, I've earned a little fun.

Ethan comes back with drinks for Fernanda and me, and to my delight, he doesn't only focus on me. He asks Fernanda to dance first, and she drags me to the dance floor with them.

One tequila shot.

Two tequila shots.

Three tequila shots.

And the roaring night envelops us in its clutches. Fernanda and me sandwiching Ethan on the dance floor, and when he gets tired, just me and her dancing together—him watching from his spot at our table.

I surprise myself, actually having careless fun for the first time since I've come home to Mexico.

# 34

# LOLA

We're never going dancing again, I vow in silent prayer to the hangover gods. I swear if this sickness lifts, I'll never go dancing again.

Fernanda's head is resting over the bar top, and she's holding a bag of ice to her temple. "Why did we drink so much tequila," she groans, "when we knew we had to work today?"

"Shhh," I say. "Don't yell."

She groans again, but I think it's meant to be a laugh.

We aren't open yet, and Ricardo, our main chef, is in the kitchen prepping for tonight. I swear he's banging pots louder than usual, making me wince.

Elena comes out to the lobby and finds us clinging to the bar. Her hands fly to her hips. "Will you look at this?" she asks in mock scorn. One eyebrow is raised, but I know she's biting back her smile.

"*Tía*, please," I beg. "We feel bad enough as it is."

"Right," she says and gets to work mixing some drinks. "I remember what it was like to be young."

My stomach churns when she sets the *micheladas* in front of us. "You're not serious."

"Very much so. If you two are going to be functional by lunch, we need to get you out of this hangover—"

"And your solution is more beer—" Before I finish my question, Fernanda is chugging her *michelada* until she's drained the glass.

She sets the glass down with an exaggerated belch. "She's right," Fernanda says. "Only beer will get us out of this one. And drink lots of water too."

I try not to look at the red liquid because I don't want to vomit, but I use a straw to drain my own glass.

And surprisingly, it mostly works.

Ethan mentioned last night he would stop by later in the week before he flies back to California, but honestly, I'm not holding my breath. Not after he tried kissing me goodnight, and I turned to offer my cheek instead of my lips. I don't think the night went quite how he had hoped, but probably better than he expected. We said our goodbyes last night, and it feels like we finally have closure.

As I watched him walk away from me, all the resentment in my heart lifted. I wish him nothing but the best, but I don't need to see him again. I doubt he'll come by again.

That chapter of my life is over. Finally.

Unlike this hangover.

---

THE REST of spring break week is utterly exhausting, and we constantly have a line around the block. I blame Mariela's food. I swear she casts love spells in each dish.

We make a killing, but my feet are sore and blistered. I don't remember being this exhausted, even when I used to clean houses for a living—something that now seems like a lifetime ago. So Elena and I make the executive decision to close the following Monday to give all of us a much-needed break.

I take the opportunity to go to the beach on a low-crowd day and catch some sun. Elena likes to joke that I came here looking like a ghost, and I tried explaining the Midwest winter, but it went in one ear and out the other.

I'm pretty ecstatic to get a little bit of a tan, to be honest.

As I sit on my towel, watching the waves reach the shore and retreat over and over, I let my mind wander. I hate that I think about him still, but I do. How are Karl and Pixel? Do they think of me like I do of them?

It shouldn't matter, but I can't shake the thoughts away.

And I finally understand what some people say about love and music. When you're in love, or in my case, heartbroken, every song, every painting, every sculpture, every classic novel, every poem is about you in that vulnerable moment.

And I see him everywhere.

I'll sit here, watching vacationers walk by, and if I peek a strand of loose blond hair on a tall man, I perk up, imagining it's him, but it never is.

Like a mirage deployed by my broken heart.

On my way to the bus stop to go home, I stop halfway down the boardwalk at a small shop I haven't noticed before. It is tiny, and the windows are painted black, but there's a fantastic painting on the sign above the door. It is a woman, her face painted like a skeleton, and she's swallowing the stars straight out of the sky. The sign under the spectacular painting reads *M y M*. I'm not sure why, maybe because it gives me rock and roll vibes, but I feel drawn to the little shop, so I open the door and step inside as the doorbell rings above me, announcing my arrival.

A woman greets me with a welcoming grin. "Hi. I'm Mitzy. How can I help you?"

# KARL

I haven't touched my guitar since she left and instead limit myself to writing songs. Bren's ongoing paternity leave and the band being stalled temporarily helps in my avoidance of the instrument. Instead, I limit myself to writing page after page of songs about her.

It started off as a joke.

I told myself I'd do what Bren did when he broke it off with Sofia before they finally got back together. And I understand the allure of it now.

Keeping the mind occupied with words, with ink on paper, is better than wallowing, motionless and useless. It's better than being stagnant, and waiting for . . . for what? For the heartbreak to one day magically disappear?

Because it won't. The hurt of her not loving me back will not lift its crushing weight, so instead, I harness that pain and put it into words.

Some of the songs are sweet little memories.

Some are accusatory and regretful.

But they are all true.

I'm not surprised when Bren shows up unannounced. He

still has access to the penthouse, and I have to remind myself to revoke it. But I can't begrudge him. After all, this is what I did to him when he was feeling this low. Showed up unannounced. Though, to be perfectly honest, I do think he was way more melodramatic. At least I function. And bathe. I shudder, remembering what he looked like that day I showed up at his country house in Germany.

Bren hands me a beer.

"Can I read some of those?" He points at the pieces of paper on the coffee table.

"Have at it," I say, not caring at all what he might think of them.

"This one's good," he says after a moment. He sips his beer.

"Which one?"

He hands me a single piece of paper. "Pain in my Ass," he says.

I smirk. Lola sure as hell is a pain in my ass. "I like that one too."

"Mind if we record it on the next album?"

I blink at him. Is this man serious? "No," I say casually. "I haven't written the music to go along with it."

"We're not recording for a year at least. You have time."

He hands me the piece of paper and stands to leave. "Good work, man. Keep it coming."

I stare at the elevator doors long after he's gone. I think Brenner Reindhart just paid me a compliment.

---

I KNEEL by the bed and take a deep breath. Pixel is staring at me like I'm crazy. Three months without playing guitar—the longest I've ever gone since I touched one for the first time.

It reminds me too much of her, and it is too painful. But I

need to start writing music to go along with the pile of lyrics, or I won't have anything to show Bren when he asks again.

"Here goes nothing," I breathe out and slide the guitar case from under the bed. I set it on the bed and unclasp it—only, when I open it, the blue dragon is gone.

I feel every drop of blood drain from my face. In its place is Lola's pink guitar.

"What the fuck?"

Then I laugh. Bitterly. Because of course she fucking would. It wasn't enough that she wanted to use me without loving me, or that she left like a thief in the night—my heart and guitar in her bag of spoils . . .

Only, she isn't a thief. She didn't even wait to be paid for her time under my employ.

Seeing the guitar brings back all those horrible memories from that night.

Finding both her and Pixel gone, thinking for one horrid second that she had even taken my dog.

Chase showed up right after me with Pixel, and I calmed down, but even though she didn't take my dog, she took my guitar.

The one I told her was precious and priceless.

*How much more does she intend to hurt me?* I think bitterly.

Then I see it, the envelope near the base of the guitar, with shitty penmanship in a chicken-scratch that reads, "Karl."

I swept the apartment that first night for a note when she didn't pick up her phone. She didn't even tell Sofia or Ileana she was leaving. They heard it from me, and they were both devastated they didn't get to say goodbye. Lola broke more than just *my* heart when she left.

And I damned Lola, damned her for blazing like a wrecking ball through all our lives, hurting every last person she left behind. Isael and Addy would have been devastated too, if they'd been old enough to understand.

It wasn't until a week later that Sofia called to say she'd heard from Lola. She had a new number that Sofia was asked to not share with me, of course—and that she was fine.

Well, at least she was okay.

But I wasn't.

I was devastated. Still am.

I grab a bottle of Vodka from the bar and sip from the bottle, staring at the sealed envelope.

Several long gulps of bitter alcohol later, I rip the envelope open, take a deep breath, and read.

---

Karl,

I can't begin to tell you how sorry I am for the way I acted.

Please forgive me for pushing myself on you. I didn't realize exactly how . . . unwelcome my advances were. It seemed like a game at the start, you know? I thought you enjoyed yourself those few times when you seemed to be letting go. In my room, and then in L.A.

I'm not sure what happened that you let yourself do those things with me, but I realize now that it wasn't what you wanted, and I'll always be sorry for treating you that way.

I'm always overstaying my welcome, aren't I? With Ethan, in this country. I even left Ileana's before I'd overstay my welcome there, only to overstay it with you.

I'm a slow learner, but I'm trying.

Now I'm going somewhere I think I'm wanted. I hope that's true this time and that I'm not wrong again—not like I was with you.

I've taken your blue dragon because I know it's a piece of your heart, and selfishly, I want that with me. Because that's the

thing, Karl, I think I've been falling in love with you for a long
time. I was guarded for obvious reasons, but if I can't have your
whole heart, then I'm stealing this small bit.

In exchange, I leave you my whole heart. Half of it in this
guitar you gave me that I love so much—the other half in Pixel
because that dog stole my heart the first day I met her. Hug her
for me, will you? And remind her every day that even if I'm not
there with her, I'll always love her.

Oh, and give her peanut butter treats, so she won't
forget me.

Goodbye, Karl.

Love,

Lola

FUCK, Iggy. I sniff back the building tears before they escape.
Why couldn't you just say it? Why couldn't you realize you
loved me in time?

I take the letter to bed with me to sleep off the Vodka.
Tomorrow morning, I'm getting on a plane.

Only before I get to, Roger shows up with Matt on his
heels. Chase has already picked up Pixel, and I'm almost
done getting ready to leave when they arrive.

"What's going on?" I ask, surprised to see Roger.

"I need to show you something, and when I do, I need you
to not freak out and do something stupid."

"What are you talking about?"

Roger looks at the ceiling and takes a deep breath. "Don't
make me regret showing you, Karl," he warns.

Then he hands me his phone, and I take it, my brow
furrowed with confusion.

"What is this?" I ask as I stare at a somewhat blurry photo
that was taken in some club. Two people are dancing in the

frame, and it's hard to make out the faces until I zoom in, and it's Ethan.

My teeth grind together. I zoom out again, paying close attention to the rest of the photo, to the woman whose back is pressed against his chest, dancing. His hand is on her naked waist, revealed by a small strip of fabric that could hardly pass for a top.

She's a brunette, all smiles and having fun, enjoying herself. It would mean nothing—except for those deep green eyes I'd know anywhere. I zoom in on her face this time, and as sure as my name is Karl Sommer, the woman dancing with Ethan, grinding her backside to him, is Lola Beltran.

"Fritz has the jet ready. He and Matt are going with you—"

"I don't need babysitters," I seethe.

"It's them or me," Roger says coolly, giving me the choice.

"Fine." I push past him, and Matt and I head to the airport downtown.

How could she get back together with him after telling me she was falling in love with me? *She thinks I don't want her*, I think, answering my own stupid question.

What did I tell Ethan that day at the grocery store? You leave a girl that beautiful alone that long, you can't expect her to not be taken when you get back?

Only this time, I'm the idiot who pushed her away.

The thing is, we're the same. Both of us so damaged we couldn't believe we deserved the others' love. But we did love. *Both* of us.

And it's not too late. Not even if Ethan is back, because the minute I see him, I'm going to punch his pretty little white teeth out and reclaim what's mine.

Because, make no mistake, Lola Beltran is, and always will be, *mine*.

# LOLA

Fernanda, Ricardo, Mariela, and Elena are all staring at me, faces harsh. I'm sitting on a barstool, and it's after closing. They said they had to talk to me, but the way they're standing in front of me, severe expressions, afraid to speak, makes me think this is an intervention.

"Well?" I ask. It's been a long shift, and I'm exhausted. All I want to do is go home and crash on my bed. Finally, I have a day off tomorrow, and I plan on going to the beach after sleeping in all morning.

"Is there anything you want to tell us?" Elena asks first.

"Um, no? What's this about?" I ask, a bit annoyed, a bit amused.

Elena and Ricardo exchange looks. Fernanda looks more bored than anything, and I know Elena asked her to stay. She's not that interested in . . . whatever this is. Mariela, on the other hand, regards me with soft, empathetic eyes.

"Is it drugs?" Elena asks.

I laugh, eyes wide and alert now. "What?"

"It's not funny," Elena says, all serious.

"I'm not on drugs, *tía*. What on earth are you talking about?"

"You've been going off on these 'appointments' as you call them, the last several weeks. No one knows where you're off to when you take off, and you act really suspicious."

"I'm not doing drugs," I say.

"You're not going off to score?"

"¡*Tía*! No!" I laugh.

"Then, what is it?"

"I love you for caring about me, but some things need to stay private. This is just for me. It's nothing illegal, or that would put me in danger, I swear."

She eyes me warily, not convinced, but finally nods. "Okay. I'm going to trust you."

I stand to hug her and look over at Ricardo. He shrugs, and I can tell he was dragged into this as well—but he'll do anything for Elena.

Over the last several weeks, I've come to realize that Ricardo is in love with my aunt, and my poor aunt is entirely oblivious. It's cute, but I also feel a little sad for him in his unrequited love. If he's here tonight to support Elena, it's because he loves her. I smile weakly at him before he and Fernanda leave us.

"I promise, *tía*, it's not drugs."

And while it's true that it's nothing illegal or that would harm me, I also know she would disapprove. Especially given how I know she feels about Fernanda's nose piercing. I'll keep my appointments with Mitzy a secret from my aunt as long as I can.

---

"Do you think Elena knows Ricardo is in love with her?" I ask Fernanda as we wait for our turn at open mic night at a local gay bar she loves. I'm trying to distract myself from my nerves.

Fernanda snorts. "She is oblivious."

"You think she loves him?"

Fernanda shakes her head. "No. I don't think so."

"How long?" I ask.

"I've worked for Elena since I was seventeen, so three years now. That entire time, he's been head over heels."

"Neither of them have dated or anything in that time?"

She shakes her head again.

It's easier to distract myself with my aunt's love life than it is to dwell on the fact that I'm about to step on the first stage of my life. As confident a player as I've become in the last few months, I've never played in front of a room full of strangers.

Since it's just a duo, for now, I had to get my hands on an acoustic guitar, and Karl was right; it's a little more challenging to play with the thicker strings. It took some getting used to, and I'm not as confident as I am on electric, but I remind myself it's only temporary until we find our bass and drums.

We've peppered every vertical surface down Acapulco's coast with flyers looking for our bandmates, but no one worth noting has popped up yet. So, we decided to play just us two to get going and get used to the eyeballs.

Fernanda's English carries a strong accent, but surprisingly, she sings it very clearly. We're sticking to performing covers tonight, not yet confident in the original songs we've come up with together.

Fernanda is a surprisingly skilled lyricist, but we still only have drafts.

"Hey," I whisper. "Be cool, but check out the guy at the end of the bar."

Fernanda spins around, not at all chill, and I have to laugh. "Way to look under the radar."

The guy smiles at her. "He's been checking you out this whole time," I tell her.

"Really?" she asks. "He's kind of cute, isn't he?"

"He sure is. But come on, I need you to focus. After our set, you can go chat with him."

"Yeah, that doesn't at all make me feel nervous," she says dryly, and we both bust out laughing.

She sings a cover of "Broken Heart of Gold" by *One okay Rock* in that deep and husky voice that is so seductive, it still sends shivers down my arms. If we can find the right band, Fernanda and I could go places. I just know it.

The small size of the crowd eases my nerves, and I don't have the stage fright I imagined I would have. As for Fernanda, she is a natural on stage. Even with so few people, she has captivated her audience, taking them with her into the spell of her song.

As I strum the last chord of the song, I think about Karl. Wondering if he'd think I'm as ready as I think I am to take my playing public. Wondering if he'd be proud tonight.

Since we didn't get a prime spot, it's still early and I can still catch the sunset at the beach.

I ask Fernanda to join me, but she ditches me for the guy at the bar.

Figures.

I set my guitar case on the sand next to me, not daring to part with it enough to dip my feet in the ocean.

Karl is in my thoughts a lot tonight. I imagined him in the crowd as I played for the first time in front of people, imagining how wide he'd be grinning, how proud he'd be, how he'd call me Iggy all night. I let myself feel the nostalgia and feel sad at the memories.

It's something I'm working on with my therapist. He's helping me understand that it's okay to be sad sometimes, to feel hurt, and that, in fact, I need to let those feelings out instead of bottling them in. What's not okay is packing my bags and staying there.

So, I feel the pain of missing him, letting myself remember our date night when he took me to the *Ampersand* and *Paco's Tacos*. How he paid for Lucinda's treatment, and to this day, no one knows he did that except for him, Carolina, and me. I think fondly of Pixel too, missing her just as much as Karl and how she guarded and protected me.

Unsure why, I scan the beach on either side of me. I smile when I see a blond man walking toward me, and yet again, I imagine it's him, like I have so many times since I got home.

This man's hair is short. Buzz-cut at the sides, with longish waves mussed at the top. He's wearing jean shorts, a white t-shirt, and his sneakers dangle from his neck where he has tied the laces to walk barefoot. But his gait is familiar, somehow, just like Karl's. But it's not him. He wouldn't be here.

I look back out into the rolling waves, wishing I could dip my feet in when I see from my peripheral vision the figure standing over me. He sits next to me, and I don't have to see his face up close to know it *is* him after all. It's the smell of him—of his aftershave mixed with his pheromones—that gives him away.

It *is* Karl. In the flesh—not my imagination.

Karl with shorter hair, but still Karl. He sets his shoes down on the other side of him. My heart hammers straight out of my chest.

Wordlessly, I let my head drop to his shoulder, and our hands lace together.

I'd say it's a dream, but it isn't. He's here. Here with me.

I smile, letting myself enjoy this small moment.

"I've missed you," he whispers.

"You're here." I choke on my voice and can't keep the tears from springing up.

"I didn't see your note, Lo, I—I would have come sooner."

"You're here now."

We watch the sunset for several minutes, letting ourselves believe we're together in this moment, sharing this same space.

"I always wanted you," he says after a long moment of us just sitting there.

"Don't lie to me," I say. "My *friend* wouldn't lie to me."

"I'm not lying to you. I wanted you then, and I still want you —if you'll have me."

"Then why did you push me away?"

"I didn't think I was good enough for you," he admits easily. Too easy for my comfort. "And because I knew you didn't love me back. Not back then."

"Karl, I—"

"Shhh. I know, doll. I know you had feelings for me."

"And you turned down sex because . . .?"

"I really wanted you to love me back before we took that step. I'll admit, I was giving in that last time, but then you said . . . you said you wanted someone with experience."

We're still not looking at each other, and somehow, I think we're both afraid to look in the others' eyes, to confirm what's there. We're both afraid of the same thing, I realize. He's afraid I no longer want him, I'm afraid he no longer wants me—we're both insecure about a love I'm certain we both feel and should be confident in, but for some reason, we can't be.

Our faith is shaken.

So we keep on in our position next to each other, and I nod, shifting a bit over his shoulder. "Right," I say, trying to remember what I said to him before he pushed me off him that last night.

"I don't have it," he says.

"What?" I ask, confused.

"Experience."

That's when I lift my head off his shoulder and turn to look at him.

His eyes are soft, if a bit downcast, a sad smile forming over his sculpted lips.

"What?" I ask again, confused.

He sighs, and runs his hands over his hair, missing the long strands he used to pull on when he was frustrated. "You want a man with experience, you said. And that's not me, Lola. I've never had intercourse."

# 37

# LOLA

My instinct is to laugh at the ridiculous notion. The man hailed as the sexiest by any publication that curates such lists, coveted bachelor, rock god/sex god as proclaimed by all the tabloids. All the pictures of him with women.

At parties.

All orchestrated by Roger.

Staged.

It was all staged.

The women too?

I can't laugh because his face is so serious; I know he's not lying. "You're a virgin?" I say more to myself than to him.

He laughs. He's facing me now, and he draws one index finger from the bridge to the tip of my nose. "I don't think of myself as a virgin because I've done other stuff . . . it's just that intercourse, um—well, it was a line I could never cross with anyone." He pauses, cupping the back of his neck, his other arm now wrapped around his knees. "I'm not the sex god our P.R. team proclaims me to be. Most of that is Roger playing up my image for press purposes."

"Oh." I don't know what to say. "But the rumors—"

He laughs. "The only truth to those rumors is the one about my tongue. There are worse things than having oral make up the biggest part of your sex life."

Heat creeps up my neck and settles on my cheeks. I can certainly attest to that. All the times Karl ate me out were unlike anything in this world.

"But you had Sandy, and that redhead who showed up . . ."

He's shaking his head before I finish my thought. "Ah, Sandy, she was there to . . . relieve some of the pressure, but I didn't have intercourse with her. As for Scarlet, I just needed you to stop coming on to me. I thought it'd push you away to hear us, but we didn't do anything of a sexual nature. I swear."

Only one word comes to mind at his revelations. "Why?"

"Why what?"

"Why haven't you had sex if you've done everything else?"

"You sure you want to hear all the details?"

I nod.

"Fine. You once accused me of being a romantic, remember?"

"Yeah."

"Maybe that's it."

"Is it?"

Karl circles his finger on the top of my hand. "No. I mean, I am a little. By the time I made it, when I joined the band, and all the women were flinging themselves at me . . . they didn't want *me*. You understand?"

I shake my head.

"Every one of them wanted something, but not a one had feelings for me. They went to bed with me for bragging rights, to be photographed with me, or expecting expensive gifts and dinners. When I got my sign-on check, the first thing I did was invest in an apartment and a sports car. I'd watch how their eyes sparkled when they saw the swanky place and expensive car, but they wouldn't light up like that when they looked at *me*. That . . . hurt. And the ones who were in it purely for my body, they were after what you were after. The legend of the sex god, but no interest in me as a person. Make sense?"

"Oh, Karl," I say and squeeze his arm tightly to me. "I'm so sorry. I never meant to make you feel that way."

"I know, doll." He kisses the top of my head. "But that's why I wanted you to love the first person you slept with. I know first-hand what an empty feeling it is to wake up in the morning, not caring one iota for the person next to you. I was looking for the one, my girl, but every time I woke up with a stranger, I disappointed myself just a little bit more. Even if we weren't having intercourse, we were doing everything else, and I still felt empty. So I promised myself I'd keep waiting, to find the one woman who could truly love me back, the way I wanted to love her."

"But the press continued to publish stories about your sexcapades," I argue, trying to fit the pieces together.

"Ah, that. That's all Roger. Most of us in the band don't care what he does with our public image. Whatever he's doing is working to keep people interested in us, so we let him say what he wants."

Then it finally clicks. He never slept with the redhead. With Scarlett. He hasn't been with anyone since we've known each other. The thought makes me smile more than I'd like to admit. And then it fades. Has he been with anyone since I left?

"So just to be clear, nothing happened with Scarlett?"

"You heard us pretending. I wanted to get you to stop trying to tempt me because I couldn't take one more day without being inside of you, and I knew I'd be weak if you kept it up. But it's all I thought about, Lola. Taking you. Everything—anything you wanted to give me. Selfishly, I wanted it all."

"Oh," I say, and I am at a loss for words for a long moment.

I let my head fall to his shoulder again as I process this information, and this time, his cheek rests on top of my head tenderly, our bodies huddled closely together. This moment is far more intimate than any we have shared so far, and we're fully clothed.

"Have you been with anyone since, since . . ." I say finally.

I feel him shake his head. "No. I've kept that promise I made myself."

"You have?"

"Yes," he says, his voice a little weak. "I love you, Lola. I don't think I deserve you, but I know I can't be happy without you, so I'll be a selfish asshole if it means I can keep you, even when I know you can do better."

"Why do you keep saying that, that I deserve better?" I force him to look me in the eye now. "Karl Sommer"—I take his face in my hands—"you are a good man. Kind and generous. I know you're fucked up about it, and you won't believe me, but trust me, there's no one better than you."

He smiles at me, letting his forehead drop to mine, cupping my hand in his and pressing it to his chest.

"And I love you," I say finally. "More than you could ever know. I'm in love with you."

With that tender promise of love, I lean in to press a gentle kiss to his lips.

"I've missed you, doll," he says between kisses, taking my lips slowly, gently.

We're both so gentle, like we're both afraid we're imagining this and the spell will be broken, leaving us alone again in different parts of the world.

So I grip the fabric of his shirt, feeling it under my fingers. Real.

His hard muscles underneath. Real.

His hot breath on my mouth. Real.

He's here, and he's *real*.

We kiss, and we kiss for the longest time against the sunset backdrop of Acapulco Bay, the last rays still warming our skin.

When we finally break away, he brushes my hair from my forehead. "You look good as a brunette," he says, smiling.

"Thank you." I stop and think for a moment. "Um, Karl? How did you find me?"

"Sofia. Then I went to your restaurant, and your aunt told me where I might find you."

"Oh."

"Can I ask about Ethan?" he says.

"What about him?"

"I saw you together. Dancing."

"What?" I ask with panic. *Has he been following me?*

"Someone recognized you and took a picture. It was so blurry they only managed to get it in this one obscure tabloid, but Roger has his ways."

"Ah, well, yeah. He was here. And we did bury the hatchet. He left more amicably than last time, and you know, I'm glad he was here. I didn't like all the resentment I was carrying. But no, he's not back. Doubt I'll ever see him again."

"So nothing happened?" he asks.

I shake my head, smiling at his jealousy. "No, I promise."

"Thank fuck." He stands and shakes off the sand from his legs, then stretches his hand out to help me up. "I rented a house on the water. Would you like to join me?" he asks, his mischievous smile heating my very center.

My heart hammers in my chest. This is it. It's finally happening. My first night on stage in more ways than one. I gulp nervously now, but I nod and take his hand to lead me wherever he wants to.

# 38

# KARL

Lola's eyes light up when she takes in the villa and our master suite.

"You were this sure of yourself?" she asks teasingly, one brow raised as she peruses the room.

Before I left, I asked the house staff to set a romantic ambiance. The sheer white curtains around the four-poster bed are no longer tied and flow freely around the bed. The room is only lit by candlelight. They went so far as to scatter flower petals leading to the bed. The French doors open to the private beach, the ocean breeze and sounds reaching the room.

Under candlelight, Lola's skin glows golden from the tan she's gained the last several months in this coastal town. With her shorter darker hair, her features seem less soft and more angular. She carries herself more confidently too, even though it's only been a few months.

She's different . . . in so many ways.

She goes over to the window to take in the view, and I come up behind her. "You're different." I whisper my thoughts as I wrap my arms around her waist.

She nods. "I'm . . . better," she says. "I've let go of a lot, and I think that's opened up a lot of room in my heart."

"Room to love me," I say, and it's not a question.

"I've always loved you. I just . . . wasn't ready for that kind of intensity."

"It wasn't that long ago." I turn her around to kiss the corner of her mouth. "Are you sure you're ready for it now?"

My mouth trails down her jaw and her neck, pulling a soft whimper out of her. "I'm sure I'm in love with you, ready or not," she says, and I bite her neck in appreciation of her words that, though playful, are full of meaning.

"It doesn't have to be tonight if you're not ready, doll. When I finally make love to you, I want you to be ready—"

"I've been ready. For you. Please don't make me wait anymore."

"Fuck, doll," I breathe out. "Do you know how hot those words are?"

"Please, Karl. I need you. I need to feel you inside me, more than anything. I've needed you for so long. I'm aching for you, baby."

I peel off her black tank top, revealing a black bra. After pushing her hair over to one side, I lick the length of her neck. "You taste just how I remember," I whisper in her ear.

I unclasp her bra and bring her tighter to my chest, sneaking a hand to pinch a nipple, and feel her suck in a breath.

She hurries to help me out of my shirt, and her eyes widen when she glimpses my left inner bicep.

"Karl," she gasps, holding my arm out. "You didn't!"

I kiss her with open lips and taste her sweet tongue. Watermelon bubblegum—just how I remember her tasting. The flavor is familiar yet somehow exciting and oh so erotic.

Her fingers trace the new tattoo on my arm, her face inches from it now as she studies the shape of the green peanut butter jar with the letter 'I' on it. A perfect replica of her Christmas gift to me.

When she frees her grip on my arm and lets me rest it, her eyes are glassy. "When?" she asks.

"The day after you left."

"You said you were saving that for someone special."

"For you, doll. I was saving it for the woman I'd fall in love with one day. And I'd fallen in love with you."

"Even after I left you?"

"Even then."

"Take my pants off," she says, and I chuckle. "Just do it," she says again.

I kneel before her, trailing kisses from her belly button down to the waistband of her jeans. I undo her zipper, and when I yank the denim fabric down, my eyes turn glassy to match hers.

"Lola," I breathe out with so much emotion, I almost choke on her name.

I tug her pants all the way down to her ankles to fully reveal the long tattoo that spans from the side of her waist, down her right hip, and nearly to her knee.

the intricate blue dragon wraps around her thigh in the curl of its tail. Its eyes are a blue uncannily close to my eye color. "When?" I ask her the same question.

She laughs a teary little chuckle. "It's huge; it took a while. Several sessions."

I nod, licking the dragon, top to bottom, enjoying the taste of her skin.

"The artwork is phenomenal," I say, studying it again.

She nods. "Kiss me," she says, pulling my head near the apex of her thighs. "We're not here to admire artwork. You can look at the tattoo later."

"You're the art, doll," I say and dive into her wet center.

I tuck her panties to the side with one finger, and my

tongue meets her swollen lips. My eyes draw closed in something a lot like reverence. She's dripping for me. With a tentative gentle lick, I let my tongue find its way inside, and Lola's hands find the back of my head, pulling me closer to her throbbing pussy.

I moan when my tongue finds her clit, and I tease it, licking circles around it, biting it gently. This, I'm good at. I'm more nervous about what's next, but at least I'm sure I can make her come like this.

I pull away from her for a moment, peering up at her as my index and forefinger part her lips wide for me, exposing her clit to the air. When her eyes find mine, I smile at her. "Be mine," I order between licks.

"I am yours," she whispers, her eyes full of emotion.

Another lick to her center. "I need you to be mine always."

Her hand runs through my hair tenderly, reassuringly. "I am yours, Karl."

I sigh my relief into her pussy, then come up for air again. "Marry me," I breathe out.

Lola's mouth falls open when she stares down at me, shocked. I take one of her lips in my mouth and suck on it, teasing her entrance with my fingers.

"Are you serious? You're proposing while you eat me out?" Her voice is shaky as she loses all composure.

"I'm proposing over the best feast of my life," I say, and dip my tongue between her folds again, tasting every hidden corner of her sex. "Marry me," I say into her cunt, just loud enough for her to hear, then swirl my tongue over her engorged clit.

She moans out, letting her head fall back, ignoring the question.

I pull back again to look up at her. "Marry me?" I repeat myself.

"Can we discuss this later?" she screams, and I chuckle

into her wetness again for a long moment. Maybe this *is* a bad time for a proposal.

Her legs shake in my palms, and I vaguely hear her screams of ecstasy as I let myself fall into some sort of trance where all I can do is enjoy the feel and taste of her body. But I only keep licking, enjoying, feeling her come on my tongue a second time.

"Karl, I need to sit or lie down," she says with alarm, and I open my eyes. How long have I been here, between her legs? I don't even know. That's how deep I've lost myself.

"I'm sorry, baby," I say and stand to lead her to the bed.

I come up and over her, now completely naked, and kiss her gently, letting her taste her own wetness on my mouth for the most erotic kiss of my life. She moans into my mouth, and she's driving me insane.

My cock is ready to explode, and I'm nowhere near being inside her yet. Just pressing it against her smooth stomach is almost enough to push me over the edge. It's throbbing so fucking hard, I need to squeeze it to relieve pressure, but I know that simple motion will push me over before I'm even inside her. "Lola, I'm sorry," I breathe out. "I don't think I'll last long."

"Me neither," she says a little shyly and claims my lips again, darting her tongue in my mouth, encouraging me to let myself go.

We break from our kiss, and I lean back to go grab a condom when she stops me.

"Where are you going?" she asks.

"Condom," I explain.

"I'm on the pill," she says hurriedly. "And I haven't . . . and you haven't . . ."

"You want to go bare?"

She nods sweetly at me, her mouth swollen and red from the long kisses at the beach and the hungrier ones when we got here. "I want to feel you. Your skin, inside me. I don't want a condom," she says, then adds, "if you're okay with that."

I fall back to my elbows and cup her face in my hands gently, my chest pressed to hers. "I'm more than okay with that."

With one last kiss, I lock eyes with her, positioning my tip at her entrance, ready to feed it to her. Her eyes widen a little with anticipation.

"It's okay, doll," I whisper. "We'll take it slow."

She nods. "Can I see?" she asks.

I pause. "What?" I ask, startled.

"I want to see you go in me for the first time."

"Fuck," I hiss, straining to keep my control. "That's the hottest thing I've ever heard."

I come up high on my hands to provide her with ample view, and she also lifts herself on her elbows, both of us staring at the place where we join.

I kiss her forehead. "I love you," I whisper, feeding her just half an inch of me.

Her breath quickens, her stomach quivering and tightening with anticipation.

"Doll, I need you to relax," I say. "Let me in."

She nods, still watching me slowly enter. Another inch of me, and I meet resistance. Her hands fist the bedsheets at her sides.

"Relax, baby. *Please*. I need you to open up for me. Open up for me, Lola."

Lola lets out a deep breath. "I love you too," she says and lets her muscles go languid.

I push in with one long stroke, and she loses the support on her arms, letting her back fall on the mattress. "Owww," she hisses, and I stay perfectly still inside her, my restraint at a breaking point.

Because I couldn't have ever imagined it would feel this good. My mind could never conjure up a feeling this perfect. I knew it would feel amazing, but not this earth-shatteringly mind-blowing. And somehow, I just know it wouldn't have been the same with anyone other than Lola. It had to be her —it was always meant to be her.

My first.

My true love.

And I've never been so glad I waited for her than in this moment. Being in love with the first person I've ever been inside of elevates the eroticism of the moment into a higher plane of ecstasy.

"Fuck." She breathes hard. "You're so fucking huge."

I keep circling her clit with my thumb until she relaxes a little around me. Finally, her hips buck, deepening our connection.

I kiss her and pull out completely, then come back home in one long, slow, deep thrust. She moans that time. "That felt good," she says and smiles up at me, encouraging me.

"Oh, thank fuck," I say and quicken my thrusts into a slightly faster tempo.

The wet sound of me easing in and out of her slowly fills the room around us, and it's the hottest thing I've ever heard. Both of Lola's hands are now cupping my ass, pulling me deeper in her. She's clenching now, either in pain or pleasure —or both—and I grind my teeth.

"You're going to wring the cum right out of me if you keep clenching like that," I growl near her ear and then suck her earlobe.

"Yes, please," she says with a soft moan, then clenches harder, pulling a primal growl out of me. "Karl, I need to feel you coming inside me. I need that hot liquid filling me up. I'm throbbing and aching for it. Please, baby. Fill me up."

"Fuck," I growl again at her words and quicken my thrusts.

I knew fucking Lola would be the hottest thing ever. I just didn't realize that making love to her would be even hotter.

As I come the hardest I've ever come in my life, she clenches around me, milking every last drop out of me to the point where I feel light-headed.

"Your pussy is magic," I whisper, not retreating from her body.

"So is your cock," she says and kisses me.

We stay like that, with me softening inside her, but I remain cocooned in her body—warm and protected like I'm finally home. Our combined arousal drips from our point of contact, but we stay like that, kissing and whispering our 'I love yous' over and over for long minutes.

Hottest fucking make-out session of my life. Several minutes pass like that, her face flushed and happy, our bodies slick with perspiration, until I start to harden inside her again at the feel of her all wet and soft beneath me.

"Oh, fuck" she hisses when she realizes what's happening.

I chuckle at how startled she looks and pick up the slow thrusts in her again, incrementally adding force. With each hard thrust, I push her up the bed, feeling free to be a little rougher now that her expressions are all of pleasure and none of pain.

I flip us over, so she's on top of me now. "Ride me," I order, and my sweet little sex doll smiles darkly down at me.

Her hips buck as she rides me, playing with different angles, learning, her weight supported with her hands on my chest.

Her breasts bounce with each undulation of her hips, and I sit up to take one into my mouth, sucking the hard point in my mouth.

Both her arms wrap tightly around my neck while she

keeps on riding, picking up the pace. "Fuck, Karl, I'm going to come again," she screams.

My back falls to the mattress, and I grip her waist tightly, holding her in place in the air, then savagely thrust into her in long punishing strokes. With piston pace, I push her up higher on her knees with each thrust, lifting her weight with my cock but slamming her down on it with my hands, my fingers digging into her skin.

The view is magnificent, my thrusts forcing her breasts to bounce, the dragon tattoo partially concealed under my palm, which looks massive over her waist. Her entire body, breasts, abdomen, shiny with perspiration. Something snaps inside me, and when I don't think I can thrust into her any harder, I do.

Her eyes roll to the back of her head at the same time her back arches—her entire body shuddering as I split her in two with a force I didn't know I had in me.

My fingers dig into her skin harder when a second orgasm rips through me, and I watch helplessly as she lifts a little, breaking contact, so she can watch as my cum drips out of her and down my shaft.

"Fuck," she moans out. "I'll never get tired of seeing that."

"Me neither," I admit, just before she collapses over my chest, gulping for air.

## LOLA

I keep tracing the tattoo on his bicep while we lay sated and fuck-drunk. "Wow," I say when my breathing slows down enough to allow for spoken words.

"Yeah," Karl says. "Wow."

"Did you imagine it'd be like that?" I ask, incredulous at the fire we started between our bodies.

"How could the human mind be capable of imagining something like that?" he says and kisses my temple.

"I wasn't bad at it then?" I ask.

Karl chuckles. "Not that I have anything to compare it to, but it was mind-blowing, doll. I swear."

My face falls. "Would you like to?"

"Would I like to what?"

"Have something to compare it to?"

He blinks at me, his head resting on his arm. "Fuck no, Lola. Come here." He scoots me closer to his body until my naked breasts press to his chest. He kisses me once so gently, there is nothing erotic about it. It's more tenderness than anything. "If I waited this long for my forever woman, there's no way in hell

I'd settle for anything less than perfect. Because you were perfect, doll. No one else could ever measure up."

My eyes drop, and I don't realize when I bite the inside of my cheek.

"What is it?" he asks with concern.

I take a deep breath. "You asked . . . you asked me to—were you just too in the moment?"

He shakes his head. "No. I meant it. Will you marry me, Lola?"

His arm tightens around my waist, the bedsheet now covering our bodies as I stare into his eyes, seeking sincerity. "We're too young. I'm too young."

"Marry me anyway."

"We haven't really known each other that long."

"Marry me anyway."

"I live in Mexico. You live in Germany, or on the road," I add.

He smiles, that goofy little-boy smile of his. "Marry me anyway."

"I don't like to clean. I'd keep a terrible home."

He bites his lip now, trying not to chuckle. "Marry me anyway."

"I might be touring in the future . . . I'm planning on starting my own band too, you know."

"I know, Iggy. Marry me anyway."

"You really want to do this?"

He finds my hand and brings it to his face to kiss the palm of it. "I do. I'd love for you to be Lola Sommer. Mine. Forever."

"I don't think I want kids."

That makes him pause. He seems to mull that over for a few seconds, then nods. "Marry me anyway."

I sigh. This man. He would agree to anything right now, and that's not fair. He should have the life he wants too, not just what I want. "Karl," I whine.

"What is it, doll?"

"I don't feel great that you're just agreeing to everything I want. I want you to be happy too."

"There's only one thing I've ever wanted. My very own family. Marry me. Be my family."

"A family of two?"

"Well, no. There's the band, and your band when you get it. They'll become your family too. You'll see."

"You want a rock and roll family?"

"With you," he adds. "Come here." He squeezes me more tightly and kisses me again. "I've never loved anyone enough to consider forever, but with you . . . it's like there's no other alternate reality where you and I aren't together. You're meant to be mine, Lola."

I nestle under his neck, letting his body warm me from the cooling perspiration on my skin, hoping he means what he says and that he won't change his mind later on—that he won't grow tired of me.

He must notice my shiver because he tightens his arms around me. "It was amazing," I breathe out dreamily.

"I don't know how we'll ever stop," he says, his fingers sliding gently along the ridges of my seam.

My thighs tighten, and I force myself to look him in the eye because I shouldn't be as embarrassed as I feel. "I'm a little sore," I admit.

"Oh," he says, still caressing my entrance gently but not intruding. Then he waggles his eyebrows. "Want me to kiss it better?"

I giggle into his chest. "No. But a bath would be nice."

I don't give him an answer to his question, and he doesn't press again.

I'm up before sunrise and leave Karl sleeping after ogling his naked body for far too long. I guess I'll always have a penchant for watching him when he doesn't know I am—a tradition that started so long ago when I passed his bedroom with my laundry basket.

I grab an oversized beach towel to do yoga in front of the dawn. As much as I'm averse to exercise, my therapist tasked me with choosing something physical to do. He insists exercise can be one of many tools to deal with depression. Yoga seemed like the least effort, so I've picked it up these past few months—and I won't lie. I kind of fell in love with it.

Looking around, the beach is empty in front of his villa, and I realize this stretch of beach is private to this property. Instead of stretching in my jeans, I take them off and decide to risk being seen in my underwear. I can always rush to put my pants on if I see anyone.

It's decadent, being on a deserted beach with no one for miles, and I bask in the luxury of it. Stretching my body until it feels languid and strong, I flow through my sun salutations.

I'm in downward dog when Karl finds me.

"Fuck, that is the hottest thing I've ever seen," he groans out, making me laugh and lose my balance.

I fall to my knees, giggling, and he is behind me before I can sit up. "No," he orders. His hands settle around my hipbones, gently keeping me in place. "Stay like that."

"Good morning," I say with a soft giggle.

"Good morning, my love," he says, lifting my top so he can kiss the dimples on my lower back. "Have you decided if you'll be my wife yet?" he whispers into my skin.

I tense at his words, but he doesn't seem to notice, or at least he doesn't comment on it. He meant it then, when he proposed. It wasn't something stupid he said from losing his head to his orgasm. He really wants to get married.

Even though deep down I know I'm too young for marriage, I desperately want to say yes to him, despite the risks.

I know he's it for me.

With his teeth, he pulls on the hem of my underwear, and I wiggle in his hold. "Karl, someone will see us," I whisper in a panic.

His mouth lets go of the fabric for a moment. "Don't worry, doll. We're completely alone," he says, and his breath on my lower back sends shivers down my spine.

"Are you sure?" I glance around us to make sure there are no stragglers, but this early in the morning, even public beaches are probably empty.

"I'm sure," he says. "I'm also sure I woke up with a raging hard-on for my fiancé-to-be, and she wasn't in my bed."

With teeth, he peels my underwear down and his work to have me bare is done.

My heart is hammering in my chest, both from fear of being seen and excited by that very fear. What the fuck is this feeling? Whatever it is, I'm so turned on, it's scary. I don't think I'd stop him even if we realized there were people around us after all.

He runs his tongue along the length of my seam. "Your so swollen, baby," he says. "Are you excited, baby? Does the thought of getting caught in public turn you on?" I don't answer apart from my increased breathing, and Karl chuckles against my skin. "My little pervert," he says and runs his fingers just a little deeper, breaking through my lips. "Are you too sore this morning?" he asks.

"Only in the best way," I admit. "But I'm . . ."

"What, baby?" He asks against my skin. "What are you?"

"Achy. I need you in me again," I beg, remembering what it did to him when I begged last night. "I need you to stuff me up with your huge cock. Please."

Karl growls, and his tongue plunges deep in me, his hands spreading my ass cheeks wide to give him access. My initial instinct is to be horrified at what he's seeing, but the sounds of pleasure rumbling up from his chest are the reassurance I need that he's enjoying his view.

He licks and licks and teases. He's really good at that. Teasing my clit until it's ready to explode with the softest breeze from all the teasing. I lose myself to the pleasure and hardly notice when his tongue trails back toward . . . there. My other entrance.

At first, it feels good until I realize what he's doing. My body tightens, and I try pulling away from him.

"Come here, doll," he says, pulling me back by my hip bones, his thumb circling that forbidden place. "Not today," he says, circling it tenderly as if it were something precious. "Maybe one day, if you want to try it," he says as I feel the tip of his penis spreading my lips gently.

"Thank you," I whisper.

"Do you know how good you feel?" he asks, not expecting an answer. "You are so wet, dripping down your thighs—for me."

He's not thrusting into me, though, and his tip is right there, driving me insane. Impatient, I rock back on my knees, taking him deeper.

"Yes, doll," he hisses. "Engulf me. Take me deep."

And oh hell, that's all the coaxing I need. I rock back farther and farther, scooting back until he's so deep in me, it steals my breath.

I am a little sore, but nothing terrible. Even last night wasn't quite as painful as I'd imagined it being, though I know without a doubt it had utterly to do with the patient man who only wanted my pleasure that first night.

His hands massage my glutes, and I rock forward and back again. He grunts with his pleasure and leans over me to grab me by the shoulders and pull me back toward him, pinning my entire body to his penis.

"Fuck," I nearly scream at the unimaginable depth that feels unlike anything in this world.

I clench around him, enjoying him this deep, and it must snap something in him because he grows wild. I know all thoughts of my pleasure are gone along with any restraint he demonstrated last night for our first time.

It's now all about him, his dick, and his release.

If last night was for me, today is for him. One hand leaves my right shoulder and goes to my hair, gathering a partial ponytail and twisting it around his fingers so he can pull on it, forcing my head back.

It's full light out now, and it's so bright we wouldn't be missed if someone walked by. But even over the slapping sound from his rough thrusting, I do my best to commit this moment to memory, the orange and blue sunrise in front of us, the soft sound of the gentle ocean not masking the sounds of wet, punishing thrusts slapping my behind. My man behind me, wild and savage, lost to his pleasure—claiming it from my body.

# LOLA

**K**arl is wrapped around me as I rest my back on his chest now that we've relocated to our bedroom. "What a beautiful sunrise," I joke, looking out our window from the bed, and he chuckles.

"Can we stay in all day and just . . . fuck?" he asks.

"As tempting as that is, I can't. I have to work tonight."

"Lola." He whines out my name.

"And this morning we should get you over to meet my *tía*. She's my closest family now, and if we're really getting serious—"

"We are," Karl interrupts me. "You're it for me, Lola. I meant it when I asked you to marry me. Please tell me you have an answer for me, doll. You're driving me crazy."

I shake my head. "I still need to think about it. I'm sorry. There's so much we need to talk about before taking a step like that."

A crease forms between his brows.

"There's nothing to discuss," he says like he's laying down the law. "You're it. *The one*. And I know, I know it's sappy and stupid, but it's also true."

I consider him for a moment, how tightly he's holding on to my waist, how pained his features look. It's almost like he's anticipating impending rejection, and he needs to hold on tightly before I have a chance to toss him aside.

"Karl," I say as softly as I can manage. "You're the one for me too, but it's a big step. We should discuss—"

"Nothing. Whatever it is, we will work through it, as husband and wife."

I sigh. I'm never going to convince this stubborn man, so I need to just say it and let the dice fall where they may. We were, after all, always fond of games. "I don't want children," I hurry to say before he can cut me off again.

"Okay," he says, thinking.

Then I add, "Ever. And it's not one of those things where you think I'll change my mind when I'm older. I won't. Would you be okay with that, it being just us two?"

"Three," Karl says and smiles at me. "Don't forget Pixel."

I laugh. "Right." I try to be serious again. "Are you okay with never having children?"

"I'm not sure," he says. "To be honest, I never gave children any thought. Can I ask why, though? Why do you think you'll never want them? And how you're so sure at nineteen?"

"I want to play. I want to make my own band. We'll be traveling, and it just wouldn't be a good situation. But it's not as simple as that. It's not about logistics. I asked myself if I could envision a life like Sofia's and Ileana's, and I can't."

"What do you mean? I always thought you loved children. You love Addy and Isael so much. I can see it—"

"I do love them!" I laugh. "And I really like children. But children require devotion that I'm not prepared to offer. I'd be happy with many nieces and nephews. Sofia is a superwoman. She manages owning her own business and being the best mom and partner to Bren. And Ileana, well, being a homemaker is her superpower. She was born to be a mother. She always knew she wanted a family to take care of—and lots of kids. But when I think of *my* future, I'm up late writing music or playing the dragon—"

"We have yet to discuss your thievery. Don't think I've forgotten, Iggy." He side-eyes me, trying to sound upset.

"Well, if we do get married, what's yours will be mine, so I don't see a problem." I throw him an impish grin. "But back to the point. I don't see myself being a caretaker. I see myself making music. I didn't know it until you, but music is my passion. Not just listening to it, but making it. And I can't imagine having distractions from that passion, with something as important as children, and being happy. Because if I did have them, I'd be devoted to my children, and I couldn't be devoted to my playing, not with the level of devotion I intend to give it. It's what I need."

He scratches his jaw. "Makes sense."

"So you see, if you want children someday, I may not actually be *the one*, as you put it."

He brushes hair back from the side of my face, and his hand drops to caress the back of my hand like he does when he's trying to soothe me. "You're the one, Lo. I've never thought about having children, but I also didn't think about not having them—if that makes sense. I like your vision for your future, being that committed to your music. I'd like to share it if you'll let me. Maybe we could even make some tunes together."

He pulls me to his chest, and I sigh with relief, hopeful he means it and isn't trying to simply give me what I want. Only time will tell, but he's worth the wager—*we* are worth the wager.

"If you're sure—"

"I'm sure."

"No children," I repeat. "Ever."

He smiles. "Marry me anyway."

I smile back. "I'll think about it."

His eyes bore into mine. "Take all the time you need, love. I'm a patient man."

I laugh. "*That*, I know."

Naked, and flushed against him, he tightens around me and takes me in for a long kiss. When we finally break away to catch our breaths, his forehead is pressed to mine.

"You have to meet my aunt if we're considering taking that step."

"I was hoping we could elope," he says.

I shake my head. "No. My family is small but precious to me. *If* we get married, I'd like them there. Guess they'd be your family then too."

Karl smiles. "Yeah. Guess they would be." The glee on his face at realizing his new family will be bigger than he imagined breaks my heart a little, but in the best way possible.

"Let's start by introducing you as my boyfriend—let my *tía* get used to the idea."

"Make a decision soon, Iggy," Karl adds. "I want to take you on the most depraved honeymoon ever. Keep you in my bed without you having to go to work. We have time to make up for. And it's the perfect time. We can take advantage while the band is on hiatus for Bren's paternity leave."

"Soon," I agree. "Let's keep this to ourselves for now. One step at a time. Meet her first, and we can go from there."

"You lead, I follow."

And somehow, that four-word sentence warms my chest. It feels like a promise he's making of what our marriage could be. I trace the shape of the jar on his inner bicep with my index finger and smile.

"What's that thought there? That made you smile like that?" he asks.

I giggle. "I'm not sure I should say."

"*If* we get married, I'd like our marriage to be one of good communication. No more keeping things from each other. Don't hold out on me now, doll."

"Fine," I say with a sigh. "I have a confession to make."

"What's that?"

After I tackle him onto his back so I can straddle him, I grind my hips to his groin. We still have some time before we have to go to the restaurant. I dip my head and dive down for a kiss. Then I trail my lips to his tattoo and kiss it too.

"What is it?" he asks again, watching me with awe, his erection starting to harden with my attention.

I smile against his skin and peer up at him to watch his reaction. "I hate peanut butter."

When we get to *Mariscos Elena*, it's Fernanda we see first. She's walking out from the back, a tray of pre-wrapped silverware in her hands. She smiles up at me and says hello. She's about to ask who is with me when she does a double-take and drops the tray.

It lands heavily on her foot. "Ouch!" Fernanda howls with pain.

"Are you okay?" Karl asks, moving to help her, but she raises her hands so he'll stop.

"You know Karl Sommer, and you forgot to tell me?" she says in Spanish. I ask her to keep it in English for him, and she just scowls at me.

"I may have failed to tell you we dated before my move," I say sheepishly. Fernanda won't forgive me for this, but really, what was I going to say? I was in love with a rock star, and I left with his prize guitar? I wouldn't believe it if someone told me that story. "And we're back together," I add.

She blinks between us. "You're dating Karl Sommer?" she asks, not believing me.

"Just Karl, please." He steps in to offer his hand. "Are you okay? That looked painful."

Fernanda blushes and shakes her head. "I'm fine, thank you." Then Fernanda turns to me. "Does Elena know?"

I wince. "No. Now that we're back together, and it's getting serious—"

"Serious?" Fernanda's eyes widen with panic. "Yesterday, all we knew about was Ethan, and now you're serious with the world's—" Fernanda stops herself, embarrassed. "Best guitarist," she adds.

I try not to chuckle and embarrass her further. I remember what it was like that first time I met Bren at Sofia's, and I would not have appreciated someone poking fun at my ruffled feathers.

*Tía* Elena barges through the door. "What's all the noise?" she asks.

"I dropped a tray," Fernanda says.

Elena's eyes fly to Karl, then to me, then to our interlaced hands. "Who's this?" she asks, her face stony and unwelcoming, her hands firmly at her hips.

"*Tía*, this is my boyfriend, Karl," I say in English I know she understands even if she won't admit it. "Karl, this is my *tía* Elena."

"*Es un placer,*" he says in Spanish, surprising all three of us. And I won't lie, hearing him speak Spanish melts my knees a little.

"*Es Karl Sommer,*" Fernanda says near my aunt's ear. "*De Industrial November,*" she says, annoyed when there's no recognition in Elena's gaze.

"From what?"

"The band! *Industrial November!*" Fernanda's arms are flailing now.

"¡Ay! You and your rock music. You." She points to Karl, then me. "Sit over there. We're going to talk." She's completely unfazed by his presence, and I can tell Karl is amused.

Karl squeezes my hand reassuringly like he's done this before, even though we both know he hasn't. But somehow, his stoic composure is comforting. He may never have found himself in this situation before, but he sure as hell planned for it.

"So this is serious?" Elena asks, not pulling any punches, and I find myself translating one way when Karl needs it.

He wraps his arm around my shoulders. "Yes. I love Lola. Very much. It's serious."

"And you're in a band?"

"I am."

"I don't like this," she says, her mouth twisted into a frown.

"*¡Tía!*" I scold.

"Well, you know how musicians are."

Karl laughs. "I know. I was like that too. I won't lie to you. But I'm serious about Lola, and I'll take good care of her heart because it is my own."

I turn to look at him, at how serious his face is as he has this showdown with my aunt, and my eyes well at the sincerity of his words. *My heart is his own?* I shouldn't be surprised to hear it because just as my heart is his heart, his is mine.

Sensing my emotion, his hand falls under the table to squeeze my knee.

"I don't like being lied to," Elena says finally.

"I'm sorry, *tía*. I thought we were over, but we just reconnected."

"Can you at least promise me you'll be careful? Take it slow?" she asks me, completely forgetting Karl is at the table too.

"I'm sorry, *tía*. I can't promise that. I'm in love with him."

"*Ay chamacos,*" she says with a shake of her head. Then she sighs. "Well, at least you brought him by to introduce him to me."

She stands and motions for Karl to follow. She is so short next to him and has to crane her neck all the way back to look at him. "With her parents gone now, I'm her family. You understand?"

"I do," Karl says.

"Good." She then pulls him into a hug that Karl returns a bit awkwardly, obviously taken by surprise. When she pulls away, she asks him, "Are you hungry?" But it's not a question. Karl is about to feast even though he already had breakfast not too long ago—his first test.

---

THE FOLLOWING NIGHT, Fernanda and I are off from the dinner shift, and we decide to meet up with her new friends. The guy she met at the bar, Geraldo, turned out to be great, and he is bringing his boyfriend, though that surprises me given the looks he and Fernanda were giving each other at the bar.

She vouched for him, and he for his buddies, that they wouldn't give Karl away if we hung out with them tonight.

So Karl and I join their little group around a bonfire on the beach. Even with how impressed the group is by Karl being in the band—they are all metalheads in their own right and immediately knew who he was—they are more impressed with his attempts at Spanish.

I beam at him proudly. Those months apart, he must have been practicing.

"I still can't believe you're dating Karl fucking Sommer," Fernanda says as she places her beer bottle between her bare feet, half-buried in the sand.

"Trust me," I say. "Most days, I can't believe it either."

"What I don't understand," Geraldo says, "is why you're working and not just naked in bed twenty-four hours a day. I mean, look at you. It's like looking at golden beach Ken and Barbie."

Karl and I both laugh at the odd compliment.

"Believe me," Karl says. "I tried. But Lola here thought I should meet her family and friends now that we're official."

Karl takes my hand to kiss the back of it, and Geraldo's hands fly to his chest as he lets out a comical, "Awwww! Aren't they cute?" He is leaning back against his boyfriend's chest, arms snuggling him from the breeze, mirroring Karl and me.

When Fernanda reveals Geraldo is also a guitarist, Karl and I almost start geeking out with him until his friends protest that this is not a guitar convention, so we stop, but I know I'll be connecting with him later on. Maybe my band could have both a lead guitar and a rhythm guitar in it. We could do some incredible things musically with two guitars.

Hours later, the group is plastered, for the most part, and barely standing. Karl and I have managed to remain somewhat sober, though I know we're both tipsy. Earlier in the night, he'd whispered in my ear, "Don't overdo it tonight. I have plans for you." And if that isn't a reason to stay sober, I don't know what is.

Now, his hands are fisting the skirt of my yellow sundress covered in daisies, and I can feel his erection pressed behind me.

No one notices when Karl and I stand and relocate a few meters away from the group. They're all winding down into the *Chente* singing portion of the evening—the drunkest part of the night.

I sit on Karl's lap, watching the moon reflect on the calm waters, his thick length pressing hard against my behind. "We should go home," I breathe out, my skin on fire from his touch and the booze.

He pushes all my hair over one shoulder to expose the other side of my neck and draws his teeth down the sensitive skin.

"But my little pervert likes to be exposed publicly," he whispers, thrusting his hips hard against my ass.

"Karl!" I yell. "Not here. They'll see us." But despite my protest, my nipples harden painfully against the dress. Why'd I have to go braless tonight? It's all too much, and I know I don't have the will to stop this and run back to the villa.

Behind me, Karl unbuckles his pants to release his erection, taking care that the skirt of my dress covers both of us. My back still pressed to his chest, he orders me to kneel up just a little so two long fingers can scoop the fabric of my thong and pull it to the side to make room for him. "You're so wet, baby," he moans with pleasure.

Gently, he eases me down onto him. Anyone watching us would think we're just admiring the moonscape ahead of us. My breath is coming in so hard, I can hardly hear the water.

"Yes," Karl whispers into my ear—thick fingers curling around my jaw. "My little pervert. You like this, don't you? You like feeling exposed? It excites you."

I nod. "Yes."

I try to ride him, using my legs for momentum, but he stills me. "No," he orders. "You can't ride so high; they'll see us. Move slowly, doll."

I glance over at the group with panic, but they're all engaged in their own debauchery. Geraldo is making out with his boyfriend and Fernanda is watching them while the rest of the group is singing, not caring what they all do.

Because I can't ride him, I grind against him, small circles with my hips that hopefully aren't too noticeable to any potential onlookers.

This is so reckless. What if he was recognized and someone took a photo?

"Relax, doll," he whispers near my ear as if he can sense my worries. "You need to let go. We're both covered with your dress, and it's so dark. No one can see under it. Let go, doll. Let go and come for me."

I take a deep breath and try to relax, but my heart keeps pounding with excitement. How did I go from being a virgin one day to getting a taste for indecent public exposure the next? Whatever the hell it is, it's hot as all fuck.

"I need you to touch my nipples," I breathe out, feeling the fabric graze them as if the nerves were on fire.

Instead, Karl grips my waist tightly. "I can't, doll. That'd be too obvious."

The need to ride harder is extreme, and I can't take it much longer. Onlookers be damned because I need that delicious friction. Just picturing the thick veins along his shaft creating resistance as he enters me is enough to send me over the edge. Three quick hard thrusts, and I clench around him with my release. My pussy convulses around him with my orgasm while he holds me tight to him.

"Fuck, Lola," he gurgles out. "Just—holy fuck."

I feel his dick twitch inside me when he comes, he's breathing hard as his chest expands against my back. "My little pervert," he whispers. "My little sex doll." He bites my shoulder blade playfully. "I love you so fucking much."

I give him time to zip up again before I turn around to face him, still straddling him.

"I love you too, but, um . . . Karl, that was really reckless."

He smiles at me. "It was. And exciting."

His grin is so wide, I laugh. "You're dumb."

"Marry me anyway."

This time, when I answer him, I answer with all my heart. "Yes."

# 41

# KARL

Within one week of breaking the news to Elena and Roger, the entirety of *Industrial November*, Sofia, Addy, and their entourage descend upon Acapulco. Their collective travel doesn't go unnoticed by media outlets, and sightings of the band in Acapulco have alerted the Mexican media that, I too, must be here in Acapulco.

Within a day, I was made, despite the haircut.

I made sure they brought Matt, Lola's bodyguard along, now that the world knows that she and I are here. Of course, they brought Pix with them. Lola and I had been missing her immensely. Lola cried when she first saw her and then had a full-blown meltdown, bawling her eyes out, when she saw Sofia and Addy.

*Mariscos Elena* is booming with business. Elena has been ecstatic, claiming the attention from the band's fans has driven even more business than spring break.

She hired two more cooks and three more waitresses despite it being the off-season when job opportunities start to dwindle.

That warmed her up to me more than anything. Had I known, I would have given myself away sooner. But it also means Lola couldn't keep working, not without being constantly hassled. Elena was more than understanding and released her of her duties. Lola will continue to stay on as an investor, but Elena will have to find someone else to partner with and train to manage the restaurant. She's thinking of one of her cooks, Mariela, who is relatively young and has lofty culinary ambitions from what I understand.

It's all working out fucking perfect—everything falling into place.

Tonight is our rehearsal dinner that Sofia has insisted on hosting at the villa she and Bren rented just down the beach from Lola and me. So everyone is here convening at her house early in the day. Lola insisted on showing up early to help, but Sofia won't hear it, so she planted Lola, Adrian, Fritz, Addy, and me in front of the television with snacks.

Lola is nestled next to me, Addy in her lap. "Are you happy?" I ask her in a whisper only she can hear.

She nods, bouncing Addy on her lap. "I'm only sad Ileana and Isa couldn't be here. But her brother is in town, which is really rare, and she treasures that time. It was just bad timing."

"We'll have her visit us after the honeymoon," I say.

"I'd like that."

The cartoon Addy was watching ends, and Adrian changes the channel. He perks up when he lands on a soap opera. "*Who* is that?" Adrian asks, elbows pressed to thighs as he leans toward the television with a little too much interest. Next to him, Fritz stiffens, and I think I see his jaw twitch.

"That's Erica Moran," Lola explains. "She's probably the most popular telenovela actress in Mexico at the moment. Oh, this one's good. It's called *Curvas Peligrosas*. Dangerous Curves. She's the antihero. They call her a man-eater because she uses men to get ahead, outsmarts them, and steals their fortunes. It's really good."

Adrian obviously can't understand what the characters are saying, but he's fixated on the gorgeous woman on the screen, and I can't blame him. The actress, Erica, is curvy, soft perfection, with huge knockers.

"Hot, isn't she?" Lola asks pointedly. Adrian is so stunned, he might be drooling soon. I laugh. "Get in line," Lola tells him, and he blinks at her, finally peeling his attention away from the screen.

"What?"

"They say she's a man-eater in real life too. She dates the wealthiest celebrities and businessmen in Mexico, as well as powerful politicians, leads them on, and every single one of them ends up with a broken heart. She's gotten like five proposals, diamonds you can see from space, and she always says no. She's notorious." Lola laughs. "Some tabloids even claim she has a magical vagina that bewitches men. Ridiculous," she scoffs, amused at Adrian's stunned expression.

"No way," Adrian says, looking back at the curvy actress.

"Even during my few months in Mexico," Lola explains, "I've come to understand that Erica Moran took the television industry by storm here. Until her, there had never been a plus-sized main character in a major telenovela, from what I understand—at least not one depicted as sexy. And the fact that they hyper-sexualized her character and played off her real-life reputation makes her one of the most desired women in the country. Though if I think about it, you *are* the drummer for *Industrial November*. You could potentially have a shot with her if you wanted it. You're famous enough—"

"Will you change the channel!?" Fritz barks, and we all turn to look at him.

Huh. The knuckles wrapped around his beer bottle are white, and his nostrils are flaring. He's been a little jumpy lately, something I attributed to the bands extended down-time. He's getting restless, and I know the second Lola and I get back from our honeymoon, we'll be practicing, getting ready to record.

"What the f—" Adrian starts to say, then glances at Addy in Lola's arms. "What's your deal?" he asks instead.

"Just shut that shit off," Fritz says.

"Language, man," Adrian snaps, pointing at Addy. "We got a kid now."

Lola and I glance at each other, and I know what she's thinking. *What's up Fritz's ass now?* I shrug. *Hell, if I know,* I answer her telepathically.

I love our little silent conversations that are happening more and more now.

I can already picture us getting old and gray together. When my mind starts to go, she will finish my sentences for me. We have a great life ahead of us—I can feel it.

SOFIA COMES in and shuts off the TV before the argument goes any further.

"Lola, can I have a chat with you?" she asks. "Sure," Lola says, and Sofia whisks away my bride-to-be.

Sofia takes Addy and hands her to Lupe, who will be helping with Addy during the ceremony tomorrow night.

Bren joins us as the women leave and whips out a humidor filled with Cuban cigars.

"Now that's what I'm talking about," Fritz says, looking more relaxed now.

We all light up and sit back to enjoy.

"Gotta hand it to you, man," Bren says, looking at me. "Never thought I'd see the day you'd settle down. And those songs you sent me are great. We'll be recording more than a few of them. I have some notes, we might need some minor changes, but we'll talk when you get back from your honeymoon." Bren finishes his praise with a slight nod.

"I never thought I'd see the day when I'd get a compliment out of you," I shoot back, and he throws me one of his crooked smiles.

Pride swells in me. I'm doing it. Finally. I have people who love me for the first time in my life and the respect of my heroes. Everything is falling into place.

To think, it all started with a bet.

# 42

# LOLA

Sofia leads me to a sitting room on the other side of the house where the guys won't hear us. She chews on her thumbnail nervously.

"What is it?" I ask as I sit down.

She takes in a big gulp of air. "You're not pregnant, are you?" she rushes out and lets all the air out of her lungs.

I throw my head back with laughter. "No!" I reassure her.

When I first called her about the engagement, as expected, she was dead set against it. She only conceded when the alternative was for her to sit out my wedding altogether. Ileana had a similar hesitation to the idea, but in true fashion, she encouraged me to follow my heart. And my *tía* Elena? *Ni se diga.* She blew a gasket but ultimately wants nothing but my happiness.

Sofia, on the other hand, can't let it go, it seems.

"You're just so young. And you had a breakup. You've barely gotten yourself together. Don't you think you should spend some time together to really get to know each other? Move in, find out if you're suited to that level of companionship?"

I study her for a moment. "Are you sure you're not projecting, Sofia?"

Sofia went through heartbreak not that long ago, and Bren has finally accepted that she will never marry. She has so many hang-ups about the institution. I understand her distrust. But I don't share it.

"Sofia, I love him, and I know he's it for me. And I know you don't trust marriage, but that just hasn't been my experience. My parents, they were so in love. I watched them all my life, how they supported and respected each other. How they lifted each other up when there were tough times. I have a great example to draw from. And I know, I know Karl doesn't, but we learn from each other. It's how our relationship works. He teaches me love for music, and I teach him how to be loved. It's beautiful, and I want it for life. And I want it with his last name."

My eyes get teary at the thought of my parents. I've been avoiding letting myself go down that path. Avoiding thinking about how Dad can't walk me down the aisle tomorrow night and how Mom can't be having this talk with me now. Though a sister is a great second. I know Sofia is concerned because I'm so young. To be honest, I would be too, if our roles were reversed.

But I'm just that sure.

"You sound a lot older than nineteen," Sofia says.

"These past few years have aged me so fast," I explain. "All that pain, all that rejection, losing my family, being forced out of the only home I'd ever known . . . it puts things in a different perspective. This is my happy, and I want to grab it with all the enthusiasm I can manage. I want to hold it tightly because I know how precious and rare it is and that I have to savor it while I can keep it."

"I guess there's always divorce if it doesn't work out like you're hoping," Sofia says, all serious, and I burst out laughing.

"I love you for caring. But you should have more faith in us than that. Have you forgotten what a great guy Karl is? Pixel and Addy both adore him. Kids and dogs, they can tell when a person is an asshole, or when they're a friend."

It's Sofia who laughs now. "Well, then. If he has the approval of his dog and my toddler, then I guess I have no arguments now." It's said with sarcasm, but Sofia's eyes are welling a bit now, and I'm so sure it's with happiness for me.

---

*Tía* ELENA GASPS when she sees me in the dress.

I'm wearing my hair down in loose waves. It's blond again, though not as long as I like it, so I had some extensions put in for tonight to return it to its former length for the pictures.

My dress is a sweetheart neckline, strapless number, with a fitted bodice. The material is lace in thick patterns that make it almost look crocheted, and I'm wearing matching lace cuffs around my upper arms. The underskirt hits above my knee, but the outer skirt fans down the length of me in a mermaid silhouette that reveals my legs through the flimsy lace material. It's boho and perfect for our location.

"Don't cry, *tía*," I beg her. "Then I'll cry, and you'll ruin my makeup!"

"*Mija*, you look so beautiful!"

"Thank you." I approach her and let her wrap her arms around me.

She sniffles next to my ear. "Your mom and dad would be so proud. She'd love to be here today. I know it. She used to talk about it sometimes—"

"She did?"

"Yeah. Especially when you were a little girl, playing wedding with your dolls. She'd call me and tell me. And your dad, he would be so sad but so proud to walk you down the aisle today."

My eyes well, and I try to reel them in. *"Tía*, please. I'm going to cry."

She lets go of me and sniffles. "Okay. I'm sorry, *mija*. You just look so much like both of them now that you're grown up. It brings up a lot of feelings, you know?"

"I know."

"Okay, I'm going to head out now and watch you walk down the aisle."

"Thank you," I say. "For everything. I'm so grateful, and I hope you know how much I love you."

She nods, wipes her eyes, and her eyes go to my hands as I reach for my 'bouquet.'

"What is that?" she asks, confused.

"My bouquet," I explain with a devilish grin.

"You're not serious?"

"Dead serious," I say.

She shakes her head as she leaves. *"Chamacos locos."*

———

THE WATER WITNESSED OUR REUNION.

The ocean watched us make love for the first time through our window, and the water was there at sunrise and at moonrise when we fucked. So we knew it also had to bear witness to our vows.

Karl stands with his back to the water in a dashing light blueish-grey suit that is so light, it's almost white. An orange boutonnière with green leaves is pinned to his lapel, and he's wearing a deep blue tie over a crisp white shirt.

He looks so perfectly handsome, waiting for me by the water, it steals my breath as I take my first step on the pathway to my future. I smile when I see Adrian standing next to Karl, a leash in his hands, and Pixel sitting like a good girl next to him.

"Sympathy for the Devil" by *The Rolling Stones* plays as I walk slowly. The handful of people invited stand to look at me, and I don't miss their expressions turning curious when they see what's in my hands, but it's Karl's reaction I care most about.

When his eyes fall to the object in question, he throws his head back with laughter. He shakes his head as I get to him, his pupils dancing with amusement. Then he sobers, and his hand goes to his heart—his eyes now full of emotion and love.

When I get to him finally and hand Sofia the 'bouquet,' Karl whispers in my ear, "Peanut butter, Iggy?"

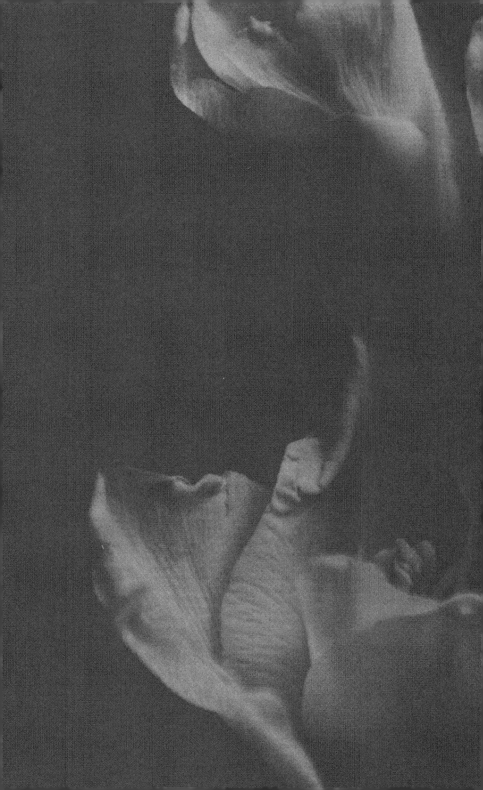

# EPILOGUE

## LOLA

We're on the third month of our honeymoon, and Karl refuses to tell me how long our honeymoon will last. Honestly, I don't think he has a plan, and we could go on like this forever if we wanted to. Except we both miss Pixel terribly. She's with Adrian now in our Acapulco villa, and I know we're both getting anxious to get back to her, so we'll probably go home soon.

From Acapulco, we went on to Vallarta for a week of nothing but making love, eating, and sleeping in, then the actual travel began. Money moves mountains in Mexico, and my passport was expedited so we were able to travel rather quickly. We spent a week in Fiji, then several in New Zealand because I fell in love with it.

After that, it was weeks in Italy where we lived on a luxury yacht most of the time, then Greece, France, and Spain. We're now at the height of the summer season, and I never want to leave beautiful Croatia.

Karl is hell-bent on showing me that the world is so much bigger than Mexico and the United States alone and that I'm a welcome global citizen. I couldn't be more in love with him for it. In turn, I treasure him like the precious man he is, showing him every day just how worthy of love he is.

I know he wanted to end in Europe so we could make a stop in Germany, and I know I'll eventually get to see his home there. *Our* home now, I guess. And he mentioned meeting lawyers to get working on my dual citizenship in Germany before we go back to Mexico.

But today, we're still in Croatia.

The callouses on my fingertips are thicker than ever from all my practicing.

Last night we went to bed late, playing music until my husband had to have me, and we were forced to stop, so I'm sleeping in now after a full night of lovemaking.

Only there's a smile on my face as my eyelids flutter open. A matching fluttering sensation between my legs.

That's one of his new favorite pastimes, waking me up with his tongue, and I have zero complaints.

"Good morning," I moan into the bright room.

"Good morning, wife," Karl says from under the covers, then comes up over my body to kiss me. "How did you sleep?"

"Wonderfully, but not better than how I woke up."

Karl chuckles. "I wasn't done, was I?"

"You sure weren't," I say, smiling at him and pushing his head down toward where it needs to be.

He chuckles at my demands but obeys and dives back down to his new home between my legs.

After he makes me come on his tongue, he starts with his second favorite pastime. When my clit is so intensely sensitive, Karl has learned to strum it like he would his guitar, just like our very first guitar lesson. With soft, gentle fingers, he rapidly dusts my clit with the most delicate of grazes. It drives me insane, and he knows it.

"Stop, please," I beg when I can't handle it anymore. That's when he comes back up and over me.

"You love it," he teases.

"I do, but now I need my husband inside me," I demand.

"You lead, I follow," he says and enters me in one long, deep thrust.

# EPILOGUE

## KARL

This is the last day of our honeymoon. Married life suits me. Never having family before, I didn't know what to expect. And despite how young Lola is, she's now my best friend and partner. I'm a lucky man to have her as my family too, and I'm so damn smart for pushing to make it legal because I intend to keep her for life.

Maybe that sounds creepy. I only mean I know we'll grow old together.

I'm pretending to write in my small notebook, but I'm really just watching her, lounging nearly naked. The lanai of our Croatian rental was inviting this evening with the warm sun rays just before sunset, so we relocated here an hour ago.

Lola is splayed on a lounge chair, topless, reading a Lou Reed biography. Her ax—the pink one I gave her—is now like an extension of her body. Even though I know she has no plans to practice again today, it rests next to her chair like she can't be away from it for more than a few minutes. I'll never get tired of this view.

I'm watching my wife do her thing when a video call chimes through her tablet next to her. She grabs the *Stone*

*Temple Pilots* t-shirt from the chair's backrest and pulls it over her head before she answers the call.

"Fernanda!" Lola squeals, and then immediately, something crosses her features. Something that looks a lot like shame. In the three months we've been gone, we've hardly spoken to anyone from the outside world, and until today, no one has reached out to us. I'm sure she's missing her friends.

And to be honest, so am I. *Tía* Elena grew on me quickly. So did Fernanda, and though we didn't get to spend much time together, I already know she'll be as good a buddy as Adrian is.

"You need to come back!" is the first thing to come out of Fernanda's mouth, even before a 'hello.'

I look up from my supposed work and throw Lola a questioning look with a raised brow.

Lola shrugs. "Why? What's going on?"

"I found our bass!"

"Yeah?"

"She's amazing!" Fernanda squeals. "She auditioned between my legs," she says dreamily, followed by a sigh.

"Fuck yeah!" I roar from my spot next to Lola.

"Thanks, Karl," Fernanda says. "But seriously. Get back here. She says she knows a kick-ass drummer who just left her old band. It's coming together."

I watch as Lola rolls her eyes. "But can she play?" she asks about the bass player. "Anything besides your *panocha*, I mean."

"Lola! Don't be so crass!"

I snort. Right. Like she didn't just tell us about her pervert audition.

Something's off, though. This excitement out of Fernanda surprises me. She didn't seem quite this excited about starting a band the few times I broached the subject at the wedding. Maybe this bass player renewed excitement within her.

I stand and go around Lola's chair to stand behind her, then duck so my face can come into the frame. Fernanda smiles at me.

"Hey, Karl," she says.

"Sorry, Fer," I say to Lola's vocalist. "Lola has to go now. If we're ending our honeymoon soon, I need to go fuck my wife."

"Wait!" Fernanda protests, "We need a band name."

Both Fernanda and I pause to look at Lola. She grins so incredibly wide at both of us while we wait for her answer. "I already have our band name."

### The End

---

Do you want more of Lola and Karl? You can read an interview deleted scene with the power couple three years after their wedding. To get access to the deleted scene from Running from the Blaze, go to ofeliamartinez.com/freebooks to download.

In the meantime, keep reading for an excerpt from *Incision*, a steamy, hate-to-lovers novella.

# ALSO BY OFELIA MARTINEZ

**The Heartland Metro Hospital Series**

Carolina & Hector's Story: *Remission*

Valentina & Rory's Story: *Contusion*

Izel & Logan's Story: *Incision* (Novella)

**The Industrial November on Tour Series**

Sofia & Bren's Story: *Hiding in the Smoke*

Lola & Karl's Story: *Running from the Blaze*

# INCISION

# INCISION EXCERPT

## CHAPTER ONE

I could be forcing the victims of a serial killer to run for their lives in my current slasher novel work in progress. But instead of my characters, I'm the one running—and not for a good reason, like to save my life, but rather for exercise. Ugh!

My sneakers paddle on the paved trail, sending a jolt of pain up my shins with each clumsy stride. It doesn't help that I'm wearing a workout top I bought a year and two dress sizes ago. The thin material rolls up my full hips and bunches at my smaller waist with the movement of my body. I gave up wrestling the hem down to my waist at the quarter mile mark. The result is an unintended crop top. And seriously, who runs in a crop top? To add insult to injury, I'm drenched in sweat, forcing the thin material to cling to my cleavage. And if *that* weren't enough, the top is white. The only saving grace is that jogging at this ungodly hour means fewer people to witness this debacle of a workout my roommate talked me into.

But Tlali, my cousin-slash-best-friend-slash-roommate, wasn't wrong when she hinted at how tight my jeans were getting around my hips and reminded me our forced modeling gig is only weeks away.

Why do I have to be such a people-pleaser? I need to work on saying 'no' more often. I cringe when I think back to how she talked me into working out.

"Izel," Tlali had whined when she got home after work and I had our favorite queso and chips at the table ready with a big pitcher of margaritas. "We can't eat like this. Mandy is going to have us nearly naked for her exhibit."

While our cousin Mandy hasn't exactly told us yet how much we'll be wearing when we pose for the day of the dead living sculpture we are modeling for, she's hinted, she's alluded, she's insinuated—it will be minimal. I don't care how much body paint she drenches me in—if she thinks I'm going to pose nude for strangers at the gallery—she has another think coming.

"But it's Friday," I'd pouted. "We always have margaritas on Fridays."

"After Mandy's exhibit, we can go back to margarita Fridays. Deal?"

I'd puffed air into my cheeks and then let it out. "I hate for this to go to waste," I'd said with a longing look at the food and margarita pitcher. "Guess I'll throw it out."

Tlali had basically lunged herself at the table to protect it. "Let's not get crazy," she said. "We'll start jogging Monday morning."

And why exactly wasn't my cousin running next to me on the trail at five this morning? She'd claimed to need her beauty sleep when I'd tried waking her. We work at the same hospital. She is a medical interpreter, and I work as a surgical technologist. We usually carpool to get to our seven a.m. shifts, so five in the morning was the best time for the run.

Mid-October in Kansas City is also too cold for her. But in truth, Tlali has the Ferrari of metabolisms and boasts perfect muscle tone on a slim figure with zero effort, while if I so much as look at chocolate, it goes straight to my hips.

I smile. Chocolate is so worth it.

While I'd never even dreamt of picking up running, Mandy coerced us into being part of an exhibit she is doing for a prominent art gallery. She calls it her Día de Muertos retrospective. And only because the three of us have been best friends since we were literally babies did Mandy convince Tlali and me into being part of her living sculpture. We'll be posing as statues during opening night. She also enlisted one of our mutual friends, Valentina, who used to be a freaking professional athlete, and two other paid models. That's right. I will be nearly naked. With body paint. On a platform. Next to four other women with perfect bodies, two of whom are professional models.

Don't care. Chocolate is still worth it.

I will overlook the fact that I don't make it a full mile up the trail before I turn around and head back. I'm winded and have terrible shin splints. Not to mention my generous bust is strapped to my chest in the most uncomfortable sports bra in the world, which also happens to be the only thing making it possible for me to run without knocking myself out with my own boobs.

It's my first run. It'll get better.

I shut off my headlamp as the parking lot lights begin to flood onto the trail. Being on this trail before dawn feels like being in a dark forest. It's wonderfully spooky and has my creative juices flowing. I note details I know will make it into a scene for one of my horror novels, like how the shadows cast by the barren cottonwood trees slither toward the path like tendrils, even as the branches shake gently in the wind.

Joy Division's *Dead Souls* plays over my earbuds as I start my cool-down walk when something coils around my right ankle. I think it's a snake and let out a yell as I fall flat on my ass on the hard concrete. Whatever was around my ankle is now gone, and I yank my headphones out of my ears so I can hear any sounds as I frantically look for my headlamp and turn it back on.

When my eyes focus, I make out the silhouette of a person on the ground.

"Sorry," a man says.

I press my hand to my heart as my pulse races with fright.

"I didn't mean to scare you. Are you okay?" he asks.

That low, husky voice is one I recognize. I flash the light on the man's face, and he brings his hand up to block the beam as he uses the other to keep himself up in a sitting position. It's Dr. Logan Williams. The surgeon I've worked under for the last four months. What the hell is he doing on the ground?

# INCISION EXCERPT
## CHAPTER TWO

"Oh my god," I say. "Are you okay?"

"I had an accident on my bike and busted my ankle when I tried to stop."

I flash the light down his blood-speckled arm. I scan his body for injuries, but he seems fine except for the scrapes on his thick bicep. He's oriented, speaking, and holding himself up.

"Help me up?"

I cock my head to the side as I study him, trying to figure out if he's serious. Dr. Williams is about six one in height and I'd bet he weighs in at two-twenty—at least. No way my five-foot-five squishy-ass frame can help him to my car. "I don't think I can carry you by myself," I say.

"Only one of my ankles is twisted. I can put my weight on the other foot."

"Hold on," I say and jog the short distance to the parking lot.

A woman is stretching by her car, and I approach her with a smile. After she gets her headphones off, I tell her what's going on, and she agrees to help.

I think about how in a different place, this could be the start of a great serial killer movie—a couple who kills, luring victims to help in a dark, wooded area. Maybe that's the plot for my next novel?

But not in this part of Kansas City. This neighborhood is one of the safest.

She introduces herself as Stacy to Dr. Williams, and between the both of us, and after a lot of grunting, we have Dr. Williams on his foot, one arm around each of us. He hops his way to the parking lot with most of his weight on Stacy and me.

"My car's just right there," he says.

"Can you even drive? Your right ankle is busted."

"I can manage."

I roll my eyes. "How about I drive you to the hospital?" I ask as I point to my car so Stacy can help us in that direction. "You need to get that ankle x-rayed."

"You wouldn't mind?" Dr. Williams asks.

I have my change of clothes in the car, and I'd planned on showering at the hospital anyway. I shake my head. "No. I don't mind."

"Okay," he says and lets us help him into my car.

As he ducks to get in, I step back, not at all checking out his perfect, hard ass in bike shorts that are basically a second skin—or at least I'd never admit it to anyone.

"Thanks, Stacy," I say before getting in the driver's side of my little Hyundai SUV, and she waves before heading to the trail. When we're alone, I think about what he'd said. "Wait, did you say you were on your bike?"

Dr. Williams nods.

"Where's the bike?"

"Forget it," he says with a scowl. "Let's just go."

"Was it expensive?"

"It doesn't matter."

Before he has a chance to protest, I get out of my car and jog over to the spot where I'd found him. I get off the trail and carefully descend down the creek bank until I see the shimmer from a piece of hardware on the bike. I lift the bike, surprised at how light it is, and roll it back up the bank.

It takes me folding down the two back seats to get the bike to fit, but I manage to get it in despite Dr. William's many objections and interruptions, ordering me to leave it.

He's a stereotypical arrogant surgeon, but that bike looks expensive, and it isn't even that busted from the accident, just a bit scratched. No way I'd leave that bike behind.

Dr. Williams doesn't say much on the drive to Heartland Metro Hospital. Other than a few grunts and winces, silence fills the car. It's not awkward, though. In the four months I've worked with him, he's hardly said a full sentence to me, unless it was about a surgical case.

The only words he's really spoken to me have been in asking for the various instruments he requires for the heart surgeries we've worked on together. Until today when he asked me to help him up.

I don't play music during our ride because he has terrible taste in music. Like most surgeons, he plays music in the operating room, but he always shuts it off when he gets to the crux of the operation and doesn't resume it until he is back on safe ground. Even with that limited musical selection, I've come to realize Dr. Logan Williams has the worst taste in music of anyone in the entire hospital.

"So, how'd you end up down the creek bank?"

He doesn't turn in my direction, and I keep my eyes on the road.

"I'd rather not talk about it," he says dryly.

I press my lips together. If he weren't hurt—and technically my boss—I'd find this a little funny. About damn time his ego got a little bruised.

"I'm going to think about it all day if you don't tell me. I'm obsessive like that. Can I at least get a hint? I mean, I *am* driving you to the hospital . . ."

Dr. Williams huffs next to me and looks out the window as he speaks again. "I was trying to avoid hitting something."

My nose scrunches up. The trail is pretty clear of people so early in the morning, but he'd said *something*. "Something?" I ask. "Shall we play twenty questions until I guess what you were avoiding?"

He grunts. "I'm not in the mood."

"Then tell me—or we can go on like this forever—"

"Fine. It was a bunny, okay?" he snaps. "A little rabbit hopped out onto the trail, and I swerved to avoid hitting it."

I bite back my smile while he stews. His thick arms cross over a form-fitting athletic shirt that doesn't leave his pectoral muscles to the imagination. Somehow, I manage not to laugh at his scowl when I think of the arrogant, grumpy, hotshot surgeon flat on his ass to save a little bunny. It's actually kind of sweet. Who would have thought?

I pull up to the emergency loading bay, and a nurse approaches the car. I get out and ask him for a wheelchair after I brief him on the patient. The nurse helps Dr. Williams to the chair and thank goodness for that because I'd almost thrown out my back getting him off the ground at the trail.

Before the nurse gets a chance to do so, I kneel to lower the wheelchair's footrests, then take Dr. Williams's injured foot and place it gingerly over one of them. While I do this, I glance up at Dr. Williams to check for any grimaces indicating pain, but his eyes are fixed on . . . something. One corner of his mouth tugs upward, and I follow his gaze all the way to my boobs. My still-drenched, wet-t-shirt contest boobs in all the glory that is daylight. It takes everything in me not to grin like an idiot at having caught him gawking at my body. I don't call him out on it, though. Any other day, I'd say *hey buddy, eyes up here*, but today he's in pain, and endorphins can help with that. So instead, I linger two seconds too long until he peels his eyes from my chest and shakes his head.

"You don't have to come in with me," Dr. Williams says, his eyes fixed to the ground in front of him as I stand to follow when the nurse wheels him in.

"I don't mind. I want to make sure you're settled and okay."

His brows furrow together, but he stays quiet.

"Dr. Williams, what happened?" The ER doctor recognizes him, and he gets the royal treatment from then on, even as he refuses pain medication. I smile when he asks for a consult with Dr. Bel from the Orthopedics department, and I make a mental note to tell Mandy her husband is a sought-after ortho god.

"Well, you're all set," I say. I'm about to tell him I'll see him later, but since he is now a patient, I guess he won't be going to work today, so I stop myself. "I'll get going." I can always arrange to get his bike to him later.

Dr. Williams turns to me with confusion etched on his brows as if he's forgotten all about me, then he remembers. "Right," he says. "And, I'm sorry, um . . . but I don't think I got your name."

My head cocks to the side. What? "I'm sorry, I don't . . ." I trail off, realization hitting me like a freight train. He doesn't recognize me. I blink once, then twice. He has no idea who I am.

This entire time . . . he thought we were strangers.

Sure, he's always seen me in scrubs, with my hair in a surgical cap and a surgical mask on my face, my body swallowed in oversized scrubs, but we've been working together for four months.

Four months.

Shouldn't he know my voice by now? My eyes? Hell, shouldn't he know what my face looks like outside of the operating room?

To be fair, Dr. Williams is classically handsome and freaking hot. Those piercing blue eyes framed by thick black brows make many a nurse swoon around him. He would be hard to forget in or out of scrubs.

But while I'm not a major babe, I do all right. Sure, I'm curvy, but I've been told I have a great rack. And even if my face is a bit round, I'm kind of pretty. I wouldn't be quite so forgettable after four months of daily interaction.

Would I?

Dr. Williams's posture becomes rigid when I take too long to answer, my jaw slack as I think of what to say.

But I don't get the chance to correct his blunder because a nurse wheels him away to x-ray.

You can read the rest of Izel and Logan's story in *Incision* when you sign up for my reader club newsletter at ofeliamartinez.com/freebooks

# ACKNOWLEDGMENTS

First, I'd like to thank my beautiful mom. I know how hard you worked to open so many doors for me that weren't open for Lola. Because of everything you sacrificed, I never lived in fear due to the circumstances of my birth like so many of my Dreamer friends.

Your sacrifice hasn't gone unnoticed, and I will always love you for it. Thank you for this beautiful life you have given me and for never once doubting a single one of my dreams.

I would also like to thank Ofelia's Escape, my reader club, and the Ofeliati. I was lucky enough to find amazing, enthusiastic readers when absolutely no one knew who I was. You took a chance on me, and I will treasure you always. Because of you, I get to live this silly little dream of making stuff up and writing it down. From the bottom of my heart, thank you for reading.

Lastly, to my partner and best friend, Robert. Though you never understood the dream, you fueled it with your encouragement and love. Thank you for putting up with me having no days off and never shutting up about my books. I love you.

# ABOUT THE AUTHOR

Ofelia Martinez writes romance with Latinas on top. Originally from the Texas border, Ofelia now resides in Missouri with her partner and their dog, Pixel.

This is Ofelia's fourth book.

She loves good books, tequila, and chocolate. She proudly shares a birthday with Usagi Tsukino. When not writing, you can find Ofelia making visual art.

Visit OfeliaMartinez.com to learn more.

facebook.com/OMartinezAuthor
twitter.com/OMartinezAuthor
instagram.com/Omartinezauthor

Made in the USA
Columbia, SC
29 January 2022

55031394R00240